Praise for J.R. Angelella's *Zombie*

"Angelella's debut novel crackles with energy and attitude."
—*Publishers Weekly*

"An irreverent and twisted coming-of-age story with one of the most shocking endings I've ever read."
—**Matthew Quick**, author of *The Silver Linings Playbook*

"Your home life's an apocalypse, school's the plague, and you're growing up in a wasteland. To survive this zombie movie of a life is probably going to take more than you've got. But a world where the dead walk is also a world with miracles. Have faith. Read this book."
—**Stephen Graham Jones**, author of *Growing Up Dead in Texas*

"Without a doubt, J.R. Angelella is a truly gifted writer, and *Zombie*, his first novel, is one of the smartest, strangest, and most beautifully crafted coming-of-age stories you will ever encounter. I eagerly look forward to see what he comes up with next."
—**Donald Ray Pollock**, author of *The Devil All the Time*

"Wow! A crazy, wicked, knock-out of a book! *Zombie* is an energetic, hilarious romp through Jeremy's world, which is full of dangers and perils both real and imagined (or are they imagined?). Remember those Zombie movies from your childhood that kept you up nights holding onto your baseball bat for safety? When you read this book, you'll go searching for that baseball bat again. A word of advice ... grab the aluminum bat. Trust me."
—**Garth Stein**, author of *The Art of Racing in the Rain*

ZOMBIE

J. R. ANGELELLA

SOHO

To my beautiful wife, Kate. For everything and the world.

∿

Published by
Soho Press, Inc.
853 Broadway
New York, NY 10003

Library of Congress Cataloging-in-Publication Data

Angelella, J. R.
Zombie / J.R. Angelella.
p. cm.
Summary: Fourteen-year-old Jeremy Barker, facing his first year of
Catholic high school and major family issues, sees the code he lives by,
gleaned from zombie movies, put to the test as he tries to set right what he
thinks are terrible wrongs committed by his father.
ISBN 978-1-61695-088-0 (pbk.)
eISBN 978-1-61695-089-7
[1. Coming of age—Fiction. 2. Family problems—Fiction. 3. Catholic
schools—Fiction. 4. High schools—Fiction. 5. Schools—Fiction.
6. Fathersand sons—Fiction.] I. Title.
PZ7.A58232Zom 2012
[Fic]—dc23
2012003803

Interior design by Janine Agro, Soho Press, Inc.
Printed in the United States of America

10 9 8 7 6 5 4 3 2 1

"I have never seen a greater monster or miracle in the world than myself."
—MICHEL DE MONTAIGNE

Jeremy Barker's
Top Ten Favorite Zombie Movies of All-Time;
Or How to Survive a Necroinfectious Pandemic:
The Zombie Survival Code!

I
Zombieland (2009)

II
Dawn of the Dead (2004)

III
Shaun of the Dead (2004)

IV
I Walked With a Zombie (1943)

V
Thriller (1983)

VI
The Greatest Story Ever Told (1965)

VII
Zombie Strippers! (2008)

VIII
Planet Terror (2007)

IX
Night of the Living Dead (1968)

X
28 Days Later (2002)

PROLOGUE TO THE APOCALYPSE

The earliest memory I have of Dad is: disappearing.

The details don't matter much now. It's more of a grainy, amateur film reel in my mind—the kind taken of some possible monster running through the darkness or a dinosaur descending down into choppy, black water. But still it's mine.

I don't remember my exact age. Maybe I was that in-between age where standing on tiptoes accomplishes things. Maybe not.

The house was empty. I walked from room to room. The lights were off. I didn't turn them on, or call out his name, for fear of disturbing whatever might be inside.

Dad was gone.

But I'm not going to start with my earliest memory. If I do that, how the fuck will we ever make it through to the end? There's so much left to come.

Like high school.

I
ZOMBIELAND

(Release Date: October 2, 2009)
Directed by Ruben Fleischer
Written by Rhett Reese and Paul Wernick

1

According to my father, there are three types of necktie knots: the Windsor, the Half-Windsor, and the Limp Dick.

"Jeremy, I'd bet my hand," he says, adjusting his seatbelt, "that every swinging dick at Byron Hall wears the Windsor."

"Could you not talk about dicks first thing in the morning?"

"The ladies love masculine things," he says, pinching his silver tie at the base of its knot.

"Dad, it's an all guy high school."

"It's the principle of the thing."

"What is?"

"The size of a man's knot. His bastion of strength."

"Don't say *bastion of strength*. Gross," I say, shivering.

"It's true," he says. "Fact. Proven." Dad turns, facing me, and exposes the flauntingly fat Windsor knot of his silver tie.

Welcome to Necktie 101. I will be your professor today.

According to Ballentine Barker, in order to make a Windsor, you must cross the long, fat end over the short, skinny one; double loop through the cross-over; make a tunnel over the loops; and funnel it through. The Windsor usually makes you look like a fuckwad.

What is that Bible story about the whale and Jonah? Or is his name Jonas? And Jonah is swallowed whole by some gigantic whale for whatever reason—I don't know—and Jonah lives inside the whale? And then the whale spits him out. Or is it that he swims out? Or is it that he gets blown out through the blowhole? Or does he die inside the whale? Am I thinking of *Moby Dick*?

We pass a sign on the side of the road that reads BALTIMORE: THE GREATEST CITY IN AMERICA. GET IN ON IT.

"When they say that—*get in on it*—what do they mean?" I ask.

"That Baltimore is a secret not many people know about," Dad says.

"A secret?"

"*Get in on it.* Be one of the people in the know. Be in on the secret. A part of the club."

"What secret? What club?"

"It's like referring to Baltimore as *Charm City*. The name creates a buzz where no buzz is buzzing."

"Buzzing?" I ask.

Dad says, "You ask too many questions."

Jackson used to call Baltimore by a bunch of different names. *B-town. Charm City. Crabtown. City of Firsts. Monument City. Mob Town. Murderland.* He'd say them mainly to impress girls. They'd stop by the house in the evenings. Groups of them. Whore-ds of them. Get it? *Whore-ds* of them? And ask if he was home. They would travel from far away. Randallstown. Ellicott City. Columbia. Westminster. Cockeysville. Perry Hall. Take 83 South to Cold Spring Lane or I-95 to Russell Street past M&T Bank Stadium. Travel just to see him. They'd stink of perfume, wearing short skirts, tight tops, big hair, lipstick-red lips. Jackson would emerge from his room, sometimes wearing only a robe, and descend down the stairs like some Casanova Fuck. "Welcome," he'd say, "to the *City of Firsts.*"

What an ooze.

We drive past a middle-aged woman speed walking in pink Spandex shorts and a black tank top. She has medium boobs, her butt cheeks shifting back and forth with each step. The Spandex cups her ass and hips such that she might as well be wearing underwear. I immediately feel guilty, like I just lied to a priest. I think about her tits. Amazing.

Dad taps his horn. "Ballentine likes what he sees," he says. Dad refers to himself in third person from time to time, including on his voicemail messages. I am constantly reminded where Jackson gets his ooziness. "A little beep-beep now and again keeps them feeling young, son. Lets them know they still got it."

"Do you think she has kids?" I ask.

"Not all mothers are *your* mother," he says.

I'm surprised Dad mentions Mom at all, especially on the first day of school as it always used to be her day. She would get up early, make a big breakfast of pancakes and eggs and strawberry milk. After, she'd pose me on the front steps of our house for the annual first day of school photo. She kept the photos framed in a collage on the wall, reaching all the way back to my first day of preschool. There's a black rectangle on the wall outlining where the collage used to hang. Today there was no first day of school photo. Today there was no breakfast or strawberry milk. I wonder where those framed photos are now.

"Your mother is not here, Jeremy," Dad says. "I am." Dad's car drifts into the other lane, crossing briefly over the double yellow lines before weaving around a garbage truck. "The size of a man's knot," Dad continues, "indicates his massiveness."

"Massiveness? Oh, Jesus."

"Language."

"Dad, seriously."

"Listen. You need to hear this: Windsor equals monster. Half-Windsor equals babyshit."

"Babyshit?"

"Babyshit."

Allow me to professor your ass with some Half-Windsor knowledge.

The Half-Windsor folds like a paper football, easy with perfect angles. Personally, I think it's the best knot. It's easier than the Windsor because you only make one loop over the cross-over instead of two. But getting the length right takes skill, practice, and a sense of pride. Where the Windsor, more often than not, gives you a stumpy bitch length, the Half-Windsor—if you get it right—hangs sexy and perfect right to the tip of your belt. That triangular tip of the tie skimming a silver belt buckle. It's badass. Totally badass. But I haven't figured out how to tie it perfectly yet.

We drive past a private golf course—some members-only club surrounded in a super high fence to keep the wrong kind of people out. There is a valley in the road, then a hill, which Dad accelerates through, and as we reach the peak, I see Byron Hall in the distance.

Dad says, "Survival scenario—you're in school. English. Zombies crash through the windows. Unstoppable. Sick. Savage. Your school is under siege. It's a Zombie Apocalypse."

"Crashing?" I ask.

He loosens his grip on the steering wheel, his fingers spread open and relaxed. "Crashing."

"I'm in English class and zombies are crashing through the windows?"

Dad coasts down a straightaway of red brick houses with long driveways. A man wearing a cowboy hat and mirrored sunglasses navigates a wheelchair down his driveway to the street and slides envelopes inside a mailbox. Dad rides the brake, cutting our speed down quick, and looks over his shoulder as we pass, watching the man spin and roll away from the street, retreating in his wheelchair, completely legless.

"Dad, you said zombies were *crashing* through the windows of my English class?"

"Right—crashing. They're crashing."

"Through the windows. A Zombie Apocalypse, you said."

"What is your weapon and what is your escape plan?" He looks at me longer than anyone driving should. "And no Minigun either. You always say Minigun. Use another movie other than *Planet Terror* as an example. Think outside the box."

Stopped at a red light, I see the Byron Hall campus up across from a strip mall, just like the one in *Dawn of the Dead*. His turn signal clicks.

"Break the glass of one of those emergency panels with my elbow, grab the axe, and chop my way across the street to the mall." I chop my arm from the school across the street to the mall. "Hold up there. Last-stand style. Barricade the doors with bike locks from a sporting good store and wait for the cavalry to come. I'd grab a few extra things—blowtorch, propane tank. If I have to make a bomb. Blow some shit up. What about you?" I ask.

"You couldn't pay me to go back to high school," he says.

We pass an empty football field with metal bleachers and two yellow wishbone goalposts. Dad pulls in behind a long line of cars, waiting to turn into the entrance. The sign out front reads: BYRON HALL CATHOLIC HIGH SCHOOL FOR BOYS. We jerk to a stop at the top of the circle where two Christian Brothers greet students as they enter. The Brothers wear long black tunics that brush their shiny black shoes, although if memory serves me correct from when Jackson went here the Brothers have the options to wear the long black tunic, or all black suits like a priest, or just rock the regular sport coat, button down shirt, and tie. But not these Brothers. These Brothers are old school. These Brothers look like hippie priests in their tunics. The Byron Hall mascot, an angry fighting blue jay, stands with the Brothers waving his blue-feathered wings at people passing by. The blue bird is equal parts terrifying and gay.

"Well, here we are, son," Dad says, palming the back of my head.

I knock his arm away. "You're messing up my hair."

He wipes his hand on a handkerchief. "It's like a fucking grease pit up there."

"Hair gel." I lower the overhead visor to see the mirror, to fix the brown curls he ruffled out of place, the curls I rushed this morning to not make him late. I comb a few strands of hair back into a part and adjust my thin black tie. I aim my shoulders to the door, so he won't see my knot.

"Look at you," he says, poking me in the back. He drapes his arm over the wheel. "Barely a freshman and already primping like a Revlon girl."

"Quit," I say, slamming the car visor up. I grab my book bag and push open the door when his hand grabs me by my navy blue sport coat.

"I'll quit," he says. "Sure. If you turn around."

"I'm late."

"I'm your father."

I know what he wants to see, but it's his fault for rushing me this morning, goddamnit.

"I'm really going to be late for homeroom. You're going to make me late." Dad's words from my lips.

Dad smells like aftershave and coffee and bleach. He disappeared again last night. Showed up at the house early—scattered, paranoid, rushed. Like always, Dad disappeared and no one knows anything about it. He thinks he'll be able to keep it a secret. He thinks he will be able to scare people away, but I follow the Code—**Zombie Survival Code (ZSC)**. The ZSC is a list on how to survive a necroinfectious pandemic, otherwise known as a Zombie Apocalypse. B-t-dubs, it should be noted that I totally ripped the idea of survival rules off of *Zombieland*. Big holla to Jesse Eisenberg. I don't know if I heard this somewhere or thought it up myself, but here is the deal—rules are meant to be broken, but codes are made to be followed.

Zombie Survival Code #1: Avoid Eye Contact (ZSC #1)
Zombie Survival Code #2: Keep Quiet (ZSC #2)
Zombie Survival Code #3: Forget the Past (ZSC #3)
Zombie Survival Code #4: Lock-and-Load (ZSC #4)
Zombie Survival Code #5: Fight to Survive (ZSC #5)

"I asked you to turn around," he says. "Show me. Now."

"You want me to miss first period?" ZSC #1: Avoid eye contact—I look away.

"I want you to obey your father. It's in the Bible. Now turn around."

I'd been hiding the knot with my sport coat all morning. I refuse to answer and hope he lets it go and leaves me alone—ZSC #2: Keep quiet. I thought I'd be able to get away with it. I know what he's going to say but there's no avoiding it, so I turn around.

"Limp Dick?" he asks, slapping his forehead. "Fuck me. That's a Limp Dick."

Hey now, hey now—Prof Knot in the house.

The third and final knot—the Limp Dick—is self-explanatory. The Limp Dick has no loop, but instead folds in an impulsive movement from the cross-over to the tunnel and funnels through, dangling down limp-like. Self-explanatory. Limp Dick.

"Mom wouldn't care about my knot," I say.

"You're right. She wouldn't. When's the last time you saw her?" Dad slips the car into drive, his foot still on the brake. He makes a fist and punches the dent in the dashboard in slow motion with a sound effect of an explosion on impact. "Jeremy. After school. You and me. Necktie refresher course."

"You're such a loser," I say.

"I'm not the one rocking a Limp Dick," he says.

"Dad," I say, "where did you go last night?"

"Spent the night at Liza's." He smiles. "Don't worry so much."

"I don't believe you."

"Yes, you do." Then, raising his hands, he says, "Have a good day, son."

I raise mine too as our hands turn into fists and we bang them together like boxers tapping gloves before a fight.

2

The Byron Hall Catholic High School for Boys—nicknamed The Hall—is made up of five hallways. There is no second floor. The school has not changed a lick since Jackson graduated four years ago.

On an aerial sketch of the school, like an architect's layout, like the kind Mom used to spread out on the dining room table, The Hall would look like the number eight on a solar-powered calculator. Three mini horizontal hallways—one at the top, one in the middle, and one at the bottom of the school. Two long vertical hallways on the sides—one with even classroom numbers, one with odd. Each lined with lockers for 1,300 students, lockers so skinny and tight they would barely hold a broom.

According to Jackson, the cafeteria is called *the cafe* and sits past the mini hallway at the top of the school. Jackson told me that Dad said the cafe reminded him a lot of the Marine chow halls at Fort Drum in New York where he was stationed before being deployed to Vietnam. Simple room to describe, really—blue-jay-blue tiled walls; eggshell white linoleum floors; long, boring, brown tables seating six evenly spaced across an L shape. A sign on the wall reads: FIRE OCCUPANCY 585. I wonder what would happen if all 1,300 kids had a free period at the same time.

When I got my course schedule and locker assignment a few weeks ago, Jackson volunteered to drive me up to his old stomping ground, a phrase he likes to use like some kind of old man. He escorted me around like some big dick hotshot, head held high, walking with a swaggerly limp. He even got all dressed up—khaki

pants, white button-down shirt, plaid sport coat with an all blue
tie in a Windsor knot. Tool. It was nice, though, to get acquainted
with the layout of the school, showing me all of the hallways, which
were empty as fuck except for custodians pushing mops around
and some people in the front office. No brothers. No students. He
showed me my locker at the end of the even hallway near the cafe
and had me practice the combo. He told me to always make sure
my lock snapped shut. One of the things the upperclassmen like to
do, apparently, is find someone's lock undone and put it on backwards. Before we left, he pointed to the vending machines in the
corner of the cafe and said, "I fucked some girl once at a dance over
by the vending machines. Fuck central."

Great—fuck central.

At my locker, I look around and wait until I feel invisible. I slip
off my shoe, pull out a piece of paper with my combination and
quickly apply the three numbers in perfect left-right-left order. The
lock snaps open like a broken jaw. I slip the paper back inside my
shoe and my shoe back on my foot and the lock back on the locker.
I wonder if I'm the only student with a combination cheat sheet in
his shoe and a back-up sheet in his bedroom. My backup is in my
closet with my other secrets. I dump the contents of my book bag
into my locker and pick out my books for the day. Western Civilization. Algebra. Christian Awareness. English Literature. My locker
rattles shut with a good kick. I twist a couple of times to scramble
the combination.

I've already forgotten the numbers.

A Brother I haven't seen yet—a small, Asian man, wearing a long
black tunic and thick black hair slicked back—paces along the back
of the cafe, his hands behind his back, watching the boys at the tables,
waiting for something to happen. I imagine him to be some kind of
drill instructor, ready to scream at kids to get to class on time.

Outside of the cafe is an overhang with metal picnic benches
where kids chill and eat lunch and congregate like felons on the
prison yard and tell stories that are most certainly all lies—stories
that mainly consist of fucking girls and drugs and sometimes school

work, but mostly fucking girls and drugs. They, the boys, the young men, they all look exactly the same, unified, like an army—an academic *siege!*—with their neckties and wrinkled sport coats, all crushed together, like a rat king. Then I hear what Jackson calls *the hotness*—sweet, honey-like voices—slow and smooth and sexy. Baby, are they sexy.

A group of four girls in short plaid skirts and white short sleeve, button-down shirts pass the cafe windows and sit at one of the metal picnic benches. A gaggle of dudes swarm the girls, sharks to chum. The guys wear super baggy pants and speak in this *faux-*gangsta accent like *they thug life, yo,* like they're from the projects, which is funny because they're probably all from the wealthiest suburbs just outside of the city, living in mini-mansions owned by parents who run PR firms and are politicians. It's that kind of school. Retards.

The girls know what they're doing, how they're sitting, showing some serious leg, sitting side by side, hips cocked, the ends of the skirts pulling up past midthigh. My God their skin looks smooth like a baby's ass, so smooth you want to lick it—the three white girls with this 2% milk sheen and the black girl a dark chocolate dream. The black girl might just be a super model—I mean she is thin and tall with an incredibly angular face in a beautiful way and her big, bold eyes might as well be singing me a song. It'd be hard to execute any of the five zombie survival rules with these girls.

The hallways swell inside with dudes stopping, pressing, and pushing each other to see the girls, like it was their first time. Once guys find a clear line of vision, they freeze and hold. There has to be a name for this. Is there a word for it? Can I call it something? Hotnified? Yes. Yup. That's it. We're *hotnified.* We're hotnified, watching the girls.

My dangerous daydream continues, the girls white-pantied and strutting around in slow motion to a rock 'n' roll soundtrack, when the small, Asian Brother sprints across the cafe, bullet-like, and hurls himself through the double doors to the outside area. I expect to see him do some kind of back flip or combo leg-swipe kick or crazy mid-air jujitsu. Instead, it looks more like hand-to-hand combat. He grabs boys by their collars and elbows and flings them away from the sexy, girl zombies come to infect and devour the Byron Hall Boys. The boys laugh and slide their bags onto their backs and go back inside the building. The girls are unphased, unmoved, and extend their hands to the Asian Brother as an introduction.

I push my way through the crowd of horny high school perverts, their faces pressed to the doors and windows, practically licking the glass, the fucks. I edge my way to the front of these boner boys and head outside, pulled in like some kind of sexual riptide.

The air is dead outside, breezeless, hot and heavy with humidity, like the girls brought all of this hot, sexy air with them. I sit at a bench and, smooth as all hell, stoop to tie both shoes that are already double-knotted. The girls, still undressed in my head, circle the Brother. Seeing girls in short skirts pass by makes my pecker shiver for sure, so I can only imagine how the entire school of horny bastards feels.

"Ladies, you must leave," the small, Asian Brother says. "No girls on school." He shakes his head. "Three thirty, then you return." He taps the face of his watch. "Then girls on campus."

"What's your name, Brother?" a girl asks, a tan girl with dark, red hair. She looks over at me and without even thinking or anything I raise my fucking hand and wave to her with a big old goofball smile on my face. She doesn't smile back. Fuck me.

"I am Brother Lee," he says.

"We're looking for the drama department," the girl with dark, red hair says. She hands him a stack of papers. "We are members of the drama club at Prudence High, Brother Lee, and are working on the Byron Hall Fall drama, but we need to turn these in before auditions."

"You bring after school," Brother Lee says. "I'm no mailman." Brother Lee crosses his arms over his chest. "I look like mailman to you?"

"No, Brother," the super model says, "you don't look like a mailman at all. They have better uniforms." She smiles at him.

"I don't think this is funny," he says.

She touches his arm and says, "They are our parental permission slips. We need to give them to Father Vincent Gibbs."

"You wait to last minute," Brother Lee says, shaking his head in disapproval, but even Brother Lee is powerless against the plaid skirt and teenage shaved legs. "Follow me. No walking." He rushes down the sidewalk toward the lecture hall building, herding them away from the rest of us, like cattle away from a cliff; although in this scenario the girls seem more like the cliff and the rest of us the cattle.

The girls march single file past Brother Lee, who follows quickly behind them. The girl with the dark red hair looks at me over her shoulder again, but still without a smile, not at all like in the movies, like in those rom-coms—the movies where two souls are destined to be together and love one another and get married but for an hour and a half they keep missing each other, either by chance or fate, or by some kind of bullshit, until one rainy or sunny or snowy day their lives crash together and they see each other for the very first time. The girl passes by the boy and smiles over her shoulder and the boy returns the smile, maybe adding a wave, but she doesn't see the wave because the guy that she's with is her boyfriend who distracts her. The smile is what I'm really talking about here, the smile that says they will meet up again soon. Then, the girl falls out of love with her fuckneck boyfriend just as the boy is about to settle for some plain girl who is good enough for him, when in the nick of time the boy and the girl wind up at a public park feeding birds, or at a library browsing books in the same section, or strolling through a grocery store in the produce section—his hands squeezing cantaloupe melons as she digs her way through a bin of avocadoes—and they see each other again, but this time it will be the last time they see each other like strangers and the first time they see each other as friends.

Yeah, this girl that I like doesn't look at me like that in the slightest. This girl looks at me like she thinks I'm just another pervert, like she knows I undressed her, got her completely naked in my head.

Brother Lee escorts the girls to the lecture hall building as they disappear.

I walk back into the even hallway of the school by the cafe and realize I am still smiling and when I stop smiling it makes me feel sad for some reason. Because she never smiled back.

3

yron Hall is prime zombie real estate—one hallway in every
direction. No second floor. No basement that I'm aware of.
Just a series of interconnected hallways. I can picture the undead,
brain- and flesh-eating hoards clambering over each other, coming
at me, crashing through doors and windows, swinging their arms
around in a jerky motion, regurgitating goo. This school would be
a perfect place to set an ambush, actually, if I were a zombie. Plenty
of food in a concentrated area with few available exits and a low
ratio of hero opportunities.

An axe sleeps behind a clear glass panel, the word *FIRE* printed
across the glass in red. I make a mental note of its location—by the
cafe, next to the patio, on the wall—for defense. Just in case of a
siege. No, Armageddon.

The same two Christian Brothers and a fat furry blue jay roam
the halls now, making their way from the front entrance toward the
cafe. So far I have been able to avoid the Brothers and mascot. And
Brother Lee for that matter, who has resumed his post in the cafe,
pacing along the all, hands behind his back.

A group of bulked-up boys, six of them, dressed in plaid, punch
and slap each other in the arm and neck like a bunch of fucking
morons, in a my-dick-is-bigger-than-yours kind of way. They are
the Plaids. The other kids in the hall instinctively move out of their
way, clearing a path so as not to draw any unnecessary or added
attention. I expect to be picked up and slammed into a locker. I've
seen what they do to underclassman, but they pass by like they
don't even see me.

A white kid with one gigantic pimple in the middle of his forehead, like a Muslim or Hindu or whoever wears the religious red
dots on their foreheads, approaches me as I reenter the school and
tries to sell me an elevator pass. He wears a Half-Windsor. His pimple looks like it could erupt any second. Sound the sirens. Mandatory evacuation. Stat.

"You don't have one?" he says, all worried for my well-being.

"Nope."

"My God. It's a good thing you ran into me then. This your
lucky day."

"I didn't run into you. You tapped me on the shoulder."

"You like to run your mouth like my bitch ex-girlfriend." He
opens his hand like a puppet and quacks it at me. "One left. Twenty
bucks and it's all yours." He dangles a scrap of paper with the words
elivater pass printed in red ink.

"The school is a giant hallway," I say. "Byron *Hall*," I say, still
maintaining Zombie Survival Code #1: Avoid eye contact. "There
are no elevators. Go find yourself another monkey."

"Fucking freshman." He lowers his sad piece of paper and waits,
scanning the crowd, before approaching some other unsuspecting
kid. Poor bastards. Both of them—the douchecloset trying to make
a buck and the newbie boy lost in a wilderness of cheap cologne
and plaid apparel.

Sometimes you only need to use the first Zombie Survival Code
to get out of a jam, but other times you need to combine Codes.
For example, ZSC #1 mixed with ZSC #2: Keep quiet. It's all
about the eyes. People underestimate how frightening it can be to
engage in a conversation with a person who's actively avoiding eye
contact. That's the thing about zombies, the undead don't use eyes
like humans. Zombies' eyes are cross hairs on some high-powered
rifle, or lasers on a heat-seeking missile. Their eyes don't engage but
seek with the ultimate intention to destroy and devour.

Two Christian Brothers flank me in the hallway—the same two
at the top of the circle earlier. The giant blue jay still stands beside
the Brothers too. The blue jay's head is humongous and bobbles

around. Kids pass by and punch the blue jay's tail. Blue feathers
flutter everywhere.

"Welcome to Byron Hall," one Brother says. "I'm Brother Bill
and this is Brother Fred."

"And this is our school mascot—Byron the Blue Jay," Brother
Fred says.

The blue jay raises a wing. More feathers. It covers its beak with
a wing and laughs—the fuck. I wish I was in the zombie samurai
movie *Versus*. I'd smash its fat, furry blue jay head in with my book
bag full of summer reading I didn't bother with. I'd say things in
Chinese or Japanese or Korean and my subtitles would be in yellow
beneath me for all to see. I'd make those sounds that they make—
aye-cha and *oye-oh*. I'd be a motherfucking kung fu black belt badass.
For sure.

"What's your name?" Brother Bill asks.

"Jeremy Barker," I say, extending my hand.

Brother Bill shakes my hand, his tunic swaying over his shoes
like a skirt.

"You must be Jackson Barker's little brother," Brother Fred says.

"My word," Brother Bill says. "Can't be." Brother Bill holds his
hands up in surrender. "That's really dating me. I don't like to think
about our legacy students." He laughs. "Are you getting used to
wearing a sport coat and tie?"

The words *Limp Dick* scream in my head. I refrain from telling
them my father's philosophy on knots. Sometimes people don't
need to know everything that you know. Like how this building
would be the worst possible place to fortify against a Zombie
Apocalypse. How they need to build levels and create smaller
spaces. Like in the remake of *Dawn*. Watch *Dawn*, then schedule
a meeting with me to discuss zombie security and preventative
zombie architecture. A second level. A fortified basement with a
secret elevator to the roof for helicopter evac. More axes. I could
tell them this. But I don't. Instead, I stick to the zombie basics.
ZSC #1: Avoid eye contact. ZSC #2: Keep damn quiet.

"I bet you're really excited to be following in your brother's footsteps. I mean, you must know this place like the back of your hand?" Brother Fred says, his hands behind his back.

"What's Jackson doing now?" Brother Bill asks.

Avert eyes.

"I bet he's graduated from college. Probably has a good job." Brother Fred puffs his chest out a bit, proud to have been a part of a success story, of a solid tradition of excellence that is The Hall.

Quiet.

"We won't keep you," Brother Bill says, finally.

They walk off together with the fucking blue jay behind them. The Brothers latch onto another kid in the crowd, asking him questions, following him down the hallway and around the corner out of sight. The fat bitch blue jay follows, leaving everything behind him bluer.

Sometimes being silent is the easiest thing in the world.

The hallway is crammed with kids, pushing each other against lockers, pulling on wrinkled sport coats, combing their freshly gelled hair, tying last-minute knots before class. Kids roam in packs of plaid shirts with striped ties, plaid sport coats with solid ties. It hurts to look at for too long. Some sport coats look two sizes too big, like they were blindly grabbed off the rack, while others should be behind glass in a Ye-Olde-fifties museum. Pants don't fit like pants should fit—at the waist. Instead, they hang down to the ass, a hand at the crotch to hold them up or a wide, waddling stance. I'd never be able to pull it off. And Dad would probably kill me before I left the house.

Before school started, he took me shopping for new sport coats, buttoned-down collared shirts, and khaki pants. I learned all about French cuffs, and the subtle differences between straight, spread, tab, and pin collars. Exciting fucking times, seriously. He said, "This is how a man should dress." He said, "A man should dress like he could be buried in what he's wearing." Dad took the new clothes to this Italian tailor in Little Italy near the Inner Harbor to get them fitted or cropped or whatever. Angelo Christini—this old, silver-haired Italian with a humped back, who spoke with a thick accent and shook his hands when he spoke. He smelled like leather.

Angelo made me wear my clothes and stand on a small stool in
front of mirrors as he measured me. It didn't feel quite right when
he ran his tape measure up the inside of my legs. I looked to Dad
for help and wanted to ask him if this was at all normal—to be felt
up by an old Italian man—but Dad couldn't be bothered while he
walked around the shop, flipping through racks of vintage Italian
silk suits for sale and two-tone leather loafers. When the clothes
came back, they fit like skin. Dad said, "Don't you even think about
growing taller or getting fat. I paid a fortune for these." Now I'm
the best-dressed freshman anyone's ever seen, surviving among a
zombie army of plaid motherfuckers with pants at their asses.

Someone jogging past knocks into me. His corduroys make a
zwip-zwip sound as he passes. I say, "Excuse me," but he doesn't
even know I exist. Kids shake lockers loose and greet each other
with arm punches and big bear hugs.

I overhear summer vacation stories.

Someone fucked some local girl in Costa Rica while on vacation with his parents.

Some other guy lost his virginity to a college chick tour guide
at Princeton.

Another guy got wasted visiting his brother in Chicago and
ended up taking a dump on second base at Wrigley Field.

Another guy did his first line of coke at a movie premiere party
in Los Angeles.

One says he, his girlfriend, and her sister all got drunk off cherry-
grape Jell-O shots and ended up fucking in their parents' bed.

Another says he knows the password to get into this sick underground club where they do fucked-up shit, so that if anyone wants
to go, to let him know by Wednesday.

My summer?

Consisted of cutting the grass of all the houses on my father's realtor list. "The lawn of a home tells a story." He sold more houses this summer than any other year.

Other than cutting pantloads of grass, I:

Saw my neighbor, Tricia, naked.

4

Tricia was home from Harvard for the summer.

One night, I was sitting in the dark of my room, alone, on a wicker chair. Yes, wicker, don't get me started, something my mom put in my room. And I looked out my window and saw a light on across the way—a table lamp on a nightstand turned low. It was a bedroom—light blue walls, framed photos, teddy bears and ribbons or awards of some kind pinned to a corkboard hung from the wall. All things from another time and place. A tiny TV, blue screen glowing, and an open closet of well-organized clothes.

Then she entered.

She wore tight-fitted blue jeans that made her butt look great and a V-neck sweater, offering a nice amount of top boobage, as far as I could tell. I turned off the light in my room and moved closer to the window. Tricia closed the door behind her and removed her sweater, pulling it over her head just as she disappeared into her closet. I had been so close to seeing her bra. Her room was empty, with only the light from the TV on the end table brightening the room, when she re-emerged. She wore a lacy white bra and white thigh-high stockings. She sat on the edge of her bed and clasped her garter to the stockings. A black minidress hung from a hanger on the back of the door and she yanked it down and slid into it. There was a makeup table with three mirrors. She sat in front of it and powdered her face and applied eye shadow and lip liner and all the things those girl magazines like *Allure* and *Cosmo* and *Marie Claire* tell girls to do or not to do.

She looked into her reflection and saw something behind her.

I don't know how, but she did. She saw me, peaking though the blades of my blinds, two white eyes watching her. She walked to her window. Her room was not visible from the street or the side yard separating our houses, only my room could see into hers and hers into mine. If we were only closer in age maybe there would have been two tin cans attached on either end of a string strung between us. She stood, staring back into the darkness of my room. She said something and I thought for a second she was trying to tell me something, but she spoke over her shoulder then, yelling to someone else. She stepped away from the window and closed her bedroom door before returning to the window, sliding one strap of her bra off of her shoulder.

I turned on the light in my room. No more hiding. I was fully clothed and standing like her at my window, staring back. I raised my hand. She reached down to her nightstand and turned off the light, leaving only the TV on behind her—a blue tinted glow. Her silhouette stood there in the backlit room, still and almost naked. Not in a sexual way, though, or at least it didn't feel sexual at the time. It was more like she was educating me on how a woman's body looked, like a specimen. She pushed the other strap off her shoulder, unclasped the bra with one hand, and held her other arm across her chest with the other. Her bra fell from her body to the floor and as fast as this was all happening, her blinds flicked shut. It was over.

For the rest of the summer, I found myself sitting in front of my bedroom window, hoping that lightning would strike twice.

I watched, and then waited to watch again, and that's all that happened.

5

On my way to my first class, Algebra, I hear it. The word.

Someone calls me a name. Someone else, or maybe the same person, I can't be certain, grabs my book bag and yanks it the fuck down, forcing it to the ground. Someone kicks me in the back of my knees, snapping me shut like a metal folding chair. I hit the floor. *Avoid them. Don't look at them. Avert the eyes. Find some other focal point.* My arm burns like it's on fire, but no fire, no smoke, no burning flesh of any kind. Then I make out several voices, each saying that word, that one word that must either be the word of the day, or the word of the school, a word that St. John Baptist de La Salle, the Christian Brother who founded this LaSallian tradition of teaching delinquents and orphans, that St. John Baptist de La Salle himself would never, one hopes, have associated with his manner of education.

This is the one word heard at every corner of this school, in every classroom of this school, at every moment that exists in this school.

That word?

Faggot.

Yup.

I'd be lying if I say I wasn't surprised at the level of creativity and enthusiasm with which the word is used. It's not mentioned anywhere in the admissions literature, but you're a faggot the second you pass through the front doors of the building. Immediately faggotized. One can be a faggot for simply standing in the hallway. Or breathing. Or walking. Or watching. Or sorting through a backpack. Or answering a teacher's question. Or turning in homework.

Or answering a teacher's question incorrectly. Or not turning in
your homework.

Fag.

Faggot.

Faggy.

Fagboy.

Fagbaby.

Fagola.

Fagina, like *vagina*.

Faggotress, like *princess* except with the clever forgery of the
word *faggot* as some kind of surprising and inspired prefix.

These are the words that my attackers call me.

The Plaids stand over me—six plaid motherfuckers, one wearing more than the next. One of them clears phlegm from his throat,
sucking it back first, then pursing it out of his mouth. It forms,
icicle-like, from his lips, slowly stretching down before snapping
loose and landing on my chest. The other Plaids laugh and hit each
other in the shoulders and arms like a family of Mongoloid monkeys when the spit hits my chest.

"Fuck you, you motherfuckers," I say, swinging my leg up in
what I believe to be a roundhouse kick. I haven't the faintest idea
what a roundhouse kick is supposed to look like. Mine looks totally
sad and pathetic.

They systematically and symmetrically attack.

One of them grabs my arm.

Another grabs my other arm.

One guy grabs my leg.

Another grabs my other leg.

They lift me into the air above the hard floor, belly-up, like a
coffin being carried out to the hearse. It feels like they are going
to pull me apart limb by limb. I twist to break free, and their hands
tighten around my wrists and ankles. I can't see the faces but know
everyone around me must be smiling their asses off at the freshman
getting fucked up.

I choke on the sickening stench of cologne wafting off them, rubbed into their faces and shirts and hands and arms. I know that I should be afraid or surprised, but somehow I knew this would happen. It was just a matter of time before the plaid douchebags caught up with me. I'm more embarrassed, I think, than anything else, knowing that everyone around me is watching. The more I think about being the centerpiece of dorkdom, the more my throat burns and I become angry and can taste rage rising up inside me.

The fifth guy jerks my head up to face my feet—my legs each still held by a bitchass Plaid.

The sixth guy, this beefy bitch with buzzed blond hair, whose neck is thicker than his goddamn head, steps between my legs which are spread apart like a wishbone. He leans over me, closing his eyes, almost sweetly, and inhales. He waves his hand over my junk, smelling my dick, bringing the scent to his nose, the way you do with burning chemicals in a science lab.

Selective hearing. No audio. Silence. Peace. Tranquility. A meadow. No sound.

"God, I love that smell. Smells like," the beefy bitch says, staring into the distance, like a general surveying a battlefield. He says, "smells like freshman."

"Pussy," another says.

"Beaver," another says.

"Twat," another says.

"Cunt," another says.

"Snatch," another says.

Wow. We have a gaggle of thesaurus enthusiasts on our hands here. What original motherfuckers. If only I had a Minigun for a leg like Cherry Darling in *Planet Terror*, this would all be over. I'd mow them all down without even blinking.

The five plaid monkeys drop me to the floor again. I land on my side. I lie there, experiencing the stillness and quiet. The floor is sticky and cold. Feet shuffle around me. Khaki-ed and corduroyed legs swing past. A fire alarm is on the wall, but no axe.

I could pull the lever. I could sound the alarm. I could create a real chaos.

The sixth plaid fuckface kicks my legs, bends over, and pulls off my shoes, throwing each in opposite directions. The plaid monkeys walk away like everyone else, goddamn guiltless and gutless, blending into the mass of sport coats and knots and off-colored khakis, jumping up on each other's backs, slapping each other in the face, punching each other in the arm hard, screaming, "DEAD ARM." The blond fuck turns around, walking backwards. He points at me, where I'm still lying on the floor. He smiles as another plaid monkey smashes into him, knocking him down the middle hallway.

Brother Lee appears at the end of the hallway as the Plaids disappear. He narrows his eyes, then looks around for evidence, for someone to come forward with information, but my fellow faggots disperse. Not one faggot says a word. Like it never happened. Eyewitness amnesia. And this faggot takes the heat. Brother Lee snaps his fingers at me and I stand, still shoeless, like it never even happened. He shakes his head and taps his watch at me like he did with the girls from Prudence before he vanishes around the corner.

Zombie Survival Code #3: Forget the past.

6

I gather my shoes from off the floor, ripped from my feet and chucked down the hallway, each shoe in a different direction. The piece of paper with my combination is gone, disappeared, nowhere to be found. I slide on my shoes and am now an official enemy of my locker.

A half-eaten chocolate donut with rainbow sprinkles lowers into my sightline.

"Chocolate-chocolate, chocolate-dipped donut? Best fucking thing in the world."

I decline.

"Suit yourself," he says, taking another bite. His pants are dark khakis, not plaid, and this somehow puts me at ease. "Shake it off," he says. "They're not worth it." The kid is short, my height, with buzzed black hair. His face looks like a mountain—craggy nose, sharp chin, bulging eyes, big floppy ears. His thin black tie falls short to the middle of his chest, tied in a perfect Windsor knot. "Don't take it personally."

"Hard to take it any other way," I say.

"They love to pick on freshman." He jams the rest of the chocolate donut with chocolate icing and white sprinkles into his mouth and then speaks with his mouth full. "Cam Dillard and his Plaid Lackeys. They are the sad benchmark by which success is measured here at The Hall."

"Is it that obvious that I'm a freshman?"

"Obvious as a sledgehammer, but don't take it personally. All you need to do is see Cam and them dance and you'll feel vindicated." He does the robot dance. "They look retarded."

"I'd like to see that," I say.

"The first Hall mixer is in a few days," he says. "They'll be there in all their plaid glory. You have to come and see for yourself."

"Jocks?" I ask.

"Something like that." He looks away. "Varsity soccer." Then slapping his chest, he says, "My name's Ryan, but people call me Zink. I'm the human sieve also known as the varsity soccer goalie."

"Jock?" I ask.

"Something like that." Zink adjusts the weight of his book bag from one shoulder to another. "We're teammates, not friends. Huge difference." He extends his hand to me. "What's your name, freshman?"

"Jeremy," I say, noticing the sweet perfection of his Windsor knot.

We shake hands. Classroom doors slam shut in a staggered crescendo down the hallway. Bodies disappear. Lockers rest in their tiny frames. A short, fat, old man with thin, white hair appears. He wears a blue tracksuit and carries a clipboard. The hallway suddenly seems smaller.

"Mr. Zinkle," he barks.

"Coach O'Bannon," Zink says, startled to see this ogre of a man, this tree trunk of a dwarf, the only one not wearing a tie.

"Are we lollygagging like a Miss Fairy Mary? Let's get on to class." He slaps the clipboard with his other hand and continues down the hallway.

"Soccer coach?" I ask.

"Cam and Coach and me—we're one big happy family," Zink says. "You got class?"

"Algebra, supposedly," I say. "You?"

"Calculus waits for no man, Barks." Zink adjusts his perfect Windsor knot. "How do I look?" he asks. He looks like he doesn't necessarily belong at this school. A little too well dressed. A little too nice. A little too much of everything. "Smile, Barks. Keeps you looking fresh-faced and full of zest."

More guys pass by and knock into me, guys flowing in both directions, late to class, rushing, careless, dead to anyone else. I adjust my Limp Dick, and dust off the elbows of my sport coat. Blue feathers stick to the bottom of my shoes. When the hallway empties, I see my secret slip of paper, crumpled on the floor by a row of lockers, torn with only the last number left behind—1.

I am spit-covered and sick.

7

The bathroom by the gym is quiet and empty, a perfect place to skip my first day of Algebra. Not even a leaky spigot drips in the background—the cliché of all high school bathroom clichés. The bathroom actually smells like it has recently been cleaned, maybe disinfected is the right word. An antiseptic smell holds the air hostage. The stall walls crack unfunny mother jokes back at me. Swear words angle and curve around diagrams of drug use. Stick-figure illustrations of sexual positions fill the space between. According to my stall, my mother, as in the universal usage of *your* mother, sucks semen through a straw. This particular message is accompanied by an interesting illustration that looks less like the image and more like a walrus with a party hat. The creativity and artistry signal a higher calling—a prison-wall scribe, a graffiti tagger.

The bathroom door squeaks open as feet shuffle across the tile. Whispers spit from lips, eager and immediate. I lift my feet from the floor to the toilet seat and hug my knees to my chest.

"Check the stalls," a guy says.

"No one's here, Paul," the other guy says in a deeper voice.

"Please."

The first stall door slams opens. Whether the door was pushed or kicked, I can't tell, but judging by the force, the heavy sound, I'd say kicked. With aggression. The second door slams open. Followed by the third.

"See," the other guy says. "Nothing."

"Don't forget to check the last stall."

"You're so paranoid."

"I'll feel better once I lock this door." Then, a loud *click* echoes as the bathroom door locks into place.

Class, please note, the following will be on the final exam. This situation is not only theoretically, but also technically referred to as *being fucked*. This is not to be confused with *getting fucked*.

A hand grips the top of my stall and pushes it open, but not all the way and the guy never looks in. He walks back across the bathroom.

"Paul?" he says.

Paul shushes him.

"Paul?" he says softer.

"What?"

"How was your summer?"

"Not long enough," Paul says.

"Go on any trips?"

"The beach. Twice."

"With?"

"My parents," Paul says. "Some friends."

"Which beach?"

"Ocean City. You?"

"I worked for my father all summer."

"Doing what?" Paul asks.

"Landscaping."

I focus on keeping my breathing as quiet as possible, keeping my feet from squeaking on the toilet seat. They're quiet now, and the more I listen to the silence, the more I can hear myself think and know I am going to do something to give myself away.

I close my eyes and think *please go away, please go away, please go away*, but they don't go away and are no longer silent.

They crash into the stall next to me.

They grab and grunt and go at each other.

Their stall door closes and locks and Paul says, in a way that I know he is smiling, "Zink, let me show you what I learned on my summer vacation."

8

The rest of the day blows by in a blur with classes and lectures and roll calls and seating assignments in neckties and khaki pants, all the while I can't get that girl with the deadly red hair out of my head.

My teachers for the most part are old and irritatingly excited that school has started, except for one who doesn't show for class at all—my English teacher, Mr. Rembrandt. How random is that? First day of school and already there's a substitute in the room, putzing around with nothing to teach. In each class, the teachers seat us alphabetically in some way around the room, but in English the substitute lets us sit wherever we want. Of course, I wind up between two winners. On my left, there's this Super Shy Kid who refuses to look at me or say his name when I introduce myself as I sit down. He even flinches when I dig into my bag for a pen. Fragile bitch. And then on my right, there's the Dirtbag Boy who needed some serious cosmetic surgery. Maybe a chemical peel and a power scrub and a round of dermatologist appointments. Pimples so big they could be seen from space. I can only imagine what the Plaids are going to do to these sad suckers.

The substitute isn't like any substitute that I've ever seen before, either. Not only is he the on-call for the entire school— here every day, waiting to sub for any teacher that calls out sick or comes in late or leaves early for a family emergency—but he's also the head coach of the varsity football team. He says his name is Dennis Vojzischek, but we should call him Mr. Vo. He doesn't look like a football coach, but more like a thick-necked, post-college stockbroker in a pinstriped, three-piece suit, slicked back hair, and brown leather briefcase open on the desk. A white pocket square peeks out form the breast pocket of his sport coat. He takes off his coat and hangs it on the back of a chair, revealing his vest fully buttoned up and a Windsor knot exposed. He doesn't say much during class, except to call out our names and instruct us to read quietly. There's no trace of an accent, despite his foreign-sounding last name. He's soft spoken, but his voice is crystal clear, hitting every syllable hard. He never sits, but instead walks up and down each row and along the walls, his spit-shined shoes clicking with each step. At the end of class, he makes a fist and holds it in front of him.

"This is a Catholic school, gentlemen. Yes?"

No one answers.

He lowers his fist, flexes his fingers, and then raises his fist again. "This is a Catholic school, gentlemen, yes?"

"Yes," we say.

"Yes, sir," he says.

"Yes, sir," we say.

"And in a Catholic school we have prayer. In this Catholic school, we pray to St. John Baptist de La Salle and we pray to Jesus Christ. You will pray every day you are here. You will pray in every class of the day. Someone will say *St. John Baptist de La Salle*." He punches his fist at us. "You will say *pray for us*." He retracts his fist. "Someone will say *live Jesus in our hearts*." He punches his fist back out. "You will say *forever*." He lowers his hand. "So let's try this one time and then call it a day. St. John Baptist de La Salle."

We respond, "Pray for us."

"Live Jesus in our hearts."

We respond, "Forever."

"I'll tell Rembrandt you men did fine work today." He snaps his briefcase shut on the desk. "Get out of here."

Rumors spread throughout the halls about Rembrandt for the rest of the day. Rumors that his flight was delayed, returning from a rehab facility for heroin addiction in Phoenix. Rumors that he was seen downtown in Fell's Point tearing through the local bars on the harbor, working on a three-day booze bender. Rumors that this is typical first day of school behavior. That he always misses the first day of school every year as a way to put his students behind schedule, which forces them to buckle down and focus on their reading and critical writing.

The final bell rings and students flood the hallway, clamoring to escape back to summer. The hallway smells of cheap cologne and biting body odor—clusterfucked with bodies slamming into each other, swinging book bags like medieval weapons.

Honestly, it reminds me of one of my favorite zombie movies of all time—*Night of the Living Dead*.

George A. Romero's *Night of the Living Dead* series has six entries of the franchise to date. I like them each less than the one before it. The sequential order is:

Night of the Living Dead.
Dawn of the Dead.
Day of the Dead.
Land of the Dead.
Diary of the Dead.
Survival of the Dead.

The cowriter of *Night*, John Russo—a dickbag—rebooted the series with his own dickbag vision. Hence, *Return of the Living Dead,* a splintered and less affecting sequel to *Night*. Russo then went on to make four more with utterly dickbagish titles:

Return of the Living Dead.
Return of the Living Dead Part II.
Return of the Dead Part III.
Return of the Dead: Necropolis.
Return of the Dead: Rave from the Grave. (This is, clearly, my favorite title.)

Night has been remade twice as a standalone—the first in 1990 based on Romero and Russo's original screenplay, but way gorier. It also portrays the character Barbara as less of a hag and more of a hero. I prefer her as a hag. The second reboot was not surprisingly made in 3-D as everything is made in 3-D these days. The 3-D reboot was called *Night of the Living Dead 3-D*. Shockingly original, I know. The reboots aren't always terrible, though, like the remake of *Dawn of the Dead*. This film gets it right. I'd go so far as to say it's my second favorite in the entire family tree.

The final list is as follows:

Night of the Living Dead
Dawn of the Dead
Return of the Living Dead.
Day of the Dead
Return of the Living Dead Part II.
Land of the Dead
Return of the Dead Part III.
Diary of the Dead
Return of the Dead: Necropolis
Survival of the Dead.
Return of the Dead: Rave from the Grave
Night of the Living Dead (1990)
Night of the Living Dead 3-D
Night of the Living Dead: Origins 3-D
Dawn of the Dead (2004)

At my locker, the Plaids pass by but leave me alone, partially, I think, because I make myself disappear by standing still. I try a couple of combinations to see if I can recall it from memory. I can't and after a few failed attempts I leave everything behind. I don't have any homework yet anyway.

Outside, the girls from Prudence re-emerge on the patio off the cafe again and walk in front of me toward the lecture hall building where the theater is. I follow them as it's on my way to the front circle where Dad is going to pick me up. I keep a safe distance. I don't want them to think I'm perving all over them. The girl with dark red hair shoots me more nasty glares, not smiling even a little bit. I check my shirt for embarrassing stains. I feel the outline of my hair to see if I have some kind of cowlick or menacing swoop action happening. But I feel nothing. The girls merge together with a small group outside of the building, reading a sign taped to the door: AUDITIONS CANCELED TODAY AND RESCHEDULED FOR TOMORROW.

At the front circle, I check my cell phone and have a voicemail from Dad. He says something's come up and he can't pick me up. He says for me to take the 55 bus home. He goes on to say a lot of things, but what he doesn't ever say is *I'm sorry*.

II
DAWN OF THE DEAD

(Released Date: March 19, 2004)

Directed by Zack Snyder

Writers: George A. Romero (1978 screenplay),
James Gunn (screenplay)

9

Jackson took the 55 bus home from school when he went to Byron Hall, and it looks like the tradition will continue. I ride the 55 home just fine and am surprised to find Dad's car parked out front. He's been protecting his secrets a lot lately and while he may think he's got them all buried away, they always find a way to come tumbling out in a messy, messy flood.

Truth has a way of bitch-slapping you right in the balls when you least expect it.

Tricia sits on the deck next door, stretched out in red wrap sweater on a chaise lounge chair, reading a magazine through sunglasses the size of two grapefruits. Her dog Travis lies on the deck next to her chair. He's one of those small fat round dogs that looks like a human head with feet.

She greets me with a smile and tells me that I look sick. She's reading the September *InStyle*, an issue I don't have yet. I tell her that I'm fine and feel normal and that nothing is wrong. Tricia talks about the weather—how pleasant it's been lately and how the end of summer never used to be as cool as it is now and how I should never talk about the weather with a girl that I am interested in because weather is a state of environmental change, not conversation.

"You really don't look well," she says.

"I really don't feel well," I say. "I think I'm coming down with something." I blow hot air onto my wrist before placing it on my forehead.

"Oh, sweet Jeremy," she says, sitting at the edge of the chaise lounge chair now. "Come here, hon. Let me feel your forehead for you." She signals me to come even closer to her. "I'm not standing up, so you have to kneel down," she says.

I kneel on the wood deck. Travis sits and licks my fingers. Tricia places the back of her hand on my forehead. There's perfume on her soft skin—lavender or almond milk, I think. Our house used to smell like this when Mom lived with us. Tricia holds her hand to my forehead long enough for me to have a quick fantasy about her.

"Why aren't you back at school?" I ask, pulling away from her. "Harvard, right?"

"No fever," she says, pushing herself back on the chaise lounge chair away from me.

Is there such a thing a being *beyond embarrassment*? Please note that *embarrassment* can be easily avoided with a simple medical procedure called a *lobotomy*. Not only would this help me not look like such a fucknut in front of girls, but it would help me not to sound like one either. Some slight incision in a particular brainal lobe and I'd be good to go—*lobotomized*. Make me a legitimate zombie, for real.

"What are you thinking about right now?" she asks.

"You wouldn't believe me if I told you."

Travis continues to lick away, like he's going for my bones.

"Try me," she says. "I have a pretty big imagination." She places her glasses back over her eyes and closes her magazine, setting it on the chair next to her.

"I can't," I say. "I wish I could, but I really can't. Maybe some other time?"

The porch door to her house swings open and her father, a real fatso, stands fatly in the doorway. Tricia turns toward him, offering him her profile only, not her eyes. He doesn't say anything and just fats there waiting for her with the door wide open.

"Jeremy," she says, "I don't ever ask a question when I'm not prepared to hear the answer, no matter how unbelievable." She walks to her house and before she evaporates in the darkness, she turns back to me, offering me her eyes, and says, "Feel better."

Travis trots inside behind her.

Her father closes the door.

I think my Dad and her Dad should go bowling together.

On the chaise lounge chair, she's left me a gift—September's *InStyle*. It would make an excellent addition to my collection hidden in the closet of my bedroom.

As I cross the yard walking back to my house, I notice the grass. It's cut low and balding in places. I wonder what story our grass tells about us.

10

I enter through the side door and know Dad's home, but I don't hear a single sound. He's somewhere inside, I'm sure of it, lost in himself, not thinking about me. The house is still, but kinetic, so I keep a sharp eye and explore my house like Ben from *Night of the Living Dead* ("*NOLD*") explores the farmhouse—nervy, lost, and waiting for zombies to attack.

The dining room is empty, the antique table owning the majority of the room with a pile of recently read newspapers at the edge. Mom told me that the table was made of cherry oak, a detail she wanted to impress me with I think, along with four matching plush chairs with fairy-green seat cushions and images of cherubs carved into the wood backs. Needless to say, I wasn't. The cherubs look like evil little fuckers and have always made me hesitant to lean back in them, like they could come to life and bite the shit out of me at any moment. Dad is not here.

There used to be beautiful and vibrant paintings by local Baltimore artists hung on the walls. There used to be awesome, giant, silver candlestick holders, like in castles. Red and black and green beaded, handwoven, Chilean placemats. Real silver forks, spoons, and knives, all a different size, and multiple porcelain plates and bowls on display, formally and forever set on the table, like our family was prepared for a dinner party to break out at any moment. There used to be heavy and thick crystal vases filled with fresh flowers replaced every Sunday night, always the same—white lilies, pink primroses, or black dahlias.

We used to have all of these things, but none of these things matter because none of these things are here anymore. Mom took the crystal vases and candlesticks and silverware and porcelain and placemats. She took all that with her. Maybe she sold it all for pill money.

I just wish she'd taken those cherubs.

Our kitchen is not much better off than the dining room—no potholders, or salt and pepper shakers, or ceramic sauce spoon on the stove, or cookbooks, or magnets on the refrigerator holding up my artwork or high grades, or bottles of extra virgin olive oil on the counter. Mom took most of the kitchen shit. She left the plant and the carving knives. This is why Dad and I only use plasticware when we eat. Sorry, Environment.

Dog sleeps on her side in the corner like she's been gutshot, splayed across her red plaid pillow, her chest rising and falling as she breathes. She whimpers, occasionally, dreaming, probably of hunting rabbits or squirrels or mice. I press the palm of my hand against her chest, right where I think her heart is, and feel her heartbeat. Her shiny black coat feels warm and soft and smells like dryer sheets. Dog opens her eyes and licks her snout, lapping it with her tongue.

"Good girl," I whisper, running my hand over her ears and down to her neck. "You know where Dad is?" Dog puts her paw in my hand and groans and sighs. Mom didn't try and take Dog when she left, but I was prepared to fight to keep her here with me—Dog, that is, not Mom.

11

Dog was a gift from Santa back when I believed in Santa, the way I used to believe in a two-parent family. It was eight years ago. I remember hearing a whimper in the middle of the night. I tiptoed downstairs to investigate. There was a cage next to the fireplace—a black Labrador puppy inside, standing, its tail shaking and whacking in every direction, its ears and paws two sizes bigger than its body. She started barking when she saw me, which woke everyone up.

Mom and Dad both came downstairs, Mom smiling in her pink robe, Dad adjusting himself in his boxers.

Jackson sat at the bottom of the stairs, barely in his boxers; his head in his hands, completely uninterested, his eyes closing like a garage door.

Mom sat next to me on the floor, poking her hand inside the cage with mine.

The dog shoved its cold nose and sharp teeth at my fingers, nibbling, licking, rubbing. Its ears flopped around like two wind-blown flags.

"Dad, come pet it," I said. "It's a dog."

"It's a girl dog," Mom said.

"A girl dog," I said, repeating her words, making them my own.

"A girl dog?" Dad asked. "Corrine, you said it was a boy."

"They were out," she said.

"We're going to have puppies," he said. "I just know it. Christ."

"Not if we get her fixed," Mom said, rubbing my head.

"It's a damn, dumb dog," Dad said from his reclined position on the couch.

The dog yelped.

"See," Dad said, pointing at the dog.

The dog yelped again.

"Shut up, dog," he said.

"Ballentine," Mom said. "Language."

"Dog," I said to myself.

"It's too early for barking dogs and being corrected by my wife," he said.

"Must you?" Mom whispered.

"It'll wake the neighbors," Dad said, throwing up his hands.

"What do you want to name her?" Mom asked.

"Dog," I said, which I thought was her name anyway. I thought that every animal came into the world with a predetermined name, a future, a life. I thought that my dog's name had been preset, that it was her identity in this life to be named the very thing that she was—a dog.

12

I sweep through the first floor of our house, but there's no sign of Dad, even though I know he's here somewhere. I can feel it in my bones. I wish someone were here with me, maybe Tricia or Zink, someone to talk to, someone to be my cover. Then again, maybe not. I'll be honest—whenever I watch *NOLD* I'm reminded of how much Ben's partner-in-crime, Barbara, fucking pisses me off. She's a raging, crazy bitch that makes dumb decisions. Ben slapping her is the highlight of the movie.

When I first saw *NOLD*, I thanked Ben out loud like he was in the room. He's the original zombie killer who completely embodies the fourth Zombie Survival Code—*Lock-and-Fucking-Load*. The big joke in the original director's cut is that Ben survives the zombie nightmare, his night of the living dead, only to be shot dead by the police as he comes out of the house. They think he's a zombie. They lock-and-load and don't think twice about it. There's that bitch-slap to the balls that I was talking about. Most days, I wish I had a little bit of Ben in me. Not *in me* like in a sex kind of way, but in me like a *hero* kind of way.

I nearly drop Tricia's September issue of *InStyle* when the house phone rings. The answering machine picks up and Dad's voice shouts out his specific voicemail instructions.

You've reached Mister Ballentine Barker. He is not available, which means he is not here. Leave your message in the following order, or your message will not be returned: first name, last name, phone number, brief reason for your call, first name again, last name again, phone number again. Then hang up. You have less than thirty seconds.

There is a pause in the message and then the beep.

"Mister Ballentine Barker," a woman says, laughing. "Your message is the greatest thing. I love it so much. Oh, honey, do I love it." She sounds like she's either flirting with him or busting his balls and I can't tell which. "Oh, God," she says, collecting herself, controlling her breathing. "This is Grace, your administrative assistant." Balls. She's busting his balls. He hates it when people make fun of his message and he really hates it when Grace refers to herself as his administrative assistant. "Where the hell are you? I have been calling your—"

Before Grace has a chance to finish her message, the machine cuts off and Dad picks up. "Sec-re-tary," Dad says, annunciating the syllables. "Hear how that sounds and embrace it. You are my sec-re-tary?"

I tiptoe along the wall. I hear the sound of turning pages—a book. I reach the end of the hallway and peek around the corner to Dad's office. The lights are off except for one that hangs over him like a dentist chair lamp. He sits behind his monstrous desk—this thick, antique, wooden beast of a thing, flipping pages of a textbook, wearing glasses, the ones he uses when he has to read small print. His silver tie in a Windsor but loose around his neck, his shirt and suit pants wrinkled—same as he wore this morning. He turns back and forth between two pages.

"The difference between a secretary and an administrative assistant is that at least with an administrative assistant I would have a broad with a brain. Are you listening to me? Clearly, you are not. Clearly, I must be talking to a zombie version of my secretary," he says.

There should be a soundtrack playing behind me right now— heavy thumping bass, all loud and shit, because I'm being a sneaky and suspicious sonuvabitch. Dad is being a sneaky and suspicious sonuvabitch too, taking me to school like he did, then disappearing and leaving me to take the damn bus home. Even sneakier than me.

"I told you, I'm sick. Do you need me to cough into the fucking phone? Do you need me to fax you a doctor's note?" he asks.

He glances up from his book to the framed photo of himself hung on the wall—his Marine photo, standing next to an American flag in full Marine blues and a young chiseled *don't fuck with me* face. He looks back to his book and berates Grace some more, then drops the phone back on the receiver, like a log being dropped on a burning fire.

See ZSC's one through three—avoid eye contact, keep quiet, forget it all. I disappear into a closet, leaving it open a crack for me to peak through.

I hear Dad whistle in perfect pitch and then say, "Here, girl." He waits by the hutch, sliding his keys and wallet into his pocket. Dog's tail thwaps side to side as she trots obediently at his heels, never in front, always behind him as they leave the house. Dad snaps on a black leash, rubbing and scratching behind both of her ears. "That's my good girl."

And out the front door they go—my father and the daughter he never had.

13

Dad's office is an altar—immaculate, symbolic, final.

I sit in his high-back, black leather office chair and it swivels without having to push or set it in motion at all. My feet don't touch the ground as I spin around and I feel like a kid again. I don't give the chair any acceleration or gas. It just goes, unattended. Must be a slant in the room. An uneven floor. I scoot to the edge of the chair and plant my feet on the hardwood, wait to gather my bearings, and then shove off, spinning fast, whipping around, the wheels grinding against the floor. Then, calculating the end, I grab for the desk and come to a dead stop.

A teenaged, Marine version of Dad stares at me from the wall—an American flag behind him, no smile, dead eyes and a shorn head. A grunt. He looks so much like Jackson, something I maybe only recognize now. His Purple Heart has a purple ribbon with a gold heart shape medallion with the profile of George Washington on it. Dad has never confirmed that he was ever wounded in Vietnam, which would have been the only way for him to receive the Purple Heart that I know of.

I remember when Dad told Mom that no man or woman was ever going to tell him what to do unless they could match what hung on his office wall. They stood in the kitchen, Mom chopping lettuce for a salad, Dad washing plum tomatoes. I set the dining room table with plates, forks, knives, and cloth napkins held together in a cigar-shaped roll with silver napkin rings. I finished and sat at my Cherub-backed chair and waited. Dad followed her around the kitchen and asked her if she knew what a man had to do to get a Purple Heart and she replied as she always did about sensitive topics, which was to execute ZSC #1 and ZSC #2—avoided eye contact and kept quiet. Mom filled a teakettle with water when Dad finally said, "Match my wall and I will do whatever you want and whatever you will."

James Dean and Jayne Mansfield hang on the wall behind his desk under framed squares of glass. James Dean is wearing a red jacket with his collar flipped up and a white T-shirt underneath. He is leaning forward, narrowing his eyes. What was he looking at when the picture was taken? His arm crooks in an L-shape, hand en route to lips with a lit cigarette pinched between two fingers. Dad loves James Dean. Dad says James Dean was a real man. *Lived fast and died young. Died in a car accident. Yeah.* Dad says the same thing about Jayne Mansfield. He says Jayne Mansfield was a real woman. *Died in a car accident. Her head was cut off clean from her body. That's called decapitated. Yeah. But, goddamn, she was sexy!*

In her poster, Jayne Mansfield wears a sparkle dress. It's black and shiny and she is leaning back on a chair, holding a cigarette like James Dean except her cigarette is stuffed inside one of those thin black cigarette holders that all those super-rich women used to smoke through. Anyway, Jayne Mansfield is leaning back and smoking and her hair is super, super blonde and curled up in the front. You can't see any cleavage. Her tits are pushed down under the dress but she is wearing these gold bracelets and necklaces that show off her pale skin. Dad says that Jayne Mansfield is what all women should be.

I wonder why he married Mom. Mom has brown hair and doesn't smoke and doesn't have a Purple Heart.

I pull myself closer to Dad's monstrous wood desk and examine it like a crime scene. Yellow Post-it notes stick to the desk pad— each with a date, a number, and names.

7/25   4   Beekman, Rogers, Santiago, Williams
8/15   2   Holdsworth, Giorgiano
8/29   6   Andersen, Trout, Druller, Mapleton, Ott, McDowell
9/5   ?   ?

Doodles cover other Post-its, drawn in dark, heavy black pen, carved into the paper like they'd been traced hundreds of times. The doodles look crude and violent; body parts wearing Windsor knots—a foot, an arm, an ear, a tongue. Everywhere I look I see more body parts with fat knots. More numbers and more dates. Older dates going back before July and more names.

Everly, Kleaversdorf, Vaille, Goodwell, Robison, Price, Young.

The handwriting is small—no, not small, tiny.

There is an open book, a dissected face diagramed and cut down into specific parts, showing the layers of muscles and nerves and bone. I flip it closed with my thumb as a place-holder and run my fingers over the red fabric of the cover: *Christopher's Textbook of Surgery.* I push back from the desk and open his desk drawers, descending, starting at the top and moving down with increasing speed. I dig through pens and legal pads, a calculator and realty brochures and business cards with Dad's face and fake fucking smile, a home office medical kit filled with Band-Aids, gauze, a tiny bottle of iodine, and medical manuals on emergency field surgery. I flip through hanging folders, mostly bills and birth certificates, social security cards, and bank statements, but also Dad's not-so-secret collection of seventies *Playboys.* Mainly girls with hairy bushes and big hair. Dad doesn't know that I know about his handful of old man magazines because Jackson showed me once when I was asking him questions about boobs and why they all had different sizes. The pages are fragile, stiff and wrinkled from water damage. These magazines were the magazines that Dad carried with him when he was *in the shit,* as he likes to say, soaked through from the torrents of rain.

His magazines are nothing like my magazines.

I open his office closet. It looks like an evidence locker in the basement of a police station. A floor-to-ceiling shelving unit bursts at the seams with boxes of all sizes. Thick black words mark boxes in years—*1987, 1996, 2001*—or in names and associations—

Jackson/College, Corrine/Medical Rehab, Jeremy/Summer Camp,
Ballentine/Brochures, Dog/Veterinarian. Minimal, cold, exact.

I thumb through the more accessible boxes at the bottom of
the closet marked in years. Boring shit mostly—incomprehensible
financial paperwork with tricolored pie charts and line graphs and
percentage numbers. I move on to a few boxes marked with names
and associations, but they really interest me less, that is except for
one.

It's clearly the largest box in the closet—unmarked, anonymous,
a plain brown box. I slide it off the shelf and place it on the floor.
The box is deep and heavy and long. I unfold the flaps and find
that the box *is* marked along the inside flaps, with tiny lettering, to
be kept a secret.

Ballentine Barker's Box of War.

Inside, there's a story. First, a canteen. I shake it. It's empty, but I
unscrew the top anyway and am hit with the smell of some kind of
alcohol. Whisky, I think—something Dad said he always asked my
grandparents to send him. An envelope holding a necklace with
two silver tags, dog tags. Folded, faded maps—absolutely nothing
recognizable to me. A stack of Polaroids. Young Dad holding big
guns. Dad standing with other Marines, holding their own big
guns. Dad and other Marines with their big guns at the camera.
Other Marines with their big guns at each other. Smaller guns to
their own heads. Their big guns at photos of naked women with
big bushes taped to the wall of their barracks. Dad looks thin and
clean cut, wide-eyed, but not in a scared way, instead in a wide-
eyed, let-too-much-light-in kind of way. He smiles in most of the
photos, a similar smile to the fake fucking one he has in all of his
realtor materials. Dad wears a green T-shirt and camouflage, smokes
a cigarette, his arm around another Marine, a blond guy. They stand
in front of a jungle that's completely in flames. The caption reads:
OBLIVION. In another picture, Dad drinks a can of beer, standing
over a dead body—face down on the ground. The dead body is
missing an ear, like it had been cut clean off. Dried blood caked

around the wound from where it dripped down the side of his face. It was so clear that I could even see flies that had landed on the body. Pictures of foreign women in bars barely dressed—whores or hopeless women in short skirts with a lot of make-up. Some make kissy faces at the camera. Two girls French kiss in a blurry haze of red and green neon light. A girl hangs on Dad's arm and the girl isn't Mom. The girl is Asian. Another picture of Dad, sitting on a cot in a tent, shirtless, dog tags dangling down—above him a sign written in red paint: FUCK THIS SHIT. The last picture is a profile picture, like George Washington in the Purple Heart. Dad is sticking out his tongue through a smile.

My hand brushes up against something cold. It looks wet or frozen or recently shined. Resting there. If it had teeth, it would have bitten my hand clean off. Black handle. Pinky-finger-sized hole. A body and a chamber. Curved angles. Masterful arcs of steel. I flip it over like it's a dead fish—not wet or frozen. Heavy and recently cleaned as a streak of grease rubs onto my hand. I feel the weight of the gun in my hand. An electric charge races through my body, etching under my skin. I raise it and aim it at Young Dad. I hold it steady, not ready to let go, locking it away into my own personal prison. I release the air from my body in a long controlled exhale, a smooth and single stream, and when I don't have any air left in my body to keep me alive I pull the trigger.

The gun—click.

The front door—bang.

The gun isn't loaded.

The gun is still in my hand and Dad is coming through the door, struggling with Dog's leash. Shit. I tuck the gun back into the *Ballentine Barker Box of War*, slap the flaps down. Shit. Dad couldn't be making any more noise in the foyer if he tried, coughing, grunting, walking, moving, breathing, whatever-the-fucking. His presence sounds immediate, like he's on top of me. Like he's in the office. Like he's standing over me, towering. Shit. Dog scrambles across the hardwood floor, released from the leash, her nails scratching as she moves through the house—foyer, dining room, kitchen. She drinks her water, her tongue slapping the water—a tired dog after a hard run. I stop moving and listen for him but don't hear anything until he calls out my name. Shit. The hardwood floors creak and tremor under his heavy steps as he sweeps the first floor looking for me like I did him. Shit. I lift the box of war back to its shelf and slide it into place, pushing it against the wall.

Zombie Survival Code Three.

Erase, forget it, get gone.

Never knew a thing.

Never happened.

14

Dad shouts my name from the foyer again. Frankly, I'm surprised he remembers me at all. I sneak out of his office when his back is turned. He closes the front door and finally finds me standing in the foyer too. I could have come from anywhere and he knows it.

"I got a call from your school today," he says.

"It was only Algebra," I say.

"Did you get lost?" he asks. "The school is one giant hallway. I don't understand how you get lost in one giant hallway."

"You didn't pick me up after school," I say. "More than that, you disappeared last night and didn't come home until this morning."

Dog sits by his feet, licking her chops.

"Good girl," he says. "Good girl." Dad slaps her side in hard thuds.

"If you won't tell me where you were last night, then tell me where you were this afternoon?"

He hangs Dog's leash over the banister and steps past me.

"I asked you a question," I say. I run down the hallway, and step in his way.

"You're as neurotic as your fucking mother," he says. "Fine. You want to know. I was with Liza."

"Liza? Who the fuck is Liza?"

"Please move," he says.

"Stop lying to me."

"Please, Jeremy."

"Were you with Liza last night? Or just this afternoon?"

"I'm sorry for not telling you about her sooner," Dad says without anything behind it. "She's someone I've been seeing. She's an ER nurse at Johns Hopkins, so her schedule is always changing."

"Call her up," I say. "Get her on the phone. I want to talk to her. I want to meet her. Let's make a meet-the-family date. Chinese and an old zombie classic. *I Walked With a Zombie.* Chicks dig black-and-white, right, Dad? You taught me that. Call her up."

"I'll be in my office," he says, placing his hands on my shoulders and gently moving me out of his way.

"What's her last name? Where does she live?"

Before Dad disappears into his office, I clap my hands together. It startles him. Dad looks back at me.

"Where were you?" I ask.

He kicks his office door closed. The fuck.

I press my ear to the door. Silence simmers inside. String-based orchestral music soon slices away the nothingness, before heavy brass marches in.

"I can still hear you," I say, punching the door. "Can you hear me?" I punch the door with both hands now. "What's her last name?" My fists flatten against the wood. Holding the door steady with one hand, I slap the door with the other, machine-gunning. I bang harder and louder and call him by name—*Ballentine, Ballentine, Ballentine!* I turn the knob and push and pull, throwing all of my weight behind it, but the door doesn't budge and instead makes a *clunk-clunk* sound. I keep fucking banging and will continue to bang until he opens up and tells me about the picture of the dead body in his box of war and how he was wounded in Vietnam and the gun and how this all has to do with some whore named Liza or something else altogether.

15

The earliest memory I have of Dad is: disappearing.

The house was empty.

I walked from room to room. The lights were off. I didn't turn them on, or call out his name, for fear of disturbing whatever might be inside.

Dad was gone.

I searched. I scoured. A human flashlight, flicking on lights in every room, ridding them of nothing. Under the dining room table by the cherubs carved into the wooden chairs. Behind the couch in the living room. In his immaculate office. Under the monstrous desk in his immaculate office. In the closet next to the monstrous desk of his immaculate office. It felt like he wanted me to find him. Like we were playing hide-and-seek. I opened the front door and turned on the outside light that lit up the night in a damning shade of a dark glow, the pumpkins seemingly bigger, casting shadows. Bushes and trees looked like monster claws and demon smiles. I listened for him, recognizing nothing.

Then, I heard something new in the darkness, coming from the basement. A groan—guttural and God-awful. Monster claws. Demons smiles. I slammed the front door with both hands, fumbling with the several levels of locks and latches, turning off the light outside and turning on the one inside. The groan grew louder. I moved away from the door and retreated further inside the house. With each step, it grew—a cold silence standing between each growing groan. Then. There. I saw it—the basement door ajar.

This is my earliest memory, the memory I remember foremost.

My tiny fingers pulled back the chipped, white door without a squeak, the opposite of horror movies. The door was dead quiet, opening easy like the legs of some whore. The door swung wide and I hid behind it, peering through the thin space between the door and the frame, angling my anxious eyes down the dark stairwell to the basement, searching for the hellbeast.

I measured the groans in slow, whispered Mississippi's.

One Mississippi.
    Two Mississippi.
        Three Mississippi.
            Four Mississippi.
                Five Mississippi.
                    Six Mississippi.
                        Seven Mississippi.
                            Eight Mississippi.

A heavy shadow moved below. I wanted to flip the switch, but it was too high up on the wall, just out of reach even if I stood on the tips of my toes. The groan picked up and lasted longer, lifting louder, before it bellied up and broke into a growl, coming up out of the blackness, gaining on me. Devils and demons. Growing and growing greater.

At the basement stairs. Footsteps thumping, ascending from below, shrugging off the black, heavy and hard. Either feet or cloven hooves—something broken, something wrong, something foul. And in the moment before the devils and demons devoured me, I covered my eyes with my hands and prayed the Lord's Prayer. This was the only prayer I knew wholly, a prayer I'd heard my mother say every day, twenty times a day, whenever she'd take her pills. I said the prayer with my head in my hands, as the darkness rose up around me.

This is the earliest memory I have of my dad, the first, most part of me.

16

In my bedroom, I flip through Tricia's September issue of *InStyle*. An exotic, beautiful woman—some actress or musician or both, I'm not entirely sure—is on the cover, wearing a Japanese kimono embroidered with a purple dragon stitched into the seemingly silk fabric. She holds the kimono just below her shoulders; her head tilted back, her thick, blonde hair so curly it makes me want to lose my hands in it. Her teeth are too white and perfect. On either side of her photo are titles of articles, indicating more often than not how to do something better, whether it be lose weight, have sex, apply makeup, wear bathing suits, flirt, cook, tell if your man is lying, or avoid general embarrassment. I turn to a tampon advertisement where women hold hands as they jump off a cliff. They are barefoot and wear bikinis. There is no way this many women would jump off a cliff together at the same time. I lick my index finger and turn the page at the upper right hand corner and read a personal essay on cutting, a disorder where people cut their skin in order to feel. The article cites the disorder as a serious form of depression. I flip back to the picture of the women holding hands, jumping off the cliff. The tag at the bottom of the tampon ad reads: NO FEAR. I turn back and forth, looking at the women jumping off the cliff and the article on cutters. Then, I go on autopilot and flip through each page like a machine counting cash—fast and without hesitation. Before I finish, I'm at my closet, sorting through the two-dozen board games stacked inside, finally opening one—*Stratego*—and lay the September *InStyle* inside. I pull down *Battleship* filled with more of the same magazines, but also my backup locker combination, which I slide into my shoe. I ease *Stratego* and *Battleship* back into place and step back, admiring my collection.

Each box—void of game contents.

Each box—filled with women's magazines.

I didn't always do this.

When Mom left, she had her mail forwarded to her new address where she was living with her boyfriend, Zeke. Mom left and her magazines kept coming to the house. I found them stacked high in the recycling bin when I dragged it to the curb on trash day. There was nothing more important to me in that moment than preserving them. *Bon Appétite. House & Garden. Oprah. Body & Soul. Marie Claire.* When I finished reading them cover-to-cover, I found inserts offering discounts and deals on other magazines and sent in subscriptions under Corrine Barker. Soon all kinds of chick mags came to the house. *Good Housekeeping. Allure. Parents. Cosmopolitan.* They'd come in the mail and I'd grab them before Dad found them, or if he got home early, I'd save them from recycling. This continued for some time until creditors began calling to collect the subscription fees and Dad swore it was Corrine playing a trick on him and canceled the magazines. Now I steal them wherever I can find them and keep them in my closet, hidden away and out of sight.

Barefoot and back at my window, I search for Tricia. Her blinds are closed, but I wait. My toes curl into the carpet. I picture her walking across her room in a bra and panties. I picture her in nothing but a T-shirt. I picture her lifting her hand holding an imaginary phone, lifting it to her ear and mouth and asking me to call her.

When Mom remodeled our house two years ago, she ordered carpet for my room. She picked out a forest green because it was my favorite color back then, but when the carpet guys arrived to install it, they had brought an industrial gray. Mom and Dad argued. They argued about everything. After the men finished installing the gray carpet and left the house and with the furniture moved back into my room, Mom took me out for ice cream. She let me order a triple scoop, hot fudge brownie sundae with all the toppings, the one I always asked for and was never allowed to get. We ate in the car—Mom with her tiny cup of orange sherbet. When we got home, Dad had disappeared. Mom let me stay up that night and watch the late night talk shows. She took pills and we slept in my room—me in my bed and Mom curled up on the new gray carpet with my green fleece blanket wrapped around her.

The carpet is thin and the same industrial gray as when it was installed.

I look for Tricia. I have to have the image of her—smooth skin, soft and sweet—except her blinds are still closed, so I take it into my own hands.

I sit on my bed and picture her here in my bedroom. She tells me that I'm not ready. She tells me that I am confused about things. Tricia stands in front of me wrapped in a red kimono pushed off her shoulders. And as my belt comes undone and my pants drop, she says, "Jeremy, let me show you what I learned over summer vacation."

17

Today is unlike any other day because today I stopped taking my pill.

Dad hunts me down in the house every day and drops the pill in my palm and says to take the *goddamn thing*. I knock it back without water, without a fight. But today Dad left my room and I spit the *goddamn thing* out.

My parents have me on Ritalin. Mom says it calms my hyper-excitability and helps me to be the boy she wants me to be. I like the sound of being hyperexcitable. My mom, the pillhead, says it's just a pill to help me get through the day.

Am I not the boy she wants me to be? And if so, how not? And if so, why not?

Dad says I'm normal now. Mom says I'm her little man. I say I'm something else altogether, because today is unlike any other day because today I'm Ritalin-free and completely hyperexcitable.

Dad disappeared again last night and didn't come home until this morning. He blew through the front door, disheveled and reeking of chemicals, and administered me my morning pill, before locking himself away in his bathroom. Last night he definitely broke pattern. He didn't eat dinner with me and watch a zombie movie and wait for me to fall asleep. Instead, he left as soon as I stopped banging on his office door and retreated to my bedroom.

I can't imagine riding in a car with him this morning and engaging in bullshit conversation all the way to school, so I pull a page out of the Ballentine Barker Handbook and I, too, disappear without a note or goodbye or explanation of any kind.

I take the 55 back to school and embrace this new hyperexcitability, firing away inside me.

18

The school bell rings, signaling the end of class and five minutes until the start of the next. I close my locker and navigate
through the riptide of students in the hallway as shoulders and arms
and elbows toss me about like a buoy in choppy speedboat waves.
I have English next and need to be on time since Mr. Rembrandt
missed class yesterday. I pass the front office, a room full of cubi-
cles where Christian Brothers and secretaries poke about, answering ringing phones, filing away papers into metal cabinets, feeding
stacks of paper through a fax machine, tapping away madly at key-
boards. I wonder which one of them called Dad when I missed
Algebra yesterday.

I exit through the front doors of Byron Hall, leaving the main
building, and cut around the corner, passing the teachers' parking
lot, and reach the sidewalk that parallels the even hallway; similar to the one on the other side of the building that parallels the
odd hallway. A freshly spray-painted football field and tennis courts
wrapped in a chain-link fence border the faculty parking lot. The
field and courts are empty. Old compact cars the color of coal and
sand junk up the teachers' lot.

I run my hand along the fence, smelling a toxic mix of the
newly painted football field and freshly cut grass, when I see a man
up ahead, walking toward me in long strides. He's not a Brother,
balding with brown hair in a crown around his head and blue-
rimmed glasses and a long tan raincoat draped over his arm. The
moment I see him, something shifts. I don't know, something just
shifts inside from bad to worse, tectonic plates. Stop touching the

fence. Hands in pockets. Head down. Focus. Pick up my pace. Move faster. I don't say shit to him—rule number two, yes, keep quiet, yes, shut the fuck up. Instead, I smile the kind of smile I give to cashiers after they give me my change. He does the opposite, sort of. No, he doesn't smile, but he does wave at me in a funny kind of way. More like a salute. He raises his hand to his forehead, showcasing a deformed hand—stiff thumb, index, middle, and ring fingers, but missing his little finger, the pinky, altogether. Gone. My eyes drop to his other hand by his side and see the same deformity—the four normals and one invisible. He chops his salute at me, lowers his hand, and moves on in the other direction.

For reasons I don't understand—maybe because of that tectonic shift—I just can't help myself. I follow. There's something about him. Something wrong, other than his fucked hands. I move to an enormous nearby tree and press my back up against it. I'm a sneaky, badass private detective. I slide down the tree to its base and pivot, peering out at him. 8-Fingers sorts through keys with his sad, remaining digits, and walks to the back of his car. He pops the trunk and leans in. He rearranges whatever is inside—spare tire, ice scraper, gym bag, books, windshield wiper fluid, flares, a dead body, his missing fingers. Who the fuck knows?

At the entrance to the school by the Byron Hall sign, a familiar-looking car signals a turn, waiting for a few cars to pass, then accelerates into the teachers' lot. The car's engine runs smooth and quiet. Sunlight glints off of the windshield, creating a phenomenal glare. It stops behind the bald man, and the window goes down.

This car belongs to my father and he is right behind the wheel. The great Ballentine Barker shakes 8-Fingers' hand in that acceptable way men exchange hand hugs. Who the fuck is this guy and how does Dad know him?

8-Fingers hands Dad a thin book and a plastic case, a DVD or CD. Dad tosses them into the passenger seat. Dad salutes, his hand at his forehead, chopping it down, and 8-Fingers returns the salute with his fucked-up hand. Dad rolls up the window, slips the car into reverse, and backs out of the faculty parking lot. 8-Fingers watches my father disappear into traffic. Sickness returns to my body, a scourge of hot and cold panic sets in.

I breathe. An uneven lightness lifts my head. Tiny, white circles spiral and pop, clouding my vision. A headache roars up behind my eyes. My skin breaks out into a cold sweat. I haven't taken that *goddamn thing*, my Ritalin, today and my body is ringing me up to say hello, to inform me that I am a sick young man and need to be back on medication to regulate myself. I focus on my breathing. The spots clear away. The lightness is still there. The roar fades to an echo of a freight train churning down a distant track.

I run.

I blast through the bushes to the sidewalk.

Brother Lee. Like some kind of mini-ninja. An Asian Christian Brother assassin. His hand grips my collar, like the scruff of a cat, and eases me into the chain-link fence of the tennis courts

"Mr. Barker," Brother Lee says. "We not met yet. I'm Brother Lee. Why you not in class, Mr. Barker?"

19

Brother Lee pushes me through the odd hallway by my elbow and aims me toward a closed classroom door. "Knock, Mr. Barker."

I make a fist and place it below the vertical window in the door. I want to knock, if only to rid myself of Brother Lee, but I cannot move my fist. It remains still against the door in a peaceful state of possibility.

"Knock, Mr. Barker," Brother Lee says. Brother Lee bangs on the door himself with an open hand of fury until the door swings open.

"Brother Lee." 8-Fingers adjusts his blue-rimmed frames and leans against the doorframe crossing his arms at his chest. "To what do I owe this honor?"

I see my classmates behind 8-Fingers. They look excited to witness this embarrassment.

"Mr. Rembrandt, are you missing anything?" Brother Lee asks.

"Thank you for finding him, Brother. High school can be disorienting for some freshmen. They have a tendency to disappear."

"He was very lost."

"Where did this young man think we were having class today?"

"Tennis courts."

"Really," Mr. Rembrandt says, smiling. "Tennis courts." Mr. Rembrandt wears a bright blue necktie with white polka dots tied in a Limp Dick knot. "What's your name, son?"

"Jeremy," I say.

"Jeremy. Jeremy. Jeremy." He repeats my name. "Does Jeremy have a last name like everyone else in the world?"

"Barker," Brother Lee says.

"My name is Jeremy Barker," I say.

Mr. Rembrandt points to a seat in the back next to a big, black kid and closes the door. Dirtbag Boy and Super Shy Kid are seated on the opposite side of the room, neither looking at me the way every other student is doing.

When I'm seated, Mr. Rembrandt surveys the class, looking at each student. "Now," he says. He combs wisps of thin, brown hair over his bald spot. He adjusts his glasses and continues. "Roll call. Attendance. Who is present and who is not." Mr. Rembrandt begins. "Jeremy Barker," he says, my name the first alphabetically in the class.

I raise my hand.

"Yes?" Mr. Rembrandt asks.

I keep my hand in the air.

"Can I help you?" he asks.

"Here," I say, but would much prefer to say *fuck you*.

"Nice of you to join us, Mr. Barker." He looks back to his class list. "Welcome," he says, then salutes me, and continues to call out names. After, he stalks through the desks. "Oh, freshmen, welcome to English Literature," Mr. Rembrandt says. "Two things I want to touch on before we begin." He claps his hands in succession, startling some of us. He stops clapping, poking his thumbs into his chest. "One—I am your leader," he says. He sits on his desk at the front of the classroom. "And two," he says, lifting two fingers, "this room is the room where the real torture begins." He extends his arms out, like Jesus on the Cross. "I know that we have some ground to make up since I was unable to grace you with my presence yesterday. Gentlemen, as I'm sure you've already been taught, we will say the prayer that'll begin and end every class for the next four years."

Mr. Rembrandt, making the Sign of the Cross, says, "St. John Baptist De La Salle."

As a class, also making the sign, we respond, "Pray for us."

Mr. Rembrandt says, "Live Jesus in our hearts."

And we say, "Forever."

20

After last period, I check my phone and wait at the circle for Dad, who doesn't come.

After most of the kids disappear, I call Mom's cell, but she doesn't answer.

I call Dad's cell again, but this time it goes right to his voicemail.

Then I try Jackson, but his goddamn voice mailbox is full.

The teachers' parking lot is almost empty.

Mr. Rembrandt stands at his car.

He sees me and salutes.

Chopping air.

Bus.

21

A car full of girls—windows down, music thumping—speeds into the front circle of school. The girls are dressed in the same short plaid skirts like the girls yesterday and the same tight, white blouses. They all look the same except for one, a girl who I know, which is surprising—the girl who refused to smile or wave back at me. She looks different from the rest.

Sister Prudence High School girls.

I pretend not to see them. We, the poor bastards at the bus stop, the collective, we pretend not to see them. We pretend not to see their smooth, long legs. We pretend not to almost smell their sweet, sweet scents. (Lip gloss? Lollipops?) We pretend not to wish to GOD to have x-ray vision and see through those white blouses. We pretend all the same damn things. We pretend these things, while flipping pages of a book, or checking our watches. That's what we do. We pretend, and then we fantasize. We fantasize a glimpse of their underwear—a thong under that skirt. We just know it. We imagine what we have never known. We imagine how it must smell and how it must feel and how everything must fit together. These are the things we imagine.

No dudes swarm the girls like they did the other morning, because those types of guys have long gone home. Only the poor bastards remain, and the jocks. The jocks either run long laps around the soccer field in shin guards and shorts or crash into each other on the football field, a mass of helmets and pads collapsing together into a pile of protected body parts. Coach O'Bannon wears a red track suit and attacks his players on the soccer field, screaming at them as they pass by, calling them horrible names and throwing whatever's not nailed down in their direction. Mr. Vo, like in class, wears his trademark three-piece suit, this time with the vest partially unbuttoned, and says very little. Instead he quietly walks along the sideline, watching his men and examining the drills before huddling with what look to be assistants, dispatching orders to be carried out.

Like clockwork, Brother Lee appears through the front doors and the girls point to the lecture hall building on the even side of the building, and he escorts them, herding them away from the boys. *God, save the boys!* The administration hates it when girls visit The Hall, unexpectedly.

"Fine, fine honeys," the black kid I sit next to in English says, also a poor bastard. He aims a fancy high-tech camera at me while I watch the girls—*click, click, click.* He wears a gold stud in his ear, a neon green tie knotted in a Limp Dick, and a red shirt.

"Honeys?" I ask, pretending I haven't noticed the girls, pretending I haven't even noticed that he's weirdly been photographing me.

He lowers his camera.

"The ladies in plaid—they're nice. You know what I mean, little man?"

"Don't call me that," I say. Mom calls me *little man*, but he doesn't need to know that.

"Meant nothing by it." He extends his hand, like Mr. Rembrandt did to Dad. "Michael. You sit next to me in English."

"I like the way you said that," I say, shaking his hand.

"What the hell are you talking about?" he asks.

"You said it like an asshole—*you sit next to me,* instead of *I sit next to you,* but whatever makes you feel like the boss."

"It's always all about me," he says.

"I'm Jeremy," I say. "And that?" I ask, meaning his fucking camera.

"My hobby," he says, snapping another picture. Still staring through his camera, he says, "You were late to class today." *Click, click, click.* "What's the deal with that?"

"Fuck off," I say, looking for my girl again. When I find her, she walks with a shake-and-bounce, entering the lecture-hall building, leaving Brother Lee behind to return to his office.

"She's a drama chick," Michael says.

"You don't even know her," I say.

"No," he says. "You got it wrong. You always get things wrong." *Click, click, click.* "Those girls, those beautiful bitches over there, including the one you want to marry, they're *all* in the drama department."

"That shit's off the chain dizzle," I say, but haven't the faintest fucking idea what I just said, much less why I said it, and immediately believe with all sincerity that Michael is going to beat the living white hell out of me.

Instead, he laughs in barks. "You're a funny little man," he says, taking a picture of a crushed can of soda in the gutter that looks like it has been used to smoke weed.

"I said don't call me that," I say.

"I'm heading over there," he says, thumbing at the lecture hall.

"Then head," I say.

"You have that bad of a day?" he asks. "Or you just on your period?" he asks with another *click, click, click.*

"You wouldn't understand," I say.

"Want to hear a secret?" he asks.

"Secrets make me nervous," I say.

"I'm African American." He laughs. "I'm black, except it's more like *yo, yo, yo, I'm black*," he says, thugged-out and gangster-licious. "People picture me slinging dope down in the tenement villages across from Camden Yards." He slaps me on the back. "Lighten up and laugh, Jeremy. Their ignorance gives me more swagger."

"Can you make me black?" I ask.

Michael laughs. "Sorry, little man."

"You aren't going to stop calling me that, are you?" I ask.

"I'm not." He swings his camera to the side and shows me a stack of postcard-size flyers. "Let's go. You're coming with me. We're going to meet those girls and hand out these flyers." He hands me a stack. "An exhibit of my work." The flyer has his name spelled different than I expected, Mykel, printed with the event information over top of a collage of photos cut and spliced together. "Chicks dig black artists. Chicks also dig white dudes who look at art." Michael (or Mykel) opens his bag to reload his camera with film.

"This is a photography exhibit?" I ask.

"I avoid explaining what I do, if I can."

"And you need my help why?"

"What bus you take home?" he asks.

"The 55," I say. "When my Dad can't pick me up."

"The M-T-A." Mykel claps. "Going Jeremy's way." He claps again and sings. "*Mass Transit. Yeah. Mass transit. Yeah. Mass transit. Yeah.*"

"I don't get it," I say.

"That's because you are wound way too tight." He grabs my shoulders, like Brother Lee did earlier, and shakes me. "Loosen up, baby. Be black like me and loosen up. Swagger, son. Let's see it." He reassembles his camera and points the long lens at me like the scope of a gun. *Click, click, click.* "Come and meet the ladies with me."

"I should get home," I say, as the 55 screeches up to the curb.

"I'm going to ask you one last question—who is waiting for you at home that is so damn important that they can't wait?" Mykel puts his arm around me. He smells like cherry flavored bubble gum, but he isn't chewing anything. "It's honey time, little man. Say it with me. Come on. Feel how the words fit in your mouth. What time is it?"

"It's honey time," I say, not feeling any blacker.

22

The foyer to the lecture hall is empty and quiet and smells like Lysol, like it had just been mopped. Glass-enclosed trophy cases line the walls, housing elaborate and varied trophies topped with tiny golden men in various positions covering what looks like athletic as well as academic accolades. The trophies have multiple levels, some with tiny golden men kicking tiny golden balls or swinging tiny golden bats. There are tiny golden briefcases and tiny golden suits and ties. There are tiny golden onesies with matching headgear, and all throughout the cases arms are upthrust, claiming tiny, golden victory.

A giant green plant guards the entrance to the lecture hall. Thick spear-shaped leaves aim like arrowheads from pencil-thin branches.

"I keep expecting Brother Lee to leap out from behind something," I say.

"Did you not hear me? I'm black. Brother Lee and I are on a first name basis."

Mykel and I follow signs taped to the walls that have the word *audition* printed on them with arrows.

"He lets you call him William?" I ask.

"Better."

"Bill?"

"Fucking weird, right? Bill—about as Asian as my asshole."

"He hates me," I say.

"He hates all the whiteys."

"Thanks."

"You prefer honkeys?"

"Fuck you."

We pass the lecture hall and enter the theater where a long line of guys and girls extends out from the stage. The theater is forty rows deep, divided into five sections of red plush seats. Matching red curtains hang over the stage. Two teachers sit at a table at the front of the stage with their backs to the room, facing students performing dramatic monologues. One of them is Father Vincent Gibbs, the Byron Hall chaplain and faculty advisor. He wears all black with an all-black collar except for the exposed white collar where the necktie knot should be. Occasionally, Father Vincent fires off harsh hushes, reminding us that auditions are underway.

"Please," he says. "Please be respectful of others. Give the same level of respect for those up here auditioning as you expect to receive when it's your turn to audition." It's hard to take him seriously when he scolds us, because he says everything with such a big, broad smile.

Mykel moves in front of me and works the girls in line like a pro, approaching each with swagger, handing out his postcards, flashing his amazing smile. I can't believe his swagger actually works with these girls. They're drawn to him, surrounding him, speaking to him, wanting to be acknowledged by him.

At the front of the stage, I see Zink, working his way up the line, the same way Mykel swaggers down the line. Zink shakes their hands, kisses their cheeks, and helps them with their monologues, giving pointers, wishing them luck, writing down numbers, running his hand over his buzzed head, like a dog.

"Yo, J-Dog, come here." Mykel grabs my shirt and pulls me into a circle of recent acquaintances. He speaks with a hint of a thuggish, gangbanger accent. "Ladies, this is my boy, J-Dog," he says. "We go way back to the East Side Players." Mykel introduces me to them by name, but I can't remember them to save my life. The girls are beautiful, but that's about all I can see. I can't tell one from the other. Each holds one of Mykel's postcards.

"I have to know—is that the name on your birth certificate?" the girl, my girl, the girl with red hair says. Her skin is tan and smooth and looks like she could be on the cover of the summer issue of *Cosmo* easy. She smells like a garden, some kind of flower— a purple flower.

"I'm sorry," I say, pretending not to have heard her.

"*J-Dog*," she says. "That's what Mykel said," she says. "He called you *J-Dog*. Your parents must have had a difficult time compromising, if that's what they settled on."

"Settled on?" I ask.

"She's blowing up your spot, little man," Mykel says.

"There are just so many names to pick from—*J-Dizzle, J-Bomb, J-Diggity*." She pulls her amazing hair back into a ponytail.

"*J-Bomb?*"

"The name. Your name. Are you lost? Are you having a stroke?" She turns to Mykel. "Is your boy—is J-Dog having a stroke? He doesn't seem okay."

"Nah, girl. J-Dog's gangsta." Mykel slaps my back. "We go way back."

"Yeah, you mentioned that." She pokes me in the chest. Her nails are painted blue, or what *Allure* calls the newest *in* color— *Blueberry Crush de Jour*. "This is new for you, isn't it?" she whispers. "Talking to girls?"

"I'm a freshman," I say.

"You're like a tiny little unicorn, all brand new and shiny."

"Are you auditioning for a play?" I ask.

"I'm not an actress, if that's what you're asking."

"Then why are you here?" I ask.

"I really don't think I have ever met anyone quite like you before," she says.

"What I wanted to say was that—what I meant to say," I say, but stop saying anything and look to my feet and see her feet too. She is wearing that same *Blueberry Crush du Jour* on her toenails. "I saw you." I rub my eyes. "Yesterday. Before school and then again after."

Big, white, open circle spots flash and pop all around me. I smell purple flowers. I feel wrong. Light fills my head.

"You feel okay? Because you don't look okay." She postures her-self, her white shirt opening a bit, enough that I can see a white bra.

"You're right," I say. "I don't feel well." My dick shivers. White bra. Light in my head. My legs crumble. The floor rushes toward me, but Zink and Mykel grab me by my arms before I completely collapse and drag me to a seat.

"Barks, baby, you good?" Zink asks. "Tilt your head back." He presses a tissue to my nose. "Your nose, it's bleeding."

Mykel moves back to the line of honeys, working his magic, getting digits, pretending he doesn't know me at all. I don't know that I wouldn't have done the same thing.

"What happened?" I asked. I tilt my head back and touch my hand to my nose and see blood and the blood continues to gush. "What is this?" The mortification of the whole scene smothers me in sadness and embarrassment. I hate myself. "This never happens." I hate everyone in this room. "Jesus." Hate. "Oh, Jesus."

"You don't need to bleed to make me notice you," my girl says sitting next to me with a handful of tissues.

Zink excuses himself, slapping me on the shoulder.

"Why do you hate me so much?" I ask her.

"Who said anything about hate?" she asks.

"Doesn't seem anything like *like*."

"You like me?" she asks, smiling for the first time, but not the smile I want.

"Honestly?" I ask.

"Truthfully," she asks.

"My name is Jeremy."

"I thought it was J-Dog." She hands me a fresh tissue. "I remem-ber you from yesterday," she says.

"Tell me about your play?"

"It's about a woman who leaves her family. She leaves her chil-dren. She leaves her husband. She's tired of being someone's pet. It's called *A Doll's House*. I'm the student director. I assist the director."

"I don't understand what this has to do with hating me?" I ask.

The line of guys and girls moves along without any interruption from my bloody nose. Zink and Mykel do their swagger thing. Plaid skirts. Plaid shirts.

"I don't hate you," she says, "but all of this blood and bleeding doesn't make me like you all that much better."

"This is the first time that has ever happened to me," I say.

"Isn't that what you guys always say—that this never happens to you? Don't you want to save that excuse for our first time together?"

Oh. My. Holy. Crap. I am gutshot speechless.

Someone claps. Someone claps loud. In succession. From the stage. Standing at the edge of the stage. I think it's part of a monologue, but when I steady my sight and open my eyes, waiting for the remaining spots to clear away, I see him. It's not the priest, but the other one, standing, staring, clapping—Mr. Rembrandt.

"Ms. Aimee White, by all means, please take your time. I have all the time in the world," he says. "Tend to the wounded and whenever you're ready, let me know, let us all know and we will continue. Am I making myself clear, Ms. White?"

"Mr. Rembrandt," I say.

"The director," she says.

"Mr. Barker," Mr. Rembrandt says.

I don't know what to do. I don't know what to do next. I drop my hand from my nose and tuck the bloody tissues into my pocket and do the only thing I can think to do—I stand and raise my hand to my forehead, my fingers tight together and stiff, and salute him with a chop. Then as she rushes toward the stage with her back to me, I yell, "I LIKE YOU, AIMEE WHITE."

Jeremy Barker is black and has that thing called swagger.

III
SHAUN OF THE DEAD

(Released September 24, 2004)

Directed by Edgar Wright

Written by Simon Pegg and Edgar Wright

23

On the 55 home, I freak out about Aimee. I don't freak out, like some kind of spaz and nerd all over the passengers. But I do replay the past two days in my head and try to guess what will happen next.

My bus stops at a community college near my house where the remnants of a small carnival are in the process of deconstruction. A Ferris wheel and Tilt-A-Whirl fold up and are loaded into tractor trailers. Wooden booths break down into a pile of planks. A canvas tent used to cover the food court is uprooted pole by pole.

Our driver opens the door and greets the students and teachers stepping inside.

The last time I went to a carnival like this my Dad taught me all about my penis. And told me he had killed people. And showed me how to shoot a gun. This was a very big day.

I remember it almost too well. We stood in line for hot dogs and funnel cakes.

I poked my penis. "Is this a bird?" I said, still poking. "People in my class call it a bird. Is it?" I asked. "A bird?" Poked some more.

"It's not a bird," he said. "It's a penis." He asked me what I wanted on my hot dog and I told him just pickle relish. He made a face. He only ever ordered his with spicy mustard. "Jeremy," Dad said. "You know it's not called a bird, right?"

A kid in my gym class, Jerome, had told me that my barn door was open earlier that week and that my bird was going to fly away if I didn't close it. I didn't want to tell Dad everything Jerome had said. I didn't want him to yell at me for leaving my barn door open.

"So it's not a bird?" I asked.

"Jesus. No. It's not a bird," he said. "Am I making sense? Your penis can't fly. It doesn't have wings. Because it's not a bird. Your penis is just a normal penis like any other penis."

"My penis is like your penis?" I asked.

"Smaller than mine," he said. "But it'll get bigger as you grow." Dad warmed up to the subject as we stood in line. He said that only boys had them. He said that girls had less to work with and had something called *penis envy*. "They have vaginas," he said. "They each have a vagina. But they wish they had what we have. The dong."

"They each have a vagina," I repeated. "What's *the dong*?"

"It's just another name for a penis. Dong. Pecker. Dick. Johnson. Snake. Penis."

"But not a bird?" I asked.

"Not a bird," he said.

We got our hot dogs and walked to a tent where a man encouraged people to shoot a rifle at alien-faced balloons .

"Baltonam is under attack," a born-and-bred Baltimore man said with a hillbilly highway accent, in a backwards O's hat. "Extraterrestrial warfare has begun in the streets of Baltonam. This is a call to arms, hon. Grab a gun and join the fight. Baltonam needs your help. Five bucks for five bullets. Pop three balloons, kill three aliens, and win one prize." Gigantic panda bears dangled from hooks above the counter of rifles. "Be a hero, not a zero." He held a microphone and wore an apron stuffed with cash. His face and forearms were sunburned red. He wiped sweat from under his eyes and unfolded a fat wad of green to make change for some people who stepped up to the counter. "Baltonam. The last stand. Be a hero, not a zero."

I asked Dad what the man meant by Baltonam and Dad explained how it was a cross between the words *Baltimore* and *Vietnam*. Just another name for our city.

"You were in Vietnam," I said, watching someone else load a gun at the counter of the tent. "Baltimore isn't like Vietnam, is it Dad?"

Dad agreed with me. He said Vietnam was nothing like Baltimore. He said that the two couldn't be more different. Then he said,
"Vietnam was the hardest thing I've ever had to do."

"Did you shoot anybody in Vietnam?" I asked.

An old lady with a walker stopped at the game, a little girl at her
side. She sited down the rifle and popped three balloons in rapid
succession. Panda time.

"I did shoot people," he said. "I shot a lot of people. When our
bullets killed someone we called them *killshots*."

"Did they cry?" I asked. "The people you shot?"

"I did a lot of bad things over there, but they were things that
needed to be done," he said. "I did a lot of things that I am not
proud of, Jeremy."

"Were you sorry that you killed those people?" I asked.

"Not at the time," he said.

"Does it make you sad now?"

"It makes me sad to tell you about it."

I hugged his leg.

Dad got out his wallet and the man loaded our rifles. Dad
instructed me on aiming for the killshot—how to control my
breathing, how to inhale and exhale before squeezing the trigger.

BANG! BANG! BANG! BANG! BANG!

My shots hit everything except the wall as the kickback from the
rifle jammed my shoulder. Dad, however, held the rifle like he'd
never been without one. He raised it to his shoulder and stared
down the barrel to aim, before popping five balloons in five pellets
and winning a panda bear prize.

I wonder sometimes if I remember the details of this memory incorrectly, like maybe I learned some of the more disturbing
details of Dad's time in Vietnam years later and somehow combined
them with this memory of us at the state fair as a way to deal with
it. Then again, look at who I'm dealing with. Really, anything is
possible.

A young man runs across the school parking lot and bangs on

the side of the bus as we start to pull away. He yells to the driver to stop and open the door, but the bus keeps on rolling. We ride down the street and through a light before pulling back over to the curb.

Zombies attack the bus on all sides, slapping bloody palms and flesh-eaten fingers across the windows. Fast fuckers with gray skin, pocked with peach-sized craters of missing muscles. Hundreds of them flood the street, filling in around us. They vomit up their insides, growl through jagged teeth, and snap their jaws. The bus rocks side to side and soon will be on its side. Then the feeding will begin. Dinnertime. And there's no place else that I'd rather be.

24

Dad orders dinner but doesn't tell me when it arrives.

I can smell it up in my bedroom and my belly growls, so I go downstairs and find him in the living room already halfway through a container of moo shu pork and starting on egg drop soup. Dad loves Chinese food but hates Chinese people. He pinches a ball of rice in his fingers and drops it in his mouth. Dog pushes herself up from her bed in the corner and sniffs the floor, looking for dropped Chinese food. Dad plucks a bamboo shoot out of a container and feeds it to her. She loves him for it.

"Jeremy, cue up the movie when you come in, yeah?" He gulps from a bottle of beer, food still in his mouth. His attention and focus are on the black flat-screen TV with nothing on it, but if I were a fly on the wall and watched him I'd swear he saw something there.

"I didn't know about dinner," I say, sitting next to him on the couch. "Why didn't you tell me?"

"I called you," he says.

"No. You asked me to cue up the movie."

"You were upstairs." Dad puts down his plastic spoon and container of neon yellow liquid. He cups his hands over his mouth. "JEREMY. DINNER IS READY." He picks up his spoon and container again.

"You never listen to me," I say.

"And you lie."

"Don't change the topic, okay? I hate it when you do that."

"You lie. You skip class and don't say anything about it. I ask you to cue up the movie and you say *yeah, yeah Dad* but don't cue up the goddamn movie. Does this look cued up to you?" He points to the blank TV. "Cued . . . up," he says, turning on the TV and DVD player with the remote control. "Jeremy, is the movie cued up? *Yes, why yes it is, Dad*. Good job, son. *Thanks, Dad*." He fake smiles to no one sitting next to him. Then looks at me. "Lied. Liar. Lie. You." Chewing like a cow, he says, "Are we going to watch this goddamn movie, Jeremy, or do you want to hold hands and continue talking about our emotions until our periods sync?"

"I am asking a simple thing," I say.

"You think I don't know?"

"I know you hear me," I say.

"You really are your mother's son."

"How hard is it to come up and get me when dinner is ready?"

"Fine. I will. Okay? Are we done here? Can we get on with it?"

"I love you, Dad."

"I love you too," he says, holding out his fist for me to pound. "I'll be better about it. Promise."

"We both know you won't," I say. I make a fist, tiny in comparison, and tap it against his, but his tap feels more like a jab. I grab the DVD from the table and cue the fucker up.

"I said I promise and when I promise, I promise," he says. He finishes a bottle of beer, but has another one ready to open. He drinks half before setting it down. "In the Marines," Dad says as the FBI warning fades up on the screen, "they teach you a lot of everyday skills. They teach you important qualities that every man should own, like loyalty, honor, respect. The Marines," he says, aiming his fork at me, instead of having to look at me. "The Marines taught me the value and importance of consequence. They taught me a lot of things. A lot," he says, looking at me now. "I was the one they trusted and so they taught me how to extract the tongue from a prisoner's mouth, surgically, as a consequence for not cooperating with our interrogator." He takes a small bite of his mu shu pork and then another bigger bite. "They taught me to do this thing as a consequence. If a valuable prisoner refused to speak, then the interrogator would say it was time to send in the doctor. That's what they called me, the doctor. That poor bastard would see me walk in with a little black kit filled with the nastiest little blades and clamps, and immediately he'd sing the most beautiful song. Everything we needed to know, right there." Dad scoops up more food, but doesn't eat it. "And when he didn't sing, I did what I had been trained to do. They took the kit away from me when I returned home. Said I had no civilian use for it." He laughs. "So don't ever lie to me." He taps his temple. "I'll know, or I'll know how to get to the truth."

Dad is known for his stories. He lectures and rants and keeps strong opinions that are mostly and largely not fit for radio or cable. But *this* story, this was different. This was new. This was about what he had done. Who he had been at one time. Extracting tongues.

"Once a long time ago," he says, "way back at the beginning of everything, there was a man and he was alone with only one purpose—survival. He didn't have a choice—he was a survivalist—and that one man learned the most valuable lesson of all. He learned that there are only two types of people in the world—the hunters and the hunters being hunted."

I am goddamn thankful that *Planet Terror*, a true Zombie Apocalypse, a terrifically bad zombedy, begins.

The writer and director Robert Rodriguez has created one of my favorite heroines in zombie cinema: Cherry Darling—a go-go dancer, not a stripper as she argues throughout the movie. I love her mainly for clarifying this very issue of stripper v. go-go dancer throughout the movie. This zombedy has a phenomenal opening sequence wherein Cherry dances on a stage, shaking it out, until the very end where Rodriguez's brilliance truly shines through, revealing Cherry in all of her emotional glory as she collapses into a puddle of furious and hysterical tears, crumpled in the corner, crying on stage as all of her deep-seated emotional pain comes crashing down all around her.

If you ask me, though, she is a stripper, not that I've ever really seen a stripper. Dad thinks she's one too and I'm fairly sure he has

seen a stripper. In the 1970s a chick that danced and stripped on
stage was a go-go dancer. In the 1980s, this same thing was called
a stripper. Either way, the girl is usually showing tit, at least.

Planet Terror is the kind of movie where it's part zombie film, part
schlock, part low-budget gore fest, part skin flick. It's the complex,
complicated layers that make it great and more than some dumbass
zombie movie. Regardless, one thing remains true—zombies are
dead inside without any stake in humanity. They generally have no
emotion and carry only the need for destruction and cannibalism.
The zombie movie is a morality tale. Catholics call these parables.
Recently, Hollywood calls them box office blockbusters.

Dad and I've seen *Planet Terror* a trillion times. Shit, we've seen
every zombie movie a trillion times, but everyone has his or her
comforts.

25

There's a chemical explosion in *Planet Terror* (isn't there always?) that causes human skin to melt and liquefy into horrendous walking rotting corpses of goo. Dad calls these *Goo Babies*. They are the grossest kind of zombie you can encounter. Like melted gum on the bottom of your shoe.

"Dad, there are two things I want to say to you. I don't like the fact that you disappear every night and I don't think that Liza really exists." I've broken two of the Zombie Survival Codes. I made eye contact with him and opened my damn mouth. I sit back and wait for him to respond—shout or explode, I'm not sure which yet.

"Let's play *Zombie*. Okay? Situation—you're alone in this house."

"Is Liza here?" I ask.

"You're in the basement. By yourself. It's our basement."

"Is it day or night?" I ask.

Dad rips off the end of an egg roll. "Night," he says.

"What kind of dark?" I ask.

"Good question," he says. I love it when he says that. Makes me feel like I'm his only son. "Early morning dark—the darkest before dawn."

"Like the time of day you usually come home?" I ask. "That kind of dark dawn?"

"It's early morning," Dad says, pushing his plate away from him. "Very dark. Stop fucking around. I'm doing our thing here. This is our thing. *Zombie* is our thing. Come on."

"Where are you in this scenario?"

"I'm dead. Throat ripped out. In my office."

"What kind of zombies? Are we talking *Night of the Living Dead* zombies? *Planet Terror,* Goo Baby zombies? *White Zombie* zombies?" I ask, laughing.

White Zombie is technically the first zombie film ever made in 1932 and the zombies in it act more like people who smoked too much weed. Not scary at all. They look like they're sleepwalking because they're hypnotized.

"Not *White Zombie* zombies," he says. "*28 Days Later.* Fast fuckers. Infected. Now. What do you use as your weapon and what is your escape route?" Dad gulps his beer, like he can't drink fast enough.

I can't wait for my favorite scene where Cherry Darling has her leg amputated and replaced with a Minigun prosthetic leg to fight off the zombies, but we are nowhere near it. While I'm talking about it, the name *Minigun* is a misnomer. A Minigun is a 7.62millimeter, multi-barrel machine gun that fires 6,000 rounds per minute with rotating barrels. It's badass. Ain't nothing mini about it. It's gigantic as fuck. A megagun, more like it.

"And you can't say Minigun," Dad says. "You always say Minigun. Not this time. The zombies are descending the stairs. Go."

"Baseball bat," I say.

"Aluminum or wood?"

"Aluminum."

"Why?"

"A hatchet or handsaw or claw hammer would cause more damage, but I would have to get right up in there to cause damage. Plus, far too messy with all that hacking." Dad's tongue comment comes rushing back, but I shake it away. "Wouldn't want to risk getting that residual blood splatter in my eyes or mouth. If I had time, I'd wear a full body rain slicker too, but does anybody ever really have time to grab the things they need? So I'd use an aluminum baseball bat. This would cause severe disorientation with multiple headshots and I would be using strength, velocity, and distance, rather than just strength. Added bonus—that ping sound. Metal meeting undead body—awesome."

"Wouldn't a bat slow you down and wear you out after a while? Think about it. After every swing, you'd have to pull back and wind up. That's a lot of energy exerted over very minimal aerial coverage."

"You want to know why a baseball bat is the best weapon out of all non-firearm weaponry? Two words—choke up." I slide my hands together. "Higher up on the bat you go gives you more speed and power at less exerted force. It's physics or some shit."

"But it's only true to a point. You can choke up some, but at a certain point it's less power and less force. You understand? And if you go up too far, guess what? It's less speed, too." Dad finishes his beer. "Next—your escape route?"

"I'd fight off the first wave and pile their bodies up at the base of the stairs so that the second wave would be met by a barricade of their own undead family. Suck on that." I pantomime swinging a bat and make a clucking sound with my tongue on contact with the imaginary zombie. I go on for a while about where else I'd go, and what I'd do. I end up talking about it on and off through the rest of the movie. When the credits roll, I ask him where he'd go, what his weapon would be.

Dad sits on the edge of the couch, resting his elbows on his knees. He runs his hands through his thick wavy hair, eyes closed. "I'm too old to run anymore. I'd welcome that kind of change of pace."

26

I wake up on the couch with Dog licking my face and the TV stuck on a bright blue menu screen. Dad is gone again. I know what needs to be done.

In Dad's office—James Dean, Purple Heart, Jane Mansfield, box of war.

I shuffle through the boxes in Dad's closet until I find the business of the night. The box of war slides out easy like before. I unflap the top and dig around for the book and plastic case, but nothing new has been added. It's possible Dad didn't have time to sneak them into the house and left them in his car, maybe the glove box or under his seat.

Back at his desk, I survey the scene. Everything that had been there yesterday—the sick drawings of body parts wearing neckties, the Christopher's surgery textbook, and the notes with the names and numbers and dates—had all been removed, disappeared. I opened the desk drawers and knocked my hand around inside. Nothing.

I lift the box of war back onto the shelf and slide it against the wall. I run my hand along the back of the shelving unit, but there isn't enough space to hide anything back there. I step up onto my toes and feel around on top of the boxes, but also don't feel anything. Then, there, stacked neatly in the corner on the floor is everything I had hoped to find. Christopher's textbook of surgery, the notes of information, sickass drawings, and Rembrandt gifts—all out in the open as if to say *fuck you*.

The book—*Notes from Underground* by Fyodor Dostoevsky.

The disc—*Sublimation.*

I read the back of the book and am not entirely sure what it's all about, but the one piece of information that I retain is that the main character attempts to save a young prostitute named Liza. Dad's new fake girlfriend. I put the book back on the floor and retrieve the plastic case instead.

I place *Sublimation* in the tray of the living room DVD player. I have no idea how the guts of electronics work but hear our machine working overtime, churning the disc around, searching for a reading or data lines or whatever is imprinted on the burned DVD copy. My insides burn while I wait—my heart, my lungs, my muscles. Now my skin burns too. The DVD player whips the stubborn disc in circles, searching, and then there is a change. The timer on the player begins to roll, measuring time by the second, a bomb in reverse. An electric charge sparks through my organs. What the fuck does *Sublimation* mean? I hold one finger on the pause button and one finger on the fast-forward button, ready to press either one at any moment. I've seen enough of Jackson naked over the years. The thought of seeing Dad's dong or even seeing Dad banging this imaginary whore, Liza—or the thought of Mr. Rembrandt naked—it makes me sick.

The screen flickers. Thin, white lines streak and scroll up from the bottom, horizontally, thin at first, but widening as they reach the top. The lines grow and widen, before cutting back to a soundless black—disappearing. A screen of nothing. The black continues. Then, a buzz breaks into the background, faint, but constant and steady. The buzz, too, fades away and disappears and reveals for the first time actual sound—movement. General movement without words. Like when Dad returned from his walk with Dog—coughing, grunting, walking, moving, breathing, whatever-the-fucking. I punch up the volume and lean in close. The screen still black, a muffled voice speaks in short, clipped phrases. A calm voice. A male voice. A direct voice directing others. The whatever-the-fuck noise in the audio scrambles like tuning in an AM radio station, finally correcting itself, clearing away the cobwebs. Then the voice.

"Some call it *God's Will*. Others—*Devil's work*. Some call it *Fate*. Others—*self-directed destruction*. Maybe you prefer *Destiny*. The semblance of it amounts to utter garbage. We live a predetermined life, an inevitable existence. A name matters nothing. What we seek is absolution. What we seek is beyond a higher power. What we seek is reckoning. What we seek is an uncommon valor. A code—this is it and it is all we have—a code. Wholeness. Transgressing without the slowed process of phases. Skip the burn and get right to the healing. Fractured, bitter, endless pieces familiarized into a singular oneness. You. A man. Adam. God's creation. The first. Fuck Eve. It's about commitment. Sublimation of spirit. Will. Fate. Destiny. Bullshit. One code. Without it, we are merely base animals. Do we agree?"

A wall of deep and heavy male voices responds, "Yes."

An electric buzzing begins. A power tool. Far away. In a single tone. Then, it changes. The buzzing changes.

"Gentlemen, let us suppose that man is not stupid. But if he is not stupid, he is monstrously ungrateful! Phenomenally ungrateful. In fact, I believe that the best definition of man is the ungrateful biped. But that is not all, that is not his worst defect; his worst defect is his perpetual moral obliquity."

The men respond, "Yes."

The buzzing now screeches—slowing for a moment, before speeding up, ripping through something. I want to press pause and stop this whole thing, but my fingers don't move or can't move. The buzzing screeches and screams, ripping and ripping. Silence again. And an uneven breathing, which becomes a wall of whispers.

A new voice, almost invisible, speaks to himself. The man's voice sounds fragile, frozen, and far closer to the speakers than the other man.

"Jesus Christ, no. I—no—I. I have to—no. Shit. No, no, no." The man stops talking, but his breath picks back up—fast, heavy, and hard.

Silence resumes, which forces me to search the black screen for something, anything, and then I see it—a thin circle of light at the edges. I touch my finger to the screen and a blue spark shocks me.

I trace my finger along the light.

The main voice continues, "Things finally come down to the business itself, to the act of revenge itself." Footsteps. Walking. Shoes. Crunching of plastic underfoot. The man's voice moves closer to the camera now. His tone changes, no longer reciting words, but rather taking registration. "Month—August. Day—Twenty-Nine. Sublimation one—Ralph Andersen."

There is a dark void of silence. Until an avalanche of sound comes crashing down—a collective primal scream. Who knows how many people are involved, or what it means. The microphone pops and cuts between silence and the communal scream. A reverberating echo pounds the speakers, the screen still black.

A new voice close to the camera says, "Are you a fucking virgin at this? Take the damn cap off."

Cap. Camera. Someone has forgotten to remove it.

The circle of light disappears as the cap pops off and a hot, bright, white light crashes into the lens, causing the camera to shuffle and refocus, shocking it into disorientation. The communal primal scream now filters through mechanical camera adjustments. Everything blurs and nothing is clear. The scream stops. Choking is all that remains. The choking is violent. Maybe better described as gagging. Like someone having chopsticks shoved down their throat. The robotic sound of the camera autofocusing stops and the white light settles and the white emptiness looks like what I imagine Heaven to be.

The aggressive white rushes away from the camera as color descends. An image comes through in flashes. A man. A man's body. Thick, industrial plastic covers him like a blurry blanket. Monitors and machines run wires into him, slipping under the plastic; his eyes taped shut; a clear tube stuffed down his throat, chocking him. He is awake. His body twitches. His neck turns, pulling away, gagging, chocking. A seizure, maybe. The way he thrashes under the plastic and the plastic begins to move and slide and gains speed and clears away from the body completely and the anonymous head finally becomes a head with a body and arms and legs.

The man is restrained to the bed. Long, leather straps cross his
chest, his stomach, and his knees. The man is fully naked, his junk
exposed and all. The body extends out of the frame of the camera,
chopping him off at his knees. No one is on camera at all except
for the man—only this man in pain.

Two men dressed in pale green surgical scrubs and caps and
masks covering their faces poke around the monitors and plunge
a syringe into the IV bag. They talk to each other, checking vitals,
but their voices are inaudible. They finally exit off screen—doctors
of some kind.

The main man's voice returns. "Oh, absurdity of absurdities!"

Snuff film—is this what I am watching? Is that what this is? No.
Snuff films are not this. They are where some dude fucks a chick
and then kills her on film for serious pervs to get off on, but this
isn't that. I don't know what this is. This is something else altogether. I lean forward, lean closer, look closer.

The camera pitches again—autofocusing—and I see them. A
crowd stands in front of the man strapped to the bed and the bed is
centered on a slightly raised stage. I see them and think it's a trick of
light. I see them, all of them, standing. I hear the man's voice again.

". . . that you have not, and perhaps never will have, an object
for your spite, that it is a sleight of hand, a bit of juggling, a card-
sharper's trick, that it is simply a mess, no knowing what and no
knowing who, but in spite of all these uncertainties and jugglings,
still there is an ache in you, and the more you do not know, the
worse the ache."

The man strapped to the bed gags.

In real life, Dog leaves the living room, sleepy, moving away in a
slow walk. I wish I could follow.

The surgical tape over one of the man's eyes snaps loose, so that
one eye remains taped shut while the other is open wide, seeking,
searching the room. The eye finds the camera. I tilt my head like
people tilt their heads in horror movies, all cliché-like and shit. I try
and see the man's face, like I might know him, like I might be able
to identify him for the police or something.

I see them there. Others. Men. Their heads are covered in black masks, like executioners. Some of the men are shirtless. Some in suits. They stand in front of the stage with the bed. They just watch, doing nothing, except for a few that rub their dicks or suck on their fingers.

The main man, the leader says, "This is what redemption looks like, gentlemen. This is the real Ralph Anderson."

The man in the bed gives up, stops fighting, breathing shallow breaths, and I keep breathing, breathing for him. He closes his one eye and breathes through the tube down his throat and then exhales and opens his one eye. A surge blasts from his chest as he throws everything into a final fight, twisting his body, seizure-like. The doctors rush back into frame, holding him down. The movement startles the crowd as they shift like current away from the stage and collide with the camera. The tripod with the camera crashes to the ground, the camera still filming, but only filming legs and the heavy plastic covering the floor and the crunching of feet stepping on the plastic. Then the audio goes silent as legs moves past the camera and the screen cuts to black.

Sublimation goes back to Dad's closet like a fucking bullet. Fucking leave that bullshit behind. I wish I had never found it. I wish I could make myself forget it.

This is the savage animal ripping through my body at this very moment.

27

throw open the door to the basement and, instead of hiding behind it, I charge down the stairs, making as much noise as possible. A zombie killer. Noise, noise, noise—bounding down the stairs in heavy strides. Here I come. If this were a zombie film, I'd be making a major faux pas and would most likely be dead in a matter of minutes. However, in this instance, I break my Zombie Survival Code Number Two—keep quiet—and embrace the chaos and calamity of my shitfuck life.

I pass antiques, wrapped in plastic, stacked in corners. I pass bicycles hung from the ceiling. I pass Dad's toolshed. I pass luggage. I pass Dog's cage. If this were back in the day, the basement would have been the jungle. It would be *the shit*. I would be in *the shit*. Dad says that in the Marines, they were told to scream *kill, kill, kill* or *ooh rah*. I say neither in the basement. In the basement, I say neither. In the back, I find the trunk where Dad keeps all of our sports equipment, collected together from over the years—deflated soccer balls and footballs; stiff, leather baseball gloves; chipped lacrosse sticks; three sets of used golf clubs that Dad bought for us but that we never used; camping equipment from when Jackson tried to be a boy scout but got kicked out because he kept getting caught fucking around with some girl scout or fighting with another boy scout in his troop; broken lawn furniture; soft seat cushions used for Orioles and Ravens games; Byron Hall Blue Jay water bottles; and wrap-around protective eyewear. All of this means nothing to me. All of this is exactly where it is supposed to be—out of sight and at the bottom of our lives. None of these things connect to us anymore.

Jackson—moved out.

Mom—moved out.

Dad—moved on.

Jeremy—still here.

What I want is still down here—an old, rubber kitchen trash can next to the trunk, filled with my big, bad, beautiful bastards—baseball bats. Covered in cobwebs, I slap them away. These are my zombie weapons. I'm the American version of Shaun in *Shaun of the Dead*. If they made a version based on me it'd be *Jeremy of the Dead*. Instead of a cricket mallet or pool cues to smash the living dead to goo, I'd simply substitute a baseball bat. If Shaun could whack them, so can I.

I grab the handle on the side of the trash can and drag it, like a dead body, across the cement floor of the basement, making an amazing scratching sound that would raise the dead. I lift the trash can and its contents up the basement stairs one step at a time, dropping it occasionally to rest, each drop making a tremendous thud that thunders throughout the house with great reverberating echoes. Every time I drop the fucker, wooden and aluminum bats *thwark* and *ping* against eachother. I drag that fucker across the hardwood of the first floor, scraping the fuck out of it. I pass Dog, who could give a shit what any of us do in this house so long as she is fed and walked. I rest in the foyer, catching my breath, looking outside to the street. Nothing. Only the shadows under the street lamp, but nothing real. I lift the trash can up to the second flight of stairs without stopping once and hustle through my bedroom door with a *28 Days Later* poster tacked to the front, the contagious symbol warning all who enter to beware.

In the zombie film *28 Days Later*, the main character, Jim, wakes in an abandoned hospital room, still attached to saline bags and shit. He is alone. There are no doctors. There are no nurses. No staff of any kind. No patients. Everyone is gone, disappeared, dead. If not, then they are rage-infected zombies. Jim learns this sad fact as he wanders the looted and lost streets of London. He survives off of vending machine food—candy and soda. He keeps to himself until he meets up with other survivors, like himself, and finds a reason to continue to carry on and fight—for humanity. But in the beginning, when he wakes in that hospital room, by himself, he has nothing except fear.

I kick my bedroom door closed and set the trash can lovingly next to my bed.

Lights off, I lay in bed, fully dressed and on top of the covers, cooling off and calming down. I hate that fucking basement, but now I have what I need and don't need anything else. Anyone else. Not Dad. Not Mr. Rembrandt. I close my eyes and see the man in the *Sublimation* DVD again—strapped to the bed, held down, stuffed full of tubes and liquids, one eye taped shut. I hear the bodiless man reciting philosophy like prayers or commandments.

Mybads. Oh, my beautiful bastards! I pull one and hold it across my chest. Sleep closes down on me. Fuck you, Sleep. I'm packing aluminum and wooden heat. Barefoot again at my window, Tricia's blinds are closed, even though her light is on. I wish I could see her and make sure she was okay. I wish I could see if she needed me to save her. I can save people. Just like Shaun.

Who needs pills, Mom?

Who needs sex, Jackson?

Who needs tongues, Dad?

Zombie Survival Code Number Four—lock and fucking load. I just have to remember to choke that bastard up.

IV
I WALKED WITH A ZOMBIE

(Release Date: April 30, 1943)
Directed by Jacques Tourneur
Story by Inez Wallace
Written by Curt Siodmak and Ardel Wray

28

The morning sun sneaking through my blinds reminds me of two things:

First thing. I have a sick fuck for a father. I can set a clock by him, but not literally, just usually. He arrives home, evasive and different, after some night out doing God knows what. I see the morning sun and I am reminded of my fucking father, coming home. From being with Liza? I call bullshit. *Notes from Underground*, Ballentine.

Second thing. The morning sun rises up and sneaks in, serving me an acknowledgement to the sad fucking fact that nothing in my bedroom is my own. In many ways, this second thing is really, like, six things packed tightly into an explosion of things. Much of my room is a reminder of Mom, or a memory of Mom I'd rather forget.

The walls are painted midnight. The carpet that industrial gray. Two armless wicker chairs bookend a wood end table with a vase of red marbles and fake red flowers stuck inside. These are my Mom.

The only aspect of my room that is inherently my own is my zombie ceiling—every classic zombie poster imaginable stuck to the ceiling, covering every inch of the ceiling. Overlapping, criss-crossing, coming down on the room. Every George A. Romero *Living Dead* movie poster, *Planet Terror*, *Dawn of the Dead* the origi-nal, *Dawn of the Dead* the remake, *I Walked with a Zombie*, *Shaun of the Dead*, *Zombieland*. Mom hated that I put them up there. She preferred I get them framed and properly hung on the wall with a drill and a hook, not tacked into the ceiling. The *Night of the Living Dead* poster, the one with the little girl, the black-and-white one where she looks fucking demonic as shit is the focal point. But it's not just U.S. film posters. I collect internationally, yo. American movies released abroad and international horror released internationally and international horror released in the States, too. British. Chinese. German. Icelandic. Dutch. Russian. African. French. Hell, even Canadian. Whatever I can get my hands on. But why do I put them on my ceiling? Simple. Because when a stranger doesn't know your ceiling is tricked out in zombie paraphernalia and they eventually look up, holy crap, it will scare the living shit out of them in a way that is simply indescribable. That and because it keeps the demon shadows off the ceiling, just like the "Thriller" poster did, way back when, kick-starting this whole thing. That story will come later.

Dad bangs around downstairs. He's home. Just before 6 A.M. Right on time.

Baseball bat in hand—wooden—I pretend to be blind with my sight taken from me by a combination of illness and freak accident. In order to survive and get along in the world, I must hone my hearing. Not my listening skills, but my hearing. My limbs are paralyzed too. It was a bad accident. And I can't move at all. I am fully functioning otherwise. I close my eyes and embrace the darkness—tracking the movement of the living dead beneath me, choking up on the warm wood. A chair scrapes against the floor. The refrigerator door slams shut. Dog's collar jingles. Dad coughs. He'll come hunting for me soon. To give me my Ritalin. Keep me normal. He's louder than usual this morning, actually, slamming all kinds of shit. I wonder if he had fun doing whatever it was he did last night. Whoever it was he did. Like Liza. I wonder if he's watched that fucking crazyass DVD yet or if he'll notice my beautiful bastards by my bed. I wonder if he knows what *sublimation* means.

Then I remember—today is a Mom day, which means that Mom is driving me to school, and on Mom days when she drives me to school, Mom is always early because Mom always wants to go to breakfast before I go to school.

Shitfuck.

Dicktroll.

I strip off my clothes, kicking them into a pile by the door and open my closet and pick up the Scrabble box when I hear Dad running up the stairs, then pounding down the hallway. I close the lid of the box and step out from the closet, still holding it. The door swings wide without a knock, revealing my whole damn self in the center of my room, naked, totally nude, but at least my closet door is closed. I cover my junk with the Scrabble box. Just as I'm naked, Dad's in a pair of white boxers and white tank top.

"Dad," I say, "you didn't knock."

"Fathers don't need to knock," he says, pinching the pill in his fingers, and aiming it toward my mouth—Ritalin. "Open." The pill hits my teeth and rattles around my mouth like a silver ball in a pinball machine. My tongue knocks it to the back of my throat as I swallow without water. "Is it down?" he asks.

I show him the emptiness in my mouth. Even make a noise like at a dentist.

"Better get dressed," he says. "She'll be here soon. Don't be like your brother. Your brother never wears any clothes. And he has emotional problems. Don't be like him. Be better than him." Dad walks away, stops, and turns back to me. "When we see him tonight, don't tell him I said that." He finally notices the board game strategically placed over my*self*. "Why are you holding a Scrabble box?" All I want to do is call him out about Liza again and tell him I watched the video, but can't get up the nerve.

"I thought we could play later."

"You know I hate that game."

"When did she say she'd be here?" I ask, putting the box on my bed, shuffling sideways.

"Early," he says. "Be on the street when she arrives. I don't want to hear her horn. And you know she is going to ask you to spend the night over there, so be ready for it this time."

"What do you want me to say?"

"Do what you want. If you want to go, then go."

"I want you to be okay."

"I'll be fine, so long as I don't hear that fucking horn honk outside. I'll be in the living room," he says.

"Where did you go last night?" I ask, the words leaking out. "I just want to know you're okay."

"Jeremy," Dad says, his back to me, his hand resting on the doorknob. He looks at the wall in front of him. "For better or worse, she's still your mother." He leaves without closing the door, pounding down the hallway, then descending the stairs.

I open the Scrabble board game and pluck out a pair of underwear and step into them, pulling them up. Mom bought me underwear as a back-to-school present a few weeks back, the kind people call *tighty-whiteys*. I hide them in the box of the board game Scrabble and keep it in my closet because I know Dad hates board games that make him think or have the potential to make him look stupid in front of someone dumber than him, so I know that he will never find them in that box. Scrabble holds my underwear and all of the other board game boxes hold my women's magazines.

Dad says that real men don't wear underwear. He says real men wear boxers. For his back-to-school gift, Dad bought me a week's worth of boxers, but I haven't worn them yet. They're all white with a button at the crotch . . . like what he is wearing. I hate how everything just hangs loose in them and you have to unbutton them to pee standing up and then button them up when you are finished. At least with underwear, you have the hole you can snake your dick through.

Sometimes it's just easier to sit down.

29

arefoot by the window, Tricia's blinds are open and there is a light on inside, but she is not there. Cars drive past our house the way old men drive, signaling turns a mile in advance . . . and dangerously slow.

The night Mom left, her and Dad had been arguing. Jackson was away at school, probably fucking some girl in her dorm room. Dad called Mom a whore and slut and Mom begged him to keep his voice down so that I wouldn't hear. Glass shattered somewhere. I heard almost everything.

"I'm unhappy," she said.

"Preach that shit to the choir," he said.

I snuck out of my room and down to the landing, peering through the bars in the railing, watching them separate, but crash back together like they had a rubber band tied between them. Mom rooted through her purse and pulled out a prescription bottle. Dad knocked it to the floor as tiny blue pills scattered, flipping and spinning. Morphine. MS Contin. Thirty milligrams. To kill the pain. Mom made a call and came upstairs to say goodbye. She sat next to me on my bed, but not really *for* me. She looked at my zombie posters on the ceiling, then covered her mouth, but didn't cry. They couldn't cover up her demon shadows.

Dad entered my room, a Marine charging a hill. Right above him was a *Night of the Living Dead* poster. The black-and-white one-sheet with the little girl zombie. Looked like she was about to fall from the sky and feast on him. Dead face with black eyes, hungry lips, and wavy matted hair flowing everywhere.

A car horn—loud and repeated blasts.

"You don't know him," she said to Dad, "but he keeps his Purple Heart in a box under the bed, not on his wall like some goddamn child." Mom ran down the stairs, and Dad followed. Then so did I. A van pulled up to the curb and a big black man got out and when Dad saw Mom's new man Dad's shoulders dropped forward like an organ had been plucked from his body, and everything else had shifted down.

"Rinny," he said. The man—who I have come to know as Zeke—had tree trunk arms, a thick neck, and wore a baseball cap tugged down low on his face, the right way to wear a baseball hat. He looked exactly like Carrefour, in the film *I Walked with a Zombie*. Mom looked like Betsy Connell, the young Canadian nurse who travels to the West Indies to care for a woman suffering from some kind of weird, walking comatose state. I remember when I first saw this movie. Everyone looked the same, that old Hollywood standard. Except for Carrefour. He was muscular, lean, with intense eyes that ate your soul. He popped off the screen, something wildly different and exciting. Which is maybe how Zeke was for Mom. Zeke opened the door to his van, lifted her into the passenger seat, slammed the door shut, and drove off with her, while dad just stood there in the doorway, watching as the van signaled a turn, traveling at a dangerously slow speed.

30

The front door is open, but Mom stands outside. She holds her purse in front of her, like she has a concealed weapon hidden away just in case. A stun gun. A pearl handled revolver. Definitely not a Minigun. Definitely not a baseball bat.

Dad yells to me from the living room. "Jeremy, your mother is outside. And I heard the fucking horn."

"I'm dressed. I'm ready," I say, running down the stairs to the foyer. "Coming." I stop at the door and wave to Mom, who smiles and waves back.

"Hi, baby," she says. She looks tired like Dad—barely alive. She opens the door and steps inside, as Dog runs over and sniffs her feet, wagging his tail like windshield wipers in a hurricane. Mom crouches down to pet her, kissing her on the nose. "Doggers! I miss you so much."

"You're not outside," Dad says to Mom. He sits on the couch still in a pair of white boxers and a white tank top. Dad has dug out his old Marine dog tags from the box of war in his office closet. The silver tags hang low and clink together as he moves. "Get back outside."

Mom stands, pulling herself away from Dog.

"Now," he says. I can tell that Dad hasn't slept. He has that glazed look of a hangover, something I've seen Jackson recover from often enough. I scan his arms and legs, looking for needle marks or bruises or cuts on his skin—some clue, some sign. Nothing. I only see his eyes—desert dry, unblinking and trained on Mom like a sniper. His beer bottles and paper plate of Chinese from last night are still on the coffee table, now neighbors to a mug of black coffee. "You don't live here anymore, Corrine. This is not your house anymore. Got it?" He gets louder—"UNDERSTAND?"—then looks back to the TV.

"Fuck you, Ballentine," she says.

Now for the uninformed, I feel I need to review a previous topic—zombie speed. When zombies attack, and I'm specifically referencing recent cinema, they are quick and agile, not cat-like, but ferociously fast. They burst through doors and windows, never hindered by the wood or glass. Like in *Zombieland*. Like in *28 Days Later*. They leap fences and scamper up hills, defying gravity and the general properties of motion. In this moment, Dad absorbs these qualities. He rockets from the couch, clawing at the air, barreling towards Mom. His breathing is controlled and quiet. He doesn't speak, instead reaches the foyer and stops, sliding on the hardwood floor. Mom flinches and holds out her hands to protect herself, but he doesn't touch her.

She says, "You haven't changed one bit."

He says, "I told you, get out of my house."

She says, "This is still my home too."

He says, "Who said this was a home, let alone your home?"

Mom studies him a moment, then turns and walks outside.

Dad goes back to his TV.

All I want is to climb a tree and wait for them both to leave again—Mom to Zeke's and Dad to wherever he goes. On the flat screen is a reenactment of a man rock climbing, and then through a series of quick cuts, he falls and gets trapped under a giant boulder—his arm pinned down, trapped. A dramatic voiceover describes how the man is contemplating cutting off his own arm to survive. Dad raises his fists and I raise mine. We pound them together.

Dad says, "You know I'm not stopping you from seeing her." Dad doesn't look away from the TV. "She is your mother. Just not my wife."

The apocalypse is at hand.

31

Another State Fair memory. Same trip as the last one. Long before Dad told me how he shot people, though.

We were on our way to the pavilion to watch the cattle auction when we passed one of those strong man kiosks where you slam the rubber mallet sledge hammer against the platform as hard as you can to make the silver ball fly up the track and ring the bell. Dad stopped us, pulled out two bucks, and handed them to me. He told me to give it to the overweight man with the orange visor.

"Let's see how strong you are," Dad said.

"Ballentine, this is silly. He's only a child," Mom said, arms folded across her chest.

"You're a child?" he asked.

"No," I said.

Mom smiled.

"I thought you were a grown up or fourteen, at least," Dad said.

I took the rubber mallet sledgehammer from the overweight man in the orange visor and wrapped my fingers around the handle. Pain snapped in my shoulders. I strained my body, shaking, trying to lift the mallet to show Dad I could do it. The mallet thundered to the ground, nearly ripping my arms from their sockets.

"Jeremy, be careful, honey. Those mallets are heavy," Mom said.

Dad stood next to me, fists clenched, saying, "Come on, son. You can do it."

"I can't lift it, Dad. It's too heavy."

"Not yet," Dad said.

"Ballentine, he wants to go."

"This time," Dad said, squatting down, our eye-lines level, "I want you to use more leg muscle." He slapped his thighs.

I closed my eyes, straining with every last bit of strength to hit the platform with the mallet. I pushed up from my feet, using whatever leg muscle I had. The mallet, not far off the ground, thumped back down.

"That's okay," he said. "You gave it your best. Now watch. I want to show you what you were doing wrong." He grabbed the handle in both hands, lifted it up over his head like he was about to chop a log of wood. Like he was going to behead someone. He growled and slammed the mallet against the platform. The silver ball sailed up the track, just missing the bell.

"So close, sir," the overweight man said, turning dollar bills around in his hand so they all faced the same way before stuffing them deep into a pocket of his orange apron. He readjusted his matching orange visor over his balding, freckle-spotted scalp, wiping sweat from his brow with his forearm.

Dad lifted it again, grunting, before slamming the platform harder this time. The silver ball flew up, but again fell short of the bell. "Fuck," he yelled, saliva spitting from his lips.

"Ballentine, these games are rigged," Mom said, her arms wrapped around me now like a cocoon. I watched his eyes turn onto Mom, dark green marbled eyes, swamp-water green. Her hands gripped my shoulders, like she was squeezing a sponge.

And that was that. I remember that we never made it to the cows. I remember Mom walked away and Dad took me to Baltonam. I remember the car ride home was silent. I remember Dad slept on the couch that night. I remember Mom took pills and slept on the floor of my room next to my bed.

I remember back then there was no carpet. Only a hardwood floor.

32

The first words out of my mother's mouth are about my father. She asks me about his health, if he is doing okay. I want to tell her about him disappearing, about the homemade video, or about his tongue extraction days in the Marines, but I don't think Mom would even know how to help with any of it. Mom looks okay, I guess, still like my mom, but more tired and scattered. She keeps checking her cell phone and looking out the windows for cars in her blind spots. She's mucho paranoid today.

We are quiet for much of the drive down to Fell's Point, moving through neighborhoods that get increasingly worse and then better and then worse again, sometimes driving for blocks at a time where the windows and doors of the row homes are boarded up with cinderblocks.

"It kills me that I couldn't take you to school the other day," she says. "Kills, kills, kills."

A woman in a miniskirt, tight black tank top, and high heels paces at a traffic light downtown. She, too, looks tired and scattered, but is looking for cars to approach, rather than avoid, like Mom and her blind spots. The woman runs her hand through her hair, looking up and down the street, waving at cars and blowing kisses. Mom looks at the woman like she is observing a rare animal, something she has heard about but never seen before. The woman leans through a window of a car that has pulled over to the side of the road.

"She must want to die, the whore," I say. "Doing something dangerous like that." I immediately think of Liza the whore in the

Rembrandt book *Notes from Underground* and Liza the whore that
Dad is apparently dating. I know it's a lie. I know it. In my gut.

"You sound just like your father."

"That's funny. Dad says the same thing, except how I sound just
like you."

The light flicks green. Mom turns into the tall buildings of Centre City. Steam curls through grates in the street, ascending into the
graying sky.

"I call them hopeless," she says. "They are without hope." Mom
passes a city bus and continues along the outside of the harbor over-
flowing with tourists. A small line for the aquarium curls around
like a snake's tail. Large groups of kids stand together in front of
antique boats. A wrought-iron fence with giant spikes protects a
playground. A giant green jungle gym towers over a turtle-shaped
sand box, but children aren't using either. They're just standing
there. Enormous buildings reach up from the sidewalks into the
sky, new buildings within abandoned and condemned city blocks,
buildings wrapped in orange construction tape. Yellow tractors and
dump bins are parked along the street. Police tape knotted to the
door of a row house snaps loose in a breeze.

"I want to show you something at the end of this street." We
approach a tower of windows. The building rises right the fuck
up into the sky and for a moment it seems that the building could
just go on and on, an endless ladder of clean, blue glass. The bottom of the building spreads out wide, spanning the majority of the
city block. Mom parks Zeke's van in the half-circle driveway at the
building's entrance.

"The Prince Edward," I say, reading the signpost above the
lobby doors.

"It's the name of the building."

"Where does it come from?" I ask. "The name—*The Prince
Edward.*"

"The financers named it. I think it's British." We get out of the
van and Mom walks to the end of the street. "I designed it. The
apartments and office spaces inside. Designed the floor plan. Fire

exits. How big the bedrooms should be. Conference rooms. Bathrooms. Furnished it. Picked out the carpet. Everything." She tucks her hair behind her ears.

Across the choppy waters of the Inner Harbor a half-dozen replica Revolutionary War Era ships are tied to a dock. People pay to go onboard and see how life used to be. People will spend money on anything that sounds remotely boring. Fell's Point reflects in the water. Red brick buildings with chimneys spitting smoke. Rows of homes lining streets, glued together. Every part of Baltimore looks small and fragile and darker from here.

"You used to be interested in my projects."

"I liked the drawings. The plastic copy of the drawings."

"The Mylar copy." Mom looks tired, big eyes with tiny wrinkles at the sides.

I want to tell her about everything going on with me, in my life, at school, and maybe this is our moment, that moment in movies when the camera zooms in and the music gets super-fucking loud and you are supposed to feel a swelling in your throat or heart or in your lungs. This is the moment right before the zombies attack. I want her to ask about me.

"Would you like to go up and see the view from the top?" Mom asks.

"Are we allowed?" And by *we*, of course, I mean are *you* allowed, because who in their right mind would let that pillhead anywhere near a building like this.

"Please," she says. "If I'm not allowed inside, then who the hell is?"

33

The lobby of the building is near completion with a concierge desk and plush sofas and chairs and square end tables and hanging plants, although almost everything is still covered in plastic. There is a security guard by the concierge desk and he has a gun and baton in his belt. As we pass, Mom digs through her purse, making herself obnoxiously busy, shooting him a friendly, cute, little smile. He's a big boy, overweight, but not in a fat way, rather in the kind of way that he might really have big bones and would probably crush me if I leapt for his gun, not that I want to at all. Who leaps anyway? I can't remember the last time I *leapt* anywhere. His badge says *Security Officer George*. Mom finds her laminated pass and shows it to him and he waves her on.

I wonder if he could hear all the pills crashing and bottles clinking in her purse like I could.

We ride an elevator that overlooks the Inner Harbor through a glass wall; rising up, up, up, up to the top floor of the high rise, skyrocketing up over Baltimore, twenty-two floors up. This must be what a bottle rocket feels like. The elevator stops and the doors open and we step out into a long narrow hallway, a dark green carpet covered in heavy, industrial plastic.

Mom leads me to an open door at the end. It's dim by the elevator, but the room at the end is overexposed with light cutting through more blue windows. This is a zombie's wet dream as far as attack spaces go—there is no exit! You get half a dozen living dead fucks on either end of the hallway and each of these doors are locked, forget about it. End of game. Game over. I look at Mom and

her weak body, her heavy eyes and sluggish speech. She's too fucked
up to fight. I'd have to carry this one on my own, but I didn't even
bring my big bastard with me.

"They keep them off during the day to save money since it's not
move-in ready. They're still selling units."

"It's a big building."

"One of the tallest buildings in the entire city. It's been a great
job. People will wake up in a room I designed. They will work every
day in spaces that I invented. And the financers are even thinking
that if the spaces rent as quickly as they hope, that as a thank you,
they'll give me my very own suite for free." Mom covers her mouth
with her hands. "How amazing is that? My own suite." We stop
mid-hallway. She grabs my shoulder and turns me toward her. She
looks confused or heartbroken or both, I don't know. "You can
come and stay with me. What do you think? They love the work
I've done. Let me show you what the suites look like. Make up your
mind after that. This is the model unit they are showing—the one
with all of the light."

She walks faster, tripping on the plastic. She enters the suite and
disappears. I step carefully on the plastic where it bunches. I reach
the doorway and cross over and feel hands grab me and pull me
through, casting me into a wall of light. This must be what it's like
to be born—burning hot, white, white light blasting and shocking
me into life.

It's hot and humid up here, no ventilation, and I gasp for air—
one whole side of the apartment covered in windows without
shades. I no longer hear that crunching of plastic under my feet
and instead it is soft—wall-to-wall green carpet. The room comes
into focus now, the little white circles leaving my vision, and I see
the whole fake setup—the fake, hollow, plastic couch across from
the fake, hollow, plastic entertainment unit with fake flat-screen TV.
The plants are fake and the tables and dining room table and chairs
are fake. I knock them with my fist and they echo inside. Hollow.
The kitchen is real and the kitchen island and chopping block on
the counter are real and the big bowl next to the sink is real, but

the fruit in the bowl is fake. Mom leads me back through a small hallway past a bathroom with real toothbrushes in a real toothbrush stand, to the bedroom, which is just more of the same fake, hollow, plastic shit—queen size bed, dresser, lamps with fake light (I'm not even kidding—fake, yellow light!) and a fake TV. I look to Fell's Point and see dark clouds forming and raindrops tapping against the windows. Everything still looks like plastic and smells like dust.

"All of this looks almost real," I say.

"It's supposed to give prospective buyers a vision of their own stuff in the space."

"This place is yours?"

"That's what they said."

"They?"

"The investors." She walks to the window, her hands on her hips, then adjusts fake flowers in a real vase. "I'm your mother. You are supposed to root for your mother. Not treat her like a spy who's committed treason."

I don't know why I am drilling her on all of this, really. I could give a fuck at the end of the day. Fuck this place. Fuck her. Fuck Zeke. Fuck Dad. Fuck it all. But she speaks with such fucking hope.

"This is what I'm telling you," she says, her arms out to the room. "This is what I'm working on." She slaps the wall—it is real, no echo. "This is the best I have right now and I want you to be a part of it, Jeremy. I want you here with me."

Mom digs through her purse again, finds it, opens it, pops it into her mouth—a movement that should have been invisible but wasn't. Not even a little bit. Tiny blue pills turn to dust between her teeth. And she doesn't even say the Lord's Prayer. This is something new—a change.

34

Jimmy's—a Fell's Point diner best known for their Breakfast Bowl: grits, scrambled eggs, hash browns, bacon, and cheddar cheese heaped together and soaked in hot sauce—is predictably slammed. The small dining area is packed with every type of person imaginable. No one is too good for Jimmy's. Construction workers. Businessmen. Businesswomen. Teenagers like me in groups. Old folks with walkers. Homeless folks, nickel-and-diming. Everyone's drinking coffee and shoveling food into their mouths. The waitresses scream orders to the line cooks who crash into one another at the grill, serving plates and slapping them on the servers' station to be delivered to tables.

The table is covered with a red and white-checkered plastic tablecloth, sticky from maple syrup or spilled apple juice. Our waitress is older than I had expected any waitress to ever be. Her silvery-blue hair doesn't move when she walks. She limps a cup of coffee over and sets it down in front of Mom and lowers a tall glass of chocolate milk in front of me and asks if we are ready to order. Her voice is a super-shaky old lady voice, cracking so much that I think for second she might actually die on us right here. Mom says that we're waiting for her other son, before we order. The granny waitress smiles and her whole face lights up in a beautiful glow as she walks over to the counter nearby and sits on a stool, breathing heavy, rubbing her knees.

"I want you to spend the night at my apartment tonight." Mom puts up her hands, stopping me from responding. "Don't say anything now. Think about it. I can call your Dad and arrange every-

thing. We can watch movies and eat pizza and stay up late and make
ice cream sundaes like we used to do when you were little."

"What about Zeke?" I ask.

"What about Zeke?" Her hand reaches across the table and
grabs mine and I let her. She looks to the front door. "I wonder
when Jackson will get here. He's usually early."

"Why did you leave?" I ask.

"It's complicated," she says. "Hard to explain."

"Well, which one is it?" I ask. "Is it complicated? Or is it hard
to explain?" I ask.

"Both," Mom says, checking her watch, then the door. "Neither. I don't know." Mom roots through her purse, pulling out the
damn phone, buzzing again. She flips it open, speaks softly. She
stands and kisses my cheek without a sound and vanishes.

"You ready to order, hon?" our old lady waitress asks, sitting on a
nearby stool. Her face hangs heavy, wrinkles from ear to ear. Brown
spots splotch across her arms and neck. Her nametag reads Rhonda.

"Not yet. I think we're still waiting for my brother. He's always
late."

"My daughter was like that. Not a punctual bone in her body."

"You have a daughter?"

"Had."

"I'm sorry," I say.

"Are you psychic?" she asks.

"No."

"Then how would you know, hon?"

"What was her name?"

"Becca. Really it was Rebecca. My husband, Kirby, and I called
her Becca, God rest his soul. She was more of a Becca than a
Rebecca anyway."

Not only did I bring up one painful loss for her, but I also
brought up her dead fucking husband. I am a lump of cold crap. I
take a sip of my milk and set the cold glass down next to Mom's
purse. I pull out a wallet, red pen, travel pack of tissues, Revlon
lipstick, over-sized Ray Ban sunglasses, and a checkbook. I pull out

three prescription bottles. Each has a different name. None of them Corrine Barker.

Thirty milligram bottles of MS Contin. Morphine pills. Baby blues. Prescribed to other women or fake women, ultimately women that are not her—Jane Barker, Joanne Barker, Jill Barker. I line the bottles up like soldiers and sit back in my chair, facing them.

I close my eyes again and make a wish—that God would come down from Heaven and, in a moment of divine intervention, take my sight. Pluck out my eyes like apples from a tree. I want to say a prayer, some kind of new prayer, some kind of random hodge-podge of words that could pass as religious. With all the faith a non-Catholic, Catholic school kid can muster, I open my eyes and see her sitting there in front of me, my glass of chocolate milk and three prescription pill bottles between us.

She closes her eyes. Then, she verbalizes her prayer. "Jesus Christ," she says.

35

Mom drops me off at school, leaving me enough time to get to my locker, open it without incident from my back-up secret combination still in my shoe, then to first period with Mr. Rembrandt. Jackson didn't show for breakfast, of course, but we waited for him anyway, Mom making excuses for him the whole ride to school. I enter the class early today and on my own will, no need for Brother Lee to escort me again. Although, as soon as I sit down I am reminded of the DVD in Dad's closet and that this motherfucker gave it to him.

The last to arrive, Mr. Rembrandt walks in and says, "Welcome, watch, and listen." He writes *POV* on the board and claps chalk dust from his hands. "Point of View, gentlemen," he says. "The point from which to best tell your story." He combs wispy, brown hair over his bald spot and readjusts blue-rimmed glasses high up on the bridge of his nose, which make him look like he reads three newspapers a day. "It tells us what we see, but also—and equally as important—what we don't see." He wears a polka dot tie in a Windsor.

Mr. Rembrandt—Mr. 8-Fingers. Seriously. I've heard kids call him Four-Fingered Faggot. Let's examine some sick-shit theories:

1. The most popular and leading theory is that his mutant hands are the product of defensive wounds from a knife fight, the emergency room unable to reattach the pinkies to the heart of each hand.

2. Another speculation is that he was born with webbed hands. The story continues that a plastic surgeon was brought in to cut away the webs and, in order to save both hands, was forced to cut away the pinkies.

3. A more interesting and recent development is a gay rumor that, in order to hide the fact that he is a homosexual, he cut them off himself to keep them from lifting up into the air whenever he sips from a cup.

"We've all read Act One of *Hamlet*. Question—is Hamlet crazy? Is there a mental disorder in place? Is he mad or simply depressed and heartbroken? Is he really seeing the ghost of his dead father? What is your point of view?" He stalks the classroom, walking between rows, his mutilated hands behind his back. He points to the greasy-haired Dirtbag Boy in the back row.

"I think he's a whole bag full of crazy from the start. He says: 'O, that this too too solid flesh would melt / Thaw and resolve itself into a dew! / Or that the Everlasting had not fix'd / His canon 'gainst self-slaughter!' He wants his flesh to melt and thaw? Self-slaughter? He's twisted. He's a nutbag."

Super Shy Kid raises his hand and Mr. Rembrandt calls on him.

"It's a fine line though. His dead father's ghost has just told him to enact revenge on his behalf. If we are talking about POV and Shakespeare is showing us this crazy scene, but also showing us sane scenes without Hamlet, then the ghost could very well be fact, just as the Hamlet-less scenes are fact. We either believe it all as real or all as fake. It's a point of view."

"What about this ghost of the father?" Mr. Rembrandt says. "Why is this important?"

A kid that is either baked out of his mind or extremely sleepy speaks. "Hammy's got Daddy issues."

"Explain," Mr. Rembrandt says, adjusting his glasses, moving them farther up his nose. Then tightens up the knot of the fattest Windsor I have ever seen.

"His dad is dead. You have to let that shit—I mean stuff—go. But Hammy doesn't. He not only sees his father's ghost, but the ghost tells him to kill his uncle. It's obvious to me that Hammy's projecting. He wants his dad back, but can't have his dad back, so goes all *Cuckoo's Nest.*"

Someone behind me asks, "What do you think, Mr. Rembrandt?"

"What I think is not important. It's important what *you* think. So in an effort to explore that a bit more and get a good grasp on POV, we're going to do an interactive exercise," he says. "We're going to use questions to help us tell a story from a unique point of view."

He calls out names in pairs.

Mykel's in the class, and he's who I'm partnered with. Mykel smiles at me and says, "Yo, Little Man."

Mr. Rembrandt continues. "One of you is the subject and one of you is the biographer. Ask as many questions as you need to write your portrait. Let's go. Let's go. Let's go."

"Do you care what you are?" Mykel asks.

"How about I ask the questions?" I ask.

"Good," he says. "I like being the subject." Mykel wears tan corduroys, a pink shirt, and green and white striped tie in a Limp Dick. No plaid. I want to write these details down. I had completely forgotten about his odd name.

"My first question," I say, "is about photography. You take the bus home from school. Stand out by the street. Wear those oversized headphones clamped around your head like a vice. That big camera." I mimic the way he holds that enormous camera with an extra long lens in his hand that looks like a boner. "You take pictures at the bus stop of parked cars and old ladies holding brown paper bags full of groceries and shit."

"I didn't hear a question," he says. He turns a big, gold stud in his ear and leans farther back in his chair.

"Find your unique point of view?" Mr. Rembrandt says, rubbing his nubby hands together. I never noticed it before, but his hands look like guns, two fleshy firearms, his nubs like triggers. BLAM. BLAM.

"How long have you been into photography?" I ask.

"Chopography," he says, handing me a postcard that reads *Chopography Exhibit by Mykel*, advertising his art show at the Daily Grind downtown in Fell's Point. It's similar to the flyers we handed out the other day, but this is smaller and has a word I've never seen before. "chopography," I say.

"I take pictures of shit, then chop them up and piece them back together. Chopography."

"I know this place," I say. "It's near my brother's apartment."

"You should come."

"What is it that you do exactly?"

Mykel makes scissors with his fingers and clips them along a line in front of his face.

"How do you chop pictures up?"

"Do I hear hard-hitting questions?" Mr. Rembrandt asks, walking behind us, clapping his hands. Nasty nubs. I look at his freak hands and want to ask *him* a hard-hitting question.

"We're good," Mykel says. He hands Mr. Rembrandt a postcard.

"This is great, Mykel," he says, waving the postcard like a fan.

"You should come," Mykel says. "Might see something you like."

"I just might."

Mr. Rembrandt moves on to a pair of guys picking out rims in a car mag.

"What do you get out of chopping people up in pictures?" I ask Mykel.

"Satisfaction," Mykel says. He sits up in his chair, rubbing at a dark stain in the wood of his desk. "Satisfaction in the act. I feel good when I do it."

"Why do you do it?" I ask.

"Why do dogs bark?"

"But you chop up pictures and reassemble them like Frankenstein's monster," I say. "Why?"

Mr. Rembrandt announces that we will be presenting our

partners at the front of the classroom. He asks who wants to go first. He asks who has the stones to be the first to face the firing squad. He says, "Volunteers. Volunteers. Volunteers."

Mykel's hand goes up and volunteers on my behalf. Mr. Rembrandt gets giddy with excitement, clapping his hands, calling us up; waving us on with his freak hands. As we approach the front of the room, I ask Mykel again why he chops up photographs. I ask him what he gets out of it.

"Honestly," he says, blowing hot air into closed fists, "so I don't do it for real."

Immediately, I think of tongue extractions.

36

The cafe is curiously quiet—tables crowded with bodies, sport coats hung from the backs of chairs, book bags held between feet, hands delivering fistfuls of food to anxious mouths. It doesn't take a seasoned anthropologist to be able to analyze the dynamics of the high school watering hole. Like any animal in the wild, the Byron Hall boy stays to his own kind, careful not to stray too far away from the pack.

Stoner table by the lunch line for obvious reasons—shaggy hair, baggy clothes, smoke heaps of weed behind the lecture hall building. Barely a Limp Dick all around.

Band table next table over—awkward kids in thick-rimmed glasses, hair gelled in strict parts, acne attacked and boil-ridden foreheads. A Half-Windsor and Limp Dick split.

Miscellaneous jock tables all over the place—plaid jackets, plaid shirts, plaid ties, plaid pants. Chatter about getting laid and wasted on cheap beer and expensive vodka. Windsor knots.

Sorry, sad-sack loser table near the fire exit—normal kids who don't play instruments, or participate in sports, or excel in skate-boarding, or smoke weed, or drink anything but energy drinks. Clip-on ties and Limp Dicks.

Computer geek table in Fuck Central near the vending machines—super smart kids that carry calculators the way most people carry car keys. Limp Dick, absolutely.

Drama club table—the loudest kids in the school with coiffed hair and a fine knowledge of the latest dance music. Expertly knotted Half-Windsor's.

Debate table—future lawyers and bankers of the world. Windsors tied with precision.

Blue Jay Weekly table—the newspaper kids in crisp, white shirts, perpetually ink-blackened fingers. Windsor knots loose around necks.

Artist table—bright colored shirts that don't match their bright colored pants. Big, fat ties in Limp Dick knots.

Jeremy Barker table—nonexistent. I walk with my head down past the soccer jock table, where Cam Dillard and the plaid monkeyfuck bastards sit flicking each other in the ear. I want to punch the douchebag and his gang of retard robot monkeys. At a table in the middle of the room I see Mykel and an open spot across from him.

"Anyone sitting here?" I ask him, pulling the chair back. I drop my brown bag lunch on the table. "You hear we got Mr. Vo today in Christian Awareness? Brother Larry's out."

"Nice," Mykel says. "Mr. Vo's cool as shit."

"Who are you?" a kid says. "And what the fuck are you eating?"

"Jeremy," I say. I open the tinfoil from my pepperoni sandwich and take a huge bite.

"You're white," he says.

"I'm friends with Mykel," I say and feel completely weird about him saying that I am white. Because he's black and if I had said what he said to me, but said "you're black" instead of "you're white," what would have happened?

"Nice to meet you," I say.

"Jimmy Two," he says.

"Jimmy what?" I ask, leaning closer to him.

"His name is James James," Mykel says. "We call him Jimmy Two."

"The fuck kind of sandwich is that?" Jimmy Two asks. He puts his hand on my shoulder and pushes me away from him.

"Large-cut pepperoni sandwich on whole wheat with mayo and lettuce." The tinfoil of my sandwich is open on the table like a body during surgery. It's smells spicy and sweet.

"Smells like shit," Jimmy Two says. "Don't bring that shit to our table. Goddamn guinea food at the BAC table, boy."

I wonder for a moment what the fuck BAC means and when I look at the faces of the guys sitting around me I get it. Fuck. Double fistfuck.

The Black Awareness table—every black kid in school belongs to this club. And no one sits at their table unless they are, well, black. Well-dressed. Gold chains with crosses looped around necks. Chunky watches, loose on their wrists. Trimmed facial hair cut close to the skin, well-manicured like a lawn. Ties tied in different knots, tied with the utmost care and attention. Casanovas. The rowdiest table in the cafe. The center of the room. The table nobody fucks with. The BAC—the Black Awareness Club.

"Smells bad, Jeremy," Mykel confirms. "Seriously, close that shit up." He bends the edges of the tinfoil over my sandwich.

"I can't sit here anymore," Jimmy Two says. "Fucking sandwich is making me sick." He stands and pushes out his chair, but it tips back and crashes to the floor, rolling sideways, rocking back and forth on its legs before settling into a cold silence.

This is when it begins—the entire cafe screams the word *dork*.

Starts small, at first, a few kids from the band table saying it into fists covering their mouths. The jock and artist tables follow suit. The stoners and debaters after that. The newspaper boys and computer and sad sack kids. Every table, all tables, joined in a total collaborative union. A choir of kids howling. The stoners and sad sack losers spit *motherfuckingdoooooork*. Half a dozen voices mix in a few high-pitched *geek*s, stretching the *eeeee* like bubbles rising up from the bottom of the ocean.

"Jimmy Two got dorked," Mykel says, laughing.

"What's happening?" I ask Mykel.

"How do you not know about dorking?" Mykel asks.

The cafe: *doooooooooork, doooooooooork*.

"I don't know," I say.

The cafe: *geeeeeeeeeek, motherfuckinggeeeeeeeeeek*.

"Dork, motherfucker," Mykel says to Jimmy Two, punching the

air. "You got fucked up, son. Motherfuckinggeeeeeek."

The *dorking* shifts again as someone yells *faggot bitch* beneath the other voices. It doesn't have anything to do with Jimmy Two, I don't think, but has everything to do with him. Jimmy Two climbs on to the table, standing on the table now, and throws his arms out like he is commanding an army. He looks terrifying up there, like a giant ready to crush us all.

Rightly so, the cafe goes silent.

"All y'all motherfuckers," he says, grabbing his junk, turning to show the entire cafe his hand on his dick, jostling it for effect. "All of you, on my dick!"

The cafe is dead, everyone trying to act as though nothing ever happened.

Brother Lee stands on top of a chair in the middle of the room and slaps the side of a cowbell with the butt of a drumstick. How he has ready access to a cowbell and drumstick I'll never know.

Jimmy Two hops off the table, picks up his chair and sets it upright. Brother Lee rushes to his side. He's a full half a person shorter than Jimmy Two.

"Anyone interested in joining Mr. James in detention today can feel free to continue acting a hoodlum," Brother Lee yells.

"Brother, the chair was an accident," Jimmy Two says. "It wasn't on purpose, I swear."

"Mr. James, do you jump on tables at home?"

"No, Brother."

"Two days of detention—one for chair and one for table."

"Brother, Jimmy Two didn't mean to knock over his chair," Mykel says.

"I appreciate your concern," Brother Lee says. "You have good friends, Mr. James. Now you have something to confess to today." Brother Lee walks across the cafe, patrolling from table to table, doling out detention like food to the homeless, taking Jimmy Two with him, making him push in chairs along the way.

"What did he mean *confess*?" I ask, dropping my sandwich into my bag.

"Reconciliation, man," Mykel says.

"Reconciliation?" I ask, completely unaware.

"A sacrament," he says. He zips up his book bag. "Like marriage. And baptism." Mykel hands me a sheet of paper.

"What's this?" I ask.

"It's mandatory," Mykel says.

"For what?" I ask.

"Mandatory to be forgiven," he says. The rest of the BAC pack up their lunches, slide on their sport coats and leave the cafe for class. "Today is the first one of the year."

And apparently this goddamn thing is madatory.

37

There are no new jokes in my bathroom stall, but there is some new graffiti.

A stick figure with big tits and a hairy vagina stands in front of a smaller stick figure with a large penis pointing in her face. A thought bubble above her head says, "I'm Jeremy Barker and I heart big dick." I spit on the cuff of my sleeve and rub the picture, smearing the ink, making the tits and penis look bigger by accident. Fuck. Me.

I stole a *Vogue* from my dentist's office last month and am reading it now. Every model looks tall and skinny, practically naked, high heels, never smiling. I look through the advertisements like a scientist for a photo of a model smiling. The only one I can find is of a man smiling. He sits on the edge of the bed, naked, a white bedsheet pulled over his lap. Behind the man is a naked woman, who rests her hands on his shoulders, pressing her tits against his back in bed as she whispers something in his ear. He is looking at a silver wristwatch on the nightstand. She is not smiling, but he sure is. The advertisement is for some expensive-looking brand of watch, but the tag line at the bottom says, "A man never needs convincing."

The door opens and two guys enter, standing at the urinals, one urinal open between them. I lift my legs to the toilet seat, holding my breath.

"I've heard rumors that this is the bathroom where dudes come to get it on."

"Who told you about that? You know what? Never mind."

Both urinals flush. Water sprays from the spigots as they wash their hands. The kids pull paper from the dispensers, wiping their hands like they're trying to rip away their skin before tossing the crumpled towels into the trash and leave. The bathroom resumes a quiet state as the flushed water fades away inside in the tiled walls.

I slip *Vogue* into my bag next to the remnants of my pepperoni sandwich and walk towards the door to leave just as it opens. For some reason, I'm startled and turn around and walk back towards the urinals, like I had just come in here. It's Zink and he stalks a urinal into submission. I approach the line of urinals, dead focused on urinal etiquette, something I learned from Dad years ago. Urinal etiquette dictates at least one open urinal should exist between each man—the buffer urinal. I settle on the urinal closest to the wall, leaving two open between us, and unzip my fly, locking my stare on the words *Stop Looking At My Dick, Faggot* scratched into the wall in front of me.

"Given Friday's mixer any thought?" he asks, arching his back, hosing the urinal cake.

I've done well at avoiding Zink since the bathroom incident, that is, until now.

"Got to be there, baby." Zink shakes his dick. "It's like religion. It's like a sacrament— *fraternization*."

"Will *you* be there?" I ask.

"Everyone will be there," Zink continues. "Chicks and dicks. Fights and dikes." Zink flushes the urinal, pressing the silver handle with his elbow. He walks to the sink and washes his hands, leaning into the mirror, peering at the pores of his nose.

I flush the handle with my elbow too.

"Have you given any thought to what you're going to wear?" he asks.

"I have this red sweater."

"Barks. A sweater? No. You have to wear something awesome. Don't wear khakis. Khakis are for holidays and hospitals." Zink shakes the excess water from his hands and then wipes them on his corduroy pants. "A button down shirt unbuttoned with a wife-beater underneath. Or a polo shirt. Spike your hair up. Open your clothes up. Throw a necklace on. Glow stick. Something. But for God's sake, no sweater."

I wash my hands.

"If you have a pierced ear, that's good too," he says. "I don't have my ears pierced, but I know guys who do and they say it works like gangbusters."

"Gangbusters?"

"If you decide to get your ear pierced, make sure it's your left ear. Not your right. Left is right and right is wrong. It's this whole thing."

"Someone is a homosexual if they have their right ear pierced and heterosexual if they have their left ear pierced?" I ask.

"I have my left nipple pierced," Zink says.

"Nipple?"

"Nipple."

"Does the left and right thing apply to nipples too?"

"Don't be a dick, Barks," Zink says, thumbing his fly to be sure it is closed.

"Do you know what people are saying about this bathroom?"

"Yes." Zink's smile lights up his face. "Funny how a fear-based rumor will not only make them believe it, but also encourage them to perpetuate it. Curiosity is killer. It's this whole predictable thing."

"I don't understand."

"They were just in here. Together. And everyone saw them. They came in together and they left together."

"But they didn't do anything in here like that."

"No one else knows that."

Neither of us says anything. No follow-up questions.

We walk to the sinks next to the urinals and stand shoulder to shoulder, staring at the other's reflection in the mirror.

"How the hell do you get your knots so perfect?" I ask, pointing at his necktie knotted perfectly in a Windsor.

"It's pretty badass," he says, reaching his hand up and unclipping the tie from his collar. He holds the mutant, pre-knotted, clip-on tie in his hand like a recently caught fish and shakes it. There is no loop at the top, holding the knot. The knot simply stands alone, allowing the rest of the tie to dangle down. "Clip-on, Barks. Motherfucking clip-on."

"Did your Dad ever teach you how to tie a knot?"

"He was always more interested in teaching me how to block penalty kicks."

"It's pretty easy, if you would like to learn."

"How can it possibly be easier than a clip-on?" he asks, and flicks the clasp at the back of the knot.

"Tying a really good knot is way more important than a goddamn clip-on. It's this whole thing," I say, stealing Zink's phrase.

"I like the knot you're wearing. Teach me that one."

I look at my Limp Dick and undo the knot, pulling it from around my neck.

He hands me his clip-on and I snap it over my collar—perfect fucking Windsor knot.

Zink says, "Everybody has a thing. Everyone has at least one thing. This is your thing."

I say, "According to me, there are three types of necktie knots: the Windsor, the Half-Windsor, and the Limp Dick."

38

In our religion class, Christian Awareness, a band kid in front of me, the one with all the acne, says my loafer's look like moccasins. He calls me Pocahontas.

"Where are your braids, Pocahontas?" he says, picking a zit on his chin.

"Pocahontas liked to suck fat dick," a soccer player says.

"Pucker those lips, Pocahontas," a stoner kid says.

Mr. Vo stands at the front of the room filling in for Brother Larry who, we are told, has come down with *the bug*. No one is sure what that means.

"Language," Mr. Vo says, pointing a fist at the stoner. "I don't want to hear it anymore. Let's be mature, okay, gentlemen."

"Poor Pocahontas," the band kid says, and kicks my chair.

"Mr. Jeremy Barker." Mr. Vo looks at the classroom chart of names and points to an open seat in the back. He wears a light yellow tie with blue sailboats knotted in a Windsor. His vest is buttoned up and a gold clip holds his tie to his shirt. "Back of the class."

I straighten my posture like a Marine, fearless-like, collect my belongings and switch seats. Semper Fi and all that shit.

"I will say this only one time," Mr. Vo says, soft and low. "We don't have a whole lot of time before you men go off to Reconciliation. I see here in Brother Larry's assignment book that he asked you each to write a one-sentence statement beginning with the words: I am." He walks along the back wall of the classroom as we turn in our seats to track him. "I want to hear what you men came up with." He points with a fist to the first kid in my row. "You. Go."

"I am the Orioles," a student council kid says. "And I badly need relief pitching and better batting deep into the lineup."

"I am the Ravens," a football player says, punching the student council kid in the back. "Fuck baseball. Pussy sport."

"I am doing your mom," a lacrosse player says.

"I see we are taking this seriously," Mr. Vo says. "Brother Larry will be thrilled."

"I am laying a lot of pipe these days," a drama club kid says, adjusting his knot, a Windsor.

"I am writing a novel," a newspaper kid says.

"You are a fucking nerd," the band kid with the acne says.

"I am a big time dealer," a stoner kid says.

"I dealt your mom last night and she liked it," a lacrosse player says.

"Lovely." Mr. Vo rubs his eyes. "Gentlemen, this is unbecoming of a Hall man."

"I am your biological daddy," a football player tells the stoner.

"I am tripping my balls off," the stoner says back.

"Let's try you," Mr. Vo says, pointing to Mykel. "What do you have for us?"

"I am chopography," Mykel says.

No one says anything to Mykel.

"Chopography," Mr. Vo says. He leans against the chalkboard, white dust covering the back of his vest. "What is that? Clearly, it's not photography?"

"Chopography," Mykel says. "I take pictures and then cut them together."

"Like collage," Mr. Vo says.

"Not really." Mykel stretches back in his chair, extending his arms over his head, kicking his long legs out to the chair in front of him. "It's more like dissection."

"Interesting," Mr. Vo says, rubbing his temples now, then points his fist at me and asks the same question.

Many things cross my mind. My women's magazine collection hidden away in my closet, tucked away in the shells of empty board game boxes. Mom leaving me for pills and leaving Dad for Carrefour. Dad and his knots. Rembrandt and his video. Dad disappearing. The great Zombie Apocalypse. And all the shit at school.

I say, "I am not who I used to be."

V

THRILLER

(Released Date: December 2, 1983)

Directed by John Landis

Written by John Landis and Michael Jackson

39

The line for Reconciliation crawls out from the lecture hall and on to the sidewalk outside, funneling along the school. It reminds me of the dance sequence in Michael Jackson's fourteen-minute music video for "Thriller"—a zombified, undead, shuffle of bodies. There is a leader, but it's unknown to us in line, moving along as instructed. Following orders. The sky is overcast, symptomatic of an approaching rain, that sweet rain smell carried in on a sharp wind. I button up my sport coat. A teacher holds his hand palm up, checking for drops, but none found. Some kids wear their jackets over the shoulders on the hook of a finger. Some wear them like rich old ladies, draped over their shoulders. The teachers patrol the line, enforcing the dress code in that respect, zapping kids to attend detention after school with Brother Lee. Detention, as described by Jackson, is two hours in a classroom listening to Brother Lee lecture, nonstop, completely in Mandarin—the lecture topic unknown. Which sounds more like Hell than detention.

A teacher hands me a prompt—this tiny sheet of paper, a script that reads:

> *Forgive me, Father, for I have sinned. It has been (say a number) (say one of the following: days/weeks/months/years) since my last confession. I am sorry for the following: (insert sins here). Father, please forgive me for these sins and the sins unspoken. Amen. (Sign of the Cross and exit Lecture Hall immediately, QUIETLY).*

I look for the nearest teacher or brother or priests or someone, anyone, a Catholic at the very least, to flag down and explain to me in detail what I'm about to participate in. Questions come fast, questions about sins and confessing these sins to a complete stranger, in order to be prepared for Heaven. It reminded me of a body being prepped for surgery. The line snails forward. When I'm about halfway through, a door opens. Rembrandt. He adjusts his blue-rimmed glasses, exposing his fucked-up hands to me. He could be flashing his deformed hands or his penis; it'd feel no different. Mr. Rembrandt, the smug fuck, checks the sky again, before stepping out onto the sidewalk. We smile. We remember. Passing each other by the teacher's parking lot. He looks down on me, but only because he's taller.

"Mr. Barker," he says. "Glad to see you outside when you're supposed to be outside." Mr. Rembrandt steps in line, excusing himself to the computer geek behind me who's done nothing but recite his script from memory since we've been outside. The sweet pre-rain breeze picks up again, but this time delivers a sharp chemical stench. Same heavy antiseptic smell as Dad. It's Rembrandt. "When your little script says *insert sins here*," he says, pointing to the script, "what do you think you'll say?"

"To be honest, I haven't given it much thought. But one thing's for sure, whatever sin I say, it won't be any worse than what the priests have already heard at this school," I say and fold the script in half, sliding it into my pocket.

Two jocks in front of me—one football, one soccer, both as indicated by the athletic letters on their letterman jackets—spontaneously trade punches like sparring partners. The jacked-up football jock pounds the soccer kid in the upper arm, which the soccer jock absorbs only to return with appropriate force, hitting him in the same location. This continues for a few more rounds in an organized fashion, before Mr. Rembrandt intercedes.

"My dear, dear boys," he says, startling them, unaware that they were under surveillance. "Why must two educated and talented young men, such as yourselves, succumb to physical violence?" He makes a *tisk-tisk-tisk* sound, like my mother used to do when I was a child. "Oh, absurdity of absurdities."

The jocks apologize, their cheeks flushed red.

"What drives a man to allow himself to be hit repeatedly without question?"

The football jock says, "It's a game, sir."

"And how does one win a game like this?" he asks.

The soccer jock says, "It's called *Deadarm*. It goes until someone quits."

"Because they have a dead arm," Mr. Rembrandt says. "Yes. I see." He clears his throat and leans forward into my peripheral vision. "Have you ever played such a game, Mr. Barker?"

I can hear the computer geek behind me, still reciting the script to himself. There are no other teachers in sight and no one else who witnessed the jocks playing Deadarm. Words flee. He knows I've seen it. It's the only explanation. Like a gift from God, the line shifts forward again, this time at a good clip, and funnels through the double-doors and into the lobby of the lecture hall and when I finally turn around, ready to retaliate, though I'm not sure with what, Mr. Rembrandt is gone.

Oh, absurdity of absurdities.

40

The lecture hall is empty except for a few priests spread out, each in close conversation with a student. Priests make the Sign of the Cross. They bow their heads. They close their eyes. Some hold necklaces with big beads. Some hold their hands together in their laps. Sometimes they smile. Sometimes they nod, either in recognition or simply feigned understanding. They dispense penance like Pez—penance, a flashy word for punishment—some mutant alien shit.

Kids exit though the art studio behind the lecture hall, otherwise known as the penance palace. There, kids kneel. They recite different prayers, numerous times, like they're memorizing lines in a play, repeating their way back into Heaven. There is a teacher monitoring the art studio/prayer palace, but not really monitoring. I can see kids quietly fucking around from the lecture hall, slapping each other in the middle of the back with open hands. Fucktards.

A priest in the front row motions to me—a pencil-thin priest with a neck beard and a messy mop of black hair. He's a young guy, maybe a few years older than Jackson, and looks like if it weren't for a standard all black uniform, he'd be a hopeless mess. He's definitely more of a nerdy, virginal version of Jackson without any muscle and with a white collar. He sits in his chair the way the broom leans against the wall of our kitchen—stiff and patient.

I fumble in my pocket for my script but decide I don't need it thanks to the neurotic computer geek still mumbling behind me.

"Forgive me, Father, for I have sinned," I say. "It has been forever since my last confession."

"Jeremy Barker?" he asks.

How the fuck does he know my name? I could hit the door in seconds and be out of the foyer and at the circle, before anyone has a chance to stop me.

"You're not in trouble," he says. "You were at our auditions for the play, but didn't audition. I'm Father Vincent Gibbs, faculty advisor to the drama department with Mr. Rembrandt." This is the first time in a while when I haven't shook hands with someone after an introduction. "I'm sorry if he embarrassed you the other day." He rolls his eyes. "You know how he can be—loves any opportunity to get bent out of shape."

"I really don't know much about him, other than his . . . you know." I wiggle my pinkies.

"Oh my goodness." He slaps his cheeks. "Do you know what happened?"

"Only rumors."

"Can you tell me one?" Father leans forward to listen. "No. Of course you can't. Don't tell me." He closes his eyes and leans back into his seat, but that smile can't be drowned and it comes bobbing back to the surface. "Well, maybe you can tell me *just* one rumor."

It's harmless fun to be gossiping with Father Vincent, but I want to try and be normal, like the other students here confessing sins. I reboot and try again. "Forgive me, Father, for I have sinned," I say. "It really has been forever since my last confession. This is my very first time."

"You are an earnest, young man. I apologize for my behavior. Continue, please."

The Reconciliation script fades from my memory. I've been so busy and excited and nervous preparing for this important and bizarre Catholic rite that I never sketched a backup plan. Right now, I need a backup plan.

"I'm listening, my son."

I can't believe the simple call-and-response language has completely disappeared. I run through the recent alleyways of my mind, through the cafe, and Mykel and Jimmy Two, but I can only think of one thing worth discussing. My nightmare comes screaming out.

"My dad disappears at night," I say.

"Where does he go?" Father Vincent's voice is soft, but serious.

"We watch zombie movies together every night with dinner. I fall asleep and when I wake up he's gone. He doesn't return until morning when he takes me to school. Brings me here."

"What has your mother done about it? What does she say?"

A response fires before I can censor myself. "My mother is dead," I say.

"I'm sorry," he says. "Have you ever asked him point blank? *Dad, where do you go at night?* Because it's possible there's a simple explanation for all of this. Maybe he has a girlfriend. Maybe he's protecting you from something."

I mentally step outside of this conversation to test the strength and weight of my fears, but they are not enough to scare me away from continuing.

"I found a homemade video in his office. The word *sublimation* was written on the disc."

"What a word. My goodness." Father rubs his head. "I'm not confident I fully understand what it means."

"It means two things, Father." I extend one finger on my hand. "It refers to a chemical process where an object in a solid state transforms into a gas state, but does so by skipping the liquid state completely."

"Do you mean *phase*—skipping the liquid *phase* completely?"

"No. It's *state*. They are states of being. That's the whole point— sublimation is the phase or lack of phases between the states."

"This is bizarre. I had no idea such a thing existed." He rubs his temples, like a headache appeared. "That definition still doesn't help much in the way of explaining things at all, does it?"

"The second is just as odd. It had to do with impulse control."

"You mean, like, an addiction? Someone's an addict and works on *sublimation*, controlling their impulses."

"Not exactly. It's is when a person channels their negative and unacceptable impulses into activities deemed more socially acceptable."

"I see," he says, but I don't think he does.

"The socially acceptable activity is supposed to force a change for the good."

"Have you seen what is on the disc yet?"

"There was a man strapped to a bed and the bed was on a stage. Other men watched as two doctors prepped the man for some kind of black market surgery."

"Jeremy, I don't know what to say." He looks around to see if anyone is listening to us. "I'm sorry. I don't. I'm at a loss." Father pats his pockets, looking for something. "You said you and your father like to watch zombie movies?"

"Yes."

"Lucky for you, that's something we have in common."

"That's not sacrilegious for a priest?" I ask. "To watch zombie movies?"

"Zombies have more in common with Catholics than people care to admit." He stops patting his pockets.

"What's your favorite zombie movie?" I ask him.

Father Vincent's smile resurfaces.

"Hands down, no contest? *Night of the Living Dead*," he says.

"I have the original *Night* movie poster on the ceiling of my bedroom. The black-and-white poster of the little girl zombie."

"Zombies represent our greatest fears. Humans must seek salvation in order to survive. This is not all that different from what Catholics believe in."

"Father, I'm going to be honest with you, as much as I love zombie movies, I don't see how any of this has to do with me or my father."

"*The Greatest Story Ever Told*," he says. "It's the life of Jesus Christ—crucified, died, and buried. He rose from the grave three days after his death and ascended into Heaven to save us from our sins. Basic Catholicism 101. This death and resurrection is also the

Catholic holiday of Easter. That's why sometimes people refer to it as Happy Zombie Jesus Day."

"Jesus was a zombie?" This priest has to be off his meds, like me.

"I believe that Jesus was the second zombie known to mankind. But if you watch *The Greatest Story Ever Told*, you will meet Lazarus and Lazarus was zombie number one. Lazarus was dead for four days until Jesus brought him back to life."

"Raised him from the dead?" I'd never thought about Jesus in those terms before, as a zombie, and the whole undead connection. "What you're saying makes a lot of sense. There are a lot of similarities, and I see what you're trying to do—get me to see things from a more Christian perspective and all. What it comes down to for me are my five simple codes to survive the Zombie Apocalypse."

"Codes?" A moment of recognition crosses his face as he repats his pocket, this time inside his sport coat. "Bingo," he says and pulls out a little pencil and a tiny booklet and scribbles a note on the blank pages. The cover has contrasting splotches of color, like a sunset maybe, or sunrise, I'm not sure. "Are they similar to commandments?" He lifts his booklet. "I'm intrigued by your idea of codes and want to make a note of them."

"No. They're Zombie Survival Codes. Nothing like commandments." I stand before this continues any further.

"You said you couldn't see how all of this Catholic and zombie talk could help you or your dad. If you listened to nothing else I've said, then listen to this—no matter how far gone you believe a person to be, there's always the possibility of a miracle to bring them back to life."

"The possibility of a miracle," I say.

Father Vincent makes the Sign of the Cross and absolves me of my sins, even though I didn't confess shit and didn't ask to be saved.

"Do you know the Lord's Prayer?" he asks.

"I do," I say.

"For your penance, I want you to say the Lord's Prayer three times. Once for your mother, once for your father, and once for yourself. And maybe sometime you can stop by the chapel and tell me all about your codes." He closes his booklet and slips it back inside his pocket. I don't know for sure what he wrote in that book, but my gut tells me he wanted to know my codes and that book won't let him forget.

"No problem," I say. "My mother used to say the Lord's Prayer all the time." This isn't a complete lie. She used to say it right before she took a fistful of pills. Mom doesn't say the Lord's Prayer anymore. Now she takes her pills with a smile.

41

I walk to the back of the lecture hall. Brother Fred waves me into the penance studio. He whispers that we are on a *time budget* and I have absolutely no idea what that phrase even means. Kids kneel at metal folding chairs, hands at their heads, eyes closed, mouthing prayers. I kneel and accidentally knock the leg of a chair against another, which makes an unflattering *clang*.

"Don't even think about it," Brother Fred says. "You were all just forgiven your sins. I will send you back to do it again. There is to be no *dorking* in here. Understood?"

I pretend to say the Lord's Prayer because I don't care enough to say it for real.

The other kids around me do the same.

Two baseball players finish praying at the same time.

When Brother Fred turns his back, one player pretends to strangle the other, gripping hands around the other's neck.

The kid getting choked flails his arms.

A debate club kid laughs, and snot shoots out his nose.

Baseball players laugh at the dangling snot.

Brother Fred snaps his fingers on both hands like he's firing a six-shooter.

A kid across from me with a Limp Dick knot, the band kid with all the acne, who made fun of my shoes and called me Pocahontas, he finishes his penance and opens his eyes. He smiles at me with crooked teeth and says, "You are such a fucking dork."

42

I wait in the lobby of the theater after school under the giant green plant between the lecture hall and theater doors, right where we lined up for Reconciliation only a few hours ago. It didn't smell like Lysol earlier today, but it does right now.

Students float through to the theater in mixed gender groups. Prudence girls are in the house. Mykel sniffs through too, slapping me five as he passes by, chasing skirt. I expect to see Brother Lee pop up like the badass, Christian Brother ninja that he is. Father Vincent stops outside the theater and waits for the others to enter, before asking me if everything is okay?

"*Planet Terror*," I say.

"Never seen it," he says. "Good zombies?"

"A girl gets her leg amputated and a Minigun attached instead."

"Consider it on my list," he says. "And *The Greatest Story Ever Told*?"

"You say early zombies. I say old and crappy Catholic movie," I say. "But I'll watch it."

"It's all that I ask." He gives me that smile and continues into the theater.

After my proclamation to her the other day, I haven't seen Aimee White on campus. But she is the assistant director of the play and has to be here. Then at last the double doors swing open and she walks in wearing her school uniform—white blouse, plaid skirt, sexy. She holds a thick, black binder in her hands and writes on a pad of paper, taking cute little diligent notes, I'm sure. The doors close behind her and I see *him*, dictating to her, lecturing about

Nora's motivation and Torvald's mistakes as a husband and Krog-stad's manipulation.

They reach the door to the theater and both stop walking.

Aimee stops taking notes. She doesn't smile when she sees me.

Mr. Rembrandt doesn't stop lecturing about subtext and emo-tional commitment. He does smile when he sees me.

I open the door for them and they pass through—first him, then her—and as they pass through and the door closes and I leave the lobby, I fantasize about Tricia, reading one of her magazines, wear-ing nothing but a bathrobe, her hair tied up in a ponytail.

43

Dad picks me up after school. I don't know right away if he's here for me or for Rembrandt, but Dad blasts his horn until I come over to the car so by process of elimination I figure it out. It seems he's here for me. I wonder if Dad is gay and dating Rembrandt. It doesn't explain the video or books but makes more sense than anything else I've come up with. We pull around the circle and see football players killing and soccer players chasing each other, all for a ball. I can't see O'Bannon or Volkavich, but I know they're out there.

Dad hits the highway and exits off of 83 South, speeding onto the cobblestone streets of Fell's Point on our way to visit Jackson. Cobblestone paves the streets just off the Chesapeake Bay. Crumpled tinfoil potato chip bags surf the choppy water in the harbor. Beer bottles bob and eventually drown to the bottom of the bay. Chipped red bricks line the sidewalks. We pass a video store called Rick's Flicks and a coffee shop called the Daily Grind—the one where Mykel is holding his art show tomorrow night—and an abandoned police station. Birds flock in and out of the station's broken glass windows, perching on ledges, nesting in nooks.

I look between buildings to see if I can see Mom's building across the bay and I sure as shit can—*The Prince Edward* peering past the Inner Harbor from Federal Hill.

Dad rolls through a stop sign. A younger crowd inhabits Fell's Point. Yuppies. Sport coats. All types of knots. Short and long skirts. Couples arm in arm. Cell phone talkers and dog walkers. Fell's Point used to be run by drug dealers, junkies, and whores, but it's all cleaned up now. That's what Dad says anyway. Dad says Baltimore moved the *bad element* back to their own streets. When Dad says *bad element*, he means black people. Obviously.

"Does Jackson's new apartment have a bathroom?" I ask.

"I'm sure it does," he says, loosening his Windsor knot from around his neck.

"The last one didn't."

"I'm sure it did." Dad approaches a red light, but doesn't brake. It turns green at the last second, like Dad changed it with some kind of mental power. "How was school today?" he asks.

"Fine," I say.

"Just fine?"

"Okay."

"Was it fine or okay?" he asks.

"My day was good," I say. This is what Dad calls executing decisiveness. I want to tell him about confession and Jimmy Two getting dorked. I want to tell him about Father Vincent and Zombie Jesus Day and Lazarus. But I don't. Fuck it. Honestly, I want to ask him where the fuck he goes at night. I want to ask him about that fucking DVD. Instead, I just say, "My day was good. It was good, good, good."

"Good is better than bad, I suppose," he says as he parallel parks in front of Jackson's red brick building. "One handed parking. Yeah." Dad spins the wheel with one hand, the other behind my head on the car seat, eyeballing the open space.

"Shouldn't you be using two hands?"

"Women parallel park with two hands."

"You're going to hit the curb," I say, peering out the window.

"You shouldn't doubt your father." Dad parks perfectly alongside the curb, tight between two cars. "You should trust your father." He feeds the meter as I shadow box behind him, watching the shadow version of myself dance across the sidewalk.

I am Jeremy "The Hero" Barker. The unsung heavyweight hero of the world. Only thing missing is an aluminum fucking bat.

44

The wood stairs in Jackson's building creak at every step. A thick banister wobbles. There are two apartments facing each other on Jackson's floor—3A and 3B.

"3B," Dad says. "That's what he told me." He knocks.

"I have to pee."

"Jackson, open up," Dad says, knocking harder. "You're brother is about to wet himself."

A door creaks open across the hall as a woman pokes her head out. "Yes?" she says. She has short, black hair and alabaster skin. Her skin looks like one of Mom's porcelain plates she uses only on Thanksgiving and Christmas. Her lips are a natural peachy-pink color. She wears a red V-neck sweater, a style that I read about in one of my magazines, flattering on women with big breasts. Tricia wears V-neck T-shirts. The longer I stare at her; the more my blood drains from my head down to my dick. "Can I help you?" she asks.

"Can you?" Dad asks.

"I'm sorry?" she asks again. A sick, hospital stench wafts from behind the door.

"I'm sorry. My name is Ballentine Barker." He extends his hand. "I am Jackson's father. Is he in, love?"

Don't call her love, I think.

"Jackson lives across the hall, Mr. Barker. In 3A."

"I'm rarely wrong about this sort of thing," he says, looking at the other door. "I was sure he said 3B."

"I am rarely wrong as well," she says. "Funny how even when we're wrong it still feels like we're right."

"Yes. Funny. I'm sorry for the inconvenience," Dad says.

"Not at all," she says.

"Sorry for the bother," I say with an English accent, like I am some kind of big-dick prince talking to some peasant girl in the market and she's selling me a ripe pomegranate.

"Nice accent," she says. "You should be an actor."

"I'm Jeremy," I say.

"Franny," she says.

We shake hands. Her skin feels cold but soft and I can feel my heart beat faster and warm fluid flush through my veins. My dick gets hard. I look into her brown eyes and want to pull her down to me and plant one on her. Her smile disappears and her eyes narrow on me.

"Oh my goodness," she says. "Your nose."

I open my mouth and taste blood, gushing from my nose and onto my lips. Fuck. I never get nosebleeds.

"Let me get you some tissues," she says.

"That won't be necessary," Dad says, pulling out his handker-chief. He clamps it to my nose. "He gets these from time to time. Low iron levels. Needs a banana. Thanks again."

Franny smiles and closes the door, her smile a bullshit smile, a sympathy smile.

Dad gives up the handkerchief and knocks on Jackson's door.

"You okay?" Dad asks. "The nose, it's okay?"

"Iron levels," I say. "Probably the bananas."

Dad slaps me on the back.

Jackson finally opens the door and combs his fingers through his greasy hair. His eyes are almost completely shut, probably because he's stoned. He's also completely fucking naked. I hate it when he does this. He has this need to walk around naked. Hates to wear clothes. Says they slow him down. His shaggy brown hair, the hair on his head, tangles in crazy curls, spiraling in all directions as if he just woke up. His body is lion-like, muscular. And while describing my brother's body sounds like a faggy thing to do, it's the only way I know how to explain what he looks like. People always ask him if he's a model. He just eats that shit up.

My boner disappears right on cue.

"Stop knocking so loud," Jackson says, resting his head on the doorframe.

"Don't put on any clothes on our account," Dad says. "Expecting company?"

"Not until later." Jackson struggles to keep his eyes open, affected by the light. He adjusts his junk, scratches, then walks away, his vanilla white ass nodding with each step.

You should know that Jackson recently named his junk Roscoe. He told me about it after he'd graduated from college a few months back. At his graduation dinner, actually. Mom, Dad, Jackson, and I had dinner at this fancy Italian restaurant called De Amici in Baltimore's Little Italy, a few streets over from Fell's Point. Dad said that De Amici was Italian for *among friends*. It was weird, all of us being together again after the separation. Mom got up to go to the ladies' room and Dad went to the bar to hit on our waitress, which was when it happened. Jackson said he had to tell me something about his dong.

"I named it," he said.

"You named it?"

"I named that shit." He raised his hand for me to high-five, but I didn't.

"Gross."

"It's not gross, Stumps. It's awesome." It drives me up the fucking wall when he calls me Stumps, but I know he only does it to get a rise out of me. Why Stumps? Because I'm as-short-as-a-stump. Yup. I'm not sure he will ever call me Jeremy ever again. Mom said he would grow out of this childish phase of his life after he graduated college and entered the real world. I guess we are all still waiting.

"Why would you name your dick?"

"Why wouldn't I name it?" Then, he said, "I named him Roscoe." Jackson smiled, eyeing a girl at the table next to us, black hair to her shoulders, glasses. Dad leaned over the bar to the female bartender, pointing to a specific bottle of vodka that he wanted. And Mom never came back to the table at all, sneaking out the back entrance, I think.

What exactly is wrong with my brother that he named his penis
Roscoe?

Maybe Jackson is just hyperexcitable, like me, and needs to be
put on Ritalin, like me. I wonder if Dad knows about Jackson's
dick? I want to make it rhyme now—Roscoe Domingo eats black
flamingoes, instead of baby dingoes. Yup. Would he think Jackson
was normal, like he thinks I am normal on my medicine? Maybe
when they find out that I've stopped taking the medicine then
they'll see just how fucking hyperexcitable I truly am.

45

Jackson lives in a studio. He has everything pushed into it: single bed, desk, three-legged table, micro-kitchen, and a stool in the corner instead of a chair. His clothes are both stacked in a corner and flung across the floor, his sheets tangled and twisted at the foot of his bed. I stand in the only uncovered space of floor and tip my head back, still pinching my nose. I don't see a bathroom. For some reason, all I can think about is the Titanic—bigass boat, tipping up on one end and sinking beneath freezing water. White foam water.

"Jesus," Dad says. "You smell like Las Vegas."

"What a nice surprise," Jackson says, back on his bed under the only window. The window is covered with a black sheet, tacked into the wall. "Stumps, what's wrong with your nose?"

"Late night?" Dad asks, walking into the micro-kitchen to see if there is a girl tucked away somewhere, naked, recently sexed. He pokes through the dirty dishes piling out of the sink, knocks around an empty bag of cookies, and leans into an ashtray, inspecting the ash and beige butts.

"Earlier than usual," Jackson says.

"What did you do last night?" Dad asks.

"Some girl." Jackson clears his throat and rubs his temples with his knuckles. His attention is clearly fractured, his focus fuzzy at best. "I wine and dine. Hit it and quit it. Jackson Barker Power Hour up in here. Sometimes two, if I take a certain baby blue pill."

"Classy," Dad says, stomping across the apartment. He doesn't like to talk about prescription pills. "It's dinner time. Time for dinner. Now get dressed."

"You guys want to watch this zombie movie I got?" Jackson asks. "*Zombie Strippers!* Jenna Jameson's in it. Porn queen extraordinaire."

"Porn is for the perverted," Dad says. "Get dressed."

"Stumps, you have Coach O'Bannon yet?"

Dad smells something in the corner of the room—a pile of dirty clothes. "It is amazing to me that you get anyone up here at all. You live like a heathen."

"I am who I am," he says.

"If you spent as much time on a job search as you do on your fuckability statistics, you'd be a CFO by now."

"My general rule of thumb is this—if I find a girl who's a six, above average, and it's after 10 P.M., then that's it. I shut it down. I don't get greedy. Chances are I won't find much better. I call it the Six-by-Ten rule." Jackson claps at me. "So what size Speedo did Coach O'Bannon make you wear? Small?" Jackson asks.

"I haven't had gym class yet," I say. I forget that we had most of the same teachers at Byron Hall. "What do you mean *what size Speedo?*"

"Tell that little Asian mushroom, Brother Lee, that Jackson says *yo,*" Jackson says. "He'll die."

"Where is your bathroom?" I ask, annoyed as fuck. I look at the blank white ceiling, keeping my head tilted. No zombie posters here.

"The fuck's wrong with his nose? No one answers my questions," he says.

"Your brother has a bloody nose," Dad says.

"You get in a fight?" Jackson raises his fists. "Knockout king? Stumps could never—"

"Jeremy could hold his own in a fight, if he had to fight," Dad says.

"Is this bloody nose a masturbation injury?" Jackson asks. "Too much rub-and-tug?"

"Fuck you," I say.

"Language," Dad says. "What's her name, the girl across the hall?"

"Franny," I say, checking the handkerchief for my blood.

Dad's phone buzzes. "Ballentine here," he says. "Wait. Let me get someplace quiet." He walks out. I wonder if that is Mr. Rembrandt calling him. I wonder what he'd be calling about. Adults always seek privacy during phone calls, ditching me for technology.

"You want to hear all the juicy porno details about Franny?" Jackson asks. "You know I'm going to tell you anyway, right?"

"Stop. Don't. Where is your bathroom?"

"We run into each other at a bar and we start slinging them back and she's all grabbing at my jeans, clawing up underneath my shirt. She's digging for the boy. She wants Roscoe. So she pulls me outside to that abandoned building. We find this hole in the fence and slip under and go inside and she pushes me up against the wall. Dirty abandoned building sex." Jackson crawls to the end of the bed and grabs the DVD. He holds it out to me. "I only picked this up to see some titties and trust me, this one has a lot of good titties. You know what a good titty flick does for a sex addict like me." I don't take it from him, so he throws it at me, instead. "Watch it when the old man's not around."

"Jackson, I have to tell you something," I say, looking at the door, still closed. "He's going to be back soon, so please listen, okay? I think Dad's in some kind of trouble."

"What is it?" Jackson looks intrigued. Jackson makes a circle with his thumb and index finger and then pokes his other finger through the hole. This is sex to Jackson.

"This new teacher at school gave this video to Dad and I found it in Dad's office and I watched it and it has this man on it and the man is strapped to a bed. I don't know exactly."

"What the fuck are you talking about?" he asks.

"The video my teacher gave him. It's a cult or something. I don't know exactly."

"Did you ask him about it? Because it's probably some kind of kinky sex thing he's into and doesn't want us to know about it, the old prude."

"It's not sex. It's different. I don't know. I need your help. He's different, Jackson. Something has happened to him. Please." Jackson's eyes close like drapes falling over an open window.

Dad reenters. He looks Jackson up and down like he's only now realizing he's naked. "We were going to go to dinner, but clearly that isn't going to happen," Dad says. "So now we are going to leave."

"I have to pee," I say, dabbing the handkerchief to my nose. The blood has stopped flowing. There are other red stains on it, dried, darker than my own.

"You going to The Hall's first mixer, Stumps?" Jackson asks, breaking linear thought yet again. "High school girls are ripe for the plucking. Back corner. Next to the vending machines. I call that the cooz corner. Remember that."

"It's a mixer, Jackson. It's just dancing," I say.

"Not dancing," Jackson says. "Fucking."

"Stop," I say.

"Boning," Jackson says.

"Enough," Dad says.

"Porking," Jackson says.

"Gross," I say.

"Dicking," Jackson says.

"Stop," Dad says.

"Pounding," Jackson says. "Hammering."

"I don't even think that one makes sense," Dad says.

"I have to pee," I say.

"Both of you—obey me," Dad says.

"Cumming," Jackson says.

"Did you hear what I just said, goddamnit?" Dad asks.

"Spooging," Jackson says.

"I'm going to the bathroom."

"Language," Dad says. "Language, language, language."

46

There's no lock on the door. A grimy black stain eats away at the shower curtain. The white tiled walls have turned brown, outlined in black mold where the caulk holds everything together. The medicine cabinet mirror hangs lopsided from the wall. A condom floats at the bottom of the toilet bowl, and a second clings for dear life to the seat. It dangles long and wide and I use toilet paper to knock it into the water, flushing quickly. Did he fuck one girl twice? Or two different girls once? The toilet water sucks down in a swirl and refills the bowl with more brownish rusty water. I drop the *Zombie Strippers*! DVD and rush my fingers over my belt, unbuckle, unzip, drop my underwear to my ankles, and sit down— my underwear bunched at my ankles.

I hear Jackson and Dad in the other room.

"Can I borrow some green to get me through?" Jackson asks.

"How is the job search coming along?" Dad asks. "Any offers?"

"I'm considering my options," Jackson says. "I'm also considering going back to school."

"Business?" Dad asks.

"Law," Jackson says.

"How much do you need to get you through?" Dad asks.

"Five hundred ought to do." Jackson continues. "What's this I hear about a homemade video of surgery?"

"Are you asking me something without asking me?" Dad bangs on the bathroom door. "Jeremy. Out here. Now."

I say nothing. I do nothing.

"I don't know," Jackson says, laughing. "I'm asking you about this homemade video?"

"Are you coked out of your fucking head?" Dad bangs again. "Jeremy. Jeremy."

I do absolutely nothing. I absolutely say nothing.

Fuck.

"I can't keep up with you. You're just like your mother, completely fucked in the head."

Fuuuuuuuuuuuuuuuuuuuuuuuuuuuuuuuuuuuuuuuuuuuuuuuuuuuuuuu uuuuuuuuuuuuuuuuuuuck.

Fuck. Fuck. Fuck. Fuck. Fuck. Fuck. Fuck. Fuck. Fuck. Fuck. Fuck. Fuck.

FUCK.

"Jeremy," Dad says. "Jeremy? Jeremy? You finished?"

I don't fucking answer at all. Fuck no. No way.

"Why are parents so uptight?" Jackson asks. I hear the sheets drag across the floor. He's out of bed and walking somewhere. "When one parent goes through what you went through with Mom, they can lose themselves. I've lost myself before. I know how it goes. It can take something pretty big to snap you out of it." Jackson snaps his fingers. Leave it to him to be literal. "So Mom banged this other dude and left you for him—so what? You went out and found this creeped out thing and you want to keep it a secret. I get it. It's cool. Don't freak out about it. You're lonely. Call it what it is. Be honest."

"I know less about you than I thought I knew," Dad says.

"Your perverted little secret is safe with me," he says.

Dad doesn't knock this time. Instead, he opens the door and looks down at me sitting on the toilet, pants at my ankles, underwear bunched up at my feet. I pull everything up.

"Were you sitting down?" he asks. He picks up the movie still on the floor.

I stare at a black amoeba-shaped stain on the wall. It's the size of a basketball if a basketball was made out of water and grunge. Maybe someone spilled something on the wall. Coffee. Or tea. Or a pipe burst inside the wall and bled out. But why would someone have coffee or tea in the bathroom? Moreover, why would they have coffee or tea in *this* bathroom? And if a pipe did burst, how come the wall was never repainted? Aren't landlords supposed to repaint an apartment every year?

"Honor thy father," Jackson says from the other room, back in bed.

"Why are you wearing squeezers?" Dad asks.

"Tighty-whitey power," Jackson says.

"Jeremy?" Dad asks. "Answer me."

"Sits like a woman," Jackson says. "Like a proper young lady."

I want to say something nasty, something really nasty, but don't say anything. I dodge past Dad and grab the movie out of his damn hands. Out of the bathroom and standing in Jackson's apartment, I see him on his bed like a Greek Prince, the only thing missing a handful of grapes. He's wearing his sheet like a toga and eating a corndog. Where the fuck did he get a corndog?

"What is wrong with you?" Dad asks.

"Stumps, you're acting very vaginal," Jackson says. "Vag-tastic with great vag-ilities."

Dad and Jackson flank me in this fucking studio apartment, the walls coming down on me. I open the door and run down the stairs.

Zombie Survival Code in full execution.

47

skip several steps at a time and hope with all the hope in the world that I trip and fall and tumble down the stairs and break my fucking neck and die. I hope that Dad and Jackson have to ride my corpse to the hospital where a doctor will tell them just how dead I am.

I crash through the building's door and onto the sidewalk and run away from those fucks. I pass an alley where trash cans roll on their sides, spilling garbage across the wet pavement.

Dad and Jackson would leave the hospital together and drive to a bar where they'd get so drunk they'd drive off a bridge into a body of ice-cold water. The water would pour in through the cracks in the windshield and fill up the car fast, as they scramble to escape, the car slowly sinking. The electric locks would short circuit and the water level would rise up and they'd cling to each other, weeping like little bitches, and they'd feel sorry for themselves. They'd suck down their last breaths and shut down their ears and eventually die.

Asphyxiation.

Later, we'd meet up in Heaven or in Hell or that place in between. I would pretend I didn't recognize them, like I never even knew who they were or that they even existed at all.

No, that's wrong. I would look at them.

I'd look them both dead square in the eyes and say, "Suck my fucking dick."

VI
THE GREATEST STORY EVER TOLD

(Release Date: April 9, 1965)

Directed by George Stevens

Some Additional Scenes Uncredited to David Lean
and Jean Negulesco

Book by Fulton Oursler

Source Writings by Henry Denker

Screenplay by James Lee Barrett and George Stevens

Uncredited writing by Carl Sandburg

48

I call Mom and she picks me up in front of Jimmy's. She doesn't say a word when I get into the van. Mom rolls through a stop sign and looks over at me with a forced smile. Her cell phone buzzes, and she reaches into her purse and digs until she finds it. It's Dad. I can hear his voice, but not what he's saying.

"You can tell him I said he can go fuck himself," I say.

"Language," she whispers to me. Then into the phone, she says, "Now that you've had your turn, I'm going to have mine. I have two things to say to you and then this call is finished. Are you, are you, no, are you listening? Good, well, good. Two things. First, my son called *me*. Don't you dare think for one second that I orchestrated a darn thing. Okay? You hear me, Ballentine? And second is same as the first, Jeremy called me. *Your* son chose me. You hear that? Am I being clear?" She waits, but he doesn't respond. "Then this phone call is finished. He's staying with me tonight and I will drop him off at school tomorrow." She closes her phone. "He's just a bull with butterfly brains." Mom looks at me as she crosses an intersection.

"Zeke know I'm coming?" I ask. "Is he mad?"

"He knows and of course he's not mad," she says. "Zeke doesn't get mad. Everything's going to be okay. Fine, even," she says, brushing my hair with her hand. "You worry too much for a teenager."

"I don't want to worry," I say. "It's just what I do. It's my thing."

"We need to find you another thing," she says. I wonder if she would count my women's magazine collection as a *thing*. "And to alleviate any additional worry from you, I want you to know that

I know what this is," she says. "You finally coming to stay with me under these circumstances, it's not by choice, so much as by necessity. I know this isn't an uninfluenced decision."

"I want it to be," I say.

"I hear you," she says, putting the phone back into her purse. "Roger that." She handles a brown pill bottle like it's an extension of her hand. A few of the baby blue MS Contin tumble into the pit of her palm—MS Contin aka Morphine.

She is gone—again.

And so am I.

49

In Zeke's apartment, I sit on the couch, waiting for him to return with dinner. Fast food, Mom says. She says they weren't expecting company. She says they rarely keep fresh food in the fridge. She says that Zeke'll be back any minute.

If this were the Dawning Age of Man with dinosaurs and shit, Zeke would most certainly be a gatherer. Fruits and berries and bark and roots and crunchy crap like that. He doesn't have the swagger of a hunter. He doesn't have the balls. You have to be able to follow the Code and he clearly doesn't know the Code even a little bit. If this were a Zombie Apocalypse, I'm certain he wouldn't survive. Mom would survive, but only because she isn't going to let a damn thing keep her from popping her pills, zombie or otherwise. Sent out into the harsh, real world to procure food, the best Zeke can do is fast food. It could be argued that Dad isn't any better, what with his favorite Chinese restaurant, Panda Express, on speed dial, but the fundamental difference between the two men comes down to the night Mom left—Zeke honked his horn and waited outside. Zeke didn't come up to the house. Zeke didn't storm in to save the love of his life. Zeke didn't confront Dad in any way. Instead, he stood by his van and waited for Mom to come to him. He can't hunt shit.

"I'm starving. Aren't you starving?" Mom says. She sits next to me on the couch, in one of those awkward, crushing silences that encourage bullshit chitchat. Mom doesn't know how to talk about uncomfortable things, so she executes the Code—Zombie Survival Code Three—and executes it often. She forgets the past, throwing in a dash of ZSC #2 for good measure, and shuts the fuck up. I don't dignify her with a response.

I shift positions on the couch and a sound like a shotgun blast of flatulence shoots out from underneath me. I freeze mid-shift and look at Mom.

"That wasn't me," I say, slapping the wholly plastic-covered couch.

When I was a kid I had a weirdo friend, Rex, who liked to try and kiss me on the lips when he got really excited. His parents had two living rooms in their house—one next to the foyer and one in the basement. The one in the basement was awesome. It had a ridiculously enormous plasma TV mounted on the wall; a red felt billiards table with hand-woven, leather pockets; as well as every gaming system imaginable across from an oversized, L-shaped, monster of a couch. If their basement living room had a reinforced steel door at the top of the stairs and the walls were made out of cinderblock, it would have made the perfect Zombie Apocalypse Survival Room. Rex and his mom spent all of their time in the basement living room. But never in the living room next to the foyer. Rex and his mother called that living room the *family room,* where every inch of every stick of furniture was shrink-wrapped in plastic. It was a very different kind of living room.

"Does Zeke call this room his *family room?*" I ask.

"What is that supposed to mean?" she asks, all snappy. I start to tell her to take a *chill pill* but think that would be in poor taste.

Zeke's apartment is a gatherer's apartment, if the gatherer was Jesus. A bookshelf is filled with religious knickknacks—ceramic Virgin Marys and tiny crucified Jesuses. The few books that he does have are all either large-print annotated bibles, the liturgical sched-ule of gospel readings, or guides to Catholic Saints. Religious CDs: Gregorian chants, a full Sunday mass in Latin by one of the dead Popes, an audio recording of the rosary. On the walls are paintings and sketches and pictures of Caucasian Jesuses. Some have a beard. Some don't. And there are religious DVDs and VHS cassette tapes. *Jesus of Nazareth. Romero. The Greatest Story Ever Told. The Passion of the Christ.*

"I need to know what happened, Jeremy? What happened? What did Ballentine do?"

"I just needed a break," I say.

"Why?" she asks.

"To get away," I say.

"From?" she asks.

"Less of a break. More of a stress fracture."

"I know what a break is, Jeremy—I took a permanent one from your father. I want to know why you feel you needed to take a one."

"I found something," I say.

"I know," she says. "I found it once too. I know what you are going to say."

"How do you know what I'm going to say when I haven't even said it yet?"

"I've known about it for a long time."

"Why aren't you listening to me?"

"I'm listening. I know all about it."

"You *don't* know about it. This is something new. This isn't something old."

"You found out about the tongues," she says. "What he did in Vietnam." She shakes her head, her eyes closed. "I know. Disgusting. Inhuman. Sick." She makes the Sign of the Cross.

"This isn't about the tongues. I know about the tongues. I found a homemade video," I say, but before I have a chance to explain, the front door swings open and that Carrefour-looking motherfucker comes strolling into his Plastic Chapel, carrying a bag of burgers and fries. He's a tall bastard with a nice smile and wears an Orioles baseball hat the right way. He has one of those smiles that makes it very hard to dislike him. Mom stands (farting too!) and throws her arms around his waist. She buries her head into his wide chest as his tree-trunk arms wrap her up. He kisses her and slips her a little bit of tongue. They kiss and hug like they're on the Titanic going down, like a whore on a Saturday night.

"I'm sorry if me being here is any kind of inconvenience," I say.

He breaks away from Mom.

"Jeremy, you've made your mother happier than you'll ever know."

"He needed a break," she says.

"Stress fracture," I say.

"Life can get like that. Life can be that way. You're always welcome here, no matter the reason." He holds me at my shoulders and says, "God bless you." Then, wraps his tree-trunk arms around me. "God bless you, my son."

50

At the kitchen table, Zeke grabs Mom's hand and my hand and nods for us to grab each other's hand to complete the new family circle. He closes his eyes and draws in a slow breath and locks it away like a prison. Then he bows his head and says, "Father Almighty, we are humbled to be here together tonight in your presence, sharing in your abundance and light. We are thankful for this family. We are thankful for this food. Thank you for sending down your only son, Jesus Christ, to deliver us from our sins. In the Heavenly Father's name, we pray."

Mom and I say *amen*, but Zeke says *ah-men*.

"This is nice," Mom says. "My two boys."

"What about Jackson?" I ask.

"It's nice to be a family again," she says.

Mom, nontraditionally, works her way around the cheeseburger with a fork and knife, careful not to eat too fast or too much, only taking small bites. Zeke watches Mom, helping her, keeping her on point. He is her Jesus and she is his sin. She looks happy here, happier than when she was with Dad anyway. Really, he's blinded by her junked-up shit. He's waiting for the day when Mom loves him more than she loves the MS Contin. If he hangs around long enough, if she hangs on long enough, they will both be saved. Or something.

Mom excuses herself from the table to go to the bathroom. She magically produces a tiny cup of tea from thin air and takes it with her. I know exactly what she is doing and Zeke's eyes tell me he knows too. Zeke takes his first bite of the hamburger, before spitting it into his napkin, excusing himself from the table, and rushing down the hallway to the bathroom, knocking loud enough to make it sound important, but not urgent. She opens the door and they whisper, but I can hear them—Zeke negotiating with her, begging her not to disappear. Don't do it for him. Don't do it for her. But do it for her son. A son needs his mother. Like I'm not fucking here. Like I can't fucking hear them. There is another crushing silence, nothing. Maybe it's a moment spent pondering a change, but I doubt it. Maybe it's a flash of another way to live, but that's hardly realistic. They resume—Mom laughs and says she will be right out and hands Zeke the cup of tea. He returns, stopping in the kitchen to dump it out.

"The tea breaks them down faster," I say. "Also," I say, pointing to her plate. "Food absorbs the good stuff. More there is in the stomach, less those puppies work. Empty belly, feel like jelly."

"You know a lot," he says.

"I wish I didn't," I say.

"Right," Zeke says. "Right. Right. Right."

"She'll be fine."

"That a question? Or a fact?" He isn't looking for an answer. He's looking for someone to take away the pain. He's looking for the healthy version of what Mom has become. He's using the Code and doesn't even know it. Avoiding eye contact. Keeping quiet, relatively speaking. Forgetting the past, or wishing like hell he could. Locked-and-loaded with God on his side. Fighting to survive. Well done, Zeke. Well done. Maybe you *are* apocalypse-ready.

"Mom says you keep your Purple Heart under your bed."

"She told you about that?"

"I overheard it."

"I do."

"How did you get it?"

"I did a lot of bad things I can never be forgiven for."

"I had my first Reconciliation today," I say.

"Your school wastes no time," he says.

"Father Vincent, the priest today, he said that Lazarus rising from the dead is the oldest zombie story ever told. He said that Jesus rising from the dead is the second oldest."

"*I am the Resurrection and the Life. He who believes in Me shall live, even if he dies. And everyone who lives and believes in Me shall never die in eternity.* Gospel of John. Jesus said that before he moved the stone from the tomb and raised Lazarus of Bethany."

"By that logic then, Lazarus *was* a zombie."

"Logic is not the word you mean," he says. "The word you mean is *faith*. Faith is the foundation of everything. Without it, there is no religion. There is no Judaism or Catholicism or Buddhism or Hinduism or Islam. All religion is based in varying degrees of faith—believing in something outside the realm of belief. Lazarus is not a zombie," he says.

"Zombies have more in common with Catholics than people care to admit." Father Vincent's words fall freely from my lips.

"Jesus is most certainly not a zombie. Jesus rising from the dead and ascending into Heaven is not some sci-fi, dime store, pulp novel. My belief in Jesus is just that—my belief in Jesus, not sublimation. You're talking about the greatest history in the world, not some schlocky cinema."

"What did you say?" I ask.

"Schlocky—it means cheap."

"No, not that. Before that."

"Schlocky—loathsome, repugnant."

"Wait, stop, listen. Please. That word. What was that word?"

"Schlocky—contemptible, despicable, cut-rate."

"Jesus Christ," I say, standing, frustrated. "Schlocky—I know what it means. The other word you said. Sublimation—why did you use that word? Why won't you listen to me?"

Mom appears from the bathroom. "Jeremy, I've been thinking and I want to take your picture," she says. "I always used to do that and I missed it this year. But we can still do it. We can do it tomorrow."

"Fine," I say. "Sounds fine."

"Did I miss something?" she asks.

"I'm going to bed," Zeke says.

"Jeremy," she says. "What happened?"

"Jesus is a zombie," I say.

"Zeke," she says. "What happened?"

"Apparently, Lazarus is a zombie too," Zeke says.

Mom sits back down at the table. "One time," she says. "I would like to leave a room and reenter that same room and have everything be better than I left it. Just one time."

Zeke leaves dishes in the sink and goes to the bedroom, closing the door behind him. Mom and I sit at the table across from one another. Neither of us says anything. Finally, my hands slip inside of hers, cupped together.

"I love you, Mom," I say.

"I love you too, Jeremy," she says.

"Zeke is not my family," I say.

"Ballentine is not mine," she says.

"There it is," I say.

"There it is," she says.

51

I turn the couch into a bed with a stack of itchy blankets Mom left out for me and put on *The Greatest Story Ever Told*. The smell of mothballs engulfs me.

The credits begin to roll and they just keep on rolling and rolling. Then these images of Jesus and cherubs appear, like the kind of cherubs carved into the dining room chairs, and then finally light and darkness emerge and the sky appears. It takes some time—a LOOOOOONG fucking time—but I finally get to the scene where Jesus raises Lazarus from the dead. Jesus says, "Come forth!" And Lazarus comes forth. And everyone goes apeshit because the bastard is alive—Lazarus. Nothing really happens. There is a lot of sky and rocks and swelling music, but nothing close up where we see the resurrection of a zombie.

Jesus, though—he's, like, the ultimate unbeatable, holy zombie. Tortured to death and nailed to a cross. Buried for three days. Then rises and ascends to Heaven. He's for sure a total zombie. *This is the body and blood of Jesus Christ*. Catholics eat his body and drink his blood. Either Catholics are all cannibals or the whole thing is fucking zombie.

I put away *The Greatest Story Ever Told* and find *Zombie Strippers!* in my bag. I mute the TV, press play, and keep a finger on the off button just in case. The movie begins and zombies appear and I'm alone. The movie is utterly nonsensical. No wonder Jackson had it.

Buckets of B&T.

Buckets.

Blood.

Tits.

52

It's early morning and Mom's already stoned. She gulps down three mugs of green tea, insisting on driving me to school, chewing up pills between promises.

Corrine Barker, the Painkiller Queen of Baltimore.

Before we leave I stop and hang back, waiting to see if she remembers. She leaves and waits for me in the van. When I get in she asks me what took so long. I say nothing and let go of the memory of us and my picture of the first day of school. She is another person now, someone I'll never know.

She coasts through Federal Hill and the Inner Harbor, through nothing but green lights, just below the speed limit, occasionally drifting into the next lane. She takes a sharp turn onto 83 North and opens up the engine onto the highway. She nods off at the Baltimore Sun offices. Her head drops—another dope wave crashing over her. She snaps back to awareness as we pass the Baltimore City Jail. She's mastered the white-knuckled grip of the steering wheel, post dope doze. I no longer fear riding in a car with her when she's behind the wheel and whacked out on junk. I used to fantasize disaster apocalyptic scenarios, death and dismemberment, but she's been high for so much of my life now that it's almost all I've ever known. Almost.

Zombie Survival Code #3: Forget the past.

Mom exits off 83 North, cutting through the same suburban streets as Dad did the other day. She takes a corner a little too fast, knocking down a plastic trash can. I buckle my seatbelt. Mom approaches a double-parked car with flashing hazard lights and speeds up, passes it, swerving back into our lane.

"For better or for worse," she says, "you need to know something."

"Whatever it is," I say, "I probably already know."

"Here it is then," she says. "I failed as a mother."

"Is that an apology?" I ask.

"It's a confession," she says.

If my mother believes she has failed as a mother, what does that say about me?

"You're father used to be a better person too," she says.

We near Byron Hall.

Mom slows down as she white knuckles past a speed-walking woman—the same Dad honked at. The woman runs with the traffic. She looks over at me. We're only separated by a few inches. I'm close to her, damn near close enough to touch her if I roll down the window. Touch her beautiful, full lips. Touch her perfect breasts. I don't touch though. I just stare. She looks away and laughs. She's obviously flattered. I tap the glass for her to look back. Finally, she does, still laughing, and says, "Your nose."

Mom slaps my arm.

"Jesus Christ, Jeremy, your nose is bleeding," Mom says. She digs through her purse, pill bottles rattling. She finds a pack of tissues and tosses them into my lap.

"I never get nosebleeds," I say.

"Things change," she says.

I zone out, staring at the identical houses and tiny lawns, each one sadly deteriorating and different only in color. Each one with the same stoop, same faded red brick, same square lawn. Men exit houses in suits and flannel shirts and ripped jeans and T-shirts, carrying bananas, newspapers, briefcases, and equipment bags. Women stand in doorways, waving goodbye, or exit houses in suits and heels, carrying children and coffee mugs. Mom slows to a stop in the middle of the street as one woman parallel parks. She's dressed in all white—a nurse—probably getting home from the night shift at the hospital. She reminds me of Ana the Nurse in the opening to the remake of *Dawn of the Dead*.

53

Here is the story of Ana the Nurse.

Ana the Nurse pulls into the driveway of her suburban house where she sees Vivian, the cute little girl next door, who has just learned to roller-skate backwards. *Aw, how sweet!*

Ana moves inside and climbs into bed with her husband and they get it on, knock boots, bang it out. *Oh yeah!*

The next morning, they wake to find the little shit Vivian standing in the doorway. She is in their house, in their bedroom, just staring. Vivian's all fucked up. When the husband approaches her, she bites his ass like a rabid animal. Vivian's the first zombie victim the audience is introduced to in the film—*bam!*—right off the bat—a child.

What I'm saying is this: I see the nurse parallel parking, and the first thing I'm looking for is a goddamn little girl on roller skates. Cute zombie neighbor kid!

And so that's the story of Ana the Nurse.

54

We pass the empty football field. The sign out front reads: BYRON HALL CATHOLIC HIGH SCHOOL FOR BOYS and below it a new message has been added—BHC FALL DRAMA – A DOLL'S HOUSE – TICKETS ON SALE NOW. Mom stops the minivan at the top of the circle. No Christian Brothers. No Brother Lee. No douchebag blue jay. Even the faculty parking lot is vacant. Mom looks at the untied tie in my hands.

"When I met your father he was dressed in a three piece wool suit and wore the biggest darned knot you've ever seen." She rests her head against the window. "It was a bar. He was sitting by himself, so I went over to him and said only a moron wears a wool suit in summertime." Mom laughs. "He'd come from play practice. He was in a play. He was an actor. Your father." She looks at me. "That was the play he was in. Same one."

"My friend is the assistant director," I say. I want to tell Mom all about Aimee, but Mom's got frogeyes—glassy, fucked up, gone.

"Torvald. Dressed in that darned wool suit. Said it helped him feel connected to the character. I saw him again almost a year later. Same bar. Except this time he wore this full Marine get-up."

"Uniform," I say.

"Sword and all. I just thought he was in another play." She nods, bobbing over dope waves. "He'd been drafted. It was Vietnam. And you know what happens next."

I tie a full Windsor, pinching my knot at the base, tightening it up. An intoxicating honest urge consumes me and with complete satisfaction, I say, "Mom, you need to know something about me." I say, "It's not that you failed as mother. You're just a fucking junkie."

55

I make it to Algebra on time today. I suffer through Natural Science and World Civilization, and survive Christian Awareness. After, I rush down the hallway, dodging plaid fuck after plaid fuck, all the way to the gymnasium, but when I get there I see a note taped to the door. It says, *Physical Education will be held at the pool today.* Signed—Coach O'Bannon.

Fuck.

Physical Education during the day fucking sucks. Some kids have it as the last class of the day, which is awesome because they can go home right after and don't have to change back into their sport coat and necktie monkey outfit. Others have it as the first class of the day, which totally blows. They come to school looking like the Incredible Hulk, their gym shirt and shorts on under their monkey clothes—bulky bitches. However, having it in the middle of the day is the assiest of all because I not only have to rush from class across campus to the gym, but then change into the required blue shorts and shirt and be on the bleachers in five minutes flat.

Inside the pool, the air is heavy and sharp, chock full of chemicals.

"Ladies," O'Bannon says to a group of us walking in together, including Super Shy Kid and Dirtbag Boy from my English class. "What the Lord took so long?" Coach O'Bannon stands by the diving board, slapping a clipboard in a gray tracksuit with black stripes up the sides. He pauses, waiting for one of us to answer, I think, or just to make us squirm. "If I told you ladies that there was a harem down here giving away free BJs, you would've been lightning fast. Do you know what a harem is?" He points to me. "Little girl, do you know what a harem is?"

"A group of whores, sir," I say.

"Yes," he says. "A group of whores. Correct. I bet if I told you that Susie Rottencrotch was down here from that diseased, sister school Prudence High, you would've damn near broken the speed barrier to be down here."

"Do we have to swim?" Super Shy Kid asks, the fucking moron.

"What did you say, Artsy Fartsy?" Coach O'Bannon's words echo. "Artsy Fartsy, do you have a question?" Super Shy Kid nods yes and Coach says, "Jesus, Mary, and Joseph." He makes the Sign of the Cross.

"I don't have a bathing suit," Super Shy Kid says.

"News flash—you ballshwanks are getting wet like a pussy in heat. No one gets out. Unless you are on your period. Are any of you on your period?"

No one answers.

"Bathing suits are in the back." He points to the locker rooms with the clipboard. "And don't forget to shower before you come out. I don't want any of that gel you ladies use in your perms getting in my pool water."

None of us move.

He stops pacing. He grits his teeth. He winds back, aims, and follows through—his clipboard slicing the air like a throwing star, clearing our heads. It hits the back wall and crashes to the deck.

All of us move. Some of us slip.

56

Waiting for us in the locker room are stacks of white towels and sealed plastic bags each with a Byron Hall Speedo—a blue jay on the ass—the bags with the word *SMALL* or *MEDIUM* or *LARGE* printed on the front in big white block letters. Kids throw the small bags around, teasing each other about a small dick size. The jocks steal the large bags right away, missing the point of what *large* actually means.

One jock rolls up his dress socks and stuffs them inside his Speedo, pumping the air in circles, so all can see. A short kid kicks him in the sock, which sends Sock Boy to the floor. Even I laugh at this. Sock Boy gets off the floor, twirls up a towel, and snaps it at Short Kid, who dodges the snap and locks Sock Boy up in a complex hold, before slamming him to the floor. Jocks jump in and separate them. They leap at each other like rabid dogs, calling each other creative names, but are kept apart. What Sock Boy didn't know until now was that Short Kid is the only freshman on the Varsity Wrestling squad. Wrong plaid to towel snap.

Undressing in the locker room is an art form. The idea is to stay covered at all times. I'm surprised to see how quickly even the jocks change out of their plaid costumes and into their large Speedos. Even they are ashamed of their dongs flopping around like uncooked sausage.

I leave my button down shirt and tie on while I take off my pants and put on my Speedo—medium. (I got lucky and grabbed a medium when the smalls were being whipped around.)

A line forms in the communal shower. The jocks drench themselves in the shower first and, lovingly, turn the water to completely
cold for the next person. As they pass the rest of us in line, they
shake the water from their bodies like a dog after a bath. The fucks.

57

Coach O'Bannon gives the color commentary over the aquatics intercom, depicting how we each look in our Speedos.

"Big dick, Randall. I bet your Susie Rottencrotch is a well-satisfied lady. Jeremy Barker, sporting the medium—not quite big, not quite small—the Goldilocks of dicks." When Super Shy Kid and Dirtbag Boy come out, the last two to change, Coach O'Bannon really opens up the vents. "Looks like we got everyone's favorite duo, Fatman and Robin. You ladies help each other get dressed?"

Dirtbag Boy clearly needed a large, but must have only been left with a small, his gut hanging over the front of his Speedo, the elastic waist cutting into his skin.

"St. John Baptist de La Salle," Coach says.

Everyone says, "Pray for us."

"Live Jesus in our hearts," Coach says.

Everyone says, "Forever."

"You two ballshwanks," he says to Dirtbag Boy and Super Shy Kid. "You're going to demonstrate the proper techniques for diving."

The two kids climb the diving board while the class laughs, and I laugh too, but as I watch them climb to the high dive, I pray hard for a Zombie Apocalypse to strike.

If zombies came crashing through the aquatics door, blathering blood from the mouth, I would jump into the water and stay in the middle, treading water, because zombies can't swim. Their eyesight is already blurry from being dead, so the chlorine would only make it worse. The best part of a Zombie Apocalypse, if it happened right now? Coach O'Bannon would be the first to go. They'd fucking feast on his belly, tear out his white hair, bathe in his blood, and beat the ground with his bones. I think that's, like, Jesse Eisenberg's first rule in *Zombieland*—cardio. That all the fatties died first in the early days of the Zombie Apocalypse because they couldn't outrun the undead.

Coach O'Bannon blows a whistle. "Get to the end," he says, nodding at Super Shy kid.

Super Shy Kid steps to the edge of the board.

"Be a pencil. Just like your dick," Coach says.

The class laughs again.

"Stiff back. Arms above your head. Bend the knees. Bounce and launch. Feet at the edge, goddamnit." When Coach blows the whistle again, Super Shy Kid finally goes for it, not so much a dive as a standing long jump. His splash is big and ugly. His arms and legs flail and fight to keep him afloat.

"Don't move. Stay out there," Coach says. "Fatman, you're next—same thing. Go."

"Coach, I don't know how to swim," Dirtbag Boy says.

"Don't care. Show me that you're not some artsy fartsy ballshwank. Show me you got a pair of stones. Now dive."

Dirtbag Boy looks to his friend in the water still treading and edges close to the diving board. He bounces up, barely, arms up, before launching himself forward. He executes the largest bellyflop I've ever seen. The class erupts into a collective groan. Dirtbag Boy pops up to the surface, fighting the water. He gulps for air, choking on chlorinated pool water. I look at Coach and my classmates and everyone is laughing. Dirtbag Boy's face turns red. He goes under. Coach isn't doing shit.

I dive from the side of the pool into the water. Perfect dive! My heartbeat thumps. I frogkick my legs under water and open my eyes and am hit with an overwhelming amount of chlorine that burns like holy fuck. I crash up through the surface of the pool and slide my arm around Dirtbag Boy and ferry him over to the side of the pool.

"I got you," I say. "Stop fighting it. I got you."

He chokes on water, coughing and spitting. His arms flail and flap at the surface. He reminds me of the man on the DVD in Dad's office. We reach the side and Dirtbag Boy pushes me away; pulling himself out of the water, dry heaving on the deck.

"I didn't need your help," he says. "Stay the fuck away from me."

"You okay?" Super Shy Kid asks, still in the pool.

Dirtbag Boy spits and says, "Yes." Then to me, "Fuck you."

"Fuck me?" I struggle to catch my own breath. "Fuck you."

Coach O'Bannon is gone. I look for him but don't see him anywhere. I stand and walk away from the fuck when I find Coach. He stands between us and the locker room, a bull kicking dirt behind him.

"Fatman and Robin. You're done. Get changed. Get gone." Coach lets them pass by, but he keeps his sights set on me. "You like to be a hero? Make you feel real good?"

"He was drowning," I say. I wipe wet hair away from my face.

"You really think I am going to let a student drown? You really think I am going to kill a student in my class? Have you lost your fucking mind?"

"He was drowning." I have no fight left. O'Bannon wants my blood.

Coach tells the rest of the class to swim thirty laps, width-wise, across the pool. He says that diving will pick up another day. He approaches me and speaks low as kids crash into the water. "Show me how a hero treads water without using his hands for forty minutes." He grabs my shoulder and pushes me into the deep end of the pool where I raise my arms over my head and tread water. I swallow so much chlorine water that when I get out of the pool at the end of class, I throw up on my walk back to the locker room.

58

In the locker room, there's a war of jocks snapping wet towels. Legs are covered in welts the size of basketballs. Kids stand around watching, dressed in various stages—pants, no shirt; shirt and tie, no pants; tie, no shirt or pants. I open my locker and see my clothes hung neatly inside, my shoes tucked away with my secret combination piece of paper still there. My Windsor hangs in my locker like a bastion of strength. I pull on my pants, button up my shirt, and loop my Windsor over my head, sliding up the knot.

Towels continue to snap. Kids push each other. Someone brandishes a tube of toothpaste from his bag, uncaps it, and tries to shove it up another kid's asshole. It becomes a thing. A group quickly forms, kill or be killed, and tries to pin this kid down so they can squeeze toothpaste up his ass. The Victim breaks free from hands and runs at Toothpaste Boy and wraps his arm around Toothpaste's head and slams him into the lockers, swinging his fists, sometimes hitting body. The hard-packing sound of naked bodies has become a familiar one in only a few short days of this place. Towels turn their chaotic attack into a uniformed one and aim at the two assholes, whipping them with loud, wet cracks.

An aluminum bat leans against the wall in the corner, my Zombie Apocalypse weapon of choice. It's an Easton. I grab the rest of my shit and move to the bench next to the bat and finish getting dressed, turning sideways—one eye on the fuckers fighting and one eye on the bat. One swing, that's all it would take. Just one swing. I will fucking do it. Velocity. Torque. One badass motherfucker with an aluminum bat.

But the morons with toothpaste and towels don't do a damn thing.

Everyone stops snapping and fighting and punching. They get dressed and leave.

59

After Phys Ed, I go to the cafe, which is quiet for deep afternoon, most of the tables empty.

Dirtbag Boy and Super Shy Kid sit across from each other. No one else is there; their table is theirs—empty and alone. They are of the group of kids that don't fit into a group. Their members live underground, afraid to show themselves, embracing ghost qualities. So they sit by themselves, each on a cell phone, neither speaking to the other. Dirtbag Boy's face is flush, splotching with red patches. Super Shy Kid sees me, but quickly averts his eyes and avoids further eye contact. Maybe he has his own version of the Survival Code. I sit at the head of the table between them. They don't look up from their phones.

"I know you guys probably don't want to talk to me. Think I'm some kind of jerkoff." I give them a moment to disagree and tell me that, in fact, they don't think I'm a jerkoff, but they don't say shit and keep dicking around on their phones. "I'm only here to say that I'm sorry if I embarrassed you," I say. "I didn't mean to make the situation any worse."

They say nothing—zip.

"Fuck you both in the ear then. I don't need this shit. I'm trying really fucking hard to be your friend here and apologize." I rifle through my book. "This is my last attempt because I'm already a fucking target. I don't need to be more of one by hanging out with you two fuck-ups." I slap the *Zombie Strippers!* DVD on the table. "I saw a movie last night that I think you both might like. It's a Zombie Apocalypse movie and it stars Jenna Jameson."

This gets their fucking attention. They look up at each other—
excited little hornballs. Not surprised at all. They are already spanking it in their minds.

"Is this an apology?" Dirtbag Boy asks.

"It's a B&T flick," I say.

"B&T?" Super Shy Kid says.

"Blood and tits," Dirtbag Boy says.

"You guys can borrow it," I say.

"How much?" Dirtbag asks.

"We have cash," Super Shy says.

"Nothing," I say. "Consider it my amends."

The boys smile. The deal is done. Super Shy Kids punches Dirtbag Boy in the arm and Dirtbag Boy returns the punch.

"We got titties," Dirtbag Boy says, doing a doofy noodle dance
in his chair, before spanking the air.

"We got titties," Super Shy Kid says, singing a little song out of
it.

They both raise an imaginary roof and I'm officially embarrassed for them when hands grab hold of my shoulders. I know
who's there by the smell alone—cheap and musky. Cam Dillard and
his Plaid Fuck Monkies. They're all wearing matching tracksuits
and tennis shoes. Must be game day. Lord do they look retarded.

"You fuckwits call each other to coordinate outfits?" I ask.

They yank me out of my chair and keep me in the middle of
their monkey plaid circle.

"I love this kid," Cam says, clapping. "What a pair of lady balls
he has." Then he says, "Someone hold this kid's thigh, please."

A plaid grabs my ankle, straightening out my leg as Cam drops
everything he has behind his punch, laying into my thigh. My muscle tightens and knots up, pain shooting in both directions. The
Mongoloids push me back into my chair hard enough to send me
and the chair crashing to the floor. On a scale of 1 to 10 with 10
being the loudest noise possible, my chair crash is a 7.3. The cafe is
quiet, but only at first. Then it begins. Slow at first. Slow and soft,
but quickly builds into a single angry voice.

DORK.
DOOOOORK.
DOOOOOOOOOOOORK.
FUCKING DOOOOOOOOOOORK.
FUCK YOU FUCKING DOOOOOOOOOORK.
DORK. DORK. DORK. DORK. DORK. DORK. DORK.

Brother Lee stands over me and grabs my elbow and lifts me with one hand, sitting me into my chair. Everyone's still dorking me, dorking their brains out like it's the last dork in the world, and he brandishes his cowbell and drumstick, hammering that sucker faster and harder than any two porn stars have ever had sex on film.

The room returns to silence and I am left alone again. Dirt-bag Boy and Super Shy Kid are gone and have taken the DVD with them. Cam and his monkeys conveniently disappear too—the cheese dicks. A handful of kids sit nearby, minding their own business, acting as though nothing had even ever happened.

Coach O'Bannon walks through the cafe. He doesn't see me, but I see him. I want nothing more than to tackle his old man ass and rip his fucking face off with my bare hands. Zink follows close behind O'Bannon, all track suited up too.

Zink salutes me as he passes. He yells across the cafe, "Mixer tonight. You better be there, Barks." Then, before he leaves the cafe he yells the final word on the matter, "DOOOORK."

60

Of course, my cell phone dies. Totally and completely sucked dry of any juice. The way things have been going lately, this doesn't surprise me even a little bit. I don't know how many times I've heard Mom or Dad or Jackson use a drained cell phone battery as an excuse. I wonder how many of their dead battery excuses were the real deal and I simply wrote them off as bullshit.

I dig out loose change from my book bag and place a call to Dad from the pay phone by the front office. Dad doesn't answer his cell, so I hang up and call our landline.

Sock Boy calls me a faggot and then punches me in the shoulder as he passes behind me in the hallway. I think about how Short Kid kicked Sock Boy in the nuts earlier. His punch was nothing compared to that, I'm sure. I felt the pain from that kick and I only watched it happen.

The answering machine picks up, and I say my name as instructed, when Dad answers.

He says he's sorry.

He says that whatever I found in his office is not what I think it is. He says there's an explanation. He says that everything's going to be okay. He explains that his car has been on the blink lately, which is why he's not been picking me up after school.

He says his phone battery is fried and doesn't hold a charge anymore, which is why he doesn't call back sometimes.

He asks me to believe him.

He asks me if I believe him.

The only thing I say the entire phone call is my name.

61

In any hallway, everyone talks about the mixer.

Moving between the even and odd hallways, teachers bitch about having to chaperon. They compare past mixer war stories, cop to lies they've told to avoid chaperoning, and question the sexual stability of the students.

In the middle hallway by the chapel, Brothers don't say much of anything about the mixer, except to remind each other that Father Vincent's daily 5:30 P.M. mass will be held an hour earlier to accommodate for the setup. They call it the *Monthly Mixer Mass*.

Outside of English class, the frequency of student conversations hums with excitement. They discuss haircuts and barber-shop straight razor shaves, plan to buy new kicks at the mall, brag about their new celebrity cologne for men called *Humpmaster*, explain the various approaches to *man-scaping* their junk, curse their whore ex-girlfriends that will be in attendance, and run down the list of fuckable Prudence High girls.

Mr. Rembrandt's room is dark; little natural light finding its way through the overcast sky. A final few lockers slam shut in the hallway. A student rushes past, carrying his book bag in the crook of his elbows like a football. Brother Lee chases him, shortly thereafter, a blazing streak of soundless, black tunic. The man is truly God's chosen ninja. Mr. Rembrandt enters the room and closes the door behind him.

"*The Tragical History of Hamlet, the Prince of Denmark*. This is the full title." Mr. Rembrandt sits behind the desk at the front of the room and puts his feet up on the corner, his hands behind his head, leaning back in his chair. "We have it right there in the title—this play is a tragedy. It's the tragical history of this devout yet damaged son, Hamlet." He is quiet again as he looks over us. He drops his feet from the corner of the desk with force, his chair slamming and scraping against the floor. He stalks the aisles of desks. "Do I have your attention?" he asks. "I wonder if my students are sometimes tragic." He places his fucked-up hand on Mykel's shoulder and raises his voice. "*To be, or not to be: that is the question: / Whether 'tis nobler in the mind to suffer / The slings and arrows of outrageous fortune, / Or to take arms against a sea of troubles, / And by opposing end them.*" He claps his hands together again in succession. "The most famous of quotations—to be or not to be." He holds up his hands, like he's about to slow someone down, then makes a revolver (minus his pinkies, of course!) with his left hand and puts it inside his mouth and pulls the imaginary trigger, pantomiming the recoil and head snap, providing what sounds to me to be a near-perfect gunshot sound effect. "Kill me now, please. How dull are those lines. We all know those lines. *To be. Not to be.* To exist. Suicide, yes. Tragic, yes. It's in the title, yes. Hamlet is a sad sack of shit, yes. But is he not more than that? At the end, I see Hamlet celebrating total redemption." Mr. Rembrandt holds out his arms like Christ on the Cross. He says, "Volunteers?" Then after a while, he says it again. "Volunteers? Volunteers?"

Students raise their hands and are selected. They speak quickly when called upon—nervous, anxious, fearful. Students answer questions that haven't been asked, quoting lines from the play as evidence to support their claims. Someone mentions the poisoned sword. Someone speaks about Hamlet's sanity, his madness of self. Someone says that Hamlet suffered from an Oedipal Complex, that the only thing he wanted to do was fuck his mother.

None of this has to do with me. Or all of it does. I'm not sure. I don't raise my hand. I don't speak at all. I don't answer any hypothetical question or quote dick from the play. From the moment he entered the room, we haven't taken our eyes off one another. At his desk. Leaning back in his chair. Stalking the aisles. Quoting Hamlet.

Fuck him. We lock in on each other. He knows that I know something, but he doesn't know what or how much.

He claps his hands together and says, "Mr. Barker. Are you with us? I am sure you have a busy weekend. Chasing skirt. But what do you think? Let's go. Let's go. Let's go. Let's go. Let's go."

I say, "The Hamlet at the end is not the Hamlet he used to be."

I say, "I think you are confusing *redemption* with *utter ruin*."

VII
ZOMBIE STRIPPERS!

(Release Date: April 18, 2008)

Written and Directed by Jay Lee

62

The five hallways of Byron Hall are fucked with kids after class.

Locker doors slamming shut, if heard just right, echo gunshots. Laughter that hacks and rolls through the hallways. Fake fighting—fists punching arms and legs, bodies checking other bodies into metal lockers. Chairs scraping across floors. Desks banging into desks. Erasers wiping boards. Cell phones being turned from silent to ring tones and beeps and buzzing and bird calls. Names yelled out, usually last names because no one ever has a first name at Byron Hall. Hence, the clusterfuck.

At my locker, I see it—my lock on backwards. Balls.

I take off my shoe, retrieve my secret paper, read the combination, kneel and feel pain shoot through my leg from where the plaid fucks deadlegged me in the cafe earlier. My cheek to the cold metal of the locker, I lift the lock as far up as it'll go, trying to read the numbers, and twist the combination as quickly as possible so as not to draw any more attention to myself. I set on the correct succession of numbers and tug, but it doesn't budge.

The overheard stories attack me like an epileptic seizure. Stories grabbing at some semblance of cool.

Someone dropped four tabs of acid and watched twenty-nine hours of dwarf porn.

Another fucked a girl in his family's minivan. He wore a cockring, but never wore a condom.

Another fucked a girl in the bathroom of a fast food restaurant where he works. He made a copy of the security surveillance tapes and is hosting a viewing party tonight before the mixer.

One did lines of coke with his dad off a tackle box while they fished at the Loch Raven Reservoir. They didn't catch a thing.

Another fucked his old babysitter, 10 years older than him.

Another traveled to Canada and bought Oxy. As a side note, his new black market pharmacy is operational.

Brother Bill and Brother Jack pass in their long tunics and squeaky black shoes but never stop to help me with my locker, even though they clearly see me on my knees, trying to hit the right combination to my backwards lock. No words of wisdom today for the new student. Fuck the freshman. No pearls of knowledge for the weak. Only mountains of bullshit.

"Mr. Barker," Brother Bill says, "we are not in the chapel. Get off your knees. Get off the ground."

"Yes, Brother," I say.

Brother Fred says, "We walk here at Byron Hall. We are not animals."

"Yes, Brother," I say.

They have no giant blue jay mascot trailing them today, like some kind of Christian zoo gang. Brother Fred looks for more infractions. The Brothers disappear into the crowd.

Do you know the story of Moses parting the Red Sea? Well, instead of Moses parting the Red Sea and saving Jews and killing Romans, the weak kids part like the sea for the Plaids to walk through. Must be a game day. Cam and his Mongoloid fucks appear in the hallway, still in their tracksuits, standing over me, this backwards lock business most probably their doing. I ready myself for a collision. I spin around, fists high, expecting to be slammed to the floor, reduced to a pile of dust. But the Plaids—they step through the parted hallway, passing me. Nothing happens. They continue down the hallway, never looking back, absorbed into a teenage current of sport coats and Limp Dicks. I lower my fists. It's then that I realize that they aren't out for me. They're out for them.

It happens like the glass of a broken kaleidoscope. Six of them. Shoulder to shoulder. That sickening stench of cologne whips around, rubbed into faces and shirts and hands and arms.

"It smells like a whole lot of faggotry over here," Cam says, pushing Dirtbag Kid and Super Shy Kid into the lockers. "Smells like a faggot girl and his faggot girlfriend are doing faggot things together in very faggot ways." The Plaid Monkeys circle around and move in on them. "God love the gays. I don't know how you do it. The asshole is such a small space."

"Queers," a plaid bitch says.

"Fairies," another says.

"Fudgepackers," another bitch says.

"Cumsuckers," another bitch says.

Cam snatches Super Shy Kid's book bag from his hands, opens it, and pulls out *Zombie Strippers!* "What the fuck is this?" Cam asks. "*Zombie Strippers!* Seriously?"

"Cam," I say, pushing my way through the crowd, trying to divert the attention on to me. "Stop. Leave them alone. It's my movie, not theirs." But no one can hear me.

"Are you two the ones we've heard all those gay bathroom rumors about?" Cam asks, pointing at each of them with the DVD box.

I call out Cam's name again and barrel through the hallway. Some shithead plaid throws a hard punch into my stomach, which knocks the air out of me but doesn't take me down. I keep my balance, hunched over, and focus on regaining my breath. But the shithead plaid follows his punch up with a knee to my face. My hands are already close to my face so I am able to protect myself, but not well enough to keep my balance as I slam into a locker.

Dirtbag Boy runs to my side and kneels and asks if I'm okay, but I can't breathe or talk or move at all.

"Cam," Dirtbag Boy says. "What I'm going to say to you I am only going to say once, so pay very close attention. Apologize."

"Let it be, Frank," Super Shy Kid says. "It's not worth it. Please."

"Not unless Cam complies," Frank says. Dirtbag Boy has a name—Frank.

"I'm sorry," Cam says to Frank. "Complies?"

Frank moves out into the middle of the circle and jumps repeatedly, like he did on the diving board, except now there's grunting and his hands turned to fists. He makes a sound after each jump. *Ha. Ha. Ha. Ha. Ha. Ha. Ha.* No one knows what to make of it, at first, but the Plaids bury their laughter and close in on him fast, but not fast enough.

Frank bends his doughy body into a power crouch, before spin-kicking his leg at a low angle, sweeping the Plaids to the floor with a single leg swipe. Cam watches his friends drop like bowling pins and charges Frank from the side. Cam cocks his right hand and aims it at Frank's face. Frank ducks and weaves away from the punch only to grab Cam's elbow and wrist, bending them up behind his back. He drops his elbow down on Cam's back.

Watching it, I can't help but tip up onto my toes to alleviate the pain Cam must be experiencing. Frank doesn't stop, though, and jabs Cam on the ribs with his free hand, now a fist. This cuts Cam down to his knees without words, gasping for air, his voice gone. Frank tightens his grip on Cam's elbow and wrist, separating them from one another. Father Vincent runs into the brawl, waving his arms around like a spazball.

"Frank, let him go." Father Vincent puts his hands on the other Plaids keeping them from going in to help. "Whatever happened, it's over. It's done. Let him go, please. Let him go."

Frank finally releases Cam, who drags his ass off the floor, stumbling into the lockers. Father Vincent checks Cam's arm before instructing one of the Plaids to take Cam to the school nurse, immediately. Cam tries to walk, but his legs are weak and buckle. Another Plaid helps to carry him off and they disappear. Father

Vincent directs the hallway traffic to resume its normal speed. He
approaches Frank and puts his arm over his shoulder.

"You know that this can't go unpunished," Father Vincent says.

"I know," Frank says.

"What happened? What did they do?"

"They didn't apologize to Jeremy," he says.

Father Vincent and Frank help me to my feet. It hurts to breath
and it feels like my lungs have been punctured with spears, but I'm
otherwise okay.

"Thanks," I say to Frank. "For everything."

"This is Anthony," Franks says, standing next to Super Shy Kid.
Anthony hands me the DVD.

"I think it's best if I give this back to you," Anthony says.

"Right," I say. "No shit." There's no hiding it from anyone
anymore.

"Father Vincent, I want to say two things to you before you go.
First, I watched *The Greatest Story Ever Told*."

He smiles and shakes my hand, like I have won some political
race.

"Jeremy, that's just terrific. What did you think of it?" he asks.

"I wouldn't go setting up any double features between it and
the latest George Romero zombie flick," I say. "But that being said,
remember that thing you said to me about the possibility?"

"I do," he says.

"I believe in the possibility now."

Father Vincent makes the Sign of the Cross and says, "God Bless
you, son." Then he says, "What's the second thing?"

I hold the DVD Anthony returned to me out to Father Vincent
and say, "The second thing—I was wondering if you wanted to
borrow *Zombie Strippers!?*"

"I think I'll pass," he says and escorts Frank toward the front
office.

63

In the bathroom by the gym, I sit in my stall, still and silent, not doing anything because I'm not alone. Someone else kicks around by the urinals. No kids are usually down here at this time of day. This is an adult. It's Mr. Vo. He hums a song while he pees, moaning as he does it, because old people have a harder time peeing, something Dad talks about on occasion. The humming gets louder, like he's getting to the climax of a song, before he bursts out with the words, "*Tryin' to stay focused on the righteous path.*" The urinal flushes with a beautiful swoosh. He doesn't wash his hands and is gone.

I sit in my stall, feet down now, not pissing like a girl the way Dad thinks I like to pee, not reading the lady magazine I stole called *Motherhood*. Instead, I hold it at the corner like a piece of trash. The pregnant woman on the cover holds her fat stomach, smiling. She stands on a beach. Tiny drops of blood drip onto the pregnant woman's face on my magazine. I touch my nose and see that it is bleeding again. I rip off some toilet paper to clamp off the leak. I open to the table of contents of the magazine and find an article on the argument: *to breastfeed or not to breastfeed.* I'm more interested in what scientific reasons they have discovered defending each side of the argument but try and trick myself into thinking that I'm really hoping to see some sideboob. The article is top to bottom words with a small picture of the author, Dr. Sandra Snow. She's the sexiest doctor I've ever seen. The rest of the magazine is filled with advertisements for breast pumps and depression pills.

Guilt, it seems, starts at birth.

As the blood quells in my nose, I roll the magazine up into a cylinder and slide it back into my bag. New graffiti covers the stall around me, but I could care less about it. Bores me now. Only so many times I can see my own name inserted into a colorful phrase before I get completely bored. I drop my feet to the floor and flush the toilet. I am not sure why I flush, but it feels like the next logical step. The water swirls around in a tight spiral, sucking down and away into a mysterious invisible pipe in the wall.

As the crescendo of the flush disappears, the bathroom door opens again. Someone else enters. They push open the stall next to mine, tip the seat down, and set in. Fuck. I slide back onto my toilet, pulling my feet back up. Maybe they didn't hear the flush. Maybe they came in after I flushed and have no idea I'm in here. I hold my breath and close my eyes and conjure the image of Aimee White, a moon hanging over the Inner Harbor behind her. God, she's beautiful in my memory. And as my image of her turns more dirty and sexual in nature with hands grabbing parts and parts sliding into holes, there's a knock on my stall.

I don't respond.

Another knock—soft knuckles on the plastic walls. Then a hand appears under the stall wall, holding a half-eaten chocolate-chocolate, chocolate-dipped donut with white sprinkles. "Want a bite?" he asks. He holds the donut steady, but when I don't respond, he dances the donut from side-to-side.

"Zink," I say.

"It's really fucking good. The best."

"Man, you scared the shit out of me."

"So no donut?" He stops making it dance and instead gives it one last shake, like a rattle in a baby's face. "Your loss," he says, pulling his hand away. He takes another bite and talks through his chews. "These little delicious treats are like sex." His chewing couldn't be more audible if he tried. "Let me get this straight," he says, pausing, waiting, I'm sure, as he forces down a painful swallow. "You want to be alone. You don't want a chocolate-chocolate, chocolate-dipped donut with white sprinkles. What's wrong with you?"

"I'm keeping a low profile," I say. "I'm regular."

"Buddy," he says. "You're pretty fucking far from regular."

"I don't know what you want me to say," I say. "I don't want your fucking donut."

"Hey, I know how it can be."

I want to paint over these stalls and wipe away the graffiti.

"I'm in hiding," I say.

"From?"

"Ultimate Fighter Frank. Plaid Fuck Cam. Mr. Rembrandt. Coach O'Bannon. Take your pick."

"Fuck," he says. "You piss all those people off?"

"Not exactly. Not quite. It's easier this way though."

"You're locked inside your head," he says.

"Locked?" I ask.

"I want you to ask me a question," he says. "You'll never get through the day if you can't get outside your head. Ask me anything. Anything you've ever wanted to know. That sexy, sugary donut has me high as a kite, so fire away. Go ahead and ask me a question about anything, and I will answer it."

Still each in our own stalls, invisible to one another, only our voices present, I say, "Why do you play soccer with those Plaid assholes?"

"Easy. I love playing the game and no one is going to keep me from that, not even dickless wonders like Cam and his Lackeys. My Dad kicked a soccer ball to me before I could walk. It's what I'm good at. It's my thing."

"Who is Paul?" I don't waste time and fire away the first thing that pops into my head.

"Jeremy," Zink says. "My friend. Good work."

"You know that I know?" I ask.

Zink laughs in such a way that makes me feel like I'm a stand-up comedian. Sometimes I say things unintentionally funny and people laugh and it feels like they are laughing at me, poking fun at me, instead of laughing with me. This used to happen a lot between Mom and Dad, usually Dad laughing at something Mom had said.

But it's different with Zink. His laugh is the sound of a friend.

"Jeremy," he says, "I've always known you've known. I saw you in the reflection of the mirror."

"You weren't nervous that I'd tell?"

"Untrustworthy people are a dime a dozen and do untrustworthy things. It's expected. They can't be controlled. But trusted people are surprising. Thank you for surprising me."

I hear him open his stall, a small squeak. I open mine too. We meet by the sinks again. He's dressed in his gameday tracksuit.

"You look very athletic," I say.

"I better," he says.

"Does anyone else . . . "

"No," he says.

"Just me?"

"And Paul."

"I want to meet Paul. You know that I'm not weird about it, right?"

"Jeremy, you're totally weird about it, but I trust you. And it's not a big deal."

"Is there anything I can do?" I ask.

"Of course not," he says. "It's a part of me, but not all of me."

"Why are you telling me now?" I ask.

"Why not," he says.

64

I call Dad again from the pay phone after last period to see where he's parked, but his phone goes right to voicemail. I call Mom. I call Jackson. I get the same response from everyone, which is no response at all.

I exit the even side of the building and walk toward the bus stop. A harem of Prudence High girls approach, dressed in their short plaid skirts and white blouses.

There she is again—Aimee White.

"J-Dog," she says. "Long time. You and Mykel back to scamming on girls?"

"Not at all," I say. "I was on my way home."

"How's the nose?"

"It's well."

"Well," Aimee says. She stops. Her girlfriends keep on for the theater. "Jeremy Barker."

"I can't believe you remembered my name."

"It's hard to forget the name of the boy who bled all over you the first day of play practice, and got you in trouble with the director. Jeremy Barker," she says, tapping her temple. "It's cemented."

"You coming to the mixer tonight?" I ask.

"Maybe," she says.

"What's a maybe?"

"A maybe is a maybe," she says.

"Aimee White," I say. "I have a few things I'd like to say to you." It still hurts to breath, but I take a breath to ready myself. "You have an awesome name. I love it. Colors for last names are just so badass."

I exhale. The words are coming easier than I thought they would. "I like you, Aimee White. And I know that's a weird thing to say to someone you don't really know, but I like you. I like you even though you really don't seem to like me at all."

"You're right, I don't like you. I'm not a fan of chronic bleeders."

"I'm coming to the mixer tonight and I would love to see you there."

"If I decide to come, I'll be sure to bring gauze and surgical tape," she says.

"And I'm sorry I bled on you."

She backs away from me, moving toward the lecture hall. She doesn't say anything and eventually turns around and vanishes.

I run across the front of the school to the bus stop just as the 55 screeches to a halt. The driver, an old man with a long white beard, opens the door and waves for me to get in. I climb in and he closes the doors and accelerates down the road, past Byron Hall. I sit right up front. "How you doing today?"

"Sixty/forty," he says. "Know how people say they are fifty/fifty, that they could go either way? You know, deciding between Mexican and Chinese or between seeing a horror film or romantic comedy. *Oh, I'm split. Can't decide. Fifty/fifty.* Well, not me. I don't see things that way. I'm sixty/forty."

"Okay, but sixty/forty about what?"

"Whatever. There's always something to be sixty/forty over."

"I'm Jeremy," I say.

"Why the hell do I care about your name?" he asks.

"Because I'm the guy who's going to steal your sixty/forty philosophy."

65

Another night at home, alone, and Dad is gone. No car out front. No half-eaten Chinese food in the living room. No voicemails on my charged cell phone. No instructions on how to cook a pre-made dinner. No curfew to keep me close to home. No parents. No siblings. No nosey neighbors keeping tabs on my activities and reporting them back to Dad. My only neighbor is Tricia and I can't wait to check in on her from my room.

With Dad disappearing, I worry about Dog being regularly fed, walked, and kept in clean water. I don't see her downstairs in any of her usual haunts, but when I search the upstairs I find her asleep in Dad's bed, curled up on the side where Mom used to sleep.

My first mixer is tonight and I have no one here to help. And it's more than just getting dressed and smelling good. What do I do when I get there? Do I just grind up on the ladies? Is it grinding? Is that what they call it? Or is it freaking?

In my room, zombies stare down at me. I look across the way to Tricia's bedroom window and her blinds are open too. I can still see her naked. All I have to do is close my eyes and there she is in all of her pink skin glory. Tonight, though, Tricia is there and stares back at me, dressed in a robe, fresh from the shower, then slides the blinds closed completely.

I dress for the mixer with Zink's tips in mind and am back out on the Baltimore streets, waiting for a Northbound 55.

There's a little boy on the bus sitting next to his Mom and he points at me and says, "Did you get in a fight? Your nose is bleeding."

"No," I say, taking out a tissue and wiping away the blood. "I'm sixty/forty."

66

The Byron Hall Catholic School for Boys calls these mixers.

DJ Doug spins a techno version of "Brown Eyed Girl" and all the girls come running to the dance floor. DJ Doug says, "I want to see some booties shake out there!" DJ Doug wears a jester's hat with bells and a black collared shirt unbuttoned halfway down his hairy chest, tucked into black pants. DJ Doug says embarrassing things a fifty-year-old man should never say. He says, "Everybody get low." He says, "Show how you'd put 'em on the glass." My favorite is when he says, "Is anybody out there gettin' lucky tonight?"

People dance to the bass-heavy music, grinding and shaking against each other under the shifting, flashing, pounding lights. A group of Plaids dance together in front of the stage, each with their own girl. They move around like retarded robots, just like Zink said they would. It's also worth noting that Plaids wear plaid outside of school, too.

Mykel snaps his camera, the flash popping like a spotlight. He dances to the music with his camera strap looped around his neck. He stops dancing to shoot the crowds. He shoots a girl holding the wall with one hand and adjusting her shoe with the other. He shoots DJ Doug, bent at the waist, tying the laces of his bright white tennis shoes. He shoots two girls dancing back to back in the center of the dance floor, twirling their arms over their heads. He shoots a guy picking a wedgie from his ass.

The room throbs like a stubbed toe.

Brother Bill and Brother Fred stand in the corner of the cafe by the fire exit, watching their Christian sons dry-hump random girls. I haven't seen Brother Lee tonight and wonder if he is like the secret weapon around here, hiding like the little ninja that he is. In their black tunics, the Brothers appear invisible, except when they step between dancers. Brother Bill and Brother Fred tag-team the grinders, working together to keep the peace and the pelvic distance between groins.

The music is loud as fuck and I can hardly think. This is all so stupid, the ditzy, half-naked, doe-eyed girls fake stripper-dancing with each other. All of it.

Zink appears in a red polo shirt and khaki pants.

"You said not to wear khakis," I say. "Only on holidays and at church, you said."

"Yeah, well, it's this whole thing." He looks at what I'm wearing. "You look like a gentleman caller."

"Fuck you," I say. "Nobody even knows what that means."

"Barks, you want women thinking of you as a big dick daddy from Cincinnati."

"I'm not really good at dancing."

"You got to turn your game on, Barks."

"What does that even mean?"

A girl with bright blue hair nudges past us. She wears purple fishnet stockings under a black skirt and a striped gray shirt with a skull on the front, tugged down over the edges of her shoulders. She looks at Zink.

"Who was that?" I ask.

"The one," he says, patting my back, following behind the punk girl. "Game on."

An all too familiar song starts and that wicked-sick bass line drops in and it's like crack to the dancing fool kids. Everyone—no matter who they are and what they're wearing—collapses onto the dance floor, doing the Michael Jackson zombie stroll until the lyrics start and a giant sing-along ensues. Michael Jackson's "Thriller." My body can't deny "Thriller" and I collapse onto the dance floor and do the damn zombie shuffle, shoulder drop and all, with everyone else. The song ends and for the fleeting moment everything was better than sixty/forty.

When I was a kid, Dad showed me the film version of the music video and it scared the living shit out of me. It was one of the earliest zombie movies I had seen. I spent that night sleeping on the floor with Dog because I believed that Dog would protect me while I slept and would scare any dancing zombies away. Little did I know that Dog doesn't get up for shit during the night. When I woke, I was back in my bed and the trees from outside cast shadows across the ceiling that looked like demon claws. Dad had found me on Dog's pillow and carried me back to bed. The next day I watched the video again and watched it again and then I wanted the whole album and the "Thriller" poster. I asked Mom if I could put the poster on the ceiling of my room and after much whining, she agreed. I positioned it right where the shadows crept into my room and this is how my posters on the ceiling began.

Jackson's cooz corner isn't empty. There's a guy sitting in a chair pressed against the wall with a girl sitting on his lap, her back to him as she grinds down on him. The girl has long blonde hair and wears a tiny white babydoll T-shirt and pink short-shorts. And of course she's grinding down on none other than Cam Dillard's lap. And he's dressed like a plaid-inspired optical illusion. Fuck me. The sight of them dance-humping in the chair takes me out of myself like a ghost, and the next thing I know I am right at their side.

"I hear your Mom takes it up the ass like a champion," I say, surprising myself that I even said anything at all. I give him two thumbs up.

"Who's a champion?" he asks.

"Your mother," I say. More thumbs.

The music fades and the girl climbs off.

"Say it again," Cam says, leaning closer. "Say it."

"I said"—my heart slams my ribcage—"your mother takes it up the ass like a motherfucking champion." I grab my dick. "She calls me her big dick daddy from Cincinnati."

Cam swings at me, but misses. He jumps to his feet, his hands poised to grab me and beat the living fuck out of me, except he freezes when he sees me—a chair hoisted over my head, daring him to come closer.

"Call me faggot again," I say. "Go on. Say it."

"Do yourself a favor," he says, "and start running." Cam's hands are fists set at his sides.

"Suck my dick," I say and chuck the chair to the floor. It crashes and slides along the floor until it hits the wall and flips over loud enough for the entire room to go completely quiet. A princess spotlight cuts over from the stage to Cam by the vending machines. He picks up the chair and sets it upright. He raises his hand as if to accept blame.

Father Vincent grabs me by the arms as I try and pass him.

"Jeremy, slow down. What's going on? Are you okay?"

"I have to go, Father," I say. I look back. Brother Lee rushes toward Cam, trying to cut off the inevitable, waving at the room, shouting, "No dork. No dork!"

"Jeremy, talk to me," Father Vincent says. "I can help you."

"I wish I could. I do. Please, Father," I say. "If you want to help me, please let me go."

Cam steps back into the crowd to slip away, but Brother Lee grabs his shirt and pulls him back, then waves his arms at DJ Doug to start the next song. But it's too late. It starts as several, single voices—loud ones. Then mob mentality takes hold and like a wave rolling towards shore, the distinct voices become pockets, which grow together into a monstrous *dork* thundering down on top of Cam with every variation imaginable.

Finally, the next song drops and the dorking stops and everyone resumes their clothed-fornication, but the damage has already been done.

Suck it, fucko!

67

My plan is to hide away in my stall of solitude, but a group of girls pour out from my bathroom, which has been temporarily converted into a ladies room. The computer printed sign on the door says LADIES ONLY. The bathroom where Zink and Paul did what they did the other day. I'm frozen, stuck, glued, nailed, fucked with nowhere to hide, when a posse of girls crash into me, knocking my ass down. The posse tramples over me, steps around me, continuing down the hallway, out of my bathroom and out of my life. Some of the posse bitches wear miniskirts, which allows me to catch a few fast moving glimpses of skimpy underwear.

"Is this a fucking roller derby," I say. "Watch where you walk. Jesus."

"Does it feel good to have been shitkicked by a harem of teenage girls?" a girl says, standing behind me. Her hair is a dark and heavy red, her lips too, her skin still tan from summer. Her shirt has sparkling letters across the front that says: *Do you have an older brother?* She wears blue jeans that flare out at the bottom. She smells like purple flowers. "You might just be the luckiest guy at this whole damn mixer," she says.

"Aimee White," I say. My smile's so wide it hurt.

"'Tis true and don't forget, that's *Aimee* spelled the weird way," she says. Aimee holds her hands down and I grab them. She pulls me up and we come together and brush against each other. "The infamous Jeremy Barker. J-Dog."

I definitely brushed against her boob—big time. I got boob.

"My Dad says that when a girl body-checks you to the floor

and causes chronic nosebleeds, that she's got a thing for you," I say.

"Jeremy," she says. "You're not going to believe me."

"You smell terrific," I say.

"Your nose is bleeding," she says. She taps her nostril. "Again."

I touch mine and see it—ripe red blood rushing out. Aimee digs through her silver-studded, black purse and hands me a tissue. I tilt my head back.

"This is embarrassing," I say. "I feel like a fucking loser."

"That's a little harsh, don't you think?" she asks. "You do get an extraordinary amount of nosebleeds though, I'll give you that. Do all the ladies have the pleasure of assisting you with your bleeds? Or just me?"

"Who has ever heard of getting nosebleeds only around girls?" I dab and look at the bloody tissue. "Only around *hot* girls?"

"Cute," she says.

"I'm trying. It's tough to look cute when you're bleeding."

"Did you know that nosebleeds are broken blood vessels?" she asks.

"All I know is that I get them whenever you're around or when-ever I think about you in any way." Neither of us says a thing. "I think about you a lot."

"They're only blood vessels, dear," she says. "I'm not magic."

"What causes them to break?" I ask.

"Why does anything break?" she asks. "They're too weak and they burst."

"Will you walk me outside?" she asks.

Ever the gentleman, I offer her my elbow, and she accepts, ever the lady, and we leave together, embracing the warm night, while I seal off the blood leak—again.

68

Disappearing is in the air tonight.

Outside, it looks like a high school used car lot. Cars parked everywhere, parents waiting for their kids, searching for their kids, leaning against trunks, circling the school, hanging out of driver's side windows. Names being called. It feels like a disaster has happened and this is the depot where the survivors are kept for identification. A car screeches to a stop and a guy gets out and thanks his friend for getting him back to school before his parents came to pick him up. He thanks the friend for taking him; that it was the sickest thing he has ever seen, that he can't believe that they got in. The car drives away and the guy disappears around the corner of the school.

"What's Prudence like?" I ask. "Because we worry about you girls over there. Those plaid skirts and white blouses. We worry."

"We worry that you Byron Hall boys think you actually have a shot with Prudence girls like us," she says.

"It feels good to be around you."

"My mom's car is over there." Smoke pumps from a tailpipe. "I asked her to wait. No parents allowed," she says, shaking her finger in a funny way.

I can't think of anything to say that doesn't make me sound like a fuckwad. This is the moment that counts, the moment where the man steps up and makes the grand gesture, where he says that thing that makes the girl swoon or whatever, but I don't have anything swoonable. She was the whole reason I came out tonight and I didn't plan a damn thing.

"Well, this is sufficiently awkward," she says. "I'm going to leave now. Goodbye, Jeremy. It was wonderful to meet a nice Byron Hall boy. See you around campus maybe. And maybe you should start carrying around napkins." She taps her nose.

"Wait," I say, thumbing the tissue she gave me. "I'm not finished yet." I'm filled with a foggy sense of myself. I can hear heartbeats all around me, some of them are mine. "There's more. I have more."

"More of what exactly?" Aimee stands in the street, waiting, but I say nothing. She finally walks back to me. "Here's some friendly advice, Jeremy. When a girl stops for you," she says, "you better have something to say and it better be good."

"I think you're beautiful."

"That's a good start. Always tell us how pretty we are."

"I love your hair, the smell of your hair."

"A little weird, but that will work for some girls. What else do you got?"

"I want to call you. Can I call you?" I am an enormous retard on roller skates.

"That wasn't half bad," she says.

"I can call you?"

"You can call me," she says, "but you have to do one more thing for me."

"Hit me with it," I say. "Anything."

"Get down on one knee and ask me again." She walks toward me. "Go on now. Get down on one knee and ask me again." Her arms hang by her sides, her hip cocked.

"You really want me to do this?"

"Really," she says.

I kneel, proposal-like and take Aimee's hand in my own hand and say, "Aimee, can I call you sometime?"

"Cell phone," she demands.

I fumble for it in my pocket and hand it over. Aimee punches her number into my address book. She walks backwards. "You did real well." She continues to walk away. "Very, very well."

"Why did I have to get on one knee?"

"Because a girl has so few opportunities to be taller than a boy," she says. "Call me." She skips to her car.

This is what a happy Jeremy looks like.

69

Aimee exits the parking lot with her mom and I am left behind.
I call Dad to come pick me up, but all I hear is screaming. It's not Dad screaming, but someone behind Dad screaming—a deep, and gross, and pleading scream.

I walk away from the building and plug my open ear.

I call him Dad.

I say his name.

He doesn't respond to either.

There is a scuffle that sounds like someone is fighting the phone. Then, the line goes dead. I call Dad back, but his voicemail picks up.

Ballentine is gone again, like vapor.

70

Zink emerges from the back of the school and offers to take me home. He drives a blue Oldsmobile, which I'm not entirely sure they even still make. It's a giant blue box with an enormous windshield. The floor is clean in the front, but the backseat is covered in blankets and empty soda bottles and plastic bags from grocery stores.

"Your car smells funny," I say. "Like oranges and maple syrup."

"That's the smell of sex," Zink says.

"Sex?"

"Hot sex."

"You had sex with The One?"

"No. Not with her. With someone else."

"Paul," I say. "I didn't know you had a car," I say.

"What was with the kneeling back there? You two set a date already?"

"I did what I had to do to get her number," I say. "Game on."

Zink looks at me like I just told him I killed a man. "Barks, you're a crazy motherfucker. You got digits. Game fucking on," he says, pulling out of the school circle and into traffic. "What did you think of your first mixer?"

"I survived," I said. "I went after Cam."

"Tell me you didn't do something stupid."

"I told him that his mother took it up the ass like a champion and then I threw a chair at him so he would get dorked."

"Why would you slap the hornets' nest like that?" he asks.

"I'm tired of being the one getting slapped. Besides, Frank took those fuckers down earlier. Why can't I?"

"Jeremy," Zink says. "Listen to me. Frank's hands are registered with the State of Maryland as deadly weapons. That's why. He can kill a man with his bare hands . . . literally. That's why. He knows how to do that kind of shit."

"I'm not worried anymore," I say. "Cam's a pussy."

"Maybe so, but he's a pussy with a posse and you are a general without an army. I'm not saying to run from the prick, but telling him that his mom . . ."

". . . takes it up the ass like a champion . . ."

"Jesus." Zink shakes his head and laughs. "What the fuck made you say that?"

"He reminded me of my brother and I really hate my brother." I roll down the window and hang my arm outside, feel the air pass over and through my fingers, the warm air cold at high speeds.

"You've got balls, Barks. *Huevoes muy grande*. In one night, you got digits, managed to dork the king of the jocks and embarrass his ass for the second time in one day." Zink guides the car through empty streets, driving faster than any other car. "*Huevos grandisimo, niño*."

"Her name is Aimee White," I say.

"When you calling her?"

"Tomorrow?"

"Is that a question or a fact?" Zink asks.

"Too soon?"

"Tomorrow is for emo puppy lovers. Tomorrow is for people who want to wear matching cable-knit sweaters and whose favorite movie is *Titanic*. Not tomorrow, but in three days. Standard protocol. Three days says you're interested, but not serious about getting serious. It says that you want to have a good time, but don't want to get married."

"What if I do want to get serious?"

"For Christ's sake, don't ever tell her that," he says. "Monogamy is like a knife wound that'll bleed you dry until there is nothing left, but skin and bones and regret."

"Lovely," I say. "You really should go into business for yourself.

Spread your sage advice around a little bit. I'd hate to hoard it all myself."

I direct Zink through my neighborhood, pointing out the massive potholes left behind from the winter ice storm, where the road at the top of certain hills makes heavier cars bottom out. He makes the final turn onto my street and pulls up in front of my house, behind my father's BMW. Ballentine's prized BMW is parked rightly in front of my very own house. The fucker is home.

"My dad," I say.

"You good?" Zink asks. "You need me to come in with you? I can. I'm good with parents. They love me."

"Zink," I say. "I have a question for you, but I don't know how to phrase it."

"Try."

"Why would you tell me that you knew that I knew about Paul, but then come to the mixer tonight and try and bag some girl?"

"Go on— you can say it."

"If you're gay, then I want you to be gay. I don't want you to hide it from me."

"Remember when I said I wasn't nervous about you telling anyone about me because you were an honest person?" He looks at me but doesn't wait for an answer. "Well, not everyone is an honest person. Actually, very few people are honest people. This is my survival technique, Barks. *It gets better*, you know?"

"Like in those campaigns?" I ask.

"Like in your zombie movies. There are rules that people live by to stay alive."

"Codes," I say.

"Exactly," he says.

VIII
PLANET TERROR

(Release Date: April 6, 2007)
Directed by Robert Rodriguez
Written by Robert Rodriguez

71

Water rushes through pipes. A creak escapes the wood in the floor. The living room and office and bedrooms and kitchen and dining room are empty except for the fucking cherubs. Dad is nowhere to be found and I wonder briefly if the cherubs came to life and devoured his brain. Maybe he took the light rail downtown. Maybe he planned on drinking and didn't want the responsibility of driving home.

In my bedroom, I kick off my shoes and start to change when I hear something, a groan—guttural and low. I hear it again—inside the house somewhere far below. I pull on my jeans and shirt and descend the stairs, stepping slowly, one foot at a time, measured and accurate. The groan echoes clear like someone forcing something poisonous out of their body. I can't locate the noise but hear it again, louder, getting louder, every time growing. Louder, louder, coming from below. From the basement.

I open the door to the basement and flip the light switch, but the light doesn't turn on. I hear the groan again. I step down the soft carpet of the stairs to the cold cement basement floor. The groan grows again. The basement is empty except for Dad's tools, a rusted bike leaning against the wall. Dog is nowhere to be found. Deeper into the basement, the darkness intensifies. Classical music. Orchestral music. A symphony plays. Heavy drums. Big brass. The groan goes again, echoing louder, coming from the room where Dad keeps all of his hammers and wrenches and clamps and saws. I pull the cord and a crude light cuts into my eyes. The bulb swings in a circle, hung from a wooden beam in the ceiling.

Finally, I see him.

Dad sits on a metal stool, still, knees bent, feet on the floor. His hands press palm down on his workbench, a handsaw and hatchet between them. The pruning shears Mom uses to cut dead limbs from trees in the spring lays at his feet. Dad does not speak. Cymbals crash and some deep-sounding string instruments hum. His hair curls and twists in every direction, as though he has been running his hands through it. He wears a white collared shirt, unbuttoned, and creased black pants. No tie. No Windsor.

"Dad?"

He breathes in controlled repetition, even movements, exhaling and inhaling. His eyes lock on the tools at the table.

"Everything okay?" I ask.

He opens his mouth, his lips peeling apart from dryness like dead skin. Wide. Wider still. The noise. The black groan—that deep, sick sound—rolls up and out of his body. He forces the noise out, pushing it from his gut. His eyes fill with water.

"Dad? DAD?"

The groan rolls again, louder this time. His chest lifts. His head tips down. He flexes his stomach muscles, forcing the noise—that awful gut-busted groan—out, again and again. He looks back to his tools.

"Dad?" I move closer to him See, in the swinging shadows, blood on the collar and cuff of his shirt. I don't see any cuts or other blood stains. I almost touch him to feel his skin, but don't out of fear.

His head turns to me, eyes hold mine in place.

"Get out of here. Jeremy. Go." His voice is not his voice.

"Dad. What's wrong? What is it?"

"Jeremy."

"DAD. I'm calling someone . . . shit, Dad."

"Get out of here." Dad pushes me away with one hand, knocking me to the floor.

I land in the doorway, the air knocked out of me.

Dad steps toward me and slaps the bare light bulb to the side.

Dull light shrouds his face in darkness. The tools out in front of him change shapes in shadows. More blood is visible on his shirt, but only in the moments when light crosses him as the bulb spirals.

"Get the fuck out of here," he says. "Leave." He sits back down at his workbench. The music fades out, but only long enough to make you think it is over before it begins again. A new piece with more brass, more strings, and heavy percussion rises up.

I run from the basement, the light bulb settling into a tiny tornado twirl from the wooden beam in the ceiling. I don't turn back. I skip steps, moving fast to my bedroom. My chest burns where Dad pushed me.

Another groan rips from the pit of the house, a growl.

It echoes inside the walls.

At my bed. On my knees.

Hands together. At my chin.

Eyes shut tight. Blocking out the world.

Our Father. Who art in Heaven. Hail Mary. Please, Mary, please.

72

I sit with my back against my bedroom door—*28 Days Later* on the other side. I open my cell phone and call Mom, but her line goes dead, disconnected. This fucking family and their cell phones, I swear. I call Jackson and he answers.

Loud music swallows his voice and I can't make out a damn thing he says, except for the word *Roscoe*. He says a bunch of inaudible words before chanting a cheer, like at a baseball game. "Roscoe. Ros-coe. Ros-coe. Ros-coe."

"Jackson? Can you hear me? I'm coming down to see you," I say. "I need your help."

More inaudible mumblings and music.

"Jackson? Can you hear me?"

"Let's do another one, baby," he says. "Excuse me, Hot Bartender? Another round."

"Jackson?"

"I can't hear you loud and clear, Jeremy. Please stop calling me," he says, before the line cuts out.

I scroll through my numbers but can't find anyone else. There is no one else in my life that is capable of helping, interested in listening, stable enough to cope. My breathing gets away from me like I've been running sprints. I scroll through for any name that I recognize, but most of them are family.

Then I come to one name I recognize. A new name. I dial and can't believe I am dialing. The phone rings and doesn't go right to voicemail like I want it to and expect it to and my alarm clock says it's recently 2 A.M., but I keep the call going anyway, until she picks up.

"Please don't hang up," I say.

"Jeremy," Aimee says. "Are you okay?" She sounds like she was asleep. I wonder what she's wearing. *Tits.* Why am I thinking about tits right now? Jesus.

"I didn't know," I say.

"Are you okay?" she asks. "This isn't a perverted phone call, is it? Because you're breathing heavy like maybe you're being perverted."

"I'm sorry. I shouldn't have called."

"You couldn't wait three days?"

"What do you mean?"

"You think girls don't know about boys waiting three days to call a girl? We know. BTW, girls don't all want serious relationships either."

"I was going to call tomorrow."

"Some of us *never* pick up a phone unless we want to. Some of us just let it ring."

"I was going to call tomorrow and make plans. For dinner. You want to go to dinner?"

"How about tea? You like tea?" she asks.

"Tea sounds good."

"Call me tomorrow, like you planned, and we'll pick a place. And for God sakes, calm down—you're going to hyperventilate if you keep breathing so fast."

I hang up and hear another moan and move to my closet and pull down a board game box. I grab a bunch of magazines and toss them into a backpack along with my phone. From the trash can, I pull an aluminum baseball bat. Time to sweep the house.

Zombie Survival Code #4: Lock-and-Load.

The house is a ghost, empty and moaning. The stairs creak under my steps. Dog hears me and trots to the front door, wagging her tail, waiting for me. She follows me as Dad moans some more and I walk to the basement door, my bat up off my shoulders, ready to swing. I choke up on the handle for good measure.

He speaks softly now, saying, "One, two three. One, two three. One, two three." Another moan, louder still. He stops, no longer counting, but quiet. He appears at the bottom of the stairs with dead eyes, looking up at me.

I grab the leash from Dad's office and snap it on Dog's collar. She walks figure eights behind me. Dad's closet door is open. So is his box of war. Like a magnet I am drawn to it. I approach and tip up on my toes to peek into its gut. The maps and photos and canteen are all still there. And so is the gun. I grab it and hold it in my hand, reintroducing myself to its texture and weight. This is Dad—the gun. His defense. Not me. I have my bat. I drop the gun back into the box, kick the closet closed and leave the house.

Dog trots next to me in the street as we make our way to the light rail station, under the cover of night, anonymous and alone.

Like Ballantine in Vietnam.

Like Dog and Jeremy in Baltonam.

73

The light rail barrels downtown like a gigantic snake, rolling along tracks through the concrete jungle of 83 South. I imagine it swallowing every car on the highway, sucking each down its throat for all of eternity. The train cuts through the new office buildings and fancy underground parking garages of Centre City, pulling into the station outside of Camden Yards.

Dog sits on the floor at my feet, waiting until it's time to move. She looks like the Sphinx. There's no one on the train except for a man sleeping across several seats, snoring. I keep the aluminum bat in my hand. The train doors open to blackness. The baseball stadium is dark and empty.

Dad used to take me to Orioles games every weekend. We would ride the light rail downtown together. At Camden Yards, Dad would buy hot dogs and fountain sodas and bags of unsalted peanuts. We'd sit in the upper deck and watch the players who looked like spiders crawling over the dirt and grass. Jackson would insult the other team. Dad would watch us both cheer when the O's would score a run. He'd high-five us. On our way home, we'd wait on the platform for the northbound light rail train and push our way to the front to get seats. Jackson and Dad would sit next to each other and I would lie across their laps, the speed of the train rocking me to sleep.

The moon crawls into the corner of the sky, pouring pale light over a parking lot full of cars. All of the surrounding office buildings are empty with only a few windows lit with light from a cleaning crew, working their way down a hallway.

Dog pulls me like a sled.

We reach the strip of land between the Inner Harbor and Fell's Point, which reminds me of a war zone. Burned out buildings and abandoned cars abound. Empty parking lots, padlocked and wrapped in a barbed wire fence. Graffiti-laden yellow school buses. Broken glass glitters up from the uneven sidewalks and pot-holed pavement, reflecting street lamplights as they buzz—a broken rainbow. A breeze blows in off the harbor and smells of a fire. Redbrick sidewalks and cobblestone streets replace the cracked streets. I approach the empty police station across from Jackson's apartment. Jimmy's is empty. Rain drizzles down again, tapping over everything. A whip of fall wind blows in off the harbor and smells of an approaching storm, swirling in the distance.

A woman on the corner in a vinyl miniskirt tries to flag a taxi that doesn't stop. She asks me if I can spare money for the bus.

"If you need money for a bus, how were you going to pay for a cab?" I ask.

"I would have found a way," she says.

Ladies and Gentleman, this is Baltimore.

74

I pound on Jackson's door, but he doesn't answer.

Dog sniffs the floor, searching for the source of that God-awful rank smell that hangs in the hallway. I pretend it is some kind of chemical warfare attack, that if I don't gain access to the mother ship in T-minus 15 seconds it will melt my insides and make my eyes pop like water balloons. No one wants to be a Goo Baby.

"Fuck off," Jackson says and throws something at the door. "I'm not home."

"Jackson," I say. "It's me. Open up. We have to talk. It's about Dad." I bang a bunch more, this time using my bat like a battering ram, before something heavier hits the door. Glass shatters. Dog flinches and looks at me like a question, *What are you going to do?* I step back, ready to kick the door in like some kind of badass cop when Franny opens her door behind me.

"Jackson?" Franny asks, squinting under the hallway light.

"I'm sorry. Did I wake you?" I ask. "I didn't mean to be so loud."

"You didn't wake me," she says. "I was pretending more than anything."

"I wish I was pretending," I say, scratching Dog's head.

"You brought your dog," she says. She crouches and pets Dog between her ears.

"Her name is Dog."

"That's a funny name," Franny says, petting her. "She is beautiful."

Franny is beautiful. She is a wedding dress away from being a beautiful bride. She wears black sweat pants and a green tank top, showing curvaceous cleavage. How about that SAT word—

curvaceous! I want her to hug me and never let go. I touch my nose, but I am not bleeding.

She stands. "It's amazing how much you look like your brother," she says.

I make a face.

"It's a compliment," she says. "Trust me."

"Could have fooled me."

"You're a smartass like your brother."

Franny leans against the door—her bare feet on the linoleum floor, her hair back in a ponytail. I take a breath and feel a burn in my lungs and I gasp for another, hoarsely. Franny holds me at my shoulders, inspecting me, then brings me in for a hug.

"Are you okay?" she asks.

"No."

"Does he know you are here?" she asks.

"He won't open the door."

She tips my face up to hers. "You can wait for Jackson, if you like," she says, opening her door. "I'm not going to send you away."

"Can Dog come too?"

"Dog can come too."

75

A copper kettle whistles on the stove. Steam shoots out from the nose. The tea attempts to cover the rank smell but doesn't even come close. Franny slides the kettle from the burner and pours three cups of tea.

"I have to take this into Sherman," Franny says, lifting a cup with all the care in the world, moving cautiously across the room and around a corner.

Dog sniffs everything, searching, finally sitting by the door, waiting, wanting to leave.

The living room is littered with books and loose papers. A bookshelf covers one entire wall from floor to ceiling, books jammed in every possible way. The spines faded and covered in dust or ash. Two brown leather recliners sit at the edge of an all-glass coffee table. A pile of pillows and blankets sit stacked neatly in the corner. The room looks like it hasn't been lived in for years. Various Van Gogh self-portraits hang from the walls, including the famous one with the bandage wrapped around his head. He looks crazy, but in a harmless way that makes me feel sorry for him.

"Sherman used to teach literature at Johns Hopkins," she says, back at my side. Her hand grazes my own and I feel my pecker shiver a bit. "Would you still like some tea?"

Dog watches, still not entering the room.

"I would love a spot of tea," I say in a British accent. I say, "I don't know why I just spoke like that."

She hands me my cup and plops down in one of the leather chairs. I take the other. I slurp the tea and burn my tongue.

We are silent for a bit, then she asks me why I'm down here. She asks if I'm in trouble.

I think about all the lies I could conjure up and all of the people I could blame and all of the wild stories I could tell, but in the end I tell Franny the truth. I tell her the truth about almost everything. About the surgery video and Mr. Rembrandt and Dad in the basement and the blood and his disappearing. Then, I tell her about my mother. I tell her that she's a pillhead junky, who's been whacked out on dope for as long as I can remember. I tell her that Jackson is some kind of sex addicted, tweaked out fuck-up and that the only real friend I have at school is Zink, but I don't tell her that he's gay. Like I said, I tell her the truth about almost everything.

Franny doesn't say anything. She just listens and occasionally agrees with a nod. I grow tired of talking, and eventually ask if she is Sherman's nurse or daughter or lover or something, and this makes her laugh. She explains that she's a former student, yes, but also his main caregiver. I ask her why he is sick and she says he has an incurable disease. I'm no moron and can pretty much guess which of the very few incurable diseases he has but don't press the issue as I can see it in her eyes—whatever is physically killing him is killing a part of her too.

"Franny, I want to ask you a question about a girl," I say.

"I'd like to help you with that very much," she says.

We both perk up and sit at the edges of our seats.

"I like this girl. Her name is Aimee. And tonight I finally got the nerve to ask for her number and I did and she gave it to me."

"That's lovely, Jeremy," Franny says.

"My friend told me I was supposed to wait three days to call her, but I called her when I got home. I woke her up."

"Everyone wants to be pursued," she says. "Besides, so few people actually give a shit that when someone like you comes along, it's a unique thing. Did she mind it when you woke her up?" Franny asks.

"Yes, but she made plans to meet me tomorrow night for tea."

"She likes you," Franny says. "No doubt about it. And tea date is much better than a dinner and movie date. You can't force a connection with people. You have to lay back and let it happen naturally. It has to click."

"Click?" I ask.

"Click," she says.

"Like a gun?" I ask.

"Like a seatbelt," she says.

76

Sherman's bathroom is goddamn yellow. Everything's goddamn yellow—shower curtain, tiled floor, bath mat, liquid hand soap, hand towels, waste basket, and wallpaper. I sit on the yellow toilet seat to pee. Next to the toilet is a yellow basket holding a stack of magazines. They're all men's magazines with half-naked women and cars on the covers. I think about flipping through to see if I want to steal any but decide that stealing from Sherman would be a pretty terrible thing to do.

I wash my hands in the yellow sink. The door swings opens and an overwhelming stench of rotting flowers fills the room. A man stands in front of me, a middle-aged man wearing a plaid robe. His hair is damp and slicked back, his eyes bloodshot. He doesn't look all that bad. I would never say that to the man's face or even to Franny, but if I passed him on the street I would have had no idea he was even terminal.

Dog barks from the living room.

"Your dog doesn't seem to like me and she's a guest in my own house," Sherman says.

"I'm a friend of Franny's. It's a pleasure to meet you, sir." I extend my hand to him and he looks at my hand and back at Dog and then to my hand again, before refusing to shake.

"Whatever it is—it's bad," Sherman says, pushing past me, entering the goddamn yellow bathroom. "You're a smart young man. I can see it in you. But whatever you're chasing, leave it alone."

I look down the hall for Franny, pissed that she talked to Sherman about all of this. I don't even know the dude. I smile and tell him that I will leave whatever I'm chasing alone.

Sherman grabs my hand and presses his palm into mine. I don't feel anything odd, like an electric charge or heat or ice or anything like that, but Sherman squeezes my hand hard and says, "Your father needs to enter alone. Your father no longer needs his son. Do not follow him. There is nothing you can do."

I step out of the bathroom and he closes the door. I can see into the bedroom that must be his. The blinds are closed and lights off, but the hallway light touches a few things. I can see a bed with the outline of a body in the sheets. A large cross above his bed with Jesus nailed to it. A statue of the Virgin Mary praying from the nightstand.

On my way out of the apartment, I ask Franny one more question.

"Did you ever, you know," I say, raising my eyebrows, "with Jackson?"

"Absolutely never," she says.

"I knew it," I say. "I just knew it."

77

I walk back to the light rail as thunder rolls off the black harbor. Black rain falls at a slant, filling the space between the cobblestones in the street. The street lamps buzz blue in the downpour like bug zappers. All signs of life have moved inside to wait for dawn or until it is dry again. No fucking zombies out tonight. I swing my bat with my free hand, holding Dog's leash in the other.

I am umbrella-less and don't care. I am careless.

I spontaneously do the "Thriller" zombie shuffle and shoulder jerk dance. I imagine forty dancers dressed up as zombies popping and locking in the middle of the rain-soaked streets with me to the soundtrack of "Thriller." I dance until I'm completely drenched and can't dance anymore from my sagging clothes, not to mention that the last thing I need is for some random person to tell the police I am bugging out on crystal meth or something.

Dog keeps looking behind us. She growls, then barks, snapping her jaw.

The woman I met earlier in a vinyl miniskirt steps out from the backseat of a car. Inside, the car is littered with trash and piled with blankets, aluminum cans, and plastic bottles. There is no one else with her.

"I need money. Can you spare any?" she asks.

"I can't," I say.

"Can you keep him back?" she asks.

"She's a girl."

"What's in the bag?"

"Not money," I say. "I have to catch my train now."

"The last light rail north left over an hour ago."

"How do you know?" I ask.

"What else is in the bag?" she asks.

"I said I don't have any money." I choke up on my grip of the bat. Exposing it under the blue lamp-lit street, showing her its length and girth like a jeweler holding a diamond ring. I point the tip of the bat at the woman and she steps back.

"A little old to be playing tee ball," she says.

"I couldn't agree more," I say.

She steps back and I lower my bastard.

"Get back in your car."

The woman gets into her car, packed with blankets and paper bags filled with aluminum cans and plastic bottles.

I pull on Dog's leash and move into the center of the street. The light rail is far away, but I will be there soon. The rain eases up but never disappears completely, dwindling to a fine mist.

I think of Franny and Sherman and say a quiet prayer for them in my head—a hybrid of a Hail Mary, an Our Father, and something about the essence of life.

Or some shit like that.

78

Our house sounds different at dawn. Everything is quiet and empty. Like *28 Days Later* when the main character wakes in the hospital room alone. Maybe a bird chirps. Maybe there's a squeak, like a door. Sun pulls itself up over a coast of trees at the end of the street. Last man standing. Little noises crackle like cereal in milk. The refrigerator clicks on and buzzes in the kitchen. A soft, electrical hum travels inside the walls, vibrating a current of power like veins running blood through a heart. Water flushes through pipes buried beneath the hardwood floors. Artificial sounds. None of them Dad.

I unclick Dog from her leash as she scrambles to the kitchen, slurping at her water bowl. Dad's office is locked up again—no trespassing. I climb the stairs to my room. One step at a time. Carefully, methodically, intentionally keeping the wood from bending and creaking, carrying my bat out in front of me, aimed and ready to strike. No lights on. No doors open. No clothes on the floor. No blood splattered along the railing. No broken glass. No busted furniture. No bodies. No gauze. No yellow police tape. No nothing. Everything normal.

But a strong chemical odor pours out from inside my bedroom, mixed with sweat and dirt and something else. I flick on the lights. Dad sits on the edge of my bed, his bare feet on the carpet, his hands in his lap, still wearing his clothes from the night before, bloodstains on his collar and cuffs, hair messy and tangled.

"I didn't realize you still had these." He stares at the wicker chairs across from him. His eyelids are heavy and flinch at the light. "Sit down. We need to talk."

"I'm sorry," I say, heading him off, dancing between all of the Codes, unsure of how Dad will proceed. I sit in one of the wicker chairs. "I didn't mean to cause any trouble."

Dad talks about real estate. He talks about subprime mortgage rates and a realtor's commission and asks me if I've ever read David Mamet's play *Glengarry Glen Ross*. He asks me if I know the ABCs of sales. I don't know any of it, but I say that I do because I'm trying to figure out where he's going with all of this.

"All of this is to say that what I do for a living, sales and property management and sourcing leads, it all directly affects you, which is why I need to know what you know about this homemade video. I won't be mad. I promise. But I need to know."

I tell Dad exactly what I saw on the DVD and not an image more.

"How did it make you feel?" he asks.

"You are never here," I say.

"But you see that I'm okay," he says. "You see that I'm all right, right?

"I saw the video, Dad. It made me sick."

"I'm still the same person," he says.

"I heard screaming last night. On the phone. What's happening?"

"You should have left the video alone, Jeremy."

"What happened to that man, Dad, the one strapped to the bed? Were you there in the crowd? Was it real? Can you answer me? I'll take any answer, so long as it is an answer to any of my questions?"

"What you saw is not what you think that it is."

"I saw Mr. Rembrandt give you the book and the movie in the parking lot of school. How could I leave it alone when you're disappearing every night?" I say.

"He said no one would see," he says.

"How do you even know my English teacher?" I make

fists and punch them into my legs with each word for effect. "What-is-happening-to-you?"

Dad licks his lips and has been for a while now. "That's an interesting question," he says. His mouth must be so dry. "I'm evolving," Dad says.

"Liza doesn't exist," I say. "In real life, she doesn't exist."

"Now, wait a second, she does exist."

"She's a fictional whore, Dad. She's a fictional whore in some old and crappy book. There's no way that you're dating a whore, like you keep lying about?"

"She's a saintly prostitute, saved and reformed."

"Once a whore, always a whore," I say.

"Jeremy, I know you didn't read your summer books, but I hope if you aren't accusing me, that you at least did your research and read this book?"

"I read the back of the book."

"Lazy like your brother. Enough. What about you? Let's focus on what's happening with you?" He aims a fist at my closet—closet open, board game boxes on the floor, board game boxes open, and my women's magazines everywhere.

My magazines. An old *Cosmopolitan* lays open on the carpet. A woman wearing a red bra and blue panties dances in front of a man in front of a full-length mirror. The caption across the top says: *101 Ways to Spice Up Your Sex Life*.

Dad continues. "I have been sitting here all night. Waiting for you. To come home. Because when I came up here to apologize last night. To explain. You weren't here. And I couldn't figure out, for the life of me, where you could have possibly gone. Sitting here trying to figure out. Trying to. What is wrong. With my son."

"Where do you go at night?" I ask. "I know there isn't a Liza. I know that's a lie."

"You're not gay, are you?" he asks, squaring himself across from me. "Well?"

I wonder if Zink's father ever asked him that question.

"Women's magazines," he says. "In your closet. I called your mother. I called your brother. She didn't hear from you. She never saw you. He never saw you. He never heard from you. Are you gay? Where did you go?"

"He wouldn't open the fucking door," I say. I choke up on my bat and wind up.

"Why would your brother ever lie to me?"

"Because," I say.

"*Because* is not a fucking answer, Jeremy. What do you think you saw last night? Why is it that you keep seeing things that aren't there? Are you taking the correct amount of medicine?"

"Whose blood was it in the basement?" I ask. "I know what I saw."

He rubs at the red still on his cuffs and collar. "I ran over a dog, Jeremy. It ran out from the woods and crossed over a median. Probably sick, diseased, and now deceased."

"Nothing about any of this is making any sense," I say.

"Remember when you were a kid and got gum stuck in your hair and Mom had to cut it out with scissors?" Dad rubs his eyes with his palms. "Jesus, Jeremy. I came up here last night to explain. Bu then I found . . ."

"They're magazines," I say.

"Women's magazines," he says.

"I met someone," I say, my eyes on the woman in the magazine with the red bra and blue panties. "Her name is Aimee White."

For the first time in some time, Dad is without speech.

"I met her at school. She's the student director of the fall play. *A Doll's House.*"

I want to scream—Torvald, Torvald, Torvald.

"Her name is Aimee," I say.

"Is she attractive?"

"I like her."

"Smart?"

"Very."

"Ha." Dad stands, excited, and stacks the magazines in a pile against the wall. "You need to call her." He closes my closet door and opens the blinds. "For a date—dinner and a movie," Dad says.

"Shouldn't I see if we click first? Should I wait three days?"

"There is absolutely no reason you can't date more than one girl. There's no need for you to tie your dingy to only one dock. You need to keep your options open." Dad unbuttons his shirt. His white undershirt is stained red with dog blood too—on the short-sleeve and collar. "You should call her. Make a date for tonight. Unless there's a reason why you wouldn't."

I dial the number and it rings and rings and rings before going to voicemail.

"Leave one," Dad whispers. "But don't sound desperate. Like you don't need to be calling. Like you got better things to do."

The anxiety of waiting for the beep forces my sweat glands to overproduce. Then, finally, after all the uber-sweat, there is the beep.

"Aimee. I was wondering if you'd like to go out to dinner and a movie tonight. If you're free. I'm free. Dinner and a movie. I don't know what's playing. But I'm sure you do. Call me. Call me back. Thank you very much and goodbye. Oh, and this is Jeremy."

I end the call.

Total. Dickbaggery.

Dad says, "I have to be honest, I'm not sure Aimee will call you back after that train wreck." Dad stands to leave when my phone buzzes in my hand and it's her.

We talk. Aimee couldn't have been happier to get my call, even though she did say my message creeped her out a bit. She kept saying, "Why are you acting like we didn't already have this conversation last night?" I try for a dinner and a movie, against all better judgment, but she, rightly, shuts the idea down. Instead, she reconfirms our plans for tea at the Daily Grind before going to Mykel's chopography art exhibit together.

Dad shakes his head the entire time I'm on the phone. He shakes my trash can full of bats. He walks to my dresser. He picks up a pill bottle. Then, when it's all said and done, he pinches a pill and aims it toward my mouth. I stop his hand with mine and open my palm.

He hesitates, but eventually drops it down. I catch it like a goddamn professional.

I pretend to swallow it before opening wide to show him the emptiness.

He leaves, his footsteps pounding down the stairs.

I spit the pill onto my comforter.

Next to a red stain.

Dog blood.

79

In the shower, I prepare to scrub my body raw.

Steam fills the room like fog from some kind of war. My conversation with Dad still has me dizzy. Somehow we talked about everything, but learned absolutely nothing. If anything, I got farther from the truth. Further from the truth about Liza and Rembrandt and the video and book and where he goes at night.

I lather with soap and shampoo. Exfoliate my face with a salt scrub sample from one of my magazines. Condition and rerinse.

I wipe condensation away from the mirror so I can see my reflection. Like a big fat cliché, I flex. My sad little man muscles are nothing to brag about, barely even noticeable.

I wrap the towel around my waist and walk to my bedroom, my chest puffed out, my towel tightly secured.

Before I pluck a pair of underwear from the Scrabble box in my closet and pull on my jeans, before I rub on deodorant and spritz myself with cologne, I first stand by the window and wait for Tricia. To see if I can return the peep show.

I wait for her, but really I'm waiting for something else altogether.

80

Tricia walks Travis past our house as I wait for Jackson to pick me up. She stops at the bushes that border our walkway. Travis blasts it with his piss. Never is there ever a more awkward moment to strike up conversation with a hot chick than when a dog takes a leak.

I fight the urge to tell her I very recently waited for her by my bedroom window half-naked. I'm not quite sure what I would have even done if she had been home.

We speak in clipped sentences, exchanging awkward every-things. We don't make direct contact, both of us following the Code. She asks if I'm feeling better, and I assure her that I am. That I no longer have a bug. That it was probably a 24-hour thing. I even touch my forehead for effect. Lame.

She says she's happy to hear I'm better. Travis isn't stingy with his piss and generously spreads it around. Tricia asks me if I have a hot date and I reassure her that we're just friends. That it's really nothing serious.

"A word of friendly girl advice," she says. "Don't tell *her* that."

Travis finally runs dry and pulls Tricia farther down the side-walk. She slows him, stops, and turns back.

"Jeremy, I meant what I said the other day—I am always here to listen. If you need it." She looks to my house, then to hers. "Things can be tough sometimes."

"Does that mean you're staying in Baltimore?"

"Travis and I will be around."

"What happened to Harvard?"

She gently pulls on the leash and Travis comes trotting back to her and sits at her feet.

"I'll be honest with you, if you'll be honest with me," she says.

"I don't know how not to feel hopeless sometimes," I say.

"Funny, I kind of have the same problem." She watches Travis sit quietly by her side, staring up at her for some kind of command. "I'm not in school anymore." She holds her hand out to me and I accept it. She squeezes my hand. "I'm a patient at Sheppard Pratt."

"Jesus. I'm so sorry. Are you sick?" I have heard of people going to Sheppard Pratt before but never really knew why. "Could they not help you at Johns Hopkins?"

She laughs. "When you're finished with my *Instyle*, just put it back on the porch." She snaps her fingers and Travis catapults himself into a trot as they both continue down the sidewalk. "I don't ever mind sharing."

"Tricia," I say. "Tonight I won't talk about the weather."

"I never thought for a second that you would." Her smile could start a war among men.

Her fat-ass father waits for her on the porch and opens the door again like some sort of parental concierge. She unhooks Travis who leads the way inside.

And they all fall away to nothing.

81

Jackson's ugly-ass mini-Smart Car, a graduation present from Dad, rolls up to the house like a giant red gumball on the loose and barely stops behind Dad's BMW. Jackson honks his horn like a maniac and throws open the passenger door.

"Get the fuck *in* before he comes *out*." Jackson watches the front door. The screen door is closed but the front door is open, and all that's there is Dog, watching us, her ears back. Jackson says the last thing he needs is another face-to-face with the old man where he tells him how to live his damn life.

We are all involuntary members of the same fucked-up club.

Jackson maneuvers his ridiculously small car past Dad's BMW still parked where it was last night—the BMW bloodless, clean and dent-free. His eyes look like a week of sleepless nights. His hair is perfect though, parted, but in a natural, non-douchebag kind of way. His clothes are wrinkled but that's not entirely surprising considering how messy his apartment looked. It smells like fast food and smoke. Jackson places the plastic tip of a thin cigar between his teeth and hands me a box of multicolored condoms.

"Dad gave me my first box when I was your age," he says. "Now I'm paying it forward." Jackson lights the end of the cigar and drags on the tip, holding the smoke in, before exhaling in a satisfyingly long stream. The car fills with smoke. He offers me a drag, careful to hold the cigar together where he had cut it open and filled it with whatever the fuck.

I've never had the urge to smoke weed, but more specifically

I've never had the urge to smoke weed with Jackson. I hold my box of multicolored condoms and politely decline his blunt.

I stand corrected. The car smells like fast food and burnt asshole hair.

He takes another pull and holds the smoke. "You'll never forget your first box of Jimmy Hats." After, he exhales. "Mine were Magnum, ribbed, and glow-in-the-dark." He smiles with the cigar in his mouth. "That was definitely a good period in my life." He smokes some more.

"Does Dad seem different to you lately?" I ask.

"You mean, like, is he crazy?" he asks.

"He was in the basement last night. He said he'd hit a dog with his car."

Jackson looks at me with some wide-ass eyes, the plastic tip of the blunt back between his teeth.

"It's why I was at your apartment. It's why he called you last night, looking for me."

"That's fucked up that he killed a dog with his car, but I don't know what you're talking about as far as the old man calling me last night, Stumps. I pretty much make it a point to avoid him, like, always."

"No. Last night. I came down to your apartment."

"I know. I had a chick with me, which is why I didn't let you in, but Dad never called."

"He said he called you and told you about hitting the dog. The dog blood. He said he was worried about me and he called you. To make sure I was okay."

"Stumps, the last time I heard from or saw Dad was when you stormed out of my apartment like a little twat." Jackson holds one toke too long and coughs his brains out like a clichéd pothead. "That . . . was . . . a . . . good . . . one," he says between coughs.

"What's Sheppard Pratt?" I ask.

"Who do you know at the Shep?"

"Tricia said she was a patient at Sheppard Pratt."

"No way!" He laughs. "The Shep is Baltimore's premiere psychiatric facility." He offers the blunt to me again, pinched between fingers. The plastic tip has bite marks on it. "It's where people go who lose their damn minds."

"You mean crazy?" I decline the cigar again.

"I mean bananas. She probably had some kind of breakdown. Happens all the time to chicks. They're so fucking emotional." He inhales and exhales with ease. "Condoms and weed, baby brother. It's what keeps us men sane."

When we get to Fell's Point and he parallel parks his ugly-ass car down the street from his apartment building, I leave the box of condoms in the passenger seat, unopened.

IX
NIGHT OF THE LIVING DEAD

(Release Date: October 1, 1968)
Directed by George A. Romero
Written by John A. Russo and George A. Romero

82

The street lights reflect against the cobblestone streets of Fell's Point and black water of the Chesapeake Bay. Nothing down here seems to stay the same, but I'm beginning to believe that about most things.

Aimee appears out of darkness. A street lamp washes her in yellow light. She wears a black skirt, above the knee, with black kitten heels and a red, long sleeve, scoop neck shirt. My magazines have prepared me in more ways than I'm even aware sometimes.

Before I have a chance to decide between greeting Aimee with a professional handshake or a more romantic hug, she grabs my hands and pulls me through an old wooden door, the entranceway to a coffee shop—the Daily Grind.

Her hand is soft and warm and for the first time today I feel hopeful about things and never want to let it go. Immediately, I worry that my damn nose is bleeding again and touch my nostrils with my free hand.

"You're fine," she says. "Don't worry so much. You carry it in your eyes. It's okay to take a break once in a while." She brushes the back of her hand against my cheek.

Aimee orders a fancy flavored tea—mandarin orange mint tea that smells like an Indian spiced fruit bomb. The barista is a dude with a tiny bird-sized bone stuck horizontal through his nostrils and he toils like each drink is the Sistine Chapel. The barista passes the hot tea to Aimee and I say, "This one's on me. My treat. I insist." I pay the barista as Aimee sources us a table.

When she is far enough away, I say, "Buddy, I need you to hook me up with whatever fancy tea a fancy tea drinker would drink."

"You got it, boss." The barista measures and scoops tea leaves into a tiny glass jar from an unmarked baggie under the counter and fills it with steaming water. "This is my own special blend. I call it *Howard's Hawthorn Horny Heroin.*" He hands me the glass jar with the tea and a mug. "Nice to meet you. I'm Howard." His teeth are yellow little fuckers and his nose bone is bothersome.

"Now when you say *heroin*," I say.

"All you need to know is that hawthorn is *the business.*"

"I'm sorry, Howard, you're going to have to help me here," I say.

Howard taps the glass of my crazy, fucked-up horny tea. "The berries, leaves, and flowers of the hawthorn plant improve a man's blood flow."

"No," I say.

"Yes," he says. "Circulation." Howard makes two fists. "This will relax your blood vessels." He loosens his fingers before tightening them back up into fists. "If you know what I mean," he says, looking past me to Aimee. Howard punches the air. "This one's on me," he says.

Aimee sits in the back room filled with tiny tables, ours with a nice wobble that causes us to almost spill our drinks when we shift our weight from elbow to elbow.

"What did you order?" she asks.

"You know, I don't know what it's called, but it's supposed to be really good for you." I pour the tea into my mug and blow on the surface. "It's way too hot right now, otherwise I'd let you have a sip." I am one God-awful actor.

Aimee takes the mug from my hands and takes a sip. She looks back at the barista. "Howard made this for you, didn't he?"

"Are we going to miss the art exhibit?" I take my mug back from her. I too take a sip and it tastes like boiled tree bark.

"Did he give it some crazy name?" She locks her eyes onto me and I am weak. I give in and tell her.

"*Howard's Hawthorn Horny Heroin.* Something about circulation. And relaxing blood vessels. I'm not entirely sure."

Aimee cups her hands over her mouth and shouts Howard's name and he looks up from behind the cappuccino machine, whipping foam or whatever, to see Aimee flip him off with two middle fingers. Howard salutes her.

"Howard likes to play practical jokes. I come in here a lot and he's always trying to trick me into trying some crazy new tea. I'm sure your blood vessels will be fine."

"Okay." Jesus my Christ, what kind of response is *okay*? I try and recover the conversation. "I like the cobblestone floors in here. Feels like olden days." I really wish I hadn't said *olden days*. God. I want to punch myself in the face.

"There used to be an amazing cinema upstairs called *The Orpheum*." Aimee dabs her lips with a napkin. "Everything changes, except maybe Howard."

"I've got to give it to him, Howard's crazy fake tea is good," I say. "It has a rich, earthy flavor to it."

"You hate tea," she says. "I can tell you hate tea. You hate it, but you'd never say you hate it, because you're too sweet."

"I need to confess something," I say.

"I love confessions," she says, leaning forward, ready for a secret. "Is it dangerous?"

"There is the potential for danger," I say.

"Will there be an adventure?" she asks.

"I've been nervous that I won't have anything to say to you," I say. "I feel like I'm talking underwater."

"With me?"

"With everyone, but you're the only one who makes me self-conscious about it. I'm tired of trying to get people to listen to me."

"I think your *Howard's Hawthorn Horny Heroin* is giving you strength of voice and power of soul." She touches my hand.

"You're making fun of me," I say.

"I am," she says. "But only because you are so serious."

"I don't know anything about tea," I say.

"Sadly, the movie theater upstairs closed down a couple years ago, so we can't see a movie and go to dinner after to talk about it."

"You like to tease me," I say.

"Love to tease you," she says.

"Everything changes," I say.

"Nothing stays the same. Huge high-rises," she says. "Faux classic architecture. Condominiums."

"My mom designed one of those buildings," I say. "She says she did. I don't believe much of what she says anymore."

"She and your Dad divorced?" she asks.

"Not technically, but practically."

Aimee blows on the surface of her tea.

"I remember when my Dad used to take me to this place called *Wonderland* out in Howard County," I say. "It was this kiddy park with rides and cotton candy and castles. I think it's a tiered parking lot and an insurance company now."

"For five dollars you could go upstairs, get a huge bucket of popcorn, and see a double feature," Aimee says. "Every night, a new double feature. Two movies and a bucket of popcorn for five bucks. Now it's a space for rent. To the highest bidder. Tonight, it's Mykel's art exhibit. Tomorrow, who knows? Next week it'll be an H&R Block."

"What movies did you see there?"

"Stanley Kubrick's *Lolita* and Martin Scorcese's *Taxi Driver*. An Akira Kurasawa double feature—*Rashomon* and *Seventh Samurai*. *White Heat* and *Chinatown*. Real quirky combos. One time I saw Stanley Donen and Gene Kelly's *Singing in the Rain* and it was supposed to be followed by Oliver Stone's *Platoon*. There was a problem with the projector. Everyone left except for me. I waited. One of the employees turned off the lights in the theater and pumped the recording of a thunderstorm through the sound system. To this day, it's one of the most memorable moments of my life."

"Did they ever fix the projector?"

"*Platoon* never looked better."

"It makes sense that you like directing," I say. "Working on *A Doll's House* must be amazing."

"I like a good story and *A Doll's House* absolutely has a good story," she says. "What I like about theater and film is breaking down characters over a few hours into their most important emotional parts."

"Like the thunderstorm in the movie theater," I say.

"Exactly." She clinks her teacup against mine.

"Do you think miracles belong in drama?"

"You've been speaking to Father Vincent Gibbs." She strangles the air. "He's already been arguing how we should interpret the ending of *A Doll's House* and we haven't even cast our play yet."

"What do you believe?" I ask.

"They exist in real life, then they exist in drama, because drama is an authentic representation of real life."

"I want to believe in miracles," I say.

"You are a little Torvald, aren't you?" Aimee folds her paper napkin and soaks up condensation on our table. "In the final moments of *A Doll's House*, right before his wife leaves him for good, Nora says, *Oh, Torvald, I don't believe in miracles anymore*, and she leaves. The stage direction for Torvald says *a glimmer of hope flashes across his face*, and he says: *the greatest miracle of all—?*"

"My dad played Torvald once. Before he was drafted. I never knew my Dad acted until recently. My mom told me. I wish I never knew."

Aimee reaches across the table and holds my hands. "No more miracles," she says.

"I have another confession to make," I say.

"Lucky me—I'm learning all of your dirty little secrets tonight," she says.

"I haven't heard of most of those movies you mentioned. I pretty much only know zombie films." I sip my tea and feel douchey. "I should know more."

She smacks my cheek with her open palm. Not hard, but hard enough. It hurts, but in a way that I like and appreciate. She folds her hands in her lap.

"I hardly know anything about zombie movies," she says. "Teach me something. What are your top five favorite zombie movies?"

Without even thinking about it: "*Night of the Living Dead, Planet Terror, 28 Days Later, Zombieland,* and *Dawn of the Dead,* the 2004 remake."

"I am not a huge fan of gore. I like violence when it's appropriate, when it builds to a crescendo, like in *Taxi Driver.* But zombie movies seem to splash around in it. Like in *28 Days Later.* Now I thought that was a political film about infection, not zombies."

"Nope. Zombies," I say. "I'd bet my hand. Total Zombie Apocalypse."

"I've seen it a few times and had no idea it was a zombie film," she says. "No one ever resurfaces as a zombie. They get infected with bad blood. That's not a zombie."

"*Necroinfectious Pandemic* is the appropriate terminology, if you want to get technical."

"You are such a little zombie snob. You're a Snombie. If the word *pandemic* didn't make you a Snombie, then the word *necroinfectious* most certainly did."

"I like zombie movies," I say.

"It's your thing," she says.

"Is this a date?" I ask.

"Isn't it?" she asks.

"There're so many rules," I say. "I don't know what this is."

"First dates usually end with a kiss," she says.

"Did I get a green light?" I ask.

"You're funny," she says.

"In a bad way?" I ask.

"I like funny."

"I like you, Aimee, and guess what? No nosebleeds." I drink the rest of my *Howard's Hawthorn Horny Heroin.* Howard gives me thumbs up from behind the counter and I give him the double middle finger, just like Aimee.

"Where do you go when you have nothing to say?" Aimee asks, crossing her arms.

"I listen, mostly."

"Don't bullshit me."

The man in the back scribbles in the margins of a book, before closing it.

"Right there—where are you?" Aimee asks, her voice calm and soothing like she's rocking me to sleep.

"I go deeper in. I listen to myself. I try to hear myself how I want others to hear me."

Aimee sits up, pulling her chair closer to the table's edge. "I think you're eccentric. Not crazy. But I think you move around like some kind of a God. Not *the* God. But like *a* God. Passing judgment. Soaking up information, a God-like, judgmental sponge, overseeing everything. Examining situations like chess pieces in play."

"If I'm a God, then you should worship me."

"I'm not finished," she says. "You're constantly starting over. You run in cycles of asserting yourself and being passive. No one listens when you tell them to stop because you don't make them listen, because you don't command it."

She wants to know where I go, but if I take her there, it's very possible she leaves and will never come back. Like everyone else. To a place with plaid jackets and sick men in fat neckties. Women's magazines in board game boxes. Giant, donkey dicks. A place without sex where sex is a currency and I am broke. Short skirts. Tight tops. Big tits. Handguns. Homemade videos. James Dean. Polaroids. Rich kids. Faggots, queers, cocksuckers, rim jobbers and cumshooters. A place where no one has a face. This is the place and this place decays and eventually everything turns to black.

"Jeremy," she says, "wherever you go, you're allowed to go there. I just want you to know that it's okay."

83

A familiar voice cuts through our conversation.

Mr. Rembrandt stands at our table, the eight-fingered freak smiling down on us.

"Aimee White and Jeremy Barker." His soft voice makes the room feel dark blue and cold, the ocean floor. "What a small, little world we live in. My favorite student and assistant director, on a date together—what a small little world indeed." He looks different outside of school—taller, more present. "I hope I'm not intruding. Father Vincent and I were on our way upstairs to see Mykel's exhibit." He holds a book dog-eared to hell in his hand—*Notes from Underground*.

Back at the counter, decked out in his priestly collar, Father Vincent is ordering drinks. He turns and waves.

"Super, small world," I say.

"Mr. Rembrandt," Aimee says.

"Please. Tonight, call me Richard," he says. Rembrandt combs white hair over his bald spot with his fingers and adjusts his blue-rimmed glasses. "It's nice to see that young men still get dressed up for dates." He pinches my knot and centers it at my neck. "And that a necktie knot is treated with respect. Your Windsor. My word." His eight normal fingers curl like spider legs. "I love its authenticity."

Father Vincent approaches with two iced coffees and passes one off to Rembrandt. "Hey, hey, you guys." His smile immediately draws one from me. "Great minds think alike," he says. Father Vincent raises his to-go cup. "Salute."

"Look, it's miracle man," Aimee says.

She's so funny that I can't help but laugh at him.

"Will you two be attending Mykel's chopography exhibit?" Rembrandt asks.

"We will," Aimee says. "Like you, Jeremy and I wanted to get some tea first."

"Richard and I had dinner at that new Mexican restaurant down the way to discuss *A Doll's House*." Father looks at the front door. "Across from The Sound Garden." He sips his iced coffee and snaps his fingers. "Important talks—casting, casting, casting." Father Vincent runs his finger around his collar. "What the heck was the name of that restaurant?"

"Lista's," Rembrandt says.

"I'll never remember that." He pulls out a tiny pencil and a little booklet from his inside pocket, the same one from Reconciliation. It's the size of his palm with unlined paper inside.

"How cute," Aimee says.

"Oh, you like this?" He sounds equal parts embarrassed and genuinely surprised. He holds it out for Aimee and I to see. The front and back cover show a crude sunset over black water.

"What do you use it for?" I ask.

"I write down the things I know I'll never remember." He slides the booklet back.

"Where did you get it?" she asks.

"In addition to being priest, I also collect antique glass bottles. The real thick ones. I make landscapes with them. I break the bottles with a hammer and crazy glue the shards of glass to a sketch that I've etched onto a tiny sheet of plywood. When I finish, I take a picture and make these." Father Vincent retrieves his booklet again from his coat pocket and opens it in full. "This was a blood moon sunset over the Inner Harbor I saw when I was a kid."

"Unbelievable," I say. "A zombie nerd, priest, and oddball artist all in one."

"Speaking of nerd, what are you reading?" Aimee asks Rembrandt, reaching for his book.

"Nothing terribly special."

Aimee turns it over in her hands and reads the back.

"What's it about?" Father Vincent asks.

"Isolation. Corruption. Redemption. Would you like to borrow it?" Rembrandt asks Aimee. "They say *Taxi Driver* is based on it. I know that's one of your favorite movies."

"Aimee, I have a copy at home you can borrow," I say. "I even have a video that goes with it." I avoid Rembrandt's stare, but I sure as shit know it's there. He can go fuck himself.

"I had no idea *Taxi Driver* was based on a Dostoevsky novel," Aimee says.

Mr. Rembrandt flips through *Notes from Underground* to a particular page. "Here, Vincent, this is for you." Then he reads. "*The long and the short of it is, gentlemen, that it is better to do nothing! Better conscious inertia! … Oh, but even now I am lying! I am lying because I know myself that it is not underground that is better, but something different, quite different, for which I am thirsting, but which I cannot find! Damn underground!*"

He closes the book and slides it into his pocket.

"No idea what it means, but sounded great," Father Vincent says. "We should go. Leave the kids alone."

They walk to the door and disappear.

"How do you think his hands got all jacked up?" I tuck my pinky fingers into my palms and wave my hands over my head, making a banshee noise.

Aimee laughs but knows she probably shouldn't as she looks around to make sure Mr. Rembrandt is really gone. I carry the glassware to the counter, handing them back to Howard, while Aimee wipes down our table with a napkin, sweeping my crumbs into her hand, and then walks them over to a trash can. She couldn't be cooler if she tried.

"He come in a lot?" I ask Howard.

"Dude with the messed-up paws?" Howard bends his little fingers. "Every now and then. Usually he's with dudes who are all messed up like him."

"Messed up like, a bone through their nose messed up?"

"No." Howard smiles. "Like, missing body parts messed up." He steps away from the counter, away from me. "Dude, the tea's working." He taps his nose.

I hold my palm under my chin as drops of blood drip down.

Aimee appears at my side like I hoped she would and runs her hand across my back, handing me another tissue. She's extraordinary. I would do anything for her. She doesn't know it, but I would fight off an entire army of undead for her like *Shaun of the Dead*. My romantic-comedy of the Zombie Apocalypse—*Jeremy of the Dead*. Instead of *Sleepless in Seattle*, *Undead in Baltimore*. Faith and love and miracles.

Aimee leads us out into the dark. Her hand laces with mine—click.

84

The art exhibit is not what I expected.

A table near the entrance serves red juice in tiny paper cups and a silver tray of Berger cookies, a Baltimore tradition of thick, cakey cookies smeared with a soft chocolate fudge on top.

Strobe lights flicker from a light system in the corner. The DJ is a chick with bleached blonde dreadlocks under headphones. I'm happy it's not DJ Doug spinning the ones and twos. She bobs her head and shakes her body like a snake moving through tall grass as trippy, mellow drum beats drop from speakers buried in the ceiling. Everyone in the room yells to the person next to them in order to be heard over the highly stylized music. It sounds like the exit song of a film score. Like in zombie movies when the entire movie has some way-too-obvious keyboard-heavy film score—all cheese and slashery and screaming *DANGER!* Then in the final scene of the movie a wildly different and entertaining and halfway decent song plays, carrying over into the credits. This is the soundtrack to chopography.

The room is small, a single white open space, packed with a lot of white people.

Kids from school are dressed down in street clothes, which is weird for me to see—T-shirts, polo's, jeans, and shorts. I got used to the neckties and khakis and sport coats, so the casual ware looks foreign. But Plaids are still Plaids.

Byron Hall teachers and Christian Brothers mill about too, the teachers in street clothes, and brothers in all black tunics.

Father Vincent is the only priest in the joint, doing his God collar thing, and spends most of his time talking with Byron Hall students, whereas the Brothers stick mainly to the other faculty members, like at the mixer.

Other art patrons look like complete foreigners—small pockets of rich, artsy people in turtlenecks and tweed blazers and dickhead soul-patch facial hair with black-and-white fedoras. My guess is that they live in the area or read about the exhibit.

Some media arrive and gather material. Reporters for the *Baltimore Sun* and *Baltimore City Paper* scribble notes into notepads about particular pieces and interview attendees to get their reactions. Local news channels send reporters to cover the event. One-man camera crews mount hulking cameras on tripods. Beautiful male and female reporters apply makeup and practice their smiles in small mirrors, checking their teeth for stuck food.

And then there are the folks that you can't really miss at all. Some are in strollers. Some are in wheelchairs. They clearly know Mykel better than white-bread Byron Hall knows him. It's the public version of the Black Awareness Table in the cafe. African American and Hispanic men and women celebrate in loud voices, shouting out his name every few words. All are well dressed—nothing but slick suits, big ties, Windsor knots, big lady hats, bright colored dresses, and enormous jewelry.

A song ends.

Conversation rises across the room.

Mykel moves through, chilled-out, all swagger, trying to talk to everyone, while everyone demands he talk to them about his art. I remember when he said that everyone loves a black artist. Jimmy Two, someone all too familiar with crowds and boisterous attention, escorts a circle of females over to Mykel, who greets them each with a kiss on the hand.

Each wall of the space features Mykel's chopography and each wall looks almost exactly the same: random photographs chopped up and mixed together like a salad and framed under thick wood. Oval squares. Small squares. Long rectangles. Even a few triangles. The frames arranged to replicate a wall of family photos, varying in shapes and sizes. On a whole, it looks very professional, but I just don't get it. The chopography. What it means. How it's considered high art and not something I learned to do when I was in kindergarten. We did shit like this when we learned about consonant combinations from Miss Lydia.

I ask Aimee a question, but she can't hear me, which is a fantastic ploy for me to move closer to her. My arm presses into her breasts. She smells like a unicorn. My dick hardens.

Miss Lydia was my kindergarten teacher and she was young and hot and had big breasts. I don't remember much, but I do remember that she was young and had big ones. My favorite part of every day was when she'd stop by my desk and I'd feel her big breast press into my arm as she checked in to see how my craft was coming along. Her kindergarten projects were really no different than Mykel's weirdo art. She'd give us a stack of magazines like *National Geographic*, *Good Housekeeping* and *Time*, scissors, paste, and a sheet of construction paper. Then, she'd ask us to cut out pictures of things that began with whatever combination we learned that day, like *wh* or *th*.

This, to me, is the G-rated version of chopography.

While similar, Mykel's version is a far cry from the same fucking thing.

Elephants with human heads.

Lamp posts bursting into classrooms.

Taxicabs parked inside basements.

Blood-covered newborn babies with ram antlers.

White people on the light rail, holding on to poles with black fingers.

Black people with white feet on a beach.

Men breastfeeding babies on bus benches.

Women holding their penises while using urinals.

Little boys jumping rope.

Little girls in Boy Scout uniforms.

Dogs fucking cats with dildos.

Cats in a crowd, hailing cabs.

Pillows giving birth to frozen turkeys.

A table of multi-ethnic erect dicks with their passenger balls playing cards.

Mykel's chopography is, no doubt, some R-rated shit.

If a mental health professional ever got their mitts on one of his chopography puppies, Mykel would be thrown in the Shep for sure. I overhear some Inner Harbor, uptight, turtleneck-wearing dildo-douchebag refer to the chopography as "disturbed and disturbing."

To be honest, I completely agree, except agree completely separate from them and only to myself.

85

I grab a paper cup of red juice for Aimee and myself, even though we just had tea, and I select the wall near the front door. Aimee receives her paper cup with a smile and she follows me through the crowd.

People are pushy as shit at art exhibits, it is pretty unbelievable—chit-chatting away without a clue who's around them. I wouldn't say that I threw any elbows or crashed into anyone, but I definitely kept some strangers on their toes.

We reach a particular piece and position ourselves in front of it. Prime real estate.

The photo is of the 55 bus approaching the stop outside of Byron Hall, except this is not your normal 55 bus. Instead, it has giant, leathery-looking, pterodactyl dinosaur wings stretching out from the sides. Spade-shaped blades spike along the roof of the bus like a stegosaurus. Tyrannosaurs feet and baby hands poke out from where the tires should be and an enormous mouth stretches below the front windshield that looks like it's filled with big, old, bad shark teeth. The piece is framed in a simple, thin, black frame with a custard-colored matt behind the chopography. The name of the piece is *Greatness*.

I step closer and see people I know inside the bus. The normal 55 driver who says *sixty/forty* is even there. I am not there.

"I have no idea what this means," I say.

"An individual's interpretation plays a major part. There's a dialogue that takes place between the art and the viewer. Like that miracle line I was telling you about at the end of *A Doll's House*. It means something different to everyone."

"I call bullshit. This is crazy. This doesn't *mean* anything. It can't possibly."

Aimee finishes her juice. "How does *Greatness* make you feel?"

"Is this, like, a therapy session?"

"In a way. Experiencing this type of art is like a therapy session." She presses herself into me from behind, directing my eyes. "How does looking at this particular chopographical piece make you feel?" She is really into this exhibit and art viewing experience, so I dig deep and try to focus on this bus with the dino parts. Her hands cup my shoulders and stop me from swaying. I focus so hard I feel like a light bulb might burst somewhere in the room, so I stare straight ahead and really focus. I need to do this for Aimee so I push again and think the word *concentrate* over and over in my head, but I think it so much that after a while the word loses all meaning and doesn't even sound like a real word and becomes the only word that I want to say at all.

"What do you feel?"

"I feel horrible," I say.

The problem is that I don't feel *horrible* from the art, but rather absolutely terrified from failing to feel anything, failing to have a dialogue with this fucked-up bus. Before she turns this into a pop quiz and asks me why I feel this way, I turn it around on her and ask the same question.

She thinks for a minute, then says, "He's captured the feeling of an insider having to take the transportation of an outsider."

A group next to us talks about it too.

"From some of the other pieces I've seen, this one seems like an early work. A bit too on-the-nose."

"I think we can easily connect the evolution of mankind to technology and the socioeconomic infrastructures constructed to prevent a return to primitiveness."

"I like the title. *Greatness*. But his images are too immediate. There needs to be more subtlety."

All I want to do is throw up. I can't find anything relatable in these glorified collages. Here's a piece of art. Let's take a look at it. It's a public bus with animal parts.

We stop at the next photo of a beautiful, wild, garden of purple, yellow, red, and green flowers under a massive black sky stuffed with interconnecting and varying sizes of copper, gold, and white plastic tubing. In the middle, a very small single line of copper tubing runs down from the heavens into the garden. The title—*Paradise Plumb*.

Aimee examines the holy hell out of the next photo, but I'm over it. This art makes me feel like I have to take a leak.

I spot-check the crowd again and don't see Mr. Rembrandt.

Father Vincent stands by the DJ's booth with Frank and Anthony, all three drinking the red juice, making their way around the room together at a turtle's pace. I am so freaking happy to see Frank and Anthony. I honestly didn't know that they'd still be enrolled as students after everything. If Brother Lee had been the one to break up the infamous hallway showdown, I'm sure they'd be gone for good. Cam and his shitbirds aren't anywhere to be found. I don't see Cam or the Plaids or Coach O'Bannon anywhere, but I know they're around. They're always around.

At the front door, Brothers Bill, Fred, and Lee greet the guests as they arrive. This isn't a school-sponsored event, but Byron Hall very purposefully positions themselves alongside him. The Brothers welcome a couple coming through the door—she has the skin of solid white porcelain and he has the skin of yellowing death.

Sherman holds Franny's arm for support as they stop at the table for some juice. He wears a plaid old-timer's cap and a heavy overcoat even though it's still summer weather outside. His clothes swallow him whole, they're so baggy, but he never stops moving, always putting one foot in front of the other. Franny doesn't look like she's all that interested in the art on the walls, but Sherman is, which makes her smile because that's all that matters to her. They pass Father Vincent and Frank and Anthony and stop at *Greatness* nearby.

She sees me, and smiles. I hold Aimee's hand again for Franny to see and she laughs. Sherman can't understand what she is whispering in his ear at first, but eventually he does and looks over at me, lifting up the brim of his hat to see better. He flashes me two thumbs up, but it's half-hearted at best as he breaks eye contact with me first and then from Franny, moving on to the next chopographical art. Franny is pulled right along with him. She almost trips but regains her balance, looking back one more time.

I wave to her and she waves back and that is that.

86

There are exactly three different techniques one can use to survive an art exhibit.

First, there's the *Chin-and-Lean*: cross one arm across the chest and bend the other arm up over the one across the chest and rub the chin. Then, after a good chunk of time passes, lean to the right. Hold this position, like stretching a muscle. This will make a person look retarded, but so long as you don't say anything and continue to shift from right to left, people will think there is some serious art-soaking happening.

There's also the *Nose-to-Art*: this starts from a standing position approximately ten feet away from the intended target. (TIP: this generally works better on larger pieces of art.) From the standing position take one exaggerated step forward, bringing both feet back together in a stationary formation. Then rest, never breaking eye contact with the art. Every three minutes take another giant step forward until you are eventually standing directly in front of the art, your nose almost touching it. Take two steps back. Rest. Then one step forward. Continue until someone approaches and follows a similar pattern of advancing and retreating. This is the electric slide of art watching.

Finally, there's the *Soft-Laugh-and-Nod*: self-explanatory. It's encouraged to mix nodding, smiling, a quick headshake, or a heavy sigh into the laughter. This will undercut everyone's own bullshit art ego because they will believe that someone understands or sees something in the art that they themselves have not yet found. Welcome to the mindfuck. Yes.

87

I follow Aimee around the room, rotating through my art survival techniques when I see myself on the wall. A small group gathers in front of it. Rembrandt is one of them.

I'm in an oval frame in the corner of the room, near the DJ booth. Without thinking, I execute the *Nose-to-Art* at an accelerated rate of motion. The chopographical art is of my world. Quite literally. It's me, Jeremy, driving my father's BMW while my father sits in the passenger seat. The photo looks too real to be a fake. I can't place the photo at first. I've never driven his car, or any car for that matter. I look closer. My father's head was cut and reattached to my body, clutching a book bag to my chest, a Limp Dick at my neck. My head on my father's body, Windsor knot wrapped tight. There is a price. $65.00. Title of the work: *Little Men.* That fucker.

Aimee doesn't get my frustration. She doesn't understand why I'm upset. My arms flail about, while she executes the *Chin-and-Lean.* I tell her how I have been plagiarized and that if she doesn't see it then she is not the girl I thought she was.

"Is that you?" she asks, shifting from her right to her left, looking retarded as one does doing the *Chin-and-Lean.*

I point to each of my heads—the real head and the chopography head. "That's me." I point to my bodies. "And that's me."

A security guard, some beefy, bald-headed fuck, approaches me. "No touching the artwork, sir."

"Who is the other person?" she asks, noting the other dissected body and head.

"My old man," I say. I lower my hands, which pacifies the security guard

"Mykel did such a good job. It's so seamless," she says. "You can't even tell."

"I don't like it," I say, tapping the canvas, first my head then Dad's body.

"It's art, Jeremy. It's expressive. It's not reality. It's the perception of reality."

"Hands," the security guard shouts.

"This is me," I say, tapping it. "Not you," I say. I flip him the middle finger. "I don't see a bald ass head in there, do you?" I tap the canvas again.

The guard comes at me.

"Okay," Aimee says, taking my hand.

"This water buffalo doesn't scare me. I have bacne that scares me more than him," I say.

"I think it's time to go," Aimee says, slipping her soft hand inside mine again. "It's time."

I look for Frank and Anthony and Father Vincent, but all I see are the Brothers.

A fucking familiar voice oozes out behind me.

"This is such a sweet scene. Like *Sleepless in Seattle* or some shit," Cam says. "Are you on a date?" he asks. Cam sees the chopography on the wall. "Little Men."

Five plaid monkeys flank us, all looking at my photo. Each wears a white polo shirt and some varying base color of plaid pants.

"Look at Gay Jeremy and his Gay Dad," Cam says. "Little Gay Men." He lisps and limps his wrist and does other shit that makes me want to cut off his hands and feet and head and throw his body in the Chesapeake Bay.

"Jeremy, I need you to listen to me," Aimee says. "Right now, in this moment, you need to decide what it is that you want to do."

She is right. I can't run forever. I can't hide forever. I can't pretend to go unseen. I need to stay in the moment. Have faith. Feel love. Hope for a miracle. Then I see my bus brother from another mother, Mykel.

Mykel counts cash at the door. A group of girls in short skirts and glittery tops hang out near him. They whistle at him every time he bends over. He takes several twenties from an older woman and hands her a red dot that she places on the art she purchased. I take my wallet out, count out cash, and hand it over to him.

"What did you think?" he asks, counting a wad of cash again for his group of admirers.

"You're good, man. I don't know how you do it. Maybe it's a black thing."

"Hey, maybe it is." He folds his cash and puts it in his pocket. "Where's your girl?"

"She's waiting for me. We're leaving. I just wanted to buy the *Little Men*."

"You can put a red dot on the frame and take it after the exhibit," he says.

"I want to take it now."

"Not possible," he says.

"Extra twenty," I say.

"After the show."

"Extra forty," I say.

Mykel checks his watch.

Jimmy Two stands with the group of girls off to the side, waiting for Mykel. The room is thinner now than it has been, as people make their way back down to the street. The girls move closer. They call out his name, sing-song. Sing it in songs and say what kind of lewd, sexual things they would do to him if they ever got him alone. He checks his watch again. Brother Lee steps between Mykel and the girls.

"Do not get distracted, Mykel," Brother Lee says, " You finish here and then you can go there."

"Not at all, Bill. I'm good. I'm right."

Mykel and Brother Lee shake hands.

"You really liked it though?" he asks.

"Little Men?"

"Because I know how much you hate people calling you that. It was all you talked about for a minute. But I had to name it a version of that name. That is you. You are it. And I needed you to know that."

"I am your little man," I say. "But your little man only."

"That's all I needed to hear, son." He takes back the red dot. "Just take the damn thing, while I get at these females."

I pull the framed piece down off the wall while Cam and his bitches heckle me through the trippy thump-a-dump music. One of them says, "Like gay father, like gayer son," or something that doesn't make any sense like that. I know I shouldn't. I know it's wrong. I know I'll regret it and will catch hell for it and know it goes against any and all art exhibit etiquette, but I hand my newly acquired art to Aimee and as we pass by the Plaid Fucks one last time and with the red mystery juice still in my hand, I flip the cup over and onto Cam's head. The red juice splashes down, soaking his hair and staining his crisp white polo shirt.

Stained fucking Monkey.

88

I run to the exit and down the stairs with Aimee following behind. We cross the cobblestone street to the abandoned police station, ducking through a hole in the fence, the same one Jackson told me about. I pull it back enough for Aimee to slip through. She passes off my art until she clears the other side and I follow. We crash through the unlocked front door, scaring a group of pigeons, putzing around inside. Feathers scatter and flutter. We close the door and press our backs to it, catching our breath. I peak through the filthy window and see the six fucks in the street looking for us. They run like the zombies in *28 Days Later*, fast, angry, though mentally they're closer in spirit to Romero's amblers. When they don't find us, they give up and return to the art exhibit.

"That was not smart," I say. "Not smart. Not smart."

"Definitely an understatement," she says.

Red emergency lights illuminate the station through windows on the second floor. I look up the long stairwell and listen for moaning and growling. Darkness devours everything.

"It's dark in here," she says.

"Horror movie dark."

"I can't imagine it during the day."

"Give me your hand," I say.

She holds out her hand and I grab it tight as we ascend the stairs from the foyer to the second floor. Cobwebs and bugs stretch and crawl along the walls. Beer bottles and condom wrappers and newspaper and rotting fruit and cans of tuna fish litter the floor.

Chairs are stacked into corners. Desks flipped over, creating forts. A mouse or a rat darts in front of us.

I feel like we're detectives investigating a crime scene. Tensions are high. Our jobs are on the line. The killer is out there. And it is up to us to solve the crime together. For the sake of all humanity. We work together, inspecting evidence, kneeling down to look closer. Check the blood, or lack thereof. Check the spatter. Spatter tells the story of the murder. Perp might still be on the premises. I'm ready to take him down to Hell.

Detective Jeremy Barker.

Aimee guides us down hallways like she's been here before, until we come upon a room overlooking the Inner Harbor. Light reflects off the black water in a halo. I imagine Franny and Jackson somewhere up here, grabbing at each other, sucking at each other, the way Jackson explained it happening, but when I see a rat the size of Dog I know he's full of shit. For one, Franny would never do anything in here when his apartment is right across the street. And for two, Jackson is afraid of rodents. Like a bitch.

We stand shoulder to shoulder, holding hands, looking out into the abyss of the harbor. I can see Federal Hill across the way and the lights of *The Prince Edward*. Sailboats and speedboats drift along, spotting the black hole with dots of light.

"I wish I could press pause right now," I say, putting *Little Men* on the floor.

"That's sweet." Her fingers lace further into mine.

"I want to be happy," I say.

"That's not asking for much," she says.

"And I want you to be happy, too."

We face each other. I know how to do this. I know what needs to be done. The how-to is imprinted in me like my DNA. I release her hand and rest mine at her waist.

"I collect women's magazines," I say. Light glints off broken glass on the floor. "I read them. I can tell you how to clean a stained toilet bowl with a can of Coke. I can tell you how to get marinara sauce out of a shag carpet. How to wear solids with stripes. Tell you what season your skin tone is color-wise. You are an Autumn, by the way. The best approaches to breastfeeding. How to break your housework up into a manageable schedule. The proper etiquette when it comes to canceling on a dinner party. I know about sex slavery. How to fight off a rapist. Which actors have the hottest abs in Hollywood. I know all of these things. And I want you to know that about me. Not later. I want you to know that about me right now."

"Well," she says. "If this is true, then you just raised the bar of first kiss expectation, exponentially."

And like a solar explosion, we kiss. Our tongues slide between lips. Stars bursting out in fading arches. It's a solar explosion, but within that, I can feel something else. Something familiar in a way that would make me miss it if we stop. We're tentative at first, then relaxed and exploratory. Wandering with a growing idea that we knew the way all along and we gain speed again. I'm a cosmic crash. This is the thing. I feel like everything could fall apart around us and we would outlast it all.

This kiss—one really long, really good, really French kiss.

Finally, a date.

89

Aimee and I wait in the foyer of the police station, peaking through the filth-stained window, looking for Cam and Plaids, but the street is empty—no one around. We leave the abandoned building and sneak back through the fence and walk along the pier of the Chesapeake. A cold breeze rolls off the chopping, black water. I take off my jacket and drape it over Aimee's shoulders. We walk to the end of the pier and cross the street. Aimee slides out of my jacket and hands it back to me as she rifles through her purse for her keys. I put *Little Men* at my feet as Aimee revs up the engine, setting out for Camden Yards to the light rail where I will take the train home. The car smells like marshmallows, some fancy black SUV monster machine that has automatic everything—TVs, DVD player, video gaming systems, the works.

"This shit's fully loaded," I say, playing with the flat-screen TV in the visor.

"My dad loves his SUV," she says. "He's a stay-at-home dad, which means he needs his tricked-out family van. Mom makes the moolah. She's a defense attorney."

"What does he do all day if he doesn't work?" I ask.

"He's a carpenter. Builds and designs stuff to-order, like hand-made furniture. He also cleans the house and makes dinner and picks me up from school and coaches my brother's high school baseball team. He used to play minor league baseball himself, so he's got a little giddy-up on his fastball, as he likes to say."

"A real family," I say. I hold my art in my lap and look at Dad and me and our fucked-up selves. No one's safe.

"I have a secret too," she says.

"I don't believe you."

"My dad's also an alcoholic." Aimee takes her hand away from mine. "He's not allowed to drive because his license has been revoked. So he stays at home and works with wood and cleans the house and makes us dinner." She laughs. "Fourteen months sober."

"What did he do?"

"He was drunk—vodka and Hawaiian Punch. He was going to drive the team bus to an away game when he ran a red light on his way to the school. There were two kids in the backseat of the car he hit. Everyone was banged up good, but thankfully they were okay. Mom left him. Took me and my brother and moved in with her mother. The judge revoked his license and he ended up serving ten months in jail."

"You are a complex thing," I say.

She says, "A compound bone fracture will always heal, but it takes re-breaking the bone to get it to heal in the right place."

90

The SUV jostles along the cobblestone street in front of the art exhibit as we slow to a stop. Several cars pull out of parked spots, holding up traffic. A door swings open and Mr. Rembrandt appears, walking quickly to a parked car, unlocking the door, checking his watch, and disappearing inside. His lights shock on and he, too, backs out into traffic, two cars in front of us. Finally, the line of traffic picks up and Aimee continues on toward Camden Yards. At the next red light, Mr. Rembrandt is only one car away from us.

"Where do you suppose he's going?" Aimee asks.

"No," I say.

"It could be fun," she says. "Come on. Let's be bad together. We don't even have to get out of the car."

"You ever follow someone before?" I ask.

"Never," she says. Then, "You?"

"We need to be sure that he doesn't see us, okay? This is serious."

"This first date just got even better," she says.

"We need to keep at least a car distance from him," I say.

"You're so nervous," she says. "This is a night of firsts. You should be excited about this. And if we're really good at this, we can open our own business."

We kiss quickly before the light turns green, but no tongue this time.

"Let's make a bet," she says. "Winner gets a kiss whenever they want, no matter the company, no matter how awkward, no matter how uncomfortable the circumstances." She thinks, stopping at a four-way stop and then proceeding through, speeding to catch up, before saying, "I bet he is en route to a booty call. Mr. Rembrandt is getting some tail."

"I bet not. I bet it's bigger than we think." I roll down the window for air—the cold air to keep me calm and collected and focused on what we are doing. "Drive slow," I say. "Drive very slow. We don't know where we'll end up."

Mr. Rembrandt moves like a shadow through the streets, past piles of garbage lining the gutters. We keep far enough back, the way we think spies would. We keep a distance in case he turns around.

He cuts through the Puerto Rican neighborhood—men and women dancing on the sidewalks to tinny salsa-type music from car stereos and boom boxes on stoops. A man smokes a cigarette and tries to coax women into joining, unsuccessfully.

Mr. Rembrandt passes the recently remodeled porn theaters and sex shops with neon-trimmed window displays with mannequins wearing purple strap-on dildos and hanging from sex swings bolted to the ceiling. The marquises to the porno theaters promote Sexy Saturdays with a matinee of one Coke, one candy, and one ticket for five bucks. The movies are *Fuck-motional* and *RoboTits III*. A street vendor sells exotic fruit next to several park benches where homeless men and women sleep sitting up, their grocery carts tied to their legs.

Mr. Rembrandt reaches the quiet community of Little Italy. Old men in slanted caps sit at glass tables outside their row homes, smoking stumpy, fat cigars, sipping on clear alcohol and tiny cups of coffee. Some play cards. Speak in Italian. Telling long-winded stories. Their friends, laughing. Old women gather inside, louder than the men, occasionally yelling through the screen doors to the men. The few children that are awake chase each other in and out of the parked cars, pointing flashlights at each other, yelling either *TAG, YOU'RE IT* or *NO, YOU MISSED ME.* Tourists step out from the Italian restaurants that smell of garlic and fried foods. Middle-aged men with slicked back hair and dark sport coats and women in bright dresses and unnecessarily tall high heels clip-clopping down the sidewalk. The men buy flowers from the peddlers selling over-priced single red roses. At a red light, a peddler approaches me and says, "Don't you want to buy your beautiful woman a rose?" I look away from him as he talks, hoping it hides what he's saying, but I'm fairly certain Aimee hears him, which makes me feel bad because I don't buy her one. The light turns green and we continue on.

We pass a parking lot and an empty building surrounded by barbed wire. Mr. Rembrandt crosses over a quiet street where a few whores flag down passing cars and pedestrians. The longer we keep going, the less I know where we are, and the farther back we need to keep in order to remain invisible as fewer cars are between us and him. He snakes through locked-up warehouses with broken glass windows and burnt brick until he finally turns down a side street where the homes are consumed by darkness and something else.

This is Tiller Drive.

X
28 DAYS LATER

(Release Date: June 27, 2002)

Directed by Danny Boyle

Written by Alex Garland

91

Aimee parks behind a dumpster, filled with debris and broken scaffolding, kills the headlights, but keeps the engine running.

Tiller Drive rolls out in front of us like a ghost town battle-field. Huge potholes crater the street like it had been bombed with heavy artillery. The street is empty except for the potholes. Immediately, I picture Goo Babies blood-screaming down the street. Two dozen abandoned row homes border the street on both sides, everything marked for demolition with notices stuck to the red brick. WARNING: WRECKING BALL. Cinderblocks and ply-wood cover where the windows and doors should be. Rembrandt's brake lights burn up in the black as he slows to a stop. Where the fuck is this guy going? In a wasteland of warehouses, Tiller Drive and the few streets that surround it will soon be leveled to dust. No one would find us back here. We are nowhere. The demolition notices don't lie—a wrecking ball waits patiently on the sidewalk, surrounded by a small army of Caterpillar construction trucks.

Rembrandt's car reaches the end of the block and parks. His brake lights stay lit, red oval eyes, casting a blood glow across the street. Aimee and I look at each other, our mouths open, our eyes wide.

"Where are we?" she asks. "I thought I knew. I thought this would be different."

"He can't be out here all alone," I say. "He's smarter than this, I know it." I look for any signs of light, from a highway or corner store or overlook or something but see nothing in any direction except blackness and the blood glow from Rembrandt's brake lights.

"Jeremy," Aimee says, her voice suddenly cracked. "He's not alone."

I follow her distracted eyes past the empty backseat to the road as a pair of headlights appear low to the ground. "What the fuck," I say. The car passes the last warehouse and the alley behind Tiller Drive when another pair of headlights pops up and another. "Get the fuck down," I say, grabbing Aimee's hand. We get low in our seats as white light shoots through the darkness and cuts through the SUV. I can hear the soft growl of each car engine as they pass us and turn onto Tiller Drive. A careful parade of cars is making its way through the bizarre backstreets of gutted warehouses to this condemned street. Aimee closes her eyes and mouths the Lord's Prayer, beginning again when she reaches the end. I time the head-lights in Mississippi seconds as they cut across the inside of the SUV and darkness rushes back in on us. I peek out through my passenger side window to see Tiller Drive reanimated.

Cars park on both sides of the street, but no one gets out. They park and wait. From this angle I can still see Mr. Rembrandt's car, but his brake lights are off. He appears to still be inside his car as well—a black shadow surrounded in darkness. Cars continue to coast onto Tiller for a bit until the entire street is full. Not an open space in sight.

Aimee opens her eyes and covers her mouth. She moves her hands only to ask me a question. "What do you see?"

"He's not alone anymore," I say. "They're everywhere."

Aimee makes fists with her hands and pushes up off her seat. We stare through the windshield, past the dumpster, to the block party.

A momentary calm settles over Tiller Drive, if only for the brief-est of moments, before the men come to life one by one. The men exit their vehicles in a staggered progression. Car doors slam. A foggy, yellow light flicks on above a stoop next to Rembrandt's car. Rembrandt stands and stretches, arching his back with his arms over his head, before pulling something over his head, covering his face. He hops a pothole and approaches the well-lit stoop. As he enters the yellow light, he looks back in our direction, like he knows he's being followed, like he can sense something's wrong. This is when we see it—Rembrandt is wearing some kind of ski mask—bright blue. Two enormous men wearing black masks flank him—monster men. Their masks are unforgettably executioner's masks, half-shading the face, sinister, protecting the eyes and mouth. They exchange words—God only knows what—before Rembrandt disappears into the foggy, yellow light.

Aimee and I sit back in our seats and say nothing, listening to car doors continue to slam down Tiller Drive. Nothing makes sense. The mathematics don't add up. Not this street. Not the men. Not Rembrandt. None of it.

"You're going to hate me," I say.

"I really, really am, aren't I?"

"Do you want me to apologize now or later?"

"Jesus Christ, Jeremy."

"Stay close."

We slip out of the SUV and work our way up the sidewalk, hiding behind the parked cars, only advancing if the cars are empty. It doesn't take long for us to find the foggy, yellow light and see the entrance into a house at the end of the block. The men approach the light too, each wearing black masks of varying shapes and sizes, some covering their whole heads, others covering only their eyes. The men enter the house like ghosts—disappearing like Rembrandt. The two beefcake motherfuckers, the monster men, they stand guard at the base of the stoop, sizing up the masked men who bow their heads before them. Some men have to bow their heads longer than others, but everyone eventually ascends the stairs. Everyone, eventually, enters the house. No matter the man.

A suit with a Half-Windsor tied loose around his neck, carrying a brief case, wears a full head executioner's mask. A man in jeans and a plain white T-shirt and shaggy hair. A man exits a jeep and stands by his car. He doesn't go in the house. Instead, he checks his fingernails, digging out dirt. He looks at himself in the window of his car and adjusts his mask. He lights a cigarette, exhales smoke, and walks to the house. Another man appears, this one black, and he wears one of those old-timer caps with his mask and carries a cane. Another man appears—old, but white with wispy hair and pants pulled up too high to his old man tits. A fat man in a tracksuit. A guy in flip-flops. A frat boy with a hemp necklace. A uniformed policeman minus his belt of weapons. An Asian man in ripped jeans and mustache. Another suit. Another cop. Men wearing sunglasses over their masks, further protecting their identity.

Gone. Gone. Gone.

Fucking gone.

All of them.

These men.

Gone. Gone. Gone.

The air hangs heavy and still on Tiller Drive, like a corpse—the stench of bleach whipping around us. Aimee grabs my shirt and points to the boarded-up windows next to the stoop. A familiar sign has been hammered into plywood, but from the looks of it the sign has been there for a long time—washed-out color, faded lettering. The sign is clearly no longer an option for this building or any building on Tiller Drive. The sign is a realtor sign. The sign is for my father. It reads: FOR SALE. PLEASE CONTACT BALLENTINE BARKER, AGENT.

"I need to get inside," I say. My father's property seems to be a meeting place for my English teacher and other whackjobs to wear executioner masks and do what exactly? Fuck each other senseless in an orgy? Fight each other for the fuck of it? Too many movie clichés present themselves as possible answers.

"I'm only going to say this once and hopefully you take me at my word. I mean this with all of the love in the world," she says. "Don't be a fucking moron."

My heart feels like a slug crawling out of a salt bath.

"You can walk away. We can forget together. Move on and never look back." Aimee touches my cheeks. "No one has to know about this but us."

I cover her hands with my own and kiss her fingers. They smell like vanilla sugar. I kiss them until she pulls away. She knows that I'm not forgetting anything anytime soon. We make our way back to the SUV, sticking to the shadows of Tiller Drive, passing only empty cars.

"There's an alley not far from here," she says. "It's your only chance to do this."

"You're going to abandon me here," I say.

"You'll just have to trust me," she says, offering me her hand. "Because you really don't have any other choice." She's right. I don't. So I accept her hand into mine and laugh at the fact that I was never going to deny her touch. Aimee revs the engine in short bursts and rolls down the windows, before banging a sharp U-turn away from Tiller Drive, before cutting a hard left into a black hole between two buildings—the alley.

The alley is narrow, barely wide enough to fit the car, the side mirrors inches from bent chain-link fences protecting the back-yards of the row homes. A stale, decaying smell lifts out of each con-crete yard from both the loose and collected garbage piling up; the discarded machinery, like refrigerators and dryers; the abandoned gardens overrun with ivy and weeds and overgrown crabapple trees. The alley street grows wider—a V-shape. Aimee turns off the headlights again, always concerned with going unseen, minimizing our exposure to the masked men. Broken glass crunches under the tires. We pass a mangled, wheel-less shopping cart, empty. Chest-high grass grows up through the cement along the rust-chewed fences. A warm breeze rolls over the broken buildings, carrying away the stale stench for a moment. There is no life back here, no sign of men in masks, only us and the remnants of the end of things

We pass the house.

Aimee pumps the brake, forcing the car to a dead-stop, jolting us forward. Baseball bats slide out from a canvas bag in the back. A chain-link fence is propped open, creating a makeshift driveway where a big, black van with tinted windows is purposefully parked, backed up against the house, facing out into the alley, ready for a getaway. Two, dying trees quarantine the van by the house. Hazy, yellow light escapes at the edges of the plywood in the windows on the first and second floor of the house. A fire escape zigzags up the back of the building, rising up to the second floor and the roof. The farther up the ladder goes, the less light exists.

This is the house.

"Keep the engine running," I say, as Aimee parks the SUV up the street from the house and out of sight. "If anyone comes out of that house, floor it and don't look back."

"Be safe," she says.

"Should we kiss?" I ask.

"When you come back," she says.

I reach behind my seat, feeling around on the floor until I find it—my beautiful bastard, a wooden, Cal Ripken Signature Louisville Slugger baseball bat.

Aimee's dad won't mind if I borrow his bat. I'm protecting his daughter. Being Chivalrous and shit.

Lock-and-load.

92

I choke up on the bat and hold it high, stepping carefully and slowly through the backyard. Masked men could be anywhere. The black van with tinted windows is backed up all the way to French double doors on the first floor of the house, the doors reinforced with thick sheets of plywood. I place a palm on the plywood and push, but nothing happens. It doesn't bend at all. No weakness exists. Foggy, yellow light lurks beneath the wood, coming from inside. Where the fuck did everyone go? What were they doing in there? There's another door on the side of the house, but that is closed off too. Every window and door appear impenetrable, the house of masked men and yellow light.

The black van is shiny in the low yellow glow of the house and dent-free with an extended back cab capable of extra storage. The license plate is nothing I've ever seen; maybe these are what people call "dealer's tags," random numbers and letters on a cardboard square of paper. I tap on the hood, feeling for heat, but the hood is cold, cold, cold, dead cold. The van has easily been here for hours, at least. Rembrandt only just arrived to the house and he seems to be the guest of freaking honor, so that begs the question—who is responsible for this van and what is inside? Are the meatheads in executioner masks the owners? I yank on the silver handle of the driver and passenger doors, but both are supremely fucking locked. I cup my hands at my eyes and press my face into the black glass of the passenger window, hoping for a glimpse of something, but all I see is darkness. For a moment, I have a daymare where the side door slides open and vicious, hungry, angry zombie dogs leap out at me, snarling, growling, gnashing their fangy teeth. They attack and rip into my flesh, but even in my daymare I can't bring myself to bash the dogs with my bat. Only humans deserve the type of pain this bat can yield. I pull on the silver handle of the side door, but this also does not open. I work my way around to the double doors of the van. I choke up on the bat and slip the base of the bat into the handle, ready to yank it open and confront whatever is inside. I Mississippi count. One Mississippi. Two Mississippi. Three Mississippi. FOUR! I throw myself into a backwards movement, pulling with everything I can muster, and the door swings free in a loud squeak and stays open. The smooth wood of the bat taps along my fingers, as they spider down the handle and cock it back. I attack the van, scaring out the big bad by swinging blindly inside, and immediately connect with a metal toolbox, which sends silver vibrations into my forearms. The back is not exactly empty, but is vacant of men.

Heavy sheets of plastic—thicker than shower-liner, tougher than leather—are folded into squares, like a comforter, and stacked neatly in the back. I open the metal toolbox and find it filled with nothing but nails. I feel around on the floor of the van and make out the shape of a nail gun. These guys have this place fortified. There's a huge amount of open space in the van, which means something else is missing, something else is being used. I move up into the front cab of the van and flip through the visors and glove box but don't find anything. My foot snags the strap of a book bag behind the driver's side. I put down the bat and unzip the teeth— various executioner masks. It's the only thing missing, so I grab one from the bottom of the bag and pull it over my head. I close up the back doors of the van and look at my reflection in the black shine. I'm one step closer to becoming one of them.

Now all that remains is finding a way inside.

93

A retractable ladder is wedged up into the small metal landing of the fire escape, running up the side of the house. Stairs rise up from the landing. I jump several times, trying to grab the bottom rung of the ladder, but my lack of athleticism and height makes this impossible. I could be at this all day and never touch the damn thing.

I center myself under the ladder. I swing the bat and hit the rung to see if it will drop with a shock. Instead, the bat makes a deep and loud *clang*. Hard vibrations shutter through my body, from my hands to my teeth to my toes. There's nothing here to stand on. No empty boxes or gardening cabinets. No chairs or loose bricks. The back of the house is pristine.

I climb up the van from the front bumper, over the hood and up the windshield. I stand at the van's back edge, just over the double doors.

First I toss the bat, which hits the side of the house and clatters to the landing.

I won't count. It needs to happen fast and be exact. My legs need to power me up and to my target. I think of Coach O'Bannon— stiff back, arms over head, bend the knees, bounce, feet at the edge, goddamnit, and launch.

I rocket toward the ladder.

But my aim is off. My forearms slam against the bottom rung and I twist and grab to take hold of the rung with my hands and as I do my arms are nearly wrenched from their sockets. Then I'm just hanging there, arms in a death grip.

I feel a shudder, a snap, a collapse, but can't tell if it's in my body or not. Then I feel it—the ladder yanks loose, unhinging from the landing of the fire escape, and slides down at an angle. Or not sliding: a single, deep slice. Another shudder. Another snap. And the ladder freezes again. White spots explode everywhere.

Then all is still. I'm just dangling, an inch or two off the ground. I can just touch the tips of my toes to the ground, holding the rung.

Hand over hand, I pull myself up the ladder until I can get a foot on the bottom rung. Then it's easy: I'm up on the landing. On two flat feet again, with my bat in my hands.

Two windows covered in plywood are within reach of the landing. I press on the first one with my hand and feel for weaknesses in the wood, but like the others, the wood is thick and nailed deep into the frame of the house. I don't even bother with it and move to the next window. I press on the wood again, expecting the same resistant result. This time the wood shifts in the sill, but only enough to notice the difference, the bottom corner denting in a bit. This is the window that'll work, if any of them work at all. In a short and fast swing, I slam the butt of the bat into the corner of the wood like a battering ram and it bashes through. Rotten wood flakes away around me. This is my savior—termites. I slam the butt into the corner above my hole and half of the plywood window now shatters away at my feet. I bash a few more times on the remaining half of plywood and snap off enough for me to fit through. I fit my arms and upper body in first, before pulling my legs up behind me, easing the plywood back into place, no one the wiser.

Inside the window frame where many years ago an actual window used to exist, darkness now was landlord. I hold my hands out in front of me and feel a cold plastic sheet, slick from moisture, pulled tight across the frame. My hands pull apart the plastic, ripping a hole wide enough for me to get though. The fuzzy, yellow light cuts through the hole. The open window is a small step down as I climb into an empty upstairs room. It, too, is completely wrapped in plastic.

I am inside the house.

94

The second floor of the house is empty and needlessly protected. There is one immediate detail, second to the vacancy, that triggers me to choke up on the bat—every square inch is covered in heavy plastic. The kind used in construction sites to keep the workers' boots from scuffing up the floors. The kind used in homes to paintproof shit from being stained with driblets and drops. It covers everything. Plastic covers the hardwood floors and expertly sticks to the stairs. It rises up the red brick walls and across the ceiling in tight overlapping lanes. It wraps the banister like Christmas garland. Not a smidge—nothing is exposed. Someone spent a patient eternity covering every inch of this damn place. I know the house isn't empty, but it is. For now. In this very moment all is noiseless. No crisp crinkling of plastic under quick feet—nothing.

I remember the homemade video. I remember the similar seeming plastic on the wall and floor on that homemade video. This is that same exact place. I am there. That is here. In the house, I feel like the inside of an IV bag.

An overpowering chemical stench—bleach—whips up and burns my eyes and the insides of my mouth and nose. I snort acidic fumes. Reminds me of how Dad describes the first time he smelled napalm, the way the petrol fumes lingered for days across the village, burning exposed skin, searing ungoggled eyes—those hazy, wavy ripples on lonesome desert highways. He said it hurt to breathe the air, but that he got used to it. He said the smell covered the smell of something much worse. The end.

Another hallway: empty bedroom, dressing room, bathroom,

and smaller room or den. More work lamps lay in corners, lighting contained patches of space, but encouraging the shadows to devour the rest. I reach the bathroom off of the hallway and step through the plastic covered doorway, patting the wall with my hand. A light switch. My fingers dig through the crisscrossed lanes of thick plastic. Flick on the light.

Sharp flourescent light cuts away the darkness. Plastic runs over the tiled floor I can see underneath. Hugs the toilet bowl and tank. Lines the in's and out's of the claw-foot bathtub. Over the walls and ceiling and small oval mirror above the sink. My reflection distorts through the plastic. I have an eggplant-shaped head and wide cucumber slices for eyes. That sick, chemical stench rears back and attacks. Stronger this time. Taste it on my lips. Smoky fire-like fumes scourge. My eyes well with emotionless tears. My nose leaks a windy trail of blood to my mouth. I spit onto the plastic. People say that blood tastes like pennies. It doesn't. It tastes like quarters. The room shifts. It tilts. I lean into the wall, steadying myself, waiting for the impairment to pass. When it does, I see it in the sink. I don't believe it at first. I think the fumes are making me hallucinate. I lower my bat to the floor and push off the wall propelling myself to the sink, placing my palms on either side of the spigot, leaning down for a closer look, waiting for it to disappear. But it doesn't. It only becomes more real. My head no longer feels connected to my neck, snapping down by force of gravity. The stench thickens. There. On the counter. Surgical equipment on a silver tray. Several sizes of scalpels in ascending order of blade length. Metal clamps. Unused gauze. A box of plastic gloves. Safety goggles.

And in the sink, the centerpiece of it all.

A hairless human foot, severed just above the ankle, rests heel down in the pit of the sink. Spongy bone pokes through the top, revealing a single clean cut. No evidence of splintered or fractured bone. Red, raw muscle hugs the insides. Five toes with trimmed, unpainted toenails. The skin color is a faded and aged piss yellow. A raw breast of chicken cutlet left out over night. Dark brown lines crack beneath the dried surface of the skin. Bloated blue veins run deeper but are visible just the same. It must be a fake. Impossibly real. I poke it with my finger and it feels warm, fresh, detached. Dry heaving sets in. Voices in the hallway. Masked men arriving below. I unflick the light and grab at the door, fucking wrapped in plastic too, and swing it shut in a single, dragging crunch of plastic. I close it close enough to all the way, leaving a tiny sliver open and stand behind it, listening for the men but overpowered by my careless breathing.

I am okay.

I am not okay.

The men in masks crunch across the plastic and up the stairs to the second floor.

" There's no way anybody got in up here."

"I know that and you know that, but for some reason he doesn't know that."

"The paranoid fuck. Thinks he's being followed."

They pass the bathroom and enter another room and codes come crashing down.

ZSC #1.
ZSC #2.
ZSC #3.
ZSC #4.
ZSC #5.

95

I open the door and am out of the bathroom, out of the black, and down the hallway. Pounding down the stairs. Through to the vacant family room.

Everything covered in plastic.

I stand in the foyer and stare straight through: foyer, fireplace room, family room, stairs, kitchen. No furniture, but a wide open, narrow space. No sound. Soft, yellow light beaming from work lamps tossed into corners. This space is void. Plastic bunches under my feet. I drop my bat, and it whacks the floor with increasing speed until it settles into a dead stop.

Leave, I hear that inner boy scream. *Leave.*

I reach the place in the house where the front door should be, but it's too late—the door is gone. I can't find it—disappeared behind a wall of plastic. I rip at the exposed edges, pulling away sheet after sheet, until I touch the doorframe and fumble at the locks—bolted shut and a padlock surgically implanted as added prevention. I move to the front windows, ripping and pulling, but can see the plywood through the plastic. The house is on lockdown. There is no way out. I pick up the bat and stare back down the hallway of the house. This must be how ghosts feel. I have to go back through.

I pass through the family room, toward the kitchen and the French double doors. The backyard. The van. Aimee. Just on the other side of those doors and through the reinforced plywood. The yellow light upstairs shuts off. Then, the kitchen. The front of the house.

I hear a man somewhere say, "It's the Blackout."

Light spills out from only one door, leading to a staircase that spirals down, all covered in plastic. I keep the baseball bat low and at my side, which is completely unseen under the darkness. I move quickly to the door and pass through alone, so no one spots my weapon.

I say, "What the fuck are you doing, Jeremy?"

I say, "Why are you talking to yourself, asshole?"

I think of all the movies—zombie and otherwise—where someone talks out loud to themselves as they do something completely moronic. I am that guy right now. Talking to myself. Being a fucking moron.

One could go so far as to call it rage.

96

I descend the small, spiral staircase. More plastic over unfinished walls of exposed pink insulation, wood beams, and electrical wiring. The chemical stench returns. At the bottom, a dirt floor covered in plastic. The room is divided somehow with yellow lighting the rafters of the basement and darkness below.

I count them, a room of thirty at least. Maybe more. Hard to say. No one talks, really. Some whisper. Some definitely whisper. The men shuffle and move, making room for each other. No one familiar or friendly enough to show signs of recognition. They all look the same. I catch one man watching me, his eyes bloodshot. He opens his mouth and wags a mangled stump of a tongue through his mask hole. I think of Dad and Vietnam and his necklace of tongues. I avoid. Masked men cram together, standing in the basement surrounded in silence, embracing the blackout like it's some kind of religious experience. I keep the bat behind me and stay towards the back of the room, avoiding any kind of direct contact.

I look to the man in front of me. To his arms. To his hands. He, missing all five of his fingers on both hands, like they'd been blown off with handgun. The man next to him, missing the lower half of his left leg, just below the knee—stump. Another lifts his mask to wipe sweat from under his eyes to reveal that he has no nose—a giant crater where it should be—like an inverted stalk of broccoli. One has an arm shaped like the tip of a hockey stick, his elbow the last bit of himself—a nub rotating around without direction. Another leans on a black metal crutch—red T-shirt and plaid shorts, one hairy leg fine with a shoe on a foot, the other leg

gone as if erased by the pink rubber end of a pencil, the fabric of
his shorts where his missing left should be pinned over to the side,
covering his hip area, all that remains. A man in a shiny, silk suit
with a Windsor knot and a gold watch around his wrist and slicked
back hair doesn't wear a mask at all, at least not yet. He removes an
eye-patch, tucking it into his pocket—his socket all that is left, no
eyeball, just a collapsed flap of black skin, no longer needed. He has
scars on his eye, wide and thick and pink over a black-red patch of
skin. He doesn't stop smiling at no one in particular as he slides a
leather mask over his face, his dead eye still peeking out from inside.
A kid in a hemp necklace lifts the side of his mask to itch where his
ear used to be but now only has a tiny maze of exposed cartilage
canals, like one of those mazes in a kids' magazine. Another man
cracks his knuckles without thumbs, missing on either hand. One
of the policemen licks his lips. He opens his mouth wide to show
bottom teeth, but none up top, only a pink ring of flesh where they
used to be as his tongue lathers it back and forth. Another man on
crutches has his pants cuffed at his ankle because he has no feet.
Another man has no lips, his face shaved back to big gums and
yellowed teeth." We could edit to be "Another man has no lips, his
face shaved back to big gums and yellowed teeth, his mask crooked
across his face, but perfectly placed to advertise his facial revision.
Another, armless with a book bag on his back. Another without
a lower jaw—gone. Only a row of top teeth to show for himself,
underlining a masked face and two angry eyes, anxious for something to begin.

A light bulb hangs from a wood beam at the front of the room
above a raised stage. We wait like teenagers wait at a concert. The
objects on the stage gutpunch—medical equipment, electrodes and
wires, a tray of IV bags, a bed wrapped in plastic.

This is the set of the Rembrandt video—*Sublimation*.

Sound picks up. Men say the word, "move." Plastic crunches
under their feet as they separate. Moses must be parting the Red
Sea as the men move aside, making room for someone to pass
through. He wears a blue executioner's mask. Him. Rembrandt. He

glides down the aisle to an opening under the light on the stage. He wears the same dark jeans and leather jacket from earlier. He paces like a general, stopping to tug on the plastic running up the wall and is content when it doesn't come undone. He moves to the left of the center of the stage and holds up the book he had been read- ing earlier, the book he had given Dad—*Notes from Underground*.

The men are silent and alive.

"I am a sick man," he says loud and heavy like a sledgehammer. There is little inflection, only volume and content. "I am a wicked man."

The men repeat the words *sick* and *wicked*, saying them over and over and over and over.

"We are sick men." He walks to the far side of the stage. "We are but wicked men." He crosses along the front now, slow. "This is what we are in our hearts as men. We are unattractive and without hope."

The men say, "Yes."

"We are base things. We don't know what to name what we are. They think they do, though. They call us what they think we are, but they don't know. The difference is that we know that it hurts. That there is no treatment for our sickness. There is no cure. We know this. But we don't let this keep us from being who we are. Do we, gentlemen?"

The men say, "No."

"Because we have this. We have others. Transgression. We are superstitious in the extremity of things. We ask the world to embrace us and our supreme wickedness, our contagious selves." He claps once. "They will not be so good to understand us, sirs, gentlemen, but we understand this. *You* understand this. We are sick and wicked men. And this is all we know how to be."

The men repeat *sick* and *wicked*.

Rembrandt loves a good call and response. The sick fuck. He continues, hovering over the surgical tray of instruments.

"I will not, of course, be able to stand here and preach to you or explain to you precisely who is going to suffer tonight or in the larger context of life out there from this wickedness; we know perfectly well that we will fuck things up. I am a wicked civilian. But do you know the point of ourselves as wicked monsters, gentlemen? How the sickness takes us away from ourselves? The whole thing, that we were simply frightening the children and pleasing ourselves with it, like rabid dogs, foaming at the mouth of experience, a stinking mess, made up of its doubts, emotions, and of the contempt spat upon it by the direct men of action who stand solemnly about it as judges and arbitrators, laughing at it till their healthy sides ache. We are at the edge of things. At the crux of it all." He throws the book against the wall. It slides down the plastic. "But now it's time." He points to a man in full green surgical scrubs next to the stage—cap, mask, short-sleeve shirt, and pants. "Doc, bring me some little man of ourselves. Maybe it'll be enough to ease us a bit and calm us down. Cure us, if only for a minute."

The man is a doctor, someone familiar with the cult of things around here. He doesn't wear an executioner's mask, but he doesn't have to. The doctor steps onto the stage and pulls back a sheet of plastic at the far end that reveals a room hidden away and knocks once before opening it. A gurney rolls through, pushed by another masked man, and the room disappears again as the door closes and the plastic drops back down into place. Another doctor. There are two of them and they bookend the gurney, tending to their own.

97

There's a body on the gurney.

It's covered in a sheet of plastic—mask on the face, a plastic tube stuffed down his throat, poking out of his mouth. The person is asleep, unconscious. The doctors lift the body from the gurney and lay it on the bed. They roll down the plastic sheet and tie the body down with long leather restraints, crossing them over the forehead, chest, stomach, and thighs. It is a man and the man is fully naked on the bed except for his mask. We can see his dick, limp. He's strapped down. Restrained for something that's coming. The doctors hook the machine up to the body—sticking electrodes to the skin, running wires into the machine to monitor shit. An IV drips down a tube and through a needle in an arm vein. It happens fast, like they've done it a hundred times before, and Rembrandt waits off to the side in his blue mask. The doctors finish prepping the body and connect the open tube coming out of his throat to a machine that keeps him breathing and position the bed on the stage.

Rembrandt then strolls out and takes point center.

I look around for a camera and find a tripod across the room, red light flickering. This is what they film. This is the Rembrandt DVD. Mr. Rembrandt approaches the bed. He unrolls a case, horizontally on the body, filled with knives and serrated objects resting safely in their sleeves. Scalpels and clamps and God knows what all else. He lifts the case and hangs it from hooks off stage right, still in clear view, the yellow light glinting now off the steel.

"We are alone, but we are never really alone. We are only one, but we are many more than that," Rembrandt says. "We must help each other, brothers. Some call it *God's Will. Devil's work. Fate. Destiny*. It amounts to futile garbage." Rembrandt hovers over the surgical tools, his fingers grazing the handle of each instrument. "We live a predetermined life, brothers, gentlemen, sirs. An inevitable existence of one, no matter how many exist under our roof." He selects a stainless steel serrated knife several inches long and holds it up into the light, reflecting. "A name matters nothing but as an identifier. What we seek is absolution from this time. What we seek is beyond a higher power, a being by choice. What we seek is reckoning in this life. What we desire is an uncommon valor under a watchful eye. A code—this is it and it is all we have—a code. Wholeness. Oneness. Transgression. Without the slowed process of phases. Skip the burn and get right to the healing." Rembrandt is at the man's head now and he lowers the knife to the man's throat, slides it up through the fabric, and cuts away the mask to reveal the face—a normal man, no different than any other man except with both eyes taped shut and a tube down his throat. He is still asleep. "Fractured, bitter, endless pieces familiarized into a singular thing. I'm talking about commitment. The Grand Sublimation. Of Spirit. Of Will. Of Fate. Of Destiny. Bullshit, I say. Bullshit, they know. One Code. One Path. Without it, we are but base animals."

The masked men shout, "Yes."

Rembrandt continues, "Do we agree, gentlemen?"

A wall of deep and heavy male voices responds, "Yes."

Rembrandt continues. "Gentlemen, we are men who gun for a goal and maybe only a brick wall can stop him dead in his tracks."

The men respond, "Yes."

Rembrandt retrieves an electric drill and slides a flat circular blade to the tip. He squeezes the trigger and the blade sings. Rembrandt continues. "We are stupid beings, I won't argue with you about that, but perhaps a normal man ought to be stupid? Perhaps it's even a very beautiful thing. There it is again, thing, a thing. Ultimately unknown."

The men respond, "Yes."

The buzzing starts as the blade spins. Rembrandt leans over the man and the blade changes pitch and screeches, slicing through skin and muscle until it hits bone. I turn away, lifting my mask in time as I vomit against the back wall—bile, dark green, fuck. This means I'll be dry heaving if this continues much longer. The man in the bed thrashes awake and fights against the restraints, gagging and choking on the tube stuffed down his throat. The doctors struggle to keep him down as the man on the bed twists. The blade never stops slicing.

Rembrandt leans into the circular blade, forcing it through the leg, but I'm not sure where on the leg until the man in front of me steps aside and lifts his mask to vomit too and it is only then that I can see and wish that I never had. Men close to the stage are covered in the man's black blood—spraying, pumping, pouring out from the jagged amputation just below the kneecap as the lower leg snaps off and away from the body. The buzzing stops, blood still flying off the blade as it spins, and as it winds down it ends in a single tragic jutting silence. Nothing more. No words. Black blood pumps out of the man's exposed knee, the lower part of his leg separated and lifeless on the table. The man fights less now, just moaning and gagging as he loses more blood.

I squat down, leaning away from the crowd. I let my stomach squeeze in on itself like a spasming muscle, but nothing comes up except gags. I cover my eyes with my hand as I turn back to the crowd and catch a glimpse of Rembrandt lifting the leg into the air like a newborn baby, blood pouring off the limb. Christ. He says, "Oh, absurdity of absurdities!"

The men respond with an avalanche of sound, rising up and crashing down—a collective primal scream. A communal prayer. One voice. A release. They raise fists into the air, pumping them. Some others rub their erect dicks, humping air. Everyone, however, screams and none of them stop screaming until Rembrandt lowers the leg, a cue, dialing down the volume.

A fever breaks out in my body, sweat pouring out of me. I lift my mask a bit to breath, but the sickfuck stench chokes me worse when my mask comes off, so I jam it back down.

He says, "How much better it is to understand it all, to recognize it all, all the impossibilities and the stone wall; that even for the stone wall you are yourself somehow to blame, though again it is as clear as day you are not to blame in the least, and therefore grinding your teeth in silent impotence to sink into luxurious inertia, brooding on the fact that there is no one even for you to feel vindictive against, that you have not, and perhaps never will have, an object for your spite."

I look away. I want to stop this whole thing, but can't. The doctors wrap him in blankets; shoot him up with God knows what. One doctor lights the end of a blowtorch, a thin blue flame firing. He aims it at the wound, searing it shut. The man on the bed rises up in a voiceless scream as the doctors fight to keep him down, and the blowtorch fully closes off the skin. The room stinks of burnt pig.

Rembrandt says, "Things finally come down to the business of revenge itself." His voice changes, taking registration. "Month— September. Day—Fourth. Sublimation one—Samuel Rustom." He ejects the blood-soaked blade from his electric drill and dips the blade in a bucket of scalding water nearby, steam pouring off the top. He raises it into the light after—a clean, brand new blade, ready for round two.

98

I take self-inventory, but all I can focus on is breathing to calm my nerves and keep from vomiting more air. No one speaks. Some hyperventilate, gasping, fighting for air. A handful have their dicks out, erect, and carefully stroke without expression. Rembrandt walks to the center of the stage and wipes his hands with a towel, then claps in succession, like in class, and keeps clapping until the plastic drape opens and the secret room appears and the door opens and another gurney is pushed through covered in plastic.

The surgical prep routine is the same as before, and I choose not to watch.

Rembrandt cuts away the mask from the man's head, but I cannot see his face from this distance. Rembrandt says, "We are but what we are—monsters—and cannot be a thing to be stopped unless presented with the opportunity of force."

The men respond, "Yes."

I say nothing.

Rembrandt eyes the surgical tools and lifts what looks to be a stainless steel S-shaped blade. He walks around the table and points to the body. . Rembrandt continues. "Beauty. Ignorance. Isolation. Rapture. These are what we know to be true."

The men respond, "Yes."

I don't say shit.

The plastic still covers most of his body. For a flashing moment, I see his thick head of hair and how his eyes are taped shut and the tube jammed down his throat into his lungs.

Rembrandt angles the S-shaped blade and chokes up on the handle. Silence cuts across the room. Not a sound. We watch, wide-eyed. Some smile. One wags his tongue. Rembrandt tilts the blade forward, then back, marking the skin with thin slices, like he's outlining his intended target. Blood seeps out slowly from the cuts. He raises the blade above his head, before lowering it slow again to the markings. Like he is chopping wood, aiming with practice swings first. He exhales and looks up. The light surrounds and swallows him. Controlled. Then. One more time. And one more test—up and down. The blade at his wrist. His eyes close. More breathing. More control. Then. They open. His eyes black. Then. A gut growl. The blade pulls back, glinting the light. The blade swings down. Rembrandt is up on his feet, his body behind the force, bringing it down with force. Leverage. Then. Contact. The blade chops through skin and bone like butter. Striking through to the bed with a heavy thud. Followed by a soft *ching*. The hand. Scrubbed raw. A dirty instrument. Now separate from his body. Flops to the floor like a wet and dirty rag.

My legs buckle and collapse to the floor, covered in plastic and sprayed with black blood. I scramble to gather myself, using the bat as a crutch. I am not the only one. One man stands dead center in front of the stage and cries, weeping uncontrollably.

Then, the man on the table erupts with life, flailing, shaking with seizure like movements, shaking blood from himself like water from a wet dog. Red streams of blood pump out in multiple sprays from his wound. Rembrandt—quiet. The only real sounds are of the plastic—the soft spray of blood in synchronized spurts as it hits. Plastic crunching under our feet. The man on the bed screams and gags and coughs through the tube. Just the way one would imagine it. A different man, one across from me, vomits onto the plastic covered floor.

Someone else says, "My Jesus."

Rembrandt picks the hand up off the floor and says, "Oh, absurdity of absurdities!"

The men in the basement explode, louder this time, in screams, war cries, bigger than before, infinite. They raise their fists, shake them, pump them, until Rembrandt lowers the lost hand.

Rembrandt says, ". . . that you never will have an object for your spite. A sleight of hand. A bit of juggling. Card-sharper's trick. It's simply a mess. No knowing what and no knowing who, but in spite of all these uncertainties, still there is an ache in you, and the more you do not know, the worse the ache. Oh, the worse." He looks over the masked men in the room. He says, "This is the business itself—to come at last to the deed itself, to the very act of revenge." Then he says, "Month—September. Day—Fourth. Sublimation two—Ballentine Barker."

99

This can't be him. That couldn't be him. Not my dad. This cannot be it.

The room of men step away, leaving the doctors to attend to the injury. The blowtorch is lit and aimed at the wound, scorching it closed. Dad screams, gagging.

"No," I say, ripping off my mask and charging the stage, slamming into men along the way, shoving them, telling them to fucking move. Rembrandt is startled and turns to see me racing toward him, but I'm sure he doesn't know it's me. I jump up on to the stage but misjudge it and crash down, hitting my shin on the edge of the stage, but keep moving, taking a limp with me. The room which had been growing louder with each amputation is suddenly quiet again. All eyes locked into place. On me. On stage.

I stand and grab my bat, swinging it back and forth—a warning to keep the fuck back. I hold it low and look up at Rembrandt, the blue-masked motherfucker standing in front of me, letting him see me for the first time.

"Take it in. Look at me, you fuck," I say, growling at him. "All of you sick fucks. Back away from me. Back away from my dad."

Men move into place around the stage, ready to watch something new, something spontaneous and off-script. Rembrandt doesn't say anything but rather tilts his head instead. I move towards Dad and swing the bat at the doctors who had been cleaning him up. They jump back, the bat making a whipping sound through the air. Dad slumps on the gurney, crying now. Tears want to surface in my face. My voice sounds like I'm crying, even though I'm not. But there's a block in me, a pressure keeping it all in. I swing the bat around me again, keeping people back, even though no one is moving in on us. Spots appear again. Maybe a side effect of Ritalin withdrawal. Maybe a side effect of what I've just seen.

"Stay the fuck back. Don't you fucking come near me." I look back at him and feel the rush, the surge of something overwhelming and powerful come over me. "Who the fuck are you people? This isn't what you are supposed to do with yourselves. Dad, no. No, no, no."

Rembrandt steps forward, his hands in the air in surrender. "I think it best if you let us help him. He is losing a lot of blood and will surely die if our doctors do not intercede."

A surge of pain rises in Dad behind me as he explodes again. His body convulsing. A chicken without a head. Flailing. Fighting to be free. I stay a ways from him. His bandage is loose and only barely begun. Dad doesn't ask for help. He doesn't say *help me* or *why* or *take me to a hospital* or *I fucking hate you* or *you fucking bastards* or *get me out of here*. Instead, he cries the word *please*. Like someone asking politely for something they will never receive. Dad sobs as he slumps off again into shock.

"Dad. Stay with me, okay? Can you hear me?" I'm screaming now, but no one can hear me. "Why can't any of you hear me? Why won't any of you help me? Please, help my dad."

Rembrandt, finally, lowers is hands and moves toward Ballentine. "The man clearly needs medical assistance and we're the ones to give it to him. Not you, boy. You are a child. Why can't you see that he will die? But we can save him. No one in the whole world will ever come to you, your name will vanish from the face of the earth—as though you had never existed, never been born at all! Nothing but filth and mud, however you knock at your coffin lid at night, when the dead arise, however you cry: *Let me out, kind people, to live in the light of day!*"

Zombie dawn. Everything goes down. Choke up. Broken codes are all around. I swing the bat and the bat makes contact with Rembrandt's head.

*

Everything stops and I know it. A freeze-frame. Still picture. Ending to *28 Days Later*. A cosmic pause on heartbeats and airways and circulation.

As I swung the bat and watched it strike my target as I intended it to strike, I collapsed in on myself and wished myself away from everything, but instead of getting zapped into another realm, everything just stopped. And this is the space we exist in for now. A kind and quiet and gentle place.

Nothing is undone here. Hands not reattached. People not un-drugged, de-sexed, un-plaided, re-booted. People simply stop. The bat looks frozen to Rembrandt's head. He does not show signs of damage. The men below the stage are mannequins, life-like, positioned and placed perfectly around like a madman's living room.

I realize now, here, in this stuck state, that there had been a rattling, snarling demon inside me, growing in strength for some time. Ready to eat its way out. I know this now because I feel nothing now. I am empty now. There is nothing. The heavy, sick darkness stuck inside my skin is gone. Evaporated. Ripped clean. Vaporized. Disappeared.

I am brand new.

There is nothing left to put back together with tape or glue or nails—this is what is left.

This space is endless. Nothing matters in this space. Zero. Nada. Zilch. Because nothing actually exists here. Everything is possible here, but nothing is certain here. There's no telling how long this moment will last, but I want it forever. Forever and forever and then a little more forever. To feel *this* protected. An endless spot in time where our decisions and our actions are nonexistent. I share this space with no one and wouldn't let anyone in if they came knocking. The anger and rage and presence of certain people in my life are all gone, leaving only a flat line of possibility.

My memory is left intact, but emotion gutted. The memory of what was said that has brought me to this place is a trail in the woods, leading from the house to the dark, unknown destination beyond the house. The basement. Where Dad disappears. To watch all this take place. Spoken about. Preached about. Prayed about. To bring us all together is what it is about. The truth is that we all have things to say and whether we are right or wrong, we say them. We say things we believe and most often we're wrong. And even if we're right, we fight so hard at making someone believe we're right, we become wrong. Words make us into monsters of ourselves.

We wake up and we go to school or we go to work or we don't work at all, and the truth is that we believe in the things that are told to us. How to dress and how to be. What to say and how to say it. Who to fuck and how to fight. That life exists with other lives. We slam into each other and share ourselves and we are chipped away.

People tell other people that miracles are real and that miracles really happen and that God has a plan and that drugs are the key to a world of normalcy and are chipped away. I was climbing farther into the forest to protect myself from what was chasing me my whole life. Now it has all been set straight. Righted and final. I have no plans to return. I am marching.

Marching, marching, marching.

Things can never be any better than they are right now.

Marching but frozen—both at once.

But even as I have all of these thoughts, there comes a new realization, which crushes all beneath it, just as—I can feel it now, at last—Rembrandt's skull is crushed by my bat: that nothing stays the same forever.

EPILOGUE TO THE APOCALYPSE

The grass on the football field is brown and the sky is an unbroken gray. The grass didn't used to be brown and the sky didn't used to be gray, but that's how they are now. Soon the players will come rushing out, grunting and hitting, as they prepare for the annual Thanksgiving football game against an all-male, Christian rival. People keep count of how many Thanksgiving wins and how many Thanksgiving losses each school has had over the years. It's something people care about. The Plaids care the most, it seems, as is evident in the formation of the Blue Jay Bandits—a group of shirtless Byron Hall crazies who coat their faces and chests in blue war paint, bang cowbells, and blast air horns at football games.

Father Vincent and I are sitting on the top bench of the bleachers, watching assistant coaches mark the field with orange cones.

"You know, you never did tell me your five codes," Father Vincent says.

"Five simple codes to survive the Zombie Apocalypse," I say.

Father Vincent retrieves a booklet and baby pencil from his black sport coat. Not the blood moon one I saw before. This one is gold and green.

"Different cover," I say.

"Cornfields by my house when I was a kid," he says. "When I use up all the pages of a notebook, I transfer the unfinished tasks to the next one."

"And my five codes are an unfinished task."

"Something like that."

"Are priests allowed to write down things they hear in confession?"

"Probably not," he says. He returns the notepad to his pocket. He's got on his God Squad uniform—black pants, black shirt, little white collar in the front. "I still want to hear them, if you want to share."

"Do you know how to tie a tie, Father?"

"Neckties are not standard issue for God's troops, my son."

"Don't be embarrassed. It's okay if you can't tie a necktie."

"Maybe you can teach me. " He checks his watch. "But some other day. I have to get over to the theater soon. We're running a final dress rehearsal with tech, makeup, wardrobe, the works." He unwraps a stick of gum and slumps back against the row behind us. "I miss the Spirit Committee." He pauses. "Do you think you can make the preview tonight?"

"Unlikely," I say. "I can't go to the bathroom without at least a dozen people signing a notarized affidavit, stipulating the date, time, location, and duration of my visit."

The blue side doors to the school swing open and slam against the wall. Kids push past each other. They kick and punch and some-times exchange intricate handshakes.

"Maybe I can speak to Phil and Nancy. Make a formal request. See if they'll break the court's rules this once."

"No," I say. "Please don't."

"I can be awfully persuading when I dress like this."

"Everyone wants to talk to Phil and Nancy. After our weekly sessions, my court-appointed family therapist asks Phil and Nancy how I'm adjusting. My teachers mail my grades and progress reports home to Phil and Nancy. The State of Maryland pays money every month to Phil and Nancy, to cover my cost of living, my expenses. Detectives, police—they ask Phil and Nancy to talk to me about everything and see if I remember anything new. Baltimore City Clerk's Office for Family Court. The office of Judge Michael Thomas Antrum. My mother's addiction specialists. All of the law-yers because we all have lawyers."

Football players jog out among the cones, helmets in hand, past some Blue Jay Bandits, fully clothed in their standard plaid attire, Cam and a few others. Soccer season ended last week. Our guys didn't make it past regionals. So they hang out at football practice now, shouting insults or squeezing off an occasional air-horn blast.

The players pull on their helmets and run drills, keeping focus— tap dancing through a hopscotch made out of string, pushing a metal bleacher around the field with their taped hands, fighting their way out from inside a circle of angry men hellbent on knock-ing the football loose from his hands. Coaches sound their whistles, regularly, walking among the players, while Mr. Vo observes. He wears a tweed top coat, black leather gloves, and a bright blue scarf wrapped around his neck. Young men tackle young men on cue. Tiny silver clouds puff from their mouths.

After that night, my life took a turn.

No one believed me, for one thing. No one wanted to hear what I did to Mr. Rembrandt with the baseball bat. No one trusts the son of a handless man. *There's nothing we can do to help him—he's Ballentine's boy.* This is what I imagine former family friends and neighbors say about me now.

The day after Dad had his hand cut off the detectives took me back to Tiller Drive to find the house. We did and it was empty, spotless, gone. I knew it would be. It looked like no one had ever been there and nothing had ever happened at all.

Mr. Rembrandt stopped coming to school. More rumors flooded the halls about him but nothing remotely close to the truth. I don't know if I killed him or not. The funny thing is—I don't expect to see him again. I'm not sure why, but I don't think I will. Gut feeling. Perhaps I just don't want to think about it—about what I would do or fail to do, if I saw him again.

Dad was released from Johns Hopkins into the psychiat-ric facilities at Sheppard Pratt in Towson. He's been on suicide watch and in isolation since it happened. His lawyers say that he's being well-cared for, but I haven't seen him or heard from him myself. All I know is that he's alive, which I guess is a good thing considering.

After Mom found out about Dad, she left Zeke and disappeared for almost a month. I found out in family court that a security officer George found her in one of the empty units of *The Prince Edward*. She'd been living in a plastic apartment and doing her dope. She's back with Zeke and Zeke tells me that she shoots her morphine now. I see her in custody court sometimes. She's far from well.

Jackson moved out of his apartment in Fell's Point and lives with one of his coozy girlfriends somewhere downtown between the Inner Harbor and Tiller Drive. He ran out of money when Dad went away. Jackson calls me when he has time. When he thinks of it. Usually a voicemail. He calls me Stumps, and then goes silent until the message runs out of space.

Tricia took care of Dog without me even having to ask. She saw all the drama and took it upon herself to make Dog a permanent part of her family. Dog and her fat little dog, Travis. I saw her the last time I was at the house. She asked if I wanted to see her, and I said not this time. She made me promise to come back and visit. I said that I would, but I think she knew I wasn't coming back.

Phil and Nancy Weber live in a ranch-style house an hour outside the city. They don't have any kids of their own. It was just me at first, but starting last week they added an eleven-year-old. His name is Matthew and he goes to public school. We share a room with all of the basics. No bunk beds like in the movies. Twin beds, each with our own nightstand, reading lamp, trunk for our clothes, and a closet we share. I gave Matt my half. He likes to hang up his T-shirts. He doesn't like them folded. I'm fine with the trunk.

The Webers don't watch a lot of TV or movies. He is a loan officer at a local bank and she is a real estate clerk for a law firm. They subscribe to more newspapers than magazines and have a garage where they park their used cars and store their tools and lawn furniture and Christmas decorations. A two car garage like a normal American family. No basement.

A yellow school bus picks Matt up every morning outside of the Webers' house. I wait with him. He never says much. Nancy then drives me to school since she works downtown. The only thing left over from before is the chopography. *Little Men.* It's hung above my bed.

"So let's hear your codes."

"I don't remember them."

"Is that so?"

I tap my forehead. "All gone, Father. Poof."

He offers me a stick of gum. I thank him, but I put it in my pocket.

"The Webers—they're only temporary," he says. "Until things change."

"Do you know what they call me?" I ask. "The students?"

He watches me. He doesn't say anything.

"Monster," I say. "Not *a* monster. Not *the* monster. Just monster."

When I first moved in with the Webers I found an unread copy of *Notes from Underground* in their living room library of histori- cal fiction and political biographies. Nancy apologized, knowing my connection to the book, but didn't know where it had come from. Phil didn't even know who Dostoevsky was, spending more time trying to pronounce the name than searching his memory of ever owning it. This and *Little Men* and zombie movies are all that remain for me. My inheritance. So I read it.

The football team stands together on the field, facing Mr. Vo, an army before their leader. They are silent, awaiting instruction. An assistant coach holds a whistle in his mouth, taking cues from Mr. Vo via subtle nods, before piercing the air. After the whistle, he shouts out the word *left* or *right.* Players slap their helmets hard with both hands open, pivot in that direction, keep pace with one another—a single unified force—while running in place as quickly as possible.

After a dozen pivots, instead of a direction, Mr. Vo shouts to the young men.

"St. John Baptist De La Salle."

J.R. ANGELELLA

"Pray for us."

"Live Jesus in our hearts."

"Forever."

"One more time. St. John Baptist De La Salle."

"Pray for us."

"Live Jesus in our hearts."

"Forever."

A description comes to mind from the text of that night, like it had been written back then, but about today. Not a literal description, but more to the center of things. Deeper underground.

I ran out into the street. It was a still night and the snow was coming down in masses and falling almost perpendicularly, covering the pavement and the empty street as though with a pillow. There was no one in the street, no sound was to be heard. The street lamps gave a disconsolate and useless glimmer. I ran to the cross-roads and stopped short. I stood in the snow, gazing into the troubled darkness.

In another light, this could have been a winterland Zombie Apocalypse—the only thing missing, the undead. *Undead Notes from Underground.*

Off in the distance, at the bus stop, I can see Mykel. He's wearing a big winter coat and a new era Orioles' baseball hat with the giant orange *O's* emblem on the front, taking photos as usual, though I can't tell of what. A car pulls into the bus lane and the passenger door opens. Mykel gets in and slams it. Zink signals and pulls out into traffic. I would never have expected them to be carpool brothers, but there it is, plain as day. Swagger.

"Miracles," Father Vincent says. "They do exist. I promise you, they do."

"I had a dream once about a miracle," I say. "Everything stopped. Time was frozen. But I was marching. And for all eternity nothing could ever change from the way it was at that one frozen moment."

Father Vincent looks at me, waiting to see if I've got more to say. But I don't. And before he can figure out how to respond, an air horn strikes the sky. It's one of the Bandits, the guy sitting next to Cam, announcing the presence of a girl.

The girl ignores the Bandits and football and turns toward me.

The Plaids and I never settled things from that night at Mykel's chopography exhibit. Cam hasn't looked at me even once since I returned to school—none of them do anymore—not that I'm complaining. I know they talk about me behind my back. I've heard the things they say, some of it true, most of it not. Nothing true ever stays a secret in these halls and even the truth has a way of sounding like a lie. Either way you're fucked here and not in the good way, as Jackson would say. But they don't see that. The Plaids don't see me—not when I'm right there in front of them. They see only what they can step on and kick, what's unapologetically in their way, and it's like I'm not part of that world anymore.

I would have thought a kid whose dad cut off his hand would have been Plaid-target #1. But that just isn't fucking so. It's like there's this fog that's settled between us, and the closest they're willing to get is a couple of half-hearted catcalls directed at the girl walking toward me along the field's edge.

Aimee.

She's layered in a peacoat with a matching knit hat and scarf—her scarf tied the French way around her neck, doubled over with the open ends pulled through the loop. Her nose is red from the cold and she climbs the metal benches with care. She drove like a professional wheelman that night. When we got to the hospital, she stuck by me until the cops made her call her parents and they took her away. The Whites had to leave behind their blood-spattered SUV, which the police impounded as evidence. We haven't seen each other outside of school since that night. Partially, the Webers. Partially, her parents, who are still waiting for their SUV. Everyone is trying to put as much distance between us and that night as possible. The collective solution is forgetfulness.

I see Aimee every day after school.

She climbs up and Father Vincent goes down.

A question in those final pages of *Notes*: *Which is better—cheap happiness or exalted sufferings? Well, which is better?*

She and I sit quiet on the bleachers and listen to the young men fighting below us. This is our reality. We do not kiss, but instead wait for things to change—for the beautiful monsters that I know will someday come.

ACKNOWLEDGEMENTS

This book has long been a troubled and disturbed project of mine. The following people not only believed in my deranged ideas and fictive reality, but worked miracles to make sure both me and this book came out on the right side of crazy.

My loving parents, Rick and Ann Angelella, and sister, Gina Angelella. Thanks for never mentioning that my five year plan to write and publish a novel actually took ten. This book, I'm certain, is proof that my plan was (mostly) never a lie.

My amazing uncle and kindred spirit, Michael Angelella, for introducing me to the sadistic art of writing and numbing me at an early age to the searing pain of a red-lined manuscript.

My cousins: Dominic Angelella, for keeping me musically current and reminding me what it means to be fearless; and Hallie Angelella, a fellow starving artist in Brooklyn and Ithaca College Bomber.

To my late-night writing partner and resident soothsayer, Jess Ashley, for giving important, poignant and perceptive feedback on my teenage landscape and for teaching me what girls actually wear.

To my teachers: Fred A. Wilcox, for daring me to write out my demons; Patricia Volk, for convincing me to resurrect this novel after I had left it for dead; Amy Hempel, for teaching me how to write a sentence and break a story; Askold Melnyczuk, for diagnosing my obsessive personality and rightly prescribing Fyodor Dostoevsky; and Bret Anthony Johnston, who challenged me to make Jeremy walk off the damn page.

To my friends at Bennington College, notably Joe Stracci, Hugh Ryan, Alka Roy, and Ian Williams, for reading early drafts of this novel and challenging me to write better and continue to create outside of the proverbial box.

For their kind correspondence, advice, and encouragement over the years, I am deeply indebted to Donald Ray Pollack, Richard Lange, Chuck Palahniuk and Will Christopher Baer.

To my editors at Hunger Mountain: Bethany Hegedus, for publishing an early excerpt from *Zombie* (formerly Alpha House); and Kekla Magoon, for her keen line-edits and tough questions.

Everyone at Random House who poured their valuable time, energy, and enthusiasm into this book. For their thoughtful, direct, and heartfelt feedback, I especially would like to thank Marcia Baumann, Brad Andrews and Lane Jantzen.

To Seth Fishman, who literally pulled my manuscript from the slush pile and forced others to read it.

My Herculean agent, Douglas Stewart, for loving Jeremy as much as I love Jeremy. For never giving up on the book, no matter the state of the draft. For never giving up on me, no matter the level of crisis. And, most importantly, for blindly believing in my work, no matter the cost.

To the artistic team behind the cover: Kapo Ng for a killer design; and Jad Fair for his brilliant paper-cuttings used as the cover art.

Everyone at Soho Press for their wild and undead support, especially Bronwen Hruska, Ailen Lujo, Juliet Grames, Dan Ehrenhaft, Michelle Rafferty, Scott Cain, Janine Agro, and my phenomenal editor, Mark Doten, who believed in this book from day one and pushed me (quite literally at times) to the very limits of my creative sanity, never settling for good enough.

My dear friend (and personal Tom Hagan), Tod Goldberg, for being the best wartime consigliere a writer could ask for.

To my beautiful wife, Kate, for being my first reader and editor, agent and shrink, fanatic and critic, heckler and cheerleader. For always being in my foxhole and endlessly leaving negativity to the fools.

Finally, to the kid dug deep into his/her troubled trench: believe me when I say that surviving is the most important step towards happiness, and survive it you will!

READING GROUP GUIDE:

1. What is the importance of Jeremy's Top Ten Favorite Zombie Movies of All-Time? Why are zombie films so important to him?

2. What does the epigraph by Michel de Montaigne mean? What does this quote say about Jeremy? What other monsters and/or miracles exist in *Zombie*? If so, how does the epigraph relate them?

3. *Zombie* opens with Jeremy quoting his father, Ballentine, on three different types of neck tie knots. What is the significance of Jeremy beginning his story with a quote from his father?

4. What role do necktie knots play in *Zombie*? According to Jeremy, what do the knots—Windsor, Half-Windsor, and Limp Dick—say about the men that wear them?

5. When we meet Jeremy, he has already developed his top five Zombie Survival Codes. What do you think (or know) fueled the creation of this list? How affective are his codes? Do they always keep him safe? Do you think he successfully survives his own "zombie apocalypse," or do his codes ultimately fail him? How so?

6. What role do the Plaids play in Jeremy's daily life? How is his life affected by them? Is it important that he stands up to them; or an unnecessary action?

7. Many of the people in Jeremy's life retain special skills and interests that on one level define them as people, however it is these very traits that cause conflict with their own identity and in how the world views them. This is something Jeremy, too, struggles with. What are their interests or special skills, and how do they affect not only their own lives, but by extension Jeremy's life as well—Zink, Aimee, Mykel, Franny, Sherman, Super Shy Kid, Dirtbag Boy, Tricia?

8. How does Jeremy perceive the adults in his life? How do you think adults view Jeremy?

9. Why does Jeremy collect women's magazines? What is his endgame?

10. Do you think that Jeremy barker is a reliable narrator? Explain.

11. Jeremy is a wallflower, an active observer, and while not entirely passive, he still tends to err on the side of invisibility to get by on a daily basis. That being said, he also has a very active imagination. When he is not killing zombies in creative ways, what other important moments does Jeremy engage with the external world around him? What propels him to engage and why does he decide to do so?

12. Why is Mykel's *chopography* important to the story? How does it relate to the overall narrative of zombies, surgery and adolescence?

13. How do you feel about Father Gibbs' belief that "no matter how far gone you believe a person to be, there's always the possibility of a miracle to bring them back to life."

14. It's fair to say that the Barker family is not the ideal picture of the healthy and happy American family. What do Ballentine, Corrine, Jackson and Jeremy do (or don't do) in *Zombie* to reconnect and mend broken relationships within the family?

15. There are two coaches that Jeremy has frequent interactions with throughout *Zombie*—Coach O'Bannon and Mr. Vo. How are these men the same? In what ways are they different?

16. Human interaction (or lack thereof) and physicality are described in great detail and to varying effects throughout the book. How do surgery and body parts fit into the landscape of this novel overall?

17. Mr. Rembrandt often quotes from Fydor Dostoevsky's novel Notes From Underground. Even Ballentine uses a plot line form the book as a lie to give to Jeremy about where he has been disappearing to at night. How does Mr. Rembrandt use the text to influence those around him? How does Notes influence the novel *Zombie* on a structural or ideological level?

18. Beyond the obvious reasons, what psychological reasons do you think the people at Tiller Drive have for congregating? What is their goal? What do they hope to accomplish or achieve? How does this activity pertain to Jeremy?

19. How do you see Ballentine and his action at the end of the book? Do you feel it is a desperate and deranged attempt to find peace? Or the act of a crazy man? Or do you think he is brainwashed?

20. The Tiller Drive sequence ends in a stark and jarring way. "Everything stops . . . A freeze-frame. Still picture. Ending to 28 Days Later. A cosmic pause on heartbeats and airways and circulation." What literally happens here? Is it a literal break? Or an emotional one? Psychological? Why do you think this freeze-frame technique is used?

21. Given the title of the book, *Zombie* is a mash-up of genres. Do you see this as a classic zombie story, or more of a coming-of-age narrative? Horror or mystery? Explain. Do you agree that there are actual zombies in this book? Or only those that exist in the movies and Jeremy's imagination?

22. What are your favorite zombie movies of all-time? What is it about them that you like? What are your least favorite zombie movies?

23. Survival scenario! You are alone in the house and asleep upstairs in your bedroom when the zombie apocalypse happens. Fast-moving goo babies crash through the front door and living room windows. What is your weapon of choice? What is your escape plan?